Sweet Vengeance

Aliya DalRae

Sweet Vengeance Copyright © 2016 by Aliya DalRae
All rights reserved.

First Edition, 2016

This is a work of fiction. All names, characters, organizations, places and incidents are either the product of the author's imagination or are used fictitiously, and any resemblance to actual persons, living or dead, places, locations, events or establishments is purely coincidental.

Cover Design by Tempting Illustrations

Image Contributor conrado/Bigstock.com

Cover Formatting by Pink Ink Designs

ISBN: 1523691425
ISBN-13: 978-1523691425

For Jessica

ACKNOWLEDGMENTS

Thank you, thank you, thank you!

To Angelica Rose Mariano of Tempting Illustrations for your amazing imagery.

To Cassandra Roop at Pink Ink Designs Co. for taking Gel's image, pulling the cover together, and giving it its final glorious touches.

To my posse of friends and family—you know who you are!— For your never-ending support and insight; for your beta reads and your participation in my relentless polls. Your enthusiasm and encouragement were instrumental in getting this story out of my computer and into print.

And To Kirk, my immortal beloved—
Thanks for believing in me.
There are no words…

Prologue

Helmut Fuhrmann watched the small pack of wolves running through the trees, leaping at each other, playfully dodging claws and teeth as they gamboled in the light of the full moon. The three young ran incautiously, unmindful of their surroundings or any dangers that might be lurking in the shadows. They trusted the adult with them to provide that protection, as young of any breed tend to do, and to her credit, she took her job seriously. The older female had a silver pelt with a white star on her forehead, and her nose was working overtime, her head swinging back and forth, scenting the air for potential threats.

Of course she could not sense Fuhrmann or any of his Clan. The spells they had cast upon themselves prevented others from detecting them in any manner—sight, sound, or even smell. It didn't just make them invisible. It made them nonexistent.

As Fuhrmann followed the small group, slipping from tree to tree, his tall, thin form blending with the shadows of the forest, he smiled to himself. This would be so easy. How the lycanthropes had ever defeated his own race in the past, he could not fathom. They were ignorant and weak, and though they had certain magic that was unavailable to his kind, theirs was a limited magic, where the Clan's magic was much more…comprehensive.

A lock of his long, white hair escaped from the leather thong he'd bound it with, and it floated in front of his eyes, blocking his view momentarily. Fuhrmann carefully tucked it back into place, securing it to keep his sight free. The amount of magic a Sorcerer carried was evidenced by the way his hair moved of its own accord. The more magic in the man, the more life in his mane. It could be distracting in situations like this, but it was a source of pride for his kind, and though he tried to keep it tamed when he walked in the human world, he relished the moments when he could let it fly free.

As the wolves continued their play, Fuhrmann watched the adult female. She was not large, which probably played into her being chosen for this task. Oh, she was large enough to provide the young protection from the usual creatures of the night. However, the larger wolves would tend to be more aggressive with the young, whereas with her there was less chance of an accident occurring. Fuhrmann also assumed she was a wolf of low standing. An Alpha wouldn't be caught dead babysitting.

The Clan had been watching this pack for many months, and so was aware that the majority of the wolves would be in their primary forest north of town, hunting larger game and probably getting into scuffles that would be too dangerous for the smaller pups. This nature preserve was like the kiddie section of an amusement park, the place they took the young ones to play during the full moon, while the older wolves partook of the wilder, more exciting attractions.

Still, decades of modern living had made these creatures lax in their securities. They always brought the young to the same nature preserve, and they always parked in the same place, their vehicle hidden along a rarely used path. So easy to follow. So easy to take.

The three young ran on, nipping and yipping, leaping over fallen trees, and hiding behind boulders to jump out at their pack mates as they scampered by. The larger of the three, a nearly black male with silver streaks around his muzzle, broke off from the group, leading the way, with a reddish male leaping on his flanks, and rolling him nearly every other stride.

The white wolf was female, tiny in comparison to the other two (though by no means small) and hesitant to jump into the middle of the fray. She took cautious nips at the older males, but seemed content to remain on the edge of their rough and tumble game. She was beautiful, really, her coat luminescent in the moonlight. And she was ideal for his purpose.

The adult would have to die, of course, and he would take the two males as spares, but the white female was his target. She was very young, and as a child in human form she had a sweet innocence about her, which he had witnessed during surveillance. The contrast between the harmless girl and the ferocious wolf she became would be awe inspiring. And these were just children. They were already larger than the largest of dogs. Any human witnessing such a metamorphosis would be stricken with terror, and their imaginations would bring them to the natural question—how big will they get? And how lethal?

When the demonstration reached the blood-letting portion of the show, the humans would be mortified by the sacrifice, but the need for the elimination of all lycanthropes and the danger they presented would be driven home. And the first step in bringing the humans into their war would be complete.

All over the globe, in small towns like Fallen Cross, Ohio, Clans were awaiting the outcome of this experiment. If Fuhrmann were to be successful in his task, then small human governments everywhere would be striking out against the Weres. Small governments would expand to include larger governments, and with luck, the animals could be eradicated within a matter of months—a year at the most. The thought made him smile.

Fuhrmann's attention returned to the present as the mood of the wolf-play changed. A large cottontail got up in front of the older males, running a zigzag pattern in an attempt to elude the predators. The hunt was on, and Fuhrmann followed, creeping in the shadows, his form invisible and undetectable, not wanting to miss the show.

He was not disappointed.

An unfortunate detour by the rabbit set it right in the path of the white wolf, who had lagged behind, and she did not hesitate. She leapt on the smaller creature, her lips curled and her fangs bared, her eyes flashing amber in the moonlight. And in less than a second, the furry creature was between her powerful jaws, blood spattering the leaves at her feet, the sounds of crunching bones echoing through the forest.

Fuhrmann nearly laughed out loud as the young she-wolf snarled at her brethren, warning them off her meal. Her white muzzle was coated in the rabbit's blood, and her fangs were impressive for a wolf her size. She looked absolutely savage. Yes she would do nicely.

It was unfortunate they would have to wait another month before staging their demonstration, but the full moon was the best time to collect their subjects, and the only time to execute their plan. The time would not be wasted, though. The cubs would need some—conditioning.

Tonight, they would wait until the wolves changed back to their human form and take them while they were vulnerable. The adults were able to change at will, although the full moon did make it more difficult for the weaker ones to return to their human form on nights such as this. The young, however, were prisoner to the moon's pull, their change initiated by the touch of the lunar light, and ending with the setting moon, at which time they simply curled up and awaited the return to human shape. Leaving them vulnerable.

The adult would stand guard, of course, but she would be easily disposed of. He would see to that personally, while his Clan gathered up the young. Special tranquilizers had been prepared, powerful sedatives mixed with a healthy dose of magic, designed especially for supernatural use. It was a complex potion—the small quantity he now possessed had taken months to prepare—but he was certain it would prove to be useful. Yes, the young beasts would be easily taken. And the cages were prepared.

But not now. The moon would be up for hours, and though he was loathe to let the pups out of his sight, he knew it was unnecessary for him to expend his energy, magical or otherwise, in pursuit of these animals. They would come to him soon enough.

With reluctance, he left the surveillance to a Clansman, and returned to the point of capture to await their return. Yet he was restless, each minute seeming to last an hour, and Fuhrmann began to pace.

He wandered along the path, or what was almost recognizable as a path, if only for the recent tracks left by the Were's SUV. Fuhrmann walked on, deep in thought, and was surprised when the path opened up into the clearing leading to the parking lot near the low slung buildings of the Nature Center, which housed specimens of plants and animals, living and dead, that prospered in the surrounding protected area.

This was where the Clan had entered, where Henry had dropped them off with orders to return near dawn with the transport they required. The lot had been empty when they arrived; however, a black Corvette was now parked in a space near the back of the car park, and Fuhrmann was instantly on guard. He contacted the Clan, letting them know through the mental thread that connected his kind that they had company and to be on alert.

Moments later, he felt Fritz's mind touch and knew that they were dealing with more than a couple of horny teenagers, thrill-seeking in the woods in the wee hours of the night. Several long moments more, and he was called to the edge of the field opposite his current location. The intruder was down.

He could have dematerialized, a magic not common among his kind except among the Elders, but a talent he had spent many years perfecting. However, their captive was going nowhere, so there was no need to rush. Besides, the night was pleasant for a change, not nearly as hot as it had been, and the air felt good on his face as he made his way through the tall grass, charcoal duster flaring in his wake.

What he found when he arrived was more than he could have ever hoped for. Lying unconscious in the grass near the edge of the wood was a man. No—not a man. A Vampire. And one he had spent many long years hunting. One who had eluded him for centuries. One he had long thought dead. He had resigned himself to that thought, to the idea that he would never get the revenge he so rightly deserved.

Yet miracle of miracles, he was here, before him, and...helpless. Several darts protruded from his back, one in his neck. It appeared the special formula worked on a variety of supernatural beings. The gods were truly smiling on him tonight. This male would die at his hand, but not quickly. Fuhrmann had dreamed of this death for most of his extensive life. If he could stretch the misery into eternity, he would, if for no other reason than to compensate himself for the interminable time he had waited.

This Vampire would suffer. And Helmut Fuhrmann would enjoy every scream that passed his cursed lips.

Regrettably, this was off project for Fuhrmann. He had to make sure his fun didn't interfere with his assignment. But a man was entitled to a little recreation now and again.

A quick message to Henry had him coming to collect their new cargo, with orders to take him to the south cabin and contain him.

No need to frighten the children they would house at the main Compound with a scary Vampire. They'd have other fears to contend with.

Chapter One

I was having trouble concentrating. My best friend, Piper, was on a roll, and when she gets going, it's really hard to get a word in edgewise. The florescent lights in the Polar King glared off of Piper's fair skin, giving it an iridescent quality. She shoveled in bites of her banana split without missing a beat. Eating while talking was like a skill set to her, one you would think would be disgusting, but she managed it with a certain flair.

"I just could NOT believe it! Seriously? I just stood there with my jaw on the floor. I was like, what kind of moron stands *me* up and then has the nerve to *text* me and ask me out again?"

I nodded in what I hoped were all the appropriate places and grimaced when it seemed like I should, but frankly, Piper's latest love tragedy was not holding my attention today.

I watched her auburn curls bounce around her shoulders as she became more animated in her story telling. Her emerald eyes flashed with wounded rage as her narrative reached a crescendo, but all I heard was a cartoon version of "mwah, mwah, mwah."

Piper was like a sister to me, but even I could take only so much of her self-absorption. It also reminded me that I was twenty-six years old, and hadn't had a date in so long, I couldn't remember what decade it was in. Okay, so there were really only two choices, but when you're my age, ten years is a lifetime, almost literally.

I gazed at my reflection in the Polar King window and searched for qualities that might be considered attractive. Nice eyes, decent hair, full lips and all my teeth. Running and Tae Kwon Do kept me in decent shape.

If you asked me, I was quite a catch. Except for maybe that vision thing, but it wasn't like that was common knowledge.

The thing is, sometimes I see things, or dream them, usually things that haven't happened yet, though occasionally the past pops in. It pretty much showed up about the time I learned to talk. Basically, I would have these visions and they would eventually come true. I predicted my birth father's desertion, my birth mother's disappearance, and the death of my poodle, Mitzi, not necessarily in that order. So, it's no fun dating when you always know how it's going to turn out, e.g. disaster. If I ever meet a guy and get the old, "happily ever after" vision, I swear I'll move heaven and earth to be with him. Even if I have to drug him, kidnap him, and hypnotize him! None of which, by the way, is in *my* skill set.

As Piper's prattling continued, I glanced around the Polar King at the other patrons.

A young couple cuddled in a booth in the back of the room sharing a milkshake with two straws, giggling like idiots when their noses touched. Across the way, an older couple sat, eating in complete silence, both staring off into space, their eyes reflecting long ago memories as they gummed their cheeseburgers to death.

My across-the-road-neighbor, Bill Stuckey, Jr. was at the counter, John Deere hat sitting at an angle on his melon shaped head, tufts of straw colored hair sticking out above the hat's green plastic sizing strip. As he shifted from one treelike leg to the other, hammy palms flat on the counter, I heard some of his order: a triple Polar Burger with cheese, extra bacon, hold the mayo, large fries, onion rings, a Chocolate-Chocolate Shake and a Diet Pepsi. Hey, a guy's gotta watch his figure, right?

Mandy Jenkins was behind the counter. She blew her perfect blonde bangs out of her eyes, her forehead creased in concentration, as her tiny brain tried to keep up. Mandy was tiny in every way, five foot nothing, tiny little figure, former Home Coming Queen and all around cute girl. But seriously, Mandy was kind of a ditz. Working at the Polar King tapped deep into her intellectual reserves. Lucky for her, her daddy owned the place.

Behind Bill Jr., old Mr. Cotterman was waiting. He had a standing order with the Polar King for a chili dog and fries to be picked up at 12:30 every day. It was 12:33. He had a little newspaper stand set up next to the grocery store about half a block away, where he sold candy, cigarettes, and of course, newspapers. The Cotter's Pen had been there since before I could remember, making him a sort of institution in the small town of Fallen Cross. As he waited, his irritation getting the better of him, his glass eye rolled up in his head making his iris disappear, leaving a big white eyeball staring out of his face. Mandy looked up and gave a little squeak when she saw him, all marble-eyed and scary-looking. Mr. Cotterman wasn't known for his patience.

"Mwah, mwah-mwah, mwah, mwah, Jessica! Mwah, mwah, mwah."

Huh?

"Jessica! Are you even listening to me?" Oops. Busted.

"Sure, Piper. Of course. So how did you leave things with, what's-his-name?" I said, feigning interest, absently chewing on an onion ring.

"I'm not talking about him anymore. Jeeze, Jessica! I was talking about the sequined dress I bought for the fundraiser at the Mayor's house this weekend. I stopped talking about Marvin, like, hours ago. Are you okay?" she asked, softening a bit.

Actually, I wasn't. I hadn't slept much since my mother passed away a couple of months ago. The grief I felt was overwhelming, losing her so soon after Dad. He was killed about a year ago in a freak crop dusting accident, when he crashed into Mr. Bentley's soy bean field. Mom was never the same. She stopped eating, stopped caring about the things she had once loved, like her restoration business, Almost New Again, her flower gardens and even the people around her. Even me. Watching her slowly disintegrate into a shell of the strong woman who had raised me since I was 6, was torture. Watching her die was all nine circles of Hell wrapped into one agonizing moment.

I walked through the funeral like a zombie, existing on caffeine during the day and margaritas at night. Piper was there for me, and so was Alexander, my other best friend, but even they didn't know how to help. Piper kept trying to take me shopping, and Alex kept making margaritas. I really loved Alex for that.

When my dad died, the whole county went into a full blown scandal-fest. A plane crash in Fallen Cross wasn't something that happened every day, so it gave the town gossips fodder for months and months. My parents were a local staple, and they were well liked in the tiny burg they had called home for forty-five years. Plus, the people of Fallen Cross never met a funeral they didn't love. Add tragedy to that and Voila!—Instant town bonding. Gave everyone a since of purpose, I suppose. It just made me feel more alone.

Then when Mom died, it was like losing Dad times a million. The town just went bonkers, stopping by and bringing me food till I thought I would puke if I ever saw another chocolate cake or tuna casserole again. I'm sure they meant well. Well, some of them did, anyway. Still, it was a nightmare I was having a really hard time waking up from.

So I didn't really know how to answer Piper. Yes, I was okay, in that I wasn't suicidal or anything desperate like that, but inside I really didn't know where I was going yet. Each new day was a repeat of the last. Wake up, work to keep Almost New Again operating, eat (maybe), go to bed, and hope that something would happen tomorrow to give my life a purpose.

I opened my mouth to tell Piper I'd be fine, but right then the door opened, letting in a gust of hot air, and saving me from telling another lie. Piper and I looked up to see Alex striding in, all tall and sexy in a Wolverine sort of way. Well, minus the muttonchops. He tried that once, and Piper and I both nixed it right quick. Friends don't let friends grow muttonchops. They just don't.

"Damn, it's hot," Alex said, plopping down in the booth next to me and grabbing an onion ring from my tray. It was late August in Southwest Ohio, and the sun gods were pulling out all the stops. "I saw your cars out front and thought I'd stop in and spend my lunch break with my two favorite girls. Are you finished with these?" That said as he crammed another of my onion rings into his mouth.

"Yeah, take them," I said, looking at his grimy hands and pushing my tray in front of him. Alex was a mechanic over at Harry's Body Shop, which was where everyone took their cars for whatever ailed them, and sometimes he was less than hygienic. I was done anyway.

"Piper has a new dress," I said, smiling brightly, hoping to take the spotlight off myself and put it back where it would be appreciated.

"Yeah?" Alex said. "You invited to the party?"

"Of course, I was invited," Piper huffed indignantly. "Mother and Daddy have been friends of the Mayor since High School. He wouldn't dare snub our family. Besides, I got invitations for you guys too. That's what I was trying to tell Jessica, before she zoned out on me...again." She gave Alex a meaningful look. I just rolled my eyes.

An invitation to the Mayor's fundraising party? Great. Lots of well-meaning people telling me how sorry they are for my loss, and even more not-so-well-meaning people goss-goss-gossiping behind my back. "Ohhh, look at poor Jessica Sweet, she's an orphan again. Such a shame, and her folks being so young, too. I mean really sixty's the new fifty right? And she looks so thin. I don't think she's eating. We should bake a cake and take it over to her. Did you hear that her birth parents left her on a door step? I heard it was at a hospital. No I'm sure it was alone in a house with fifteen starving cats that were starting to nibble on her toes." And on, and on it will go.

The truth wasn't nearly as exciting as some of the gossip suggested. My birth father walked out on my mother and me when I was about four and a half. The proverbial "went out for cigarettes and never came back" scenario. My mother tried to support us, but she was kind of a whack job, into drugs and booze and all that fun stuff. Ultimately, Child Protective Services got involved, removing me from the home until my mother could get her act together. Which never happened. Once CPS got involved, I never saw her again.

I was adopted by the Sweets when I was six, and my history had stopped being interesting among the locals by the time I was seven. However, now that I'd lost *another* set of parents, it was all prime news again. I could hardly wait for another chance to showcase my pathetic life, in front of the town's elite no less.

But how could I say no to Piper? She'd been my friend when no one else would come near me, and had defended me since we met in kindergarten. She and Alex were among the few who knew of my talent, and they were as viciously protective of my secret as they were of me. If I declined, I would totally break Piper's heart, and I just couldn't do that. Damn. Now I had to buy a dress.

Alex and Piper chatted on about the party as Alex demolished what was left of my lunch. Despite his rugged looks and blue color demeanor, Alex was kind of a social butterfly. He loved being around people, and large crowds energized him. He tucked a stray strand of his longish, brown hair behind his ear, then scratched at his beard scruff as he and Piper discussed the party and dress codes.

I always thought Piper and Alex made a cute couple, but for whatever reason they didn't see it that way. Piper's perfect auburn locks and lithe little five foot two inch body just seemed to fit well with Alex's long, lean five-eleven frame and wild brown hair. Opposites in every way, but complimenting each other as only an opposite can. However, when I mentioned it to Piper she either blew me off or suggested I date him myself. At which point, the conversation was usually over.

During my reverie, it was decided that, since Alex was going to need a tux, we would all go shopping tonight after work. As they made plans, I furiously sucked the last of my milkshake through the tiny straw. Ugh. Shopping. I could hardly wait.

Chapter Two

He ran naked through the woods, blood dripping from the numerous wounds on his vast body. It was dark, several hours before dawn, but he had excellent night vision. His breath caught in his lungs, and he ran on, faster than humanly possible, but not sure if it was fast enough to escape his pursuers. If they tranqued him again, he was done.

The trees gave way to a large pasture, hills undulating throughout. He leaned against a towering oak, taking a risk in stopping, but knowing he needed to weigh his options, and quickly.

The ones chasing him weren't human, he was sure of it, in spite of their human forms. Mere humans would never have been able to capture him, let alone torture him the way these had. He was free only by the carelessness of his guard, whom he had surprised by feigning unconsciousness, and when the moron had turned his back on him, he had wrapped his chains around the creature's neck, breaking it before the bastard could call for aid.

After a very quick search of the dead creature's pockets, he had found the keys to the shackles on his wrists and ankles. They had kept him starving and weak, else he would have been able to break the iron fetters like twigs. Having shed his restraints, he had run, the dying flora around the clearing giving way to healthier trees and underbrush that slapped and stung his bare skin.

Now, as he searched the terrain, he saw in the distance a group of buildings. His strength was fading, his blood loss great, and he knew he needed to get below ground quickly so he could heal, but where to go? If he stayed in the woods, his captors were likely to track him. But if he could reach a house, the benefits could be lifesaving. If there were people, he could feed, regain some strength and leave the humans none the wiser.

There would also be transportation, a car he could borrow to get him home, where his people could be informed of the danger lurking in their territory. The Legion must be warned!

He broke out of the woods, and ran as fast as his tortured body could bear, cursing his legs for not carrying him at his usual lightning quick speed. When he reached the first building, a large, ancient barn, he leaned against the wooden planks, red paint flaking off in his fingers as he struggled for purchase. Inside, the animals stirred, a cow stamping a restless hoof, a pig grunting nervously.

Keeping to the shadows, he stole around to the front of the barn. The livestock awakened, acknowledging his intrusion, but seemed not to be bothered by his presence. Animals could sense if there were a threat present, and though they knew him for the predator he was, they also knew they weren't on the menu. Such was the way with his people.

Scanning the property, his keen eyesight took in the remaining out buildings, then the farmhouse located at the south side of the property. The old home was shadowed in a copse of weeping willows, white paint peeling from what was once a grand residence, with verandas edging the front and sides, both upstairs and down.

He reached out with his mind and sensed the presence of three humans inside, simultaneously taking stock in the automobiles in the graveled drive. An old pickup truck, probably ran but maybe not reliable; a newer looking sedan, and a tricked out Ford Super Duty, black with black interior and running lights on the cab roof. It would be a little conspicuous, but probably the best choice for his getaway. Plus it was an awesome ride.

As he started toward the house, the hair on the back of his neck stood on end, his skin tingling as though lightning had struck nearby. He spun around to find two of the humanoid creatures behind him, tall and pale, white blond hair floating about their heads with more life than the evening's light breeze merited.

He felt the beast rising within him, alarming him nearly as much as the thought of being recaptured, so he focused his energy, mentally leashing his feral side, and lunged at the creature nearest him, fangs bared, controlled fury carrying him into a collision with more speed than he thought himself capable of in his current condition.

He and the creature flew several feet in the air before crashing to the stony ground. Then with control that came only from decades of training, he tamped down his other cravings and gave the beast its head, gave it leave to kill, and in seconds his teeth were at his opponent's throat, ripping, tearing, shredding, until all that remained was a ruined carcass bleeding in the gravel.

He spun again, his dark hair flying, normally sapphire eyes sparking amethyst with the passion of the kill, and faster than light his attentions were focused on the other creature. This one was smaller, though tall nonetheless, and apparently younger, because it hesitated, tranq gun in hand, mumbling under its breath and stabbing the gun in his direction as though the threat alone would stop him.

He was a cyclone, now, energy surging through him from the earth and the sky. A poisonous dart flew toward him, missing by a mile as he whirled behind the creature, grabbed its head in his powerful grip and twisted sharply. The crack of the creature's vertebrae echoed in the dark, sent shivers of satisfaction through his own spine, and a scarcely controlled howl of victory to his throat.

The sound of animals in full panic brought him back to the moment, helping him to reign in the beast. He reached out to them with his mind to try and calm their terror, but they were too far gone. Whatever these now-deceased creatures were, they weren't friendly to animals of any kind, and the livestock were as aware of this as he was.

With the beast tempered, his damaged body was failing him again, the encounter with the creatures taking the last of his already depleted strength, borrowed energy from the universe sinking back into the earth. He looked down at the creature he still held in his hands and realized it was changing, melting into a pile of bloody gore, which he flung to the ground, stepping back to avoid the mess. A glance over his shoulder told him its partner had already disintegrated, a puddle of red liquid all that remained.

His head whipped around as lights snapped on in the house, first upstairs and then down. There wasn't time for a proper clean-up, and by the sounds inside, the humans were afraid for their animals. He could stay and try to alter their minds, but there were two coming out now, screen door banging behind them, and he wasn't sure he had the energy to take care of them before he passed out.

The only choice now was a quick departure. With the last of his strength, he willed his body to the end of the driveway, a good quarter mile north of the commotion around the barns.

The next thing he knew he was flat on the road, the smell of tar strong in his nose. He lifted his head, a saltbox farmhouse coming into focus only twenty yards on the other side of the pavement, a strong heartbeat echoing between its walls. Dawn was coming quickly, maybe an hour and a half away, and he had to find shelter soon. These old houses usually had cellars. He would be safe there through the day. And that heartbeat was calling to him.

Chapter Three

I woke up on the couch, the TV blaring with some guy trying to eat one hundred oysters in ten minutes or something. As I wiped sleep drool off my face, I looked around the living room to see what had startled me awake. Eating a hundred oysters is scary, but that wasn't it.

The shopping had been almost fun, and productive as well. At Benjamin's, Alex had rented a rich, black fashionable tux with satin lapels, and a real tie that Piper promised to tie for him. And for me, a simple black, tea length cocktail dress with a modest neckline that showed just a hint of cleavage, and with slits up the sides of a slightly flowing skirt that, in spite of Alex and Piper's raucous catcalls, I still found to be way short of slutty. Piper had insisted on paying for everything, but Alex and I knew we'd pay her back somehow. She may come from a wealthy family, but we would never take advantage of her that way.

After a couple of pitchers of margaritas at *Los Mexicanos* Piper dropped me off at home around 12:30, and I managed to get as far as the couch, promising myself I would get up and wash my face in a little bit. I turned the television to one of my favorite food related channels and that was the last thing I remembered. I keep forgetting that tequila and I aren't the best of friends. I pretty much forget it on a regular basis. I thought about all the work I had in the shop I'd taken over when my mom got sick, and was once again thankful that my "office" was twenty yards away and my "boss" was very understanding.

Bam!

There it was again! It sounded like something was on the porch. Probably another animal found its way in. There were cats all over the place, courtesy of the farm across the street. The Stuckeys made fertilizer over there, and if you're wondering where fertilizer comes from, you can pretty much guess. It doesn't smell like crap for nothing! But the Stuckeys were real considerate and they always put their cows and pigs in the back pasture to keep the smell down for the neighbors.

Still with all of those animals, it meant lots of barns and lots of mice, hence the cats that propagate at an exponential rate. Sometimes they wander across the street and I feed them. I figure there can only be so many rats and mice, and with the number of cats fighting for the food, somebody's bound to go hungry—or go cannibal—and that's just too much to have on my conscience. If I can catch them, I follow that game show guy's advice and have them spayed or neutered. Anything I can do to help control the pet population. Plus I'm a softy for a stray, being kind of a stray myself.

I walked out to the kitchen and glanced at the clock on the microwave—4:38 am. I peeked out the window by the door and saw my reflection. Ick. My chestnut hair was tangled all around my head like Medusa and my makeup was smeared around my mouth where I was drooling in my sleep. I rubbed at my chin to try and remove the streaks, but figured there was nothing to be done about my hair. I'd worry about that tomorrow.

I couldn't see what was going on from the window so I headed to the door, which opens onto the porch. It's about fifty percent window, giving a decent view of the enclosed area to the storm door across the way, and beyond into the front yard where the limbs of a maple tree swayed in the amber beam of the motion light on the near corner of the barn. That light was pretty much a waste of a motion sensor, though, as it was always being set off by some animal or another, which means it was on most of the time.

I walked past the kitchen table, tripping over a chair I had failed to push in, and stubbing my baby toe. Hopping and swearing, I staggered to the door. Cupping my hands around my eyes, I peeked through the window to see if some lost Puss-N-Boots had found his way in through the pet door and was out there knocking my flower pots off the picnic table again. I looked at the table and saw a pot laying on its side. Yep, cats. Then I scanned the rest of the porch, my eyes finally resting on the floor. I blinked several times to make sure I was seeing what I was seeing. Then I staggered back for real.

I had seen this scene a hundred times, maybe more. This vision had started when I was little, at first just flashes of awareness of a time to come, and then as the years went on, more and more of the future—this future—was revealed. I squeezed my eyes shut, took a deep breath and reached over for the porch light switch, clicking it on.

Holding my breath, afraid to move too quickly, I leaned back toward the window and opened my eyes. Crap. It was still there. The vision, the one I had hoped was just a pain-in-my-rear recurring dream, was right in front of me, playing out in real time—a man lying on my porch, naked and bleeding.

I tried to back away from the door, my breath coming fast now, nearly hyperventilating, but I was frozen there, staring out the window. I mean, normally the sight of a naked man on my property would have my heart pounding for a totally different reason. The bleeding thing kind of put a damper on my libido, though, so I just stood there wondering what to do. My first thought was to call 911 of course, but I hesitated. I'd never seen myself doing that in the vision, which just sort of ended at a certain point. I trusted my visions, and since we weren't at that point yet I decided a little investigation wouldn't hurt. I could always call an ambulance later.

Quietly, I opened the door a little bit. Well, as quietly as I could. My house is over a hundred years old, and it tends to squeak at all the wrong times, this being one of them.

The man flinched at the sound and gave a croaky moan. At least he was still alive.

I opened the door and crept outside onto the enclosed porch. The screened walls let in a light breeze, which stirred the leaves of the few plants still upright on the picnic table. The man was lying on the floor just inside the storm door with his back to me. Besides all the blood, I noticed a lot of muscles, broad shoulders, and one heck of a derrière. He was a little pale, but...Okay, Jessica. Get a hold of yourself!

"Hey," I said, "you okay?" Well, obviously he wasn't, but my brain was set on slow at the moment, especially with a head full of tequila and that beautiful butt looking at me. I didn't remember *that* from my dreams.

I walked over and knelt down beside him, moving some displaced flowerpots out of the way, and gently placing my hand on his shoulder. The man's head whipped in my direction and he growled at me, his jaws snapping like a startled animal. I jumped about six feet in the air and as far back as the space allowed.

Okay. He was kind of scary. He didn't move again, though, just lay there with his head over his shoulder facing me and his eyes closed, so I took a minute to scan his injuries, from a safe distance.

He was good looking—well, he would be if he were cleaned up a little. Dark hair clung to his forehead and cascaded around his shoulders, making puddles of shadow on the fake grass carpet. And the man was huge. Even laying down and folded up like he was, he was taking up a lot of space. He was covered in blood, especially around his neck, his arms, and his back looked like someone had taken a cat-o'-nine-tails to him, ugly slashes crisscrossing everywhere. Not that I knew firsthand what that would look like, but I have a pretty vivid imagination. Plus, I read a lot, and in the books I read, people get whipped with a cat-o'-nine-tails all the time. Seriously, it happens.

I leaned forward again, to try and get a better look at his back, and his eyes opened, boring into mine. I jumped again, and it felt like he was inside my head, reading my every thought, making my brain itch. But of course that was ridiculous. Nobody could do that, right? Then again, nobody has visions of the future either, but there you are.

As he glared at me, I did what I would do with the feral cats I collected. I started talking in a soft, high voice, hoping it was as soothing to him as it was to the kitties. "It's okay," I whispered. "You're gonna be okay. I've got you."

"Who are you?" he demanded. His voice was low and raspy, deep like thunder and sandpaper coarse. And his eyes—O.M.G.—they were sapphire blue and bottomless as the sea, and I could easily have drown in them.

It felt like about an hour before I swallowed and said, "I'm Jessica. Jessica Sweet, and this is my house. I think I need to call an ambulance. You're pretty messed up..." His eyes flashed purple and...

I woke up on the couch, déjà vu all over again. I looked at the TV, sure I was going to see that oyster guy again, but instead it was the butter lady, cooking up some grits, and I could see the sunlight shining through my living room windows. What the heck just happened? Was it just the dream again? It had seemed so *real* this time. No, I was sure it had happened.

I jumped up and ran to the kitchen, stubbing my pinky toe on the corner of the coffee table on my way. I screeched in pain, realizing that my toe was already injured. I had done it last night, in the kitchen, tripping over that stupid chair! Right?

I hobbled out to the porch and searched for signs of the intruder. Blood. There had to be blood—he was a morbid mess! But the porch was clean. There was nothing. No blood. Nothing out of the ordinary. The flower pots I remembered being scattered on their sides were upright and where they belonged.

Now, I knew I was losing it. It's one thing to have visions and know that they are just visions, but to have a vision and think it's really happening? That's just, well, *nuts*! I sunk down into a wicker chair, usually occupied by King Cat, the friendliest of my strays, and looked around the porch, absently scratching my wrist. Picnic table—check. Clay pots full of snapdragons and petunias—check. Porch swing with rusty chains and faded flowered cushions—check.

My work shoes were sitting by the door, right where I'd left them yesterday, along with the work clothes I had hastily shed after I'd quit working on a mission chair in order to get ready for my shopping date with Piper and Alex. I absently thought that I really needed to get those clothes in the wash, or I'd be pulling steel wool splinters out of my ass for weeks.

Nothing was out of place. I looked down at my toe—black and blue for the torture it had received, and sighed. Piper and Alex knew about this particular vision, and I considered telling them about this little glitch in my otherwise imperfect system, but decided that I didn't want my friends to go all protective on me. No, this one I'd keep to myself. If it happened again, though. Yeah. Then I'd let them in on it.

After that, I'd seek psychiatric help—as soon as I found a therapist that didn't want to throw me in the loony bin the minute I mentioned "visions."

Chapter Four

The cellar was cold and musty, but it was dark, and that's what was important. The sun had been up for several hours, and he should be sleeping, but having fed recently he was full of energy. Buzzing, really. The girl who had found him lying bleeding on her porch had been a magnificent, albeit oblivious donor. His skin itched where his wounds were mending at a speed that amazed even him. As a General in the Legion, he was used to being injured, so healing was not a new process to him. However, this feeling was...incredible!

He looked around the cellar. Ancient shelves that had once held the household's provisions now stood covered in cobwebs. A few dust covered jars were scattered among the detritus of the cellar, long forgotten if their black contents were any indication. The newer water heater at the base of the rotting wooden stairs was a contradiction to the dark ramp opposite the steps that had once led to a coal shoot at the back the house, bituminous shards still lingering on the angled ground.

He had dragged himself to her doorstep, somehow opening the storm door, and had fallen to the floor, that nasty imitation grass pressing into his cheek, flower pots full of colorful blooms tumbling around him. He had made one final attempt to reach the heartbeat, the lifesaving liquid that would keep him on this earth, but had collapsed beside the picnic table before he could even pull her to him psychically.

He had awakened to her voice, sweet and gentle, talking to him like the wild animal he was. He was disoriented and confused, his hunger fighting for control. When their eyes met he was overwhelmed, by her kindness and her fear, her confidence and her insecurity, but most of all by the awareness in those ice blue eyes. Like she had been expecting him.

Who are you? he had asked. And she had said she was sweet. He rubbed his eyes, trying to remember. No, she'd said her *name* was Sweet—Jessica Sweet—but *sweet* was how he would remember her, her chestnut curls tangled around a soft, gentle face. She had said something else, but by then he was only the hunger, the beast dangerously close to the surface.

At first his need was such that he was willing to do what was necessary to survive, even if it wound up costing him in the end. He didn't even try to calm the superfluous cravings that tortured him when he fed, grabbing her roughly to him and sinking his aching fangs into the delicate skin of her wrist, consequences be damned. The first taste of her life's blood had made his veins sing, and to his surprise, the beast was not aroused, it was soothed. He tranced her into sleep as he fed, her mind so pure he had no trouble in altering it.

After slaking his thirst, he had struggled to his feet, lifting her as gently as he could, and carrying her to the sofa in the living room. He laid her on the soft cushions, her head lolling toward him, and he brushed an errant curl from her face. Her brows were drawn together, and her full lips pursed in a soft pout. Without thinking, he bent toward her, his lips barley brushing hers, electricity shooting through him as their skin touched. Her lips were like velvet against his.

He covered her with an afghan that he found draped over the sofa's back, embarrassed by the flicker of intimacy he'd poached and puzzled that he'd even bothered to make her comfortable. He was lightheaded and, deciding he must still be in shock, had withdrawn to the kitchen where he located the entrance to the cellar just inside the front door.

He executed a fast clean-up job on the patio, confident things were as they should be. The sun was just peeking over the horizon as he closed the cellar door behind him, mentally replacing the hook on the outside of the door before descending the shabby, decaying stairs.

Now, he leaned against the stone wall opposite the water heater, which was cycling up as she showered somewhere in the house above him. He listened to her movements, and it sounded like she was singing.

After many long moments, he heard the door slam closed as she left the house, probably headed to work. He rested his head against the cold stone, wondering where it was she was going and what she did to earn her living. He closed his eyes, running his tongue over his teeth and enjoying the feel of her blood flowing through him, her taste still in his mouth. Honeysuckle. She tasted like honeysuckle and wine. And, he thought as he drifted to sleep, she tasted like more.

Chapter Five

After talking myself out of hysteria, I picked up my work clothes and took them to the laundry room. Hot water, lots of bleach, and in they went. Then I went to the bathroom, jumped in the shower and washed away some of the eerie feelings and most of the leftover tequila. I dried my hair, threw on some powder and blush, and retrieved fresh work clothes from the laundry room. I didn't really have a place to store them, like a closet or dresser, because they were either coming out of the wash or going in, so why bother, right?

I threw on an old t-shirt with the arms cut off and a pair of baggy blue jeans, all compliments of the thrift shop in Centerville. Bleach spots covered the jeans, making me look like a blue and white Guernsey cow. I grabbed a bottle of water out of the fridge and, slipping on my stain covered sneakers from the porch, I headed out to the barn for some therapeutic stripping. Furniture, that is.

I was still working on the Mission chair for Mr. Peterman over in Germantown. I loved the smooth lines and flat surfaces. Made it easier to strip and finish, and I didn't have to worry too much about messing it up.

I learned this trade from my parents, the Sweets. It was really my Mom's thing—Dad was more into his airplane—but they both worked at the furniture. I'd never seen two people who could spend so much time together and never get tired of each other. Rumor had it that in the forty-five years they were married, the only nights they spent apart were when one or the other of them was in the hospital, and those occasions were rare. They loved each other so deeply, and though they argued sometimes about silly things, they were a force to be reckoned with when it came to the important stuff.

I used to love watching them work together. Whether it was in the furniture shop, cleaning the house or making a meal, it was like a well-rehearsed dance where each of them knew their part, their steps flowing together in an elegant waltz, their years together creating an effortlessness that was a true thing of beauty.

I looked up at the little sign above the office door. "Almost New Again." Mom had loved that name. Dad thought it was hokey, but he never let her know it. As I looked at the lettering, elegant curves in shades of tan and gold, I remembered watching Mom paint it, Dad telling jokes and trying to make her laugh, finally succeeding as she finished the lettering and fell back on the ground, dabbing at his face with the wet paintbrush, their giggles floating to the heavens. People spent entire lifetimes searching for the kind of love they had. I'd feel lucky to come even close.

It was Thursday, so I still had a couple of days before the Mayor's thing on Saturday. Piper had informed me over margaritas that I had an appointment to get my nails done tomorrow and she made me promise that once they were done I would not work on furniture until after the party. The way I figured it, I could get this chair stripped today; apply the first coat of polyurethane tomorrow before my appointment and then take Saturday off to preserve my nails. Sunday would have to be a work day, though. I was getting a little behind in the seat weaving department. I had a set of six ladder-back chairs that needed rush seats, and if I worked really hard I might be able to get two or three of them done, depending on how long my hands held out. And how much I drank the night before.

I turned my CD player on loud, "Phantom of the Opera" blaring from the dust covered speakers, and I sang as I worked.

For some reason as I sang, the image of a naked man lying beautiful and dying on my porch, the one I was trying hard to forget, came rushing to the forefront again.

I cranked up the volume on the stereo and redoubled my efforts on the chair, trying desperately to clear my mind of foreboding thoughts.

Chapter Six

I stripped on the chair for a couple of hours, chemical fumes permeating the air in spite of having left the doors open for ventilation. Between singing "Phantom," scraping, steel wooling and buffing the now raw wood, not to mention the eighty degree temps outside, by 1:00 I was ready for a break.

I shifted the chair to a clean patch of floor, and proceeded to clean up the newspapers, full of dirty strip and slimy old varnish. I rolled it up, bagged it all in a large black garbage bag, and set it aside to be taken to the processor for proper disposal.

I thought about going in the house for a PB and J and a quick breather, but as I wiped the last bits of residue off the back slats of the chair with a cotton rag, my mind wandered back to the night before, and I tried really hard to convince myself that it was truly just the vision again. Obviously, I'd need more than PB and J to get my mind off of that.

I sighed as I walked back out into the sunlight, pulling the impromptu bandana I'd made from a strip rag off my forehead and wiping the sweat from my face and neck.

A real break was imminent, so shower first—yes, another one—burger next. I needed to exchange some books at the library anyway, and one of Mable's famous bacon burgers, rare, was just what I needed to think through the previous night. Okay, I didn't really need it, but I wanted it, and that was as good an excuse as any.

Freshly showered, powdered and fluffed, I jumped in my silver Civic hatchback, a relic from the late Eighties that I just couldn't part with, and headed north into town, books strewn over the passenger seat, air conditioner cranked on high. I waved at Bill Jr. in his fancy truck as we passed going opposite directions, and then drove the five miles into town.

A quick stop at the library provided me with three new novels in exchange for the five I returned, and I was off to Mable's. It was such a nice day that I decided to drop my books off in the car, which was parked in front of the historical stone building that housed the public library, and walk the block and a half to the diner.

I entered Mable's to the merry tinkle of the little bell that hung over the door and saw Mr. Stuckey, Sr. at the breakfast bar talking to Mable herself. I walked up to the take-out counter, and as I ordered the burger and fries I'd been drooling about for the past hour, I tuned in to the conversation taking place at the bar.

"It was the darndest thing," I heard Mr. Stuckey telling Mable, who was pouring him a cup of coffee, silver bun bouncing on the back of her head, the pencil stuck through it (the bun, not her head) dangerously close to flying out and into the pie case. Her beady eyes were bugging out at the impending new gossip. By the looks of things, I hoped she was pouring decaf.

"Early this morning the animals just went plum crazy! I thought they was going to tear the barn down trying to get out! Like to scared Mary out of her flannels, it did! Bill Jr. and I ran out and did what we could to quiet them down, but it took the rest of the night just to get them calm. Bill Jr. got out his clarinet and that helped some."

Bill Jr. played the clarinet? *Wow*, I thought, *who knew*?

"Finally, about dawn, they seemed to come to their senses, and Bill Jr. and I headed back to the house to try and get an hour's sleep or so, and we saw it—blood all over the driveway! We looked everywhere for something that had been hurt or kilt, but nothing! Not even a blood trail. All the livestock's accounted for. I suppose it could have been a cat—"

I cringed at the thought of one of my orphans being hurt, but my skin tingled as Mr. Stuckey continued.

"—but it was an awful lot of blood for it to have come from a small animal. Chief Ned's as stumped as we are."

Ohmigod! Something did happen last night! I just knew it! But why would a naked man be over at the Stuckey's, bleeding all over the driveway and riling up the livestock? And then how would he have ended up over at my place without leaving a trail of blood? And if he *were* at my place, and it wasn't just a vision rerun, where did he go, and why was there no blood on *my* porch?

"—did you Jessica?"

What? I really needed to stop with the daydreaming.

"I'm sorry, Mr. Stuckey, what did you say?"

"I asked if you had seen or heard anything out of the ordinary last night. Something that would have got my animals all in a lather?"

My heart was in my throat, my pulse pounding in my head and I know I looked guilty, but I just said, "No, sir. I was out with Piper and Alex last night and after a couple of margaritas, you know I sleep like the dead!"

Kathy, the waitress at carryout, was chuckling as she bagged up my burger. I paid her quickly, thanked her, said, "I'm sure glad all your animals are okay," to Mr. Stuckey, and hurried out the door, the bell ringing cheerily behind me.

I was too worked up to go home, so I walked a few blocks to the little Memorial Park next to the Police Station, chewing my nails in concentration. I sat in the sunshine at an old picnic table and absently nibbled on a fry. I could hear the splashing of some folks getting in an end-of-the-summer swim at the pool behind the park, while a group of little guys huddled around a pigskin almost as big as they were, practicing for what must be their first ever year of football, peewee style.

I just couldn't figure out for the life of me what had happened last night. It was obvious that there had been more to my night than just an old vision returning for a visit. What with all Mr. Stuckey had said I knew that there really had been a man on my porch, but why couldn't I remember?

Taking a big bite out of my burger, I decided not to go looking for trouble. If Chief Ned couldn't figure it out, who was I to try? If I came forward with what I thought I knew, I'd just expose myself and my secret, and I certainly didn't want to do that. Since there was no body on my porch, there was no proof, and without proof, I'd just sound as crazy as I felt. The best thing I could do was finish my burger, go home and finish that chair, and focus on the Mayor's party this weekend.

Or maybe I'd run over to Piper's and see if she wanted to hang out for a while. With my brain working overtime like this, alone was the last thing I needed to be.

Chapter Seven

When night fell, he crept up the dusty steps and hesitated by the cellar door. The house was quiet, the heartbeat absent, so he opened the creaky door and stepped into what could only be described as an old fashioned country kitchen. The house was completely dark, but with his vision this wasn't an obstacle. With a quick perusal he saw that a small dinette set took center stage in the room, with an L of cabinets and counter space taking up one corner, an old gas range on one end and a yellow porcelain sink in the center. The range and the refrigerator were both the same goldenrod as the sink, and the border topping the walls near the ceiling was a collage of roosters and hens.

The linoleum was also on the golden side and the ceiling was done in a unique pattern that could only be explained by decades of paint chipping off in places, but never being completely removed before the next coat was added. The current color looked off-white, but you could see in the corners where it had once been blue, and green, and myriad other colors as well.

First things first. He really needed a shower. After feeding he had regained enough strength to take care of the girl and to do what he hoped was a passable clean-up job on the porch, but that had pretty much drained him of both energy and time. Her blood hadn't quite taken its full effect yet, and the sun had been peeking in the living room's bow window when he tucked himself away in that damp hole in the ground they called a cellar.

Now his wounds were healed, and with her blood still humming in his veins he was feeling stronger than ever. And he was an unholy, stinking mess. Blood was caked and cracking on his skin where his injuries had been, his hair was matted and filthy from his beatings in captivity, and the gore of the creatures he had killed left a smelly film on his hands and arms.

Scratching at his scruffy beard, he located the little bathroom with the modern tub and shower, cranked on the water and waited for the steam to rise before stepping in. He groaned with pleasure as the scorching hot water soaked into his hair, sluicing away the filth and grime and old blood. He picked up the shampoo bottle sitting on the ledge, flipped open the lid and inhaled the sweet aroma of mango and kiwi. As he lathered his hair, he thought about Jessica, the sweet smelling, sweet tasting, Jessica Sweet, who had unknowingly saved his life. She would never remember he was there, never know he existed, let alone what she had done for him. Guess a thank-you note was out of the question. Not that that was his style.

He shook his head to clear his mind, water from his nearly black mane spraying the shower walls. Thoughts like this could get a guy in trouble, and he had enough to worry about without having a woman in his head. He washed quickly, borrowing the razor on the bathtub's edge and some girly smelling shaving cream to scrape the stubble from his chin. The sooner he was out of this house, the better off he would be.

As he toweled off, it occurred to him he didn't have any clothes. Damn. This Jessica wasn't a tiny girl, but her clothes were still too small for his six foot four inch frame. Surely she had some sweat pants or something lying around. His ass wasn't *that* big. Maybe he could wear them as shorts.

He stepped out of the bathroom, a towel secured around his hips, and peeked into the laundry room. Clothes were piled on the dryer, but a quick search through them revealed there was nothing that was going to fit. As he walked out of the tiny room, a steep staircase caught his eye.

He lifted the latch on the door, oddly located at the third step up, and silently climbed the stairs, intent on searching the bedrooms. He told himself he needed clothes, but the truth was, he wanted to know more about this woman. Photos lined the wall up the narrow staircase. An older couple smiled out from the pictures, mostly taken in this house. One photo in particular caught his eye.

A young girl on the steps of a government building, an adult on each side with her tiny hands clasped in theirs, all three beaming with love and hope. Probably Jessica and her parents, though any human scents in the house other than Jessica's were faint, as though she were the only one living here on a daily basis. However, by the other photos it looked like they had lived here at one time. Perhaps the man had left some clothes behind.

The first room on the left at the top of the stairs was a smallish room with lime green carpet and wallpaper patterned with horses jumping fences, their jodhpured riders clinging to their necks. The small closet inside the door was filled with what looked like mementos—a flag pole with a colorful flag leaned in the corner of the closet, surrounded by old teddy bears and dolls, a couple of formal gowns, an old high school letterman's jacket with numbers on the sleeve, and boxes of pictures and programs from high school plays. A quick visual of Jessica's past, but nothing he could really use.

Across the hall was a larger room, this one taking the form of a sitting room. An old sofa and chair took up two walls, with a build-it-yourself entertainment center hulking across from the sofa, near the window. A stereo from the late Eighties sat on one shelf, complete with dual cassette and turntable, and a nineteen inch analog TV occupied the largest space on the shelves, a VCR on the shelf above it (VHS—at least it wasn't Betamax!) The other shelves were lined with various books, video and audio cassette tapes, and—he couldn't believe it—real record albums! Who was this girl to have such a collection of antiques? Most of the humans he'd encountered, especially the younger ones, were all about the DVDs and Blu-ray, tablets and smart phones. This room was totally retro.

He opened the doors to the narrow cedar closet, but it, too, was stuffed with antiques. Although the contents probably had belonged to the couple whose faces beamed from even more pictures scattered throughout this room, he still hadn't found any clothes.

Diagonally across from the door he'd entered was another door which lead to another room and another staircase. He'd go down that way, but there was a room back the way he'd come that he had yet to investigate.

This room looked to be the master bedroom, the place where this Jessica did her sleeping and dressing. Another narrow closet revealed various blouses, slacks, jeans and dresses. He ran his fingers through the fabrics, bringing a silky sleeve to his face to inhale her scent, the same honeysuckle as her blood. He closed his eyes and took a deep breath. *Christ!* Things were starting to stir down low, the cravings he fought on a regular basis on the rise, and if he didn't find some clothes soon and get the hell out of here, he might be tempted to stay until she returned. And that could be disastrous.

A cedar robe in the corner of the room caught his eye, and inside he found what he was looking for. The man in the pictures had been smaller than him, but not by *that* much. His search produced a pair of grey sweatpants he was just able to squeeze into, though they barely reached his ankles, and a blue t-shirt with "I Fly" in gold lettering that fit about the same. A glance in the vanity mirror told him he looked like an idiot, but it would have to do until he could get back to the Legion's Compound and his own closet.

He'd lost his cell phone when he'd been captured, so he picked up the cordless next to the bed and dialed. A deep voice answered the phone. "Who is this? How'd you get this number?" Finally.

"Viper, it's me. Raven."

"Christ, Raven, where have you been? The boss is going apeshit! We tracked your Vette to the Reserve, but you were nowhere to be found. That was three weeks ago. What the hell happened?"

"Calm down, V. People will think you care." Raven chuckled at Viper's snarl on the other end of the line. "Listen, I'll explain it all later, but right now I need a pick up. I'm at a house on Reserve Road, east end, but I don't know how long I can stay here. The owner is out, but could return at any time, and the Reserve itself isn't safe."

"What do you mean, not safe? What the fuck's going on, Raven? Never mind. Tas is in town and can be there in five. If the human comes back before he gets there, just contain the situation. We're coming for you, bro."

Raven hung up, and sat down on the bed, her scent surrounding him. Contain the situation. Yeah, right. He really had to get out of here.

He walked back downstairs the way he'd come up, the unexplored portion of the house forgotten, and exited the kitchen to the porch where he had lain just a few hours ago, inches from winking out of existence. When he sat down on the swing, it groaned under his bulk, the rusty chains protesting as he rocked his feet back and forth. Jessica notwithstanding, big trouble was brewing in the little town of Fallen Cross, and if his abduction were any indication, his people were right smack dab in the middle of it.

A breeze drifted through the screens surrounding the porch, helping to clear his senses of her scent, and a large black cat entered through a pet flap on the porch's side door. Meowing loudly, he wove himself between Raven's bare feet, rubbing soft whiskers against his calves. Without warning, the witchy looking creature jumped in Raven's lap, planted large paws on his chest and looked him straight in the eyes. Raven reached out his mind to the little guy, searching for intent, and instead found the same question in the mind of the feline. This cat wanted to know Raven's intensions?

Things were getting very strange indeed! Mesmerized by the cat, Raven nearly missed the vehicle approaching, lights blinking in old Morse code. The word it spelled was *tart*, the Legion's current code for situations like this (the codes were changed often for everyone's safety, and were subject to Merlin's wry sense of humor.) Raven dropped the cat unceremoniously to the ground, ignoring the animal's protesting growl, and was at the road in an instant. As he climbed into the black SUV he could swear he heard the black cat's inquiry repeating over and over in his head.

Chapter Eight

Raven glanced around the war room. Hours had passed since he and Tas returned to the Legion's home base, and he was tired, frustrated, and still a little itchy from his recently healed wounds.

He had explained to Mason, Warlord of their region, and to the rest of the Team assembled around him, everything that had transpired over the past few weeks, glazing over the Jessica Sweet parts, but putting full detail into the description of the creatures he'd encountered, as well as his time in captivity.

And then he explained it again.

He rubbed his eyes, sure the sun was full up by now. Gods, he was tired.

Mason sat at the head of the oak conference table, leaning back in his chair, the fingertips of his left hand tapping his temple. His stylish blue black hair was slicked back, its perfection belying his agitation. To his right, Viper, the Legion's munitions specialist, was shaking his head, light bouncing off his cleanly shaved scalp, one of his many tats peeking out the back of his black t-shirt.

Next to Viper, Merlin, the e-genius, was shuffling papers in a manila folder on his lap, a pencil between his teeth, laptop on the table in front of him. His shoulder length dark hair was tucked behind his ears, and his almond-shaped eyes were narrowed in concentration.

Raven had positioned himself at the end opposite Mason, as far away as he could get from the Warrior. The male was a friend and was the only one in the room who outranked Raven, but beneath the calm exterior was a famous temper—one that Raven's news would definitely have set to simmer. Better to keep his distance and let things play out.

Next to him, Tas ran his fingers through his golden blond hair, a smirk on his surfer boy face that had Raven wanting to kick him under the table. Raven had given him a quick rundown on the way back to the Compound, and though the Aussie was fascinated by the creatures and glad that Raven was all in one piece, he was still finding humor in Raven's spending the day in a skanky cellar, not to mention his less than fashionable ensemble and flowery scent at the time of his pick-up. At least there had been time to change before this debriefing.

Harrier, the Legion's aviation expert, stood behind Mason, leaning against the wall nearest the door. His beefy arms were crossed in front of him, russet hair falling over his brow and shielding his golden eyes, which were focused on Raven, laden with disbelief. "What I want to know," Harrier began in a thick Scottish brogue, "is how the fuck you got yourself captured in the first place? Everyone knows what you're capable of. So explain to us *again* how some skinny albino bastards were able to keep you captive for three weeks..."

Mason cleared his throat and sat up straighter in his seat. Placing the palms of his hands on the table in front of him, he stood up. "We've been over that, Harrier," he said, giving a slight glance over his shoulder at the male. Harrier glowered at his leader's back, but clamped his jaw shut, regardless.

Turning back to Raven, Mason said, "Your escape has given us valuable information. You're being captured would lead us to believe that we're being targeted. We just need to figure out the who and why of it. Merlin, are we any closer to knowing what we're up against?"

Merlin did some more paper shuffling and keyboard tapping, then moved his page of choice to the front. "I've been online—both inter and Undernet—and from what I've been able to piece together, it looks like we're dealing with an ancient race of Sorcerers, powerful magicians who were prolific in the early 1800's. The race is not well known now, and they haven't really been on the radar since their uprising in 1829 was quashed by a group of lycanthropes—Werewolves, I think.

"Early intel shows that Clans of the race have turned up in Germany and Russia, always rural, wooded areas, always fairly low key. Based on the description Raven has provided—tall, thin, floaty white hair, red eyes and all—it looks like they've decided to grace our little town with their presence."

Someone murmured *Christ* under their breath, and Mason held up a hand for silence.

"What concerns me," Merlin continued, "is that a man fitting this description has been seen in the presence of Mayor Diggs in Fallen Cross. In nearly all of the Mayor's public appearances, this man, name of..." he glanced at the paper to his right, "...Helmut Fuhrmann, has been at his side. If Fuhrmann is, indeed, of this Sorcerer race, then it's pretty safe to say Fallen Cross is in for some shit." Merlin pushed away from his computer and glanced around the room, seeming surprised to find the rest of them there. Merlin may be a Vampire, but when it came to research, he could be an über geek.

Mason looked around the room, including each of them in his solid gaze. "So it looks like the first thing we need to be concerned with is the Mayor's new assistant. What can you tell us about him?"

Merlin leaned forward, and after a few more taps and clicks said, "My sources tell me he's relocated here from Germany. His associates range from seedy to downright scary, with ties to some mafia types, both human and preternatural. They also say that a Clan of Sorcerers has turned up locally, with indeterminate numbers. Their purpose is unknown, but the fact that they are in control of a small town government reeks of conspiracy. I can't imagine Fallen Cross as their main target. More than likely it's a precursor to something bigger. The question is, what exactly are they trying to do— and what does it have to do with us?"

"Do we have any idea where this local Clan is based?" Mason had returned to his seat and was now tapping his index finger on the arm of his chair.

"No," Merlin answered. "They are obviously nearby, probably someplace secluded. We have it narrowed down to these three sectors," he indicated the map he produced on the smart board hanging on the wall behind Raven. "We started with the section of woods where Raven was held."

"I took some Soldiers to recon that area as soon as Raven got back," Harrier interjected, "and though we found signs of the camp as Raven described it, it looks like they bugged out after they lost their prisoner."

"Exactly," Merlin continued, "so we looked more around the Reserve where Raven was taken. So far nothing has turned up, but there's a lot of ground to cover and we have to consider we're dealing with magicians here. If we can glamour our grounds, chances are these guys have something at least as effective to hide their whereabouts."

"What about the third area," Mason asked.

"There's another large area of forested land north of town, near the gravel pit, that could have potential. It's Were turf, but you never know."

"How can you be sure they're hiding out in the woods?" Tas asked. "With their hands in the government, it seems to me they'd want more modern facilities."

"It's the trees," Raven said, a faint memory sparking in the back of his mind. "I think they draw energy from the trees. I can't explain it—I was pretty much out of it most of the time—but there seemed to be some connection. They seemed stronger in the woods than they were when we fought out in the open."

"Raven's right," Merlin agreed. "These Sorcerers have a connection to the trees, whether it's a source of their magic, or just a tool they use to implement it, I don't know. It's not just the trees, but the animals of the forest as well. And from what we can gather, it's not a mutually beneficial relationship.

"Our offices in Europe have reported sections of forest being completely obliterated, the discovery of which, incidentally, coincides with Sorcerer sightings in the area. Humans are blaming some sort of blight, but it seems the Sorcerers bleed the energy resources around them and then move on. Large trees and small animals have suffered the most, the theory being that they provide the greatest amount of energy with the least possible resistance. Humans, of course, would be a higher source of energy, but they produce their own set of problems in that they tend to notice when the neighbors fall ill or disappear altogether. And sometimes they try and fight back. These things we're dealing with would rather not have to work too hard for their magical sustenance."

"The question remains, what are they doing here, and why have we been targeted?" Mason was up again, pacing in the small area behind his seat at the head of the table. Harrier moved to another wall, giving the man room to process his thoughts.

"Raven, would you recognize your captors if you saw them again?"

"Sure," Raven shrugged. "Kind of hard to miss, really."

Mason shook his head. "No, I mean, did you get a mental signature from any of them? One that would be recognizable as belonging to their race?"

"Oh, yeah. Absolutely!" Raven nodded, understanding lighting his eyes. With his unique version of mind touch, he had an advantage over his fellow Vampires.

"They were kind of distorted," he continued. "It was like there was some kind of cerebral interference. Like trying to tune into a radio in the mountains. I could get a word or two, but nothing consistent. Very distinguishable."

"Fine," Mason nodded, then looked back to Merlin. "Am I correct that there is some sort of fundraising event for the Mayor tomorrow evening?" Merlin confirmed, and Mason continued, "Great. Raven, you'll go in, see if you can get close to this Fuhrmann guy and find out what's going on. Anything you can learn will be of value."

"Sure, Boss. It would be my pleasure." Raven smiled, showing some fang. He had a score to settle with these Sorcerers. This was personal now, and he was anxious to begin.

"Meanwhile, Harrier and Viper, you two fly recon over the forested areas Merlin has mapped out for us. I don't want you going in physically again until we know exactly what we're facing. Look for areas that seem to be damaged or dying. Tas, maintain normal patrol with the Soldiers, and Merlin, keep digging. We need to know exactly what we're up against, before things get out of control."

Chapter Nine

"Hurry up," Piper whined. "We're going to be late!" I was sweating and struggling to pull on panty hose that Piper insisted I didn't need, but I knew I'd feel naked without. Call me old school. I finally wriggled them into place, amazingly without putting my new acrylic fingernails through the nylon, and slipped on the little black dress Piper had bought for me last Wednesday. Thinking of Wednesday night led me to thinking about my Naked Man, but I stuffed that thought to the back of my mind and promised myself I wouldn't go there again. Tonight, anyway.

My nails were lacquered cherry red, and my hair was piled on top of my head in what Piper insisted was a stylish "updo." The dress was finally in place, and I quickly crammed my feet in my new shoes, wobbling on heels that were way higher than I was used to, and confident I would end the evening with at least one blister on each foot, if not a broken ankle. As I did up the clasp on my new necklace, a gold cross Piper had talked me into, I turned to her for final approval.

"Oh, Jessica!" she sighed, her eyes going misty on me. "You look so beautiful! You really should dress up more often," she said seriously. Then after a beat, "Now, hurry up! We've still got to pick up Alex, and we're really pushing the limits of 'fashionably late!'"

Piper trotted down the stairs ahead of me, her emerald shoes clacking on the wooden steps, then across the kitchen tile. I've never seen anyone make green look so good. Her dress was cut low at the top and high at the bottom, and was a chorus of shiny emerald sequins. I would have looked like a Christmas tree in that dress, but Piper, with her auburn curls cascading down her back, looked like a million bucks.

She ran down the sidewalk and jumped in her BMW before I even got the door locked. "Jessica, are you coming or not?" she yelled.

"Hey, I'm not used to wearing these stilts like you are," I hollered back, catching a spiky heel in a crack in the sidewalk and all but doing a face plant, as if to prove a point. Only some fancy wind-milling prevented an actual landing and the ruination of my stockings. Piper just huffed her impatience, glared at me as I climbed in beside her, and tore out of my driveway like the devil himself was behind her.

Chapter Ten

Raven drove around the circular drive, stopping beneath the porte-cochere of the Mayor's home. He was in a black Hummer tonight, though he would rather have driven his Corvette. Mason had suggested Raven's car might be recognized, assuming the Mayor's assistant was one of these Sorcerers. It could also be assumed that he wouldn't be here alone. Raven let his mind reach out, scanning the property around the house. He didn't sense anything unusual, but reminded himself that the night was young.

The valet was also young, a teenager based on the condition of his skin. He opened the Hummer door, and bowed slightly to Raven, handing him a blue slip and attaching its mate to the keys placed in his scrawny hand. Raven touched his mind and found nothing but inane thoughts of what he would do with the money he made tonight. The boy's eyes locked with Raven's, widening as his mind was probed. He took the fiver Raven held out to him, scratching his head in confusion. The human young were more perceptive of the mind touch, though they were never certain what was happening. Raven had heard it was like something was scratching their brain. For whatever reason, the sensitivity all but evaporated once a human reached their twenties.

Raven smiled as he walked toward the immense double doors, solid oak with stained glass windows and side lights sparkling from the lights both indoors and out. The party had started at 7:00, with cocktails and heavy hors d'oeuvres, but Raven's light sensitivity prevented him from being on time. The invitation Merlin acquired for him was in the breast pocket of his black designer tuxedo. He removed it smoothly and handed it to the guard at the door, who checked his name against the list he carried, then handed the invitation back to him.

The guard directed him to the doors where a butler motioned him inside and pointed him to the ball room on the left. He stood in the entryway, searching the minds of the humans around him. The echoes of dozens of heartbeats surrounded him, like a drum corps competition taking place in a small auditorium, pummeling his senses. It took some doing to concentrate on something other than the human buffet in front of him, the beast all but begging to come out and play, but centuries of evolution had brought his kind to a new level of control, the majority existing under the Legion's laws. First and foremost among these laws was to feed only when hungry, never kill when feeding, and never leave a memory behind. This law was unbreakable, the penalty extreme. Since most of Raven's atrocities had been committed before the new laws were enacted, he'd been spared the consequences, but suffice it to say he would have had to die several hundred times over to pay for the sins of his youth. Now, he not only followed the laws—he enforced them.

So with that as incentive, he tamped down the arterial tattoo, tightened the leash on his alter ego, and opened his mind to the room. It seemed all of Fallen Cross's elite were in attendance, without exception. The ballroom was quite large and very ornate, verging on ostentatious, with high, mural-painted ceilings dotted with skylights that revealed a clear, star-filled sky above. The décor was oriental, with black lacquer and mother of pearl furnishings throughout the room. On a platform on the east wall, a small cover band was playing enthusiastically, a group of young people dancing to an old Seventies tune on the milky marble floor.

Throughout the room, guests were clustered in little cliques of three or four. Raven extended his mind in a general scan and began his search.

A group of blue-blood biddies stood near him to his right, discussing their latest garden club project. The plump woman with white hair piled high on her regal head was somehow looking down her nose at a taller, birdlike lady, thinking that her companion looked like a hooker in that dress, while the bird lady felt the plump woman had gained at least ten pounds since their last meeting.

Beyond the ladies, a bar had been set up, where Raven found Mayor Diggs holding court with a group of businessmen. A tall, thin blond stood nearby, his back to Raven. He seemed like a body guard, sticking to Diggs like a puppet master to his marionette. This had to be Helmut Fuhrmann, a quick scan of his mind confirming what the Legion had feared. He was definitely Sorcerer.

Before he could investigate further, a scent in the air had Raven's eyes widening, and drew his attention away from his quarry. Honeysuckle. His blood pounded through his veins, responding to the call of a familiar floral scent and a distinctive heartbeat that now pulsed louder than all the others combined. His eyes searched for what his other senses had already confirmed.

Sweet Jessica was here.

The absolute last person he could imagine being at an affair like this. Her home was simple, her clothing off the rack. This was a black tie fund raiser for the Mayor of Fallen Cross, Ohio. Okay, so it wasn't New York City, but it was still as fancy as it got in this town. There was a pecking order, and, stunning as she was, he never dreamed she'd be high enough even in this society to make the cut.

She looked absolutely beautiful in a simple black dress and heels, and Raven was uncomfortable with the wave of pleasure that swept through him at the sight of her. This was definitely a distraction from his mission tonight, but one he found himself uncharacteristically eager to embrace.

Chapter Eleven

Walking into the Mayor's mansion I felt like Cinderella arriving at the Prince's ball. Everyone was beautiful—even the ugly people! You know that old saying about a pig in a dress still being a pig? Well, if you put enough glitz and glamour around them, you may not notice the curly tail, and if you do, it will be so dazzling you'll just think it's a fancy belt.

The Mayor lived on an estate east of town, acres and acres of grass and trees, with a house that must have been a million square feet. That's probably an exaggeration, but to me it was the biggest, most amazing place I'd ever seen. Huge, white columns framed the porte-cochere (that's what Piper called it), with large windows as tall as a person all along the front of the house.

Inside, the foyer was all marble and crystal, a humongous fountain chandelier lighting the hall, prisms from the crystals dancing all around the room. The party was being held in the ball room, and that was as magnificent as everything else I'd seen already. It was as big as a cathedral, and every bit as fancy, the Asian décor breathtaking.

Piper was in her element, laughing, talking and introducing Alex and me to Fallen Cross's posh and pompous. Of course, we knew who everyone was. The Fallen Cross Press was a very small local paper, and there weren't that many people in town who were newsworthy. Every one of them was here tonight, the high school football team being the only exception. We said hello to Piper's parents, Dr. Tom and Amber Pendleton, as well as James Stanley, Attorney at Law and his wife, Mavis; Dr. Angus Jeffries, DDS, and his "friend" Susie Marlo; Reverend Jonathon Marks from the First Presbyterian Church down on Cherry Street, as well as several other ministers, a Catholic Priest and the entire school board.

"Isn't this the BOMB?" Piper sang as we excused ourselves from an overenthusiastic campaign volunteer. "And Jessica, you look absolutely fab! I still think the purple backless would have looked fantastic on you, but I'm telling you, you look simply ravishing. I think you could definitely get a date out of this, and with someone worthy of your time—not those losers you usually date."

"Ummm. Piper. You're the one dating all the losers. I haven't had a date in—"

"Whatever," she waved me off. "But I see your first prospect already. He just walked in the door and can't take his eyes off of you, and he is H-O-T, HOT!" Piper kept nodding toward the door like a bobble head doll and I couldn't help but laugh at her enthusiasm. I think she had made it her personal goal to get me laid tonight. I waved my hand at her with the traditional get-out-of-here sign, and glanced over my shoulder. It never hurts to look, right?

Chapter Twelve

She was truly beautiful. The dress she wore was perfect, clinging to her curves with slits up both sides of the skirt, teasing but not giving anything away. She was chatting with a pretty little red-head, laughing at a shared joke, waving her hand at the smaller woman like she was full of it. Then she looked over her shoulder, a rosy blush adorning her high cheekbones as she casually scanned the room. When her gaze reached him, their eyes locked, and he couldn't believe what he saw in those ice blue pools.

Recognition.

Chapter Thirteen

No. Freakin'. Way! I blinked several times, sure I was imagining things. Nothing changed, so I closed my eyes tightly and counted to ten. When I opened them again, The Naked Man was still standing *right there* in the entryway! Okay, so he wasn't naked anymore, and from what I could see there wasn't a mark on him. He was standing in the entry to the Mayor's $500 a pop Fundraising Ball in a $2,000.00 tuxedo, looking just fine!

Truth told, he was looking more than fine. His dark hair was sleeked back and tied at the nape of his neck, and his eyes shone like sapphires, more than a little spark in them flying my direction. His face was chiseled, like a Greek God, his shoulders broad, his olive skin perfect. His chest looked like rock wrapped in silk, and I was disappointed to see his jacket was long enough to cover that magnificent tush. And the look on his face spoke volumes. He knew who I was!

I felt a little dizzy and started to sway a bit, but before I could collect myself Alex was at my arm holding me steady, and the Naked Man had disappeared.

Chapter Fourteen

Christ—she knew him! Raven crossed the room as quickly as he could without drawing attention to himself, and exited through the patio doors on the opposite side from the entrance. She had recognized him—but that wasn't possible! She had gone instantly into trance, and under his suggestion had not awakened until well after dawn. She couldn't possibly know who he was! And certainly not from their encounter of two days ago.

He wanted to convince himself that she was mistaking him for someone else, but there was no mistaking what he heard in her mind—*The Naked Man is here!*

Well, at least he'd left an impression—no, wait! It wasn't *possible* for him to have made an impression! Her memory had been erased, and after five hundred seventy-two years, he was quite certain he had that little trick down pat.

He paced the patio, dodging happy party-goers, his prime objective put on hold. If she remembered him, then she might remember what he'd done, and if she remembered that, he was in big trouble. Prime Law—No Memories, No Bodies. Well her body was intact and then some, but apparently so was her memory, and he was not about to let this little wench get him killed for exposing his race to humans. He'd come too far to allow this to happen. No matter how tasty, this little problem had to be addressed, and eliminated at all costs.

He peeked through the glass patio doors and saw her through the crowd, a tall young man standing at her arm, face contorted in worry, helping her hold a drink to her lips. Those perfect, full, honeysuckle lips. The tenderness in that man's eyes, the concern and affection as he tended to Jessica as though she were the only woman on Earth was absolutely...infuriating.

Forgetting his previous vow of self-preservation, Raven found himself being drawn back inside, absently closing the patio door to the late summer breeze.

"Hey Handsome." This from a gangly blonde standing just inside the door. She was holding what Raven was sure was not her first glass of champagne this evening, her ample bosom spilling out the top of a gold lamé slip. She reached up and grasped his arm, but he was pulling away before her disappointment could register.

He couldn't stop himself. In spite of the danger Jessica's memories posed to him, Raven wove his way through the crowd until he was nearly in front of her. He convinced himself that he needed to talk to her—to find out what she remembered of their encounter. And that it had nothing whatsoever to do with the way that lanky bastard was touching her—or the way her blood was calling to him.

Even Vampires can be delusional.

Chapter Fifteen

"Really, Alex, I'm fine. I'm just not used to these stilts!"
"Yeah, well it looked like you were going down, and it had nothing to do with your shoes. They're not that high, anyway." Alex was being a mother hen.

"He's right, Jess. My shoes are twice as high as yours, and I'm not having any problems," Piper was concerned, too. "Did you know that guy or something? I mean, I know he was super-hot, and even though I've never seen anyone actually swoon before, I think you swooned! If you've already been out with that hunk o' burning love without dishing to me about it, you are in big trouble, sister!" Piper was *really* concerned.

"No, I've never been out with him, and yes, these shoes are too high for me, and I absolutely do NOT swoon! I wear Nikes, for chrissakes. Alex, if you don't stop flitting around like that, I swear I'm going to slap you silly!" Piper had seen the Naked Man. I didn't imagine him this time!

"I wonder where he went." Piper mused, craning her neck to look around the room. "Oh, there he is, over by the patio door with Monica Musick. She's such a slut!"

I snuck a peek in the patio direction, and sure enough, Monica was going full goose blonde bimbo all over Naked Man. The last thing I expected to feel was jealousy, but the little green monster crept up, and if I'd have had laser eyes, old Monica would have been a dust pile.

"Don't look now," Piper whispered, "but he's heading this way! I swear, Jessica Sweet, you have been holding out on us!"

Piper kept talking, but I didn't hear what she said. He *was* walking toward us, and I thought I was going to not-swoon again.

"Excuse me," his voice was still deep and sexy, but some of the raspiness was gone, making him sound like rolling thunder from a storm miles away. "I couldn't help but notice that the two most beautiful women in the room were not dancing," he said in a lilting accent I couldn't place. He completely ignored Alex, and though he included Piper in his words, he never even looked at her, his eyes on me the whole time. I glanced at Piper and she was pouting a little. Lines like that were usually used on her, and for a minute I felt guiltily superior.

Then I remembered who I was talking to—Naked Man—and thought maybe I should proceed with caution. Alex placed a protective arm around my shoulder, and I could swear I heard Naked Man growl at him. Seriously! I reached up and touched Alex's hand to reassure him, though I wasn't particularly confident myself. "It's okay, Alex. I think I *would* like to dance with Mr...."

"Knight. Ramon Knight," he offered his hand to me in an old fashioned way, his palm facing down. I gave him a hesitant smile as I placed my hand on top of his. I guess this was supposed to make a lady feel like she wasn't being dragged to her doom, but going along of her own free will.

Even so, I felt like a huge door was slamming behind me, telling me that once I took this step I'd never be able to go back. My life was about to change, and there was nothing I could do to stop it.

Chapter Sixteen

She laid her hand on top of his, sending a small spark through Raven's skin as he led her out to the dance floor. The music was slow, and several couples were taking advantage of the opportunity, some moving in a graceful waltz, and others doing the modern version, hanging onto each other and swaying back and forth. The buxom blonde had found new prey, and was wrapped around a young man who looked completely conquered, and eagerly so.

Raven opted for the modern dance style which was more conducive to conversation, slipping his arms around Jessica's waist. She was hesitant, but after a couple of beats she put her hands on his shoulders, keeping some space between them. He found himself wishing she had put them around his neck.

Raven glanced over her shoulder to look again at the male who had tried to claim Jessica. The way he'd drawn her to him had sent spikes of jealousy though Raven's spine, and he was surprised at the intensity of the emotion—at the emotion itself. He reached out with his mind and knew that the male, Jessica had called him Alex, didn't trust Raven. Smart man.

"So, Jessica, how do you know the Mayor?" Did he really just say that? Next he'd be asking her astrological sign.

"I don't, and how did you know my name?" She asked.

"I heard your friends refer to you as such." Good save, Raven.

"Oh," she muttered. She glanced at the floor, then looked up into his eyes. Her gaze hardened, then became resigned. Taking a deep breath, she dropped her voice to a whispered hiss and said,

"Look, *Ramon*, or whatever your name is, I know you were the man on my porch the other night, and I know that something crazy is going on here, because I saw your wounds, you were covered in blood, and now you're fine—you're not even limping! I don't know what your deal is, but I do know there was a ruckus across the street from me at the Stuckey's farm, and there was blood there, too. I'm no genius, but where I come from two and two are still four, and you don't have to be a rocket scientist to figure out that you were involved somehow." She was a mass of clichés, but the words were tripping off her tongue, and her heart was racing full out, sending his senses into overdrive.

Raven opened his mouth to respond, but she continued, seemingly on a roll. "I've been going crazy trying to figure this out, and I had almost convinced myself that it was just another, vi… Just a dream," she corrected. "But now, here you are and I don't know what to think, so please. *Please!* Tell me what I'm missing before I have myself committed. Can you do that? *Ramon?*"

Raven just stared at her, not sure he had heard correctly. She knew him, knew she had found him on her porch, but didn't seem to know about the, umm, other stuff that had happened. Now what did he do? He had to find out exactly what she remembered, before he could determine if she were a threat to the Legion, and right now she was talking in circles.

He looked into her eyes, sapphires into icy blue, and she glared back at him, unblinking. He reached to her mind again, but her thoughts were a murky pool. She was nervous and she was afraid, and her emotions were blocking her thoughts...but her fear was not of him. It was something else. And it shocked him to realize that his greatest desire in this moment was to alleviate that fear.

Their feet were barely moving now, as she searched his face for answers, and he became lost in her gaze. Raven raised his hand to cup her chin in his palm, smoothing his thumb over her velvet cheek.

They stood there frozen for what seemed an eternity, then her eyes grew wide and pale, and for several beats her mind was completely blank to him. Raven was shocked. None but Vampire had ever been completely closed to his mind touch! He focused now, trying to regain the mental connection, but when it finally returned he found her fear and anxiety had been replaced with shock and—embarrassment? She shook her head as if denying something she could not bear.

And then she collapsed in his arms.

Chapter Seventeen

"I said, get your hands off of her!"

What was all the yelling about? I opened my eyes, still in Naked Man's, *Ramon's,* arms, but for some reason I was on the floor, people were all staring at me, and Alex was having a conniption. I swear sometimes he's such a girl! "What did you do to her, you bastard? If you don't get the fuck away from her, I swear, I'm calling the police!"

"What seems to be the trouble here?" Chief Ned had pushed his way through the crowd, his wispy hair slicked over his bald spot in a hasty comb-over, and the buttons of his slightly faded tux jacket straining with the bulk of his middle. He looked kind of funny in that suit. It had probably come from the "For Sale, Cheap" rack at Benjamin's Formalwear at the mall.

Everyone started talking at once, Alex yelling at Ramon, Piper swearing it was my shoes, other guests trying to input their version of the newest Jessica Sweet story, just in case it made the papers. Ramon, however, was not speaking. He knelt on the floor with me practically in his lap, looking at Alex like he was going to make a meal of him. He must think I'm a total nut case—Good lord, he touches me and I pass out? Jeesh!

"I'm fine," I said, but nobody was listening.

I struggled to get up, but Ramon tightened his grip on me, looking at Alex and growling again. What was with that anyway? I grabbed his lapel and tugged a few times to get his attention back on me, and a little more loudly said, "Hey—I said I was FINE! Hell-oooo! Hey, big guy, let me up." He finally stopped staring at

Alex and returned his attention to me, concerned. I struggled against his hold, and he reluctantly relented, sliding his hands gently down my arms until he was grasping both my hands, pulling me to my feet.

"Piper's right. Just a little shoe trouble! Nothing to see here, go on about your business!" I was getting a little grouchy—I hated to be stared at—and the look on my face must have said as much, because people started to disperse.

"Are you sure you're okay, Miss Sweet?" Ned was trying to be official, but the monkey suit was putting him off his game. I just smiled at him and said, "Yep, never better," as I brushed imaginary wrinkles and dust from my dress. The chief stared at me doubtfully, but finally left us to ourselves, scratching his head as he ambled back to the bar.

Ramon still had my hands, and was looking at me like I was going to start speaking in tongues or something when Alex grabbed my arm and pulled me away from him. "Hey!" I cried, and I nearly went down again—this time it really was the shoes—as Alex pulled me behind him protectively and blocked me from Ramon's view.

"I didn't hurt her," Ramon said. "Jessica, please tell your friend that he has nothing to fear from me." He said this while looking at Alex. By the look on Ramon's face, I wasn't sure that was exactly true, but sensing something ugly about to happen I wrapped my fingers around Alex's bicep and pulled him toward me, though he continued to glare at Ramon. Ramon, for his part, looked all calm on the outside, but his eyes were spitting fire. I swear, you let one naked guy on your porch and all hell breaks loose. See why I don't date?

"Alex, please, it's okay. I just had one of my little *episodes*," I said giving him a meaningful look. He tore his gaze away from his foe, and as his rugged face registered understanding, he backed off a little. Very little. At some point I was going to have to explain to him the vision I'd had while dancing with Ramon, but fortunately the number of people around prevented me from doing so immediately.

"Are you okay?" he asked, forgetting Ramon for a moment.

"Yeah," I said, and felt my cheeks reddening. Alex and Piper are my best friends, and they totally understand about my "episodes," but I wasn't looking forward to explaining this particular vision to them.

When Ramon's fingers touched my cheek there had been a spark, like an electrical current arcing between us, and what I saw...what had put me on the floor...was a vision of he and I, well, having sex! We were both quite naked with him on top of me, his face buried in my neck, and the room was bathed in lavender light. And we were having a *real* good time.

But it wasn't just the sex that knocked me out—it was more than that. The intensity of the vision was like nothing I had ever felt before, carrying me so far into it that I couldn't seem to find my way out. And when I did, I lost consciousness. As much as I tried to convince myself it was just wishful thinking, I knew better than anyone that my visions weren't merely a suggestion. They always came to pass. Piper and Alex would have a field day with this one.

How in the world was I going to explain this to Ramon? He was keeping his distance now, his expression hard to interpret. I hoped his wariness was directed at Alex, but didn't think I could be that lucky. Sometimes I wished I could read minds instead of having this psychic, vision crap. Right now, I'd really like to know what he was thinking.

Chapter Eighteen

I was still trying to figure out my next move when there was a *thump-thumping* of someone tapping on a microphone. The band had stopped playing and the Mayor was now standing on the little stage, a tall, blond man standing behind him to his right, hands folded in front of him, eyes on the Mayor. His long, white hair seemed to be struggling to free itself from the elastic bands holding it at bay. Talk about a static electricity problem.

"Ladies and gentlemen, if I could have your attention please." The chatter died down and all eyes turned toward the men on the platform.

"First of all, I want to thank you all for joining us here today to celebrate my candidacy for re-election, and for supporting my initiative for a stronger, more prosperous Fallen Cross!" The guests applauded politely as the Mayor smiled pompously from the stage. His corpulent belly was barely camouflaged by the expensive tuxedo he wore, his thick, silver hair combed smartly to the side.

"I stand before you today, a humble man, grateful for your support and honored to know that when it comes to change in our community I can count on you to help us all move forward with the policies that will keep our town safe from the evils that plague the world." The people nearest us were exchanging puzzled looks and began murmuring softly under a smattering of applause. This was Fallen Cross. What "evils" could we have here?

The Mayor continued, "With the help of my staff, and my new advisor, Mr. Helmut Fuhrmann," the blond man nodded his head once in acknowledgement, "we are committed to the changes necessary to protect the good people of Fallen Cross, and to launch our community into a new realm of wealth and prosperity!

"So, enjoy the rest of your evening knowing that your futures and the future of our town are in the best of hands! And don't forget to vote!" More applause followed, though it lacked its original enthusiasm, and people began to discuss this little speech in earnest.

Piper wasted no time returning to party mode, but Alex and I exchanged a glance before I looked over his shoulder to find Ramon glaring at the stage. The Mayor and his consultant were exiting the platform, and if I didn't know better I'd swear the tall stranger had looked right at our little group. I figured he was just looking to see who the idiot was who'd passed out earlier, but he gave me the creeps. As I watched, he pulled out a cell phone, spoke briefly, then returned it to his pocket. For his part, Ramon seemed to have melted into a shadow.

Having reached my maximum embarrassment level for the evening, I looked at my two friends and said, "Guys, I hate to be a party pooper, but I think I've had all the excitement I can stand for one night."

"No!" Piper cried. "The party's just getting started! We can't go now!" I hated to put a damper on their good time, but I just couldn't stay here any longer.

Alex could sense my discomfort and came to my rescue, offering, "I can take you home, if Piper will lend me her keys. Then I can come back and P and I can rock the rest of the night away." He pulled a goofy dance move to lighten the moment, but Piper was still sulking. Behind Alex, Ramon reappeared, clearing his throat.

"I would be more than happy to see Jessica home safely."

Alex glared over his shoulder at the larger man behind him and said, "Forget it."

Before things could escalate, I moved to stand by Ramon and said, "Thank you, that would be great. That way Alex can stay here with Piper and everyone will be happy, right Piper?"

Piper was still not happy, and Alex was looking skeptical for a totally different reason, but since they hesitated I just said, "Right. Have a great time—don't drink too much and I'll call you both tomorrow!" I hugged them both and ignoring the arm Ramon offered me, I walked toward the front door, retrieving my bag from the hat check girl in the foyer. Hopefully, some fresh air would clear my head.

As we waited for Ramon's car to be brought around I glanced at him and said, "I'm not finished with you."

"I was hoping you'd say that," he said, a roguish smile playing at his lips, and I struggled to maintain a straight face. A shiny black Hummer parked in front of us, and Ramon moved to collect the key from the valet. I just stared at him.

"Are you *kidding*?" I asked, incredulous. "A *Hummer*?"

"Company vehicle," was all he said. He held the door open for me, and I shook my head while trying to figure out the most dignified way of crawling inside, dressed as I was. I managed to flash only a small amount of skin before finally settling into the leather seat and fastening my seatbelt, while Ramon walked around to the other side and climbed in.

He slid into the driver's seat, and shifted out of park without another word. As he aimed the monster vehicle down the driveway I decided to wait and see if he'd ask for directions. I knew he was keeping things from me—his lack of denial all but proving it—but just how much he knew about me was still in question.

Chapter Nineteen

Raven pulled down the drive and took a left when he reached the country road. Jessica's presence beside him was a contradiction he couldn't wrap his mind around. He wanted her there. More than anything he'd ever wanted in all his years on the planet, he wanted her near him. But her knowledge of him was key. How could he expose his true self to her and still protect his people? Protect himself? Opening up to her with the full truth could be the death of both of them.

But she had saved his life. Though she wasn't yet aware of that, it was a fact he couldn't hold lightly, especially with her blood still dancing through his system. He had discussed the situation with Mason and the others to some degree, but that was when they assumed she would have no memory of him. Christ—Mason was going to kill him! If her memories were more than she let on, Mason would have every right to kill him.

The silence in the car was giving him too much time to think so he asked, "Am I going the right way?"

She glared at him and said, "You tell me." Okay, there was no getting around that one. She knew he'd been in her home, on the porch at least, and lying about it now would get them nowhere.

So instead he glanced at her and said, "Tell me what you remember, and please don't lie."

"I'm not the one who's been lying here," she sulked. When he didn't respond she inhaled deeply and said, "As I told you before, I woke up and found you passed out on my porch. You were covered in blood, with wounds on your neck and arms. Your back looked like it had been whipped, from top to, well…bottom." She cleared her throat and he could feel more than see the blood rushing to her cheeks. Well, he had been nude.

"I tried to approach you, to find out if you were okay," she continued, "and you growled and snapped at me. I figured you were out of your head with pain so I talked to you. I was going to call an ambulance when you asked me who I was."

She hesitated here. "Go on," he encouraged. "Everything you remember."

"Well, it felt like you were messing with my head," she said, glancing at him through her eyelashes, like she thought he'd question her sanity. "Same as it did right before I passed out earlier. You looked into my eyes and it was like you were in there going through filing cabinets or something."

He tried not to let his discomfort show, but this was not a good sign. Jessica was too old to be able to feel the mind touch. That she remembered this now—this could be a problem.

"It passed soon enough, but when I told you I was going to call for help," she faltered here, "well I woke up on the couch with the butter lady making grits."

"The butter lady?" he couldn't help but laugh at that, his teeth shining perfect and white in the moonlight.

"Don't laugh," she scolded him. "You don't know what I've gone through these past few days, thinking I was crazy—well crazier than usual. I mean, I know everything up to that point, but what I don't know is what happened after I reached for you. I came out on the porch and saw you there, just like you've always been, but then, as usual, I don't know what happened next!" She was getting frustrated, and—wait…

"What do you mean, as usual?"

"I…never mind." There was definitely more to tell, but for now at least, he didn't press. They had turned onto her road, and in moments would be pulling into her driveway. That was all the time he had to decide if this woman was going to be a threat to him, or not. She was looking at him now, her questions burning in her eyes, and so help him, he wanted to tell her everything. She looked so vulnerable. He knew he should drop her off and hope his erasure had been complete, at least past the point she had told him. He couldn't chance another alteration—her friends knew too much and if she forgot the whole night it would throw up all kinds of red flags. But what disturbed him the most, was the intense desire to just take her in his arms and tell her it was going to be okay.

Instead, he said, "Have you told me all you remember?" She nodded and when he touched her mind to determine her sincerity, she winced.

Raven pulled the Hummer into her driveway, put the vehicle in park, and turned to her. "Jessica, we have a serious problem. I like you. Gods help me, I do. But honesty on my part is going to be a problem. The things you want to know—that I truly do want to tell you—it could get me into a lot of trouble."

"What, like, you could tell me, but then you'd have to kill me? Is that what you're saying?" she joked.

"In a word, yes—but I really don't *want* to kill you, do you understand?" He cringed as the words left his mouth. This wasn't going the direction he'd hoped. Her hand was on the door handle and she looked absolutely terrified now. "Shit, I'm not saying this right—I'm not going to *kill* you, okay? Tell me you understand."

"No, I don't. I don't understand a thing."

Chapter Twenty

Ramon puffed out a breath he was holding, then got out of the Hummer and walked to my side of the vehicle, ostensibly to open my door for me. However, I wasn't about to let him play the gentleman after that last little revelation. I had been kidding with the tell me/kill me comment, but his response was way too serious.

I yanked open the door and jumped out, just as he came around the front of the—what the heck *is* a Hummer, anyway? A car? A truck? Whatever. I was still mad, still confused and a little frightened of this tall, dark stranger who spoke of killing me like it would be a minor annoyance that he would be mildly sorry for in the end. A stranger I happened to know for a fact I was going to end up in bed with.

So, when the shadow by the barn resolved itself into the shape of a person, my mind wasn't processing what my eyes were seeing.

Ramon seemed to sense the new arrival. He pushed me back toward the vehicle and was on the guy before my brain could even register what was going on. Blows were exchanged, blood was flying—I couldn't tell whose—and I stood there like a damsel, eyes like saucers, hands over my mouth to cover my gaping maw.

I remained in the driveway, frozen, knowing I should do something to help Ramon, but he and the other guy, a white haired man in what looked like a white karate *gi*, were moving so fast I was sure I'd just be in the way. The attacker seemed familiar to me, but everything was happening so quickly the thought was gone before I had a chance to grasp it fully.

In my mind I seemed to hear Ramon telling me to go inside, but useless as I was, I couldn't just leave him!

As I struggled with what to do, fate gave me no choice when another albino materialized out of the shadows, all camouflage and flowing blond hair, and he came straight for me. My heart was racing, but I was surprisingly Zen as my karate training took over. Without even thinking I went into a cat stance, my weight balanced on my back leg, my hands in tight fists held protectively in front of me. The albino hesitated, taking in the fancy dress, high heels, and my obvious attempt at battle readiness...and he laughed.

The bastard *laughed* at me! And that just pissed me off. "Come on, Blondie," I screamed. "Give it your best shot!"

"Jessica! No!" I heard from somewhere to my right, and then "Oomph," as Ramon took a hit to the gut.

But the asshole was still laughing at me, and the more he laughed the madder I got, my infamous temper flaring up again.

Finally, the albino must have decided comedy hour was over. Before I could attack out of anger and stupidity, he rushed me, his white hair floating all around him. His eyes were red (duh, albino!) but they seemed to be glowing or something. I shook my head and blinked a couple of times, sure I was seeing things. Then he roared what sounded like a battle cry as he ran toward me. It was a little overdramatic, if you ask me.

The nearer he got, the more determined I was to take the bastard out. I leaned back on my support leg, and when he was just a few feet away I hit him with the best side kick I'd ever executed! (*Sensei* would be so proud!) His forward momentum connected with my foot, and I felt his hands wrap around my ankle. Then the sound of my foot hitting his chest clicked in my brain, and it wasn't the *thunk* I had anticipated—it was more of a *crunch*. At the same time this sunk in, I realized my $90 heel was stuck in this guy's chest, his cold hands grasping my foot, and I was hopping around on the other stilt.

I had just enough time to think, *Oh, shit!* before Blondie and I both fell ass over applecart onto the gravel drive, skinning my hands and knees and tearing holes in my stockings. His face displayed pure shock, but I think I was more surprised than he was. We hit the ground together and with a squelch, I pulled my designer knockoff out of his chest. He had done nothing to break our fall, and his hands fell away from my foot, not even trying to stop me from getting away. That's when I realized that he wasn't moving at all.

Oh, my God! I'd killed him! Ohmigod! Ohmigod! Ohmigod! I scrambled away from him on my hands and feet, crab style, and backed myself into the humongo tire of the Hummer. I couldn't catch my breath, and I think I was going into shock, when things went from bad to downright impossible!

The albino lay in front of me, blank eyes staring into the heavens, and he...started to melt! No shit! Just like in the *Wizard of Oz*! If he'd still been alive I would have expected to hear the "What a world, what a world" speech of the Wicked Witch of the West, but this guy just, well, melted! His exposed skin was bubbling, and his clothes looked like there were little hoppy frogs inside trying to get out. Then the clothes started melting too! Within seconds he was nothing but a pool of bloody goo, and I felt myself sliding swiftly down the rabbit hole.

I was sitting by that big ol' tire, trying to comprehend all I'd seen and (gulp!) done, when I realized that Ramon was still fighting. Jeesh, what was taking him so long? I shook my head clear and pulled myself to my feet, stumbling to the yard to see how he was doing.

He and the other albino were grappling, and I wasn't really sure who had the upper hand. They both looked bloody, but things seemed pretty even to me. I grabbed a shovel I'd left by the trellis when I was rearranging my rose bushes, and I quietly approached the two men as they rolled on the ground. I thought about taking off my shoes, but decided they'd served me pretty well so far, so maybe I'd leave them on, even though they were sinking into the ground a little.

Just then, a pile of black and white rolled near my feet and I could see the albino was on top, his hands around Ramon's neck, and none too gently. I looked at my shoe, reconsidered, and raised the shovel over my head, bringing it down sharply on the albino's head with a resonating *gong*! This got his attention off what he was doing to Ramon, giving the Naked Man (sorry, that's just how I still thought of him) the chance to pull a reversal on him, resulting in them both kneeling on the ground, Ramon in back, with his arm wrapped around the albino's throat.

"Our race will see yours in hell, bloodsucker!" the albino croaked. Whatever that meant.

"Perhaps," was all Ramon said before breaking the man's neck. He pushed the limp body away from him and, sure enough, it started up with the bubbly, melty thing, and before you could say, "What the fuck?" it wasn't a body anymore.

That grass was *never* going to grow back.

I dropped the shovel, and followed it to the ground, my knees finding the damp grass, before I rocked back on my ass. Exhausted, I lifted my eyes, searching for Ramon's. He stood before me now, his fancy tux in tatters and spattered with blood. He swung his head toward me, and with all that had just happened, what I saw should not have surprised me, but it did.

Ramon's eyes were glowing purple (hadn't I seen that before?) and his teeth were...I tried to find another word, but sometimes you just have to call a duck a duck.

Ramon had *fangs*!

Chapter Twenty-One

I closed my eyes, trying to shake all the incongruity from my head, sure that there were cobwebs tangling up inside making me think I was seeing things that *just couldn't be*!

Ramon was by my side before I could blink, but when he reached for me, I flinched. He hesitated, withdrawing his hand. His eyes—they were blue again and his teeth were normal. He looked kind of beat up, and more than a little chagrined.

"You fought like a warrior," he said to me. "I have fought two before, but these were stronger. Though I'm sure I would have prevailed, I," he hesitated, "I appreciate your help." He bowed his head to me, touched his fingers to his lips, and then to my forehead. "I am in your debt."

"Hey, no problem," I said, contemplating that kissy thing. I looked around the yard, taking in the still bubbly forms of the creatures—I couldn't bring myself to call them men anymore—and that's when I started to lose it.

"Look, Ramon, I'm not really sure how to start this conversation. I'm probably going to stumble a bit, or maybe it's best if I just come right out with it. I guess what I'm trying to say is, *what the fuck just happened here?*" I was yelling now, and I didn't care. Perhaps I was a touch hysterical.

"Jessica, please, you're injured." I looked where he indicated and was surprised to see my hands and knees were bleeding from my fall with Blondie. "I will explain everything to you," he was saying, "but first we have to get you someplace safe."

"I'm safe in my own house!" I screamed. "At least I was until you showed up on my fucking porch three nights ago! Why? Why did you pick me?" I whined. Okay, now I was feeling sorry for myself. Seriously, I had to get a grip. I picked myself up off the grass and headed to the house, uncaring whether he followed or not. It's hard to stomp in grass in spiky high heels, but I did my best, making a show of it when I got to the sidewalk.

By the time I reached the front door and let myself into the kitchen, Ramon was beside me, begging me to go with him. "Please, Jessica, there could be more. I know they had a place in the woods across the road, and unfortunately, I know they are after me. I have killed several of them—in self-defense only!" he added at my incredulous glare. "But now I fear I've dragged you into this, and I'm obligated to protect you."

All of a sudden that memory that had been tickling the back of my brain clicked, and pointing out the door I said emphatically, "I *saw* that man. At the Mayor's party." I hesitated. "Well, I saw one of them, or someone who looked just like them. That helmet guy?" I was confusing myself.

Taking a steadying breath, I said, "Look, Ramon, I don't know who, or even *what* they are, or what *you* are for that matter," I said, waving my fingers at his chest, and he winced. "But I had my guy down and out while you were playing around with the other one, and *then* I had to help *you*! And you expect me to believe that *you're* going to protect *me*? Excuse me if I don't feel too confident in your offer."

He had the good graces to look embarrassed, but the more I talked, the more I think I was pissing him off. He seemed unaccustomed to being spoken to this way. Then again, he did rush the first guy, so he obviously wasn't afraid of a fight. And he was trying to protect me, even if he did require my help in the end. Oh, and he broke that guys neck like he'd done that sort of thing a time or two. He did say he'd already killed several of them. Maybe I was being a little harsh. I twisted a stray strand of hair around my index finger, and hung my head, ashamed but trying hard not to show it. Finally, I schooled my face into a mask of patience and looked up, fighting to keep my voice calm.

"Ramon, you show up here on my front porch, all bloody and a mess,"

"They did that to me."

Okay.

"But then I don't remember anything after finding you, like how you got better, or where you went—*when* you went? I remember nothing, except finding you. And your eyes—your eyes flashed purple like they did tonight—I remember that now! And then I woke up on the couch with the butter lady on TV!"

"You do go on about the butter lady," he chuckled.

"This isn't funny, Ramon," I cried. "This is about you, and who the hell you are, and why the hell you've been in my head all my life and then ended up on my porch!"

"Jessica, I swear, I will tell you everything—No, I promise, on my heart! There's no getting around it now. And then I need you to explain what you mean about me being in your head, all your life did you say? But we need to leave here, just for now. I can take us someplace where we'll be safe for the night and where," he hesitated again, "Where I can introduce you to my people and we can figure all this out."

"Your people? Who are your 'people'? And where is this place? Where will you be taking me?"

"I—can't tell you. I'm sorry," he rushed on at the fierce look I threw at him, "but it's for your own safety. Just, tell me you'll go with me, and we'll figure out what to do next." His eyes were pleading now, and though I wasn't sure I wanted to know everything, I knew that if I didn't go it would haunt me forever. And if one of those albinos showed up again, forever probably wouldn't last very long. Even though I was acting all tough about it, we both knew I'd been lucky tonight.

"Okay," I said, "But how are you going to keep me from knowing whe—"

Chapter Twenty-Two

Raven caught her before she fell. For all the trouble her memory was causing, she went into trance faster than any human he'd ever seen. He mentally locked the front door, then carried her to the Hummer, setting her gently in the front seat and strapping the seatbelt around her. He scanned the area where the Sorcerers had been eliminated. There was still a lot of goo, but it looked like it was dissipating. At this rate, it would be gone in twenty-four hours. Again, no time for clean-up. They needed to get out of here. If there was time he'd have Mason send someone out to take care of the mess before sunrise. If not, well, hopefully no one would be by here before the evidence erased itself.

A mental scan of the area confirmed that they were alone for now. The two Sorcs must have been alone. The only thoughts he sensed were those of the myriad cats who apparently kept residence in Jessica's barn. One feline mind burned stronger than the rest, but Raven didn't take the time to dwell on it.

He knew he needed to get her to safety, but was awkwardly distracted by the scarlet rivulets growing tributaries along the curve of her calves. The beast was still writhing within him, awakened by the recent kill, the scent of her blood making it purr, and Raven's breathing was ragged as he struggled for control. Tentatively, he ran his hands behind her knees, down the length of her limbs and removed her shoes, one heel sticky with the blood of his enemy. Her stockings had become shredded in her fall, and were easy enough to discard. With the nylon removed, her blood ran more freely, and Raven felt his fangs biting into his lower lip.

Before he could stop himself, he bent his head to her and ran his tongue gingerly along the cut on her right knee, telling himself it was only to heal her. The moment he tasted her, though, he found himself wanting more. Jessica moaned in her induced slumber, her hips moving slightly on the dark leather seat.

Beyond himself, now, he slid his mouth down the curve of her calf, catching a drop of blood with the tip of his tongue before it fell wasted to the floor mat, his eyes blazing violet and his thoughts only of her. With one hand, he explored her legs, brushing, touching the length of her thighs, while his other held her gently behind the knee, supporting her limb for his oral ministrations. Jessica arched toward him, her movements reactionary and inviting, encouraging him as he continued to lap at her legs, careful not to bite, but eager for more.

A cry from Jessica's sleeping lips brought him back to himself with a start, lightheaded from the music of her blood. His eyes finally focused on the curve of the leg he held in his hand, surprised to find Jessica's wounds not only healed, but cleaned as well. Not a drop of blood remained.

Horrified with what he had done, what he *could* have done, Raven backed away, quickly closing the door on the sight of her bared legs. By sheer determination, he hurried to the driver's side and started the engine, failing to see the black cat watching him from the side of the barn. He glanced at Jessica, who was panting lightly in her sleep, and his fangs throbbed. His grip on the steering wheel came dangerously close to breaking it, so he loosened his hold and banged his head against it instead, trying desperately to bring himself to his senses. Regaining a measure of control, he finally shoved the beast into submission. Running his tongue over his aching canines, still salivating at the thought of more of her, he aimed the Hummer in the direction of home, leaving a trail of gravel dust in his wake.

Chapter Twenty-Three

When he approached the Legion's Compound he pulled up to the gates, entering several codes to open them. As the gates swung aside, he glanced at Jessica, still sleeping peacefully beside him. He knew that her peace would be short-lived, and hated that he had brought this misery upon her. But the thought of her being in his home gave him a thrill, nonetheless. It was unlikely anything could come of it, and after what he had done in her driveway he wasn't sure it would be his most intelligent move either, but he couldn't stop the smile that crept to his lips.

He pulled into the underground garage, parking the Hummer in its designated spot. Once he had extracted his precious cargo, he nudged the door closed with his hip, barely having to shift his arms to engage the lock and alarm before heading toward the elevator at the far end of the garage. As he turned toward them, he saw the elevator doors open, Mason and Harrier heading his way, grim faced and determined.

"Raven," Mason said as they approached him. "It seems like trouble just follows you wherever you go, and I see now it's followed you home."

Raven shifted his hold on the girl, grimacing at his Warlord's comment. Mason's words were light, but his mood was most decidedly not.

Harrier nodded toward Jessica and said sarcastically, "This the one that saved your life the other night?"

"Yes," Raven answered, "and again tonight, as well."

"Christ Raven, you fed from her *again*? What the hell happened this time? You look like shit, by the way." Harrier was being his usual sardonic self toward Raven, sneering at him and the girl in his arms. Raven and Harrier were not on the best of terms on a good day, deep-seated resentment fueling most of Harrier's attitude where Raven was concerned. For Mason's part, he was beyond frustrated with them, and Raven could sense that his boss's patience was running quite thin.

"No!" Raven hissed at Harrier. "There was another attack. Look, I'll fill you all in, but not here in the garage. I need to get Jessica inside and then I'll tell you everything."

They walked in silence back to the elevators, hit the down button when the doors closed behind them, and were emptied out into a tunnel leading to the main house. Jessica was tall and lean, and though her weight was insubstantial to Raven, having her in his arms like this was uncomfortable on so many other levels. Her head was resting on his shoulder, her breath like a feather against the pulse in his neck. She snuggled into him, as if she couldn't get close enough, and when he gasped at her movement, the quick intake of air brought her scent with it, making things altogether worse.

Mason and Harrier followed him to his office in the Sub-T West Wing, where he gently laid her on the leather sofa, removed her shoes, and carefully placed a blanket under her head for a pillow. He wanted to touch her face, to fill himself with her scent, but with two sets of eyes on him, he simply turned and walked to the door. The thought of explaining something to these men that he didn't understand himself? So not where he wanted to go right now.

With Mason watching him skeptically, Raven locked the door behind him—it wouldn't do for her to wake up and start wandering around the Compound. The three of them were the only ones who knew she was there, and until the others were notified, she was safer where she was.

Mason led them to his own office, where Merlin and Viper were waiting. Tas was in Fallen Cross with a Squad of Legion Soldiers, scoping out the local hangouts and trying to get a feel for the mood in town. Taking a seat behind his roll top desk, Mason turned to Raven, folded his arms over his chest and gave him the "I'm waiting" look.

Raven explained in detail about the Mayor's party, including the fact that Fuhrmann was, indeed, Sorcerer, and also that thought Fuhrmann recognized him. He related the strange speech the Mayor had given, speaking of ridding the town of the evils of the world, and this drew curious glances from everyone.

Explaining about Jessica took a little more time. When he described Jessica's partial memory of him, Mason's eyes darkened, and Harrier swore, "Dammit, Raven, are you saying you botched the alteration?"

"No," Raven glared at him. "It's not that. There's something about this human that doesn't play out. She goes into trance like she's eager for it, and once she's under it seems her memories are easily manipulated, and she remembers nothing from that point on. Getting rid of memories prior to trance, though. For whatever reason, it didn't happen."

"Did you try and alter her tonight, before you brought her here?" Mason queried.

"No, I didn't, but there were mitigating circumstances," Raven rushed on. "I maneuvered myself into a position of taking her home, to determine just what her memories were, what the threat level was. She was still explaining things when we were attacked in her driveway."

"That explains your suit," Viper chuckled.

"Viper, can it," Mason glared. "You were attacked again?"

"Yeah, two of them, again. I only saw the first one and was in combat with him, when another went for the girl. Before I could do anything about it, the girl had...dispatched the second Sorcerer."

"When you say 'dispatched' I'm assuming you mean 'killed'?" Mason clarified.

"Uhh...yeah. Killed." Raven was squirming internally now, fighting hard not to make it a physical thing. His comrades held barely restrained laughter in check, knowing how it must have torqued Raven to have a human outpace him in battle. Not to mention a human *female*. This next part was going to send them over the edge. "And then she, uh, she hit the Sorc I was battling with a, uhh, a shovel, distracting him long enough for me to eliminate him as well."

Raven fumed as the others gave up and let the laughter come full force. Even Mason couldn't control the smile playing at his lips. "Laugh it up, assholes, but when you finally get a shot at one of these monsters, we'll see who's laughing then." He explained how Jessica had taken the Sorc out with her high heel, meaning to convey the luck that had played into it, but they just laughed harder. Viper had a little pink tear in the corner of his eye, and even Mason gave up his usual control and was holding his ribs as the mirth overtook him.

Finally regaining command of himself, Mason stood up, quieting the room as he moved to where Raven was sulking, leaning on a credenza near the door. "Raven, no one here can question your abilities. We've all seen you fight and your history alone proves you to be more than capable. This human must be exceptional to have stood beside you in battle, and to have been an asset as well. Bring her to me when she awakens. We'll give her a chance to explain herself, and then we will be able to decide how best to proceed regarding her involvement in the situation." He glanced around the room at the still smirking males, his own smile long gone. "Don't you all have some place to be?"

As the others filed out, Raven held back. Mason had returned to his desk and, realizing Raven was still there, turned an inquiring eye to him. "You know this is a problem, don't you?" Mason asked.

"Yeah, I do. Listen, Mason. I know we've been over it, but really, there was nothing I could do. And I've been thinking about some of the things she said. What she told me about what she remembers? It was strange, really. She said something about me being in her head all her life and then showing up on her porch. I think there's more to this situation than a memory alteration error, and I'm afraid if we sic the whole team on her, she's going to feel ganged up on. Let me talk to her before I bring her here, before we make any final decisions. Let me find out what she meant. I have a feeling she could be useful to us. Besides, those bastards know she's connected to me now. Even if we can find a way to make her forget about us, we can't just throw her back out there with no memory of what happened, and let them torture and kill her for things she would no longer know." His voice was shaking and he couldn't keep his apprehension hidden.

Mason studied him for a moment before asking, "What is going on between the two of you?" his voice steady, his eyes intense.

When Raven didn't respond, Mason moved his head until Raven had to look him in the eye, his question obvious.

"Ah, hell no!" Raven exclaimed, flinching as if he'd been hit, then pacing the length of the room and raking his fingers through his hair. "I mean, I fed from her that first night—I told you that. But there's just something about her, about her blood. After feeding, I was so energized I could have built a house! I know it's not rational—human blood doesn't do that, right? But I'm drawn to her, Mason, in a way I can't explain. If her memories can't be controlled through trance, I mean, I get that she could be dangerous to us, but I just don't know if I can allow anything to happen to her," he finished, his voice fading with the realization of what he was saying.

Raven looked up, expecting to see contempt, on his leader's face, or at least judgment, but instead he saw compassion. Mason's eyes had softened, but his voice was firm when he said, "Bring her to my office, and we'll talk to her, just the two of us."

Mason studied Raven for another moment. "Be careful, my friend. You know how important it is that we maintain anonymity for our race. I hope we can contain the situation, and that we can do it with no collateral damage. But if it proves the human is too dangerous, we will have to eliminate her. I presume this will not be a problem for you?"

Raven nodded, knowing that Mason was right. But her blood was still dancing on his tongue, and he knew in his heart that he'd go feral again before he'd let them harm her.

Chapter Twenty-Four

When I opened my eyes I was lying on a couch. Again. I took a deep breath and blew it out on a sigh. Was this couch thing going to be a habit?

I sat up, shaking off the remnants of an erotic dream, and taking inventory of myself. I was still in the little black dress, although it was now grass and gravel stained, and the slit on the right hand side was a little higher than it had been originally, showing a hint of the lacy panties Piper'd talked me into for the "special occasion." My stockings were gone and my shoes were standing neatly on the floor at the end of the sofa. I rubbed the palms of my hands on my knees, and flinched. My hands were still stinging from the gravel skid they'd taken, and I dreaded looking to see what kind of damage had been done to my knees. I'm kind of a wuss when it comes to blood, more other people's than my own, but still. I knew it would have to be attended to sooner or later, though, so I gritted my teeth and moved my hands aside to evaluate my knee injuries, which were...nonexistent. Okay. I looked at my hands, and was relieved to find them still scraped and damaged.

It seemed like every time I woke up on a couch, pieces of my memory were missing, and it was beginning to freak me out. I didn't know if I was losing what sanity I'd had to begin with, or if maybe my gift was pulling a reversal on me, taking away memories of the past instead of giving me visions of the future. Then again, every time I woke up on a couch lately, Ramon had been around. I blinked as an image of violet eyes and sharp fangs came to mind. I really needed to put a check on my imagination. I'd almost convinced myself that Ramon was a...cripes! Get a grip, Jessica.

Instead, I looked around the room. *This must be the "someplace safe"*, I thought. It looked nice enough, in a man cave sort of way. There was a large mahogany desk centered along an entire wall of bookshelves, a small desk lamp on the corner and some papers standing in tidy piles on either side of a desk mat calendar. The office chair was black leather and sturdy, and it matched two slightly smaller versions which sat facing the desk. The sofa I currently occupied, also leather, was on a shorter wall near the door.

I stood up and walked first to the door. I turned the antique brass knob and wasn't at all surprised to find it locked. Then I walked to the bookshelf nearest the sofa and perused the titles there. Keats. Shakespeare. Anne Rice? This guy had one hell of a collection. I trailed my fingers along the spines of the books, smiling at the titles I recognized and pulling out several I didn't, mentally adding them to my "must read" list.

I walked behind the desk, inspecting the books on the shelves, enjoying the peek into Ramon's psyche (a complete set of "Harry Potter" novels?), and when my hip brushed the heavy chair, I turned to examine the desk.

The calendar pad had puppies on it. Puppies. This month was Labrador Retrievers. A smile tugged at the corners of my mouth as I wondered what next month's puppy would be. I took a furtive look around to make sure I was alone, and, unable to stop myself, I lifted the top sheet of the calendar to get a quick glimpse of the page beneath—cocker spaniels! I couldn't help it—I laughed out loud.

Who was this Ramon guy, a man with sapphire eyes one minute, amethyst the next, apparently retractable fangs and puppies on his calendar?

And why was I so calm? Here I was, just minutes (hours? days?) out of a fight for my life against melting bad guys, in a strange place, alone and locked in a room God only knows where...and I was laughing about puppies?

I pulled out the chair and sat, elbows planted on the desk and head in hands. What in the world had I gotten myself into? I tried to convince myself that I hadn't really seen fangs on Ramon. He was bloody and had just killed a man, so of course he'd have a bit of a wild look about him, right? And I could easily have imagined him looking like a wild animal, just as he had that night on my porch. And wild animals had fangs. Right? I had to believe this, because the alternative was just a little much for me to accept.

Chapter Twenty-Five

Raven sat in the surveillance room with Merlin, his eyes glued to the monitor showing the scene inside his office. Cameras were set up in all rooms of the Compound, though the ones located in private offices and quarters were equipped with an off switch, and were really only activated in circumstances such as now.

Jessica was walking through the office, examining his things. She seemed to be enthralled with his book collection. He was an avid reader with a wide range of interests, and since library hours weren't always convenient for his nocturnal nature, he would buy the books he wanted to read, resulting in quite a library of his own. His books were like special friends to him, a refuge he had turned to when he was struggling to reclaim his life, and it touched him to see her enjoying his collection.

When she turned to examine his desk he tensed, not sure if he had left anything out that would give away his true nature. Not that he had doodled "I am Vampire" all over his calendar, but he wanted to be able to explain everything to her before she got the wrong idea about him and his people. Then again, with what she'd seen, it could already be too late for that.

She was looking at his calendar now, and smiling? He couldn't imagine what she found so funny, but her amusement continued as she glanced cautiously around the room and then lifted the top page to view the sheet below, which resulted in her outright laughter. If people didn't stop laughing at him, he was seriously considering letting his beast out, consequences be damned.

Finally, she sat in his chair, and she looked good there. Right. She also looked sad. After a moment she straightened her shoulders and rolled the chair to the bookshelf, where she removed a worn copy of Wuthering Heights. He knew the book by sight, though he was unable to read the title on the spine.

"Is she awake?" Mason had arrived and was watching the screen over his shoulder.

"Yeah," Raven said. "I was just giving her a minute to gather herself. I'll go get her. You want her in the conference room or your office?"

"My office is fine," Mason said, turning to leave the room.

"Yo, Mason," Merlin looked up from the screen in front of him, raising his hand in the air. "Got a sec?"

Mason turned back to Merlin as Raven edged past him and out the door. Mason had told him not to mention the whole Vampire thing yet, that they would tell her together. Raven wasn't sure that was a good idea. Chances are she didn't even trust him. The idea of outnumbering her and then telling her they were monsters she thought existed only in her imagination? Yeah, that was smart. But Mason always had reasons for what he did, and he'd never made a major wrong turn where the Legion was concerned. Raven just had to trust he wasn't making one now.

Chapter Twenty-Six

I was lounging behind the giant desk, thumbing through a very old copy of *Wuthering Heights*—it looked original—when the door opened, light and shadow spilling into the room. Ramon was standing in the doorway, looking a bit sheepish if that's possible for a man of his size. I laid the book gently on the desk, and leaned back in the chair, my hands tented in front of me. I felt like the Godfather behind that desk, all powerful and in control. I'd look back on that feeling wistfully in the days to come.

"Jessica, are you okay?" Ramon asked, inching toward me cautiously, like he was approaching a skittish animal that might bolt at any second.

"I'm fine," I said. "Well rested." I wiggled my eyebrows at him.

"I'm sorry, Jessica. It was necessary," he began, but I interrupted him. I was tired of apologies and ready for some answers.

"No. No. Please don't apologize to me again. Obviously there's a lot for us to discuss, so I'm hoping we can start at the beginning and just work our way forward." He walked to the bookshelf and reached up, switching something on or off, I wasn't really sure.

"Was that a nanny cam?" I asked incredulously.

Ramon nodded, said, "A camera, yes," and I swore.

"You mean, you've been watching me all this time?"

"Yes. I needed to keep an eye on you to make sure you were..."

"Yeah, safe, I know." I shook my head, trying to remember if I'd done anything embarrassing while I thought I was alone.

Then he turned to me and said, "Jessica, my Warlord has asked me to bring you to his office, where we will exchange information with you about us, about you, and about what you have unwittingly been drawn into. But before we go, I just need to tell you, I never intended to put you in harm's way." He was behind the desk, now, his hands reaching out to me, begging me to forgive him for ruining my life. In one swift motion he was kneeling on the floor, having turned me, chair and all, to face him.

"I have sworn myself indebted to you, and that means I will protect you from any who try to harm you. You need to understand this. You need to know that whatever you learn in our meeting with Mason, we're the good guys, and I above all others, will let no ill fall your way."

Sometimes he sounded like a character in one of his old books, all flowery words and avows and avers, and I was still having trouble placing his accent. But the sincerity in his eyes was truly moving, and I found myself trusting him. Wanting to trust him with my life, which from the looks of things could very well be necessary. Again.

I reached out to him and took his hand in mine, raising my eyes to meet his, hoping to see what I needed to see. And for once, my ability made a command performance. As our eyes locked, I felt his hand gently squeezing mine, and then the man before me faded and the vision I'd hoped for took his place.

We were in the middle of a moonlit glade, surrounded by colossal trees with diseased limbs, their dead leaves scattered on the ground, and blowing around us in an unnatural wind. To one side there was a man in white robes, a polished redwood staff clutched in his right hand, extended to his side. His white hair floated around him with a life of its own, flowing with and against the wind, eyes glowing red in an ageless face, first young, then as ancient as the trees. It could have been Helmut Fuhrmann, or either of the creatures who had attacked us at my home. But the manner of this man was one of immense power beyond what I had seen in his brethren, the air around him crackling with electricity.

On the opposite side of the clearing, I was lying face down on the ground in a bed of papery, dry leaves, arms stretched at odd angles above my head. I was naked and unconscious, my entire body bleeding in a network of intersecting welts and gashes.

And between us, he was there, standing tall and fierce. His eyes were flashing amethyst and his canines had elongated into elegant white fangs, emphasizing the sharpness of his cheekbones and jaw, his dark hair tangled wildly around his head and shoulders. He was dressed all in black, his shirt hanging from his broad shoulders in tatters, his body tense as a bowstring, ready to strike.

As he prepared to battle the man in white, a large black bird crashed through the dying boughs and landed clawing and pecking on the face of the man in white. With his concentration broken, the air cleared and the wind died down. The enormous bird continued its assault, giving my rescuer the opportunity to scoop me up and carry me through the trees, moving at speeds no man could obtain. The bird had joined us now, guiding us to the best path through the forest, leading us to safety.

As the vision faded into a single symbol, my eyes refocused on the man kneeling before me, worry etched in his brow. "Raven," I said, and his eyes widened in surprise. I stood up, grasping his hand more tightly in mine and pulling him to his feet. He towered over me, but I reached up with my free hand and touched his stubbled cheek, smiling at the shock in his eyes. "Raven," I said again, shaking my head. "I knew Ramon was too much of a sissy name for you."

I released his hand, which now hung limply at his side, astonishment still plastered on his face, and I walked confidently to the now unlocked door. "Are you coming?" I asked over my shoulder. "I imagine your fearless leader is waiting, and I could really use a bathroom."

Chapter Twenty-Seven

Raven was stunned. Her ice blue irises had turned nearly white, and she had totally blanked out on him, much as she had at the Mayor's party. He'd thought she was having a seizure or something, her hand had tightened so firmly on his, her nails digging into his skin. He had tried to touch her mind, to find out what was wrong, but it was completely closed to him again, an impossible feat she had now managed twice.

Then as suddenly as it had begun, she was herself again. And she'd said his name—his real name. Not just said it—knew it! Wait—did she say Ramon was a sissy name?

He joined her in the hall, laughing to himself and absently wondering if Mason would let him get new human credentials.

This female was full of surprises, and he was beginning to have an idea about just what they were facing with her. The girl had a talent, and unless he was mistaken, it was one that could come in handy, making her very valuable to the Legion.

The thought of her having value to more than just himself lightened his heart, and when she gestured for him to lead on, he did so with much less apprehension than he had carried into the room only moments ago.

As they walked side by side down the wide hallway, Raven could feel her eyes on him, and in a glance he saw that, though she was still amused by what had occurred in his office, there was also concern lurking behind those beautiful eyes, causing Raven to look away.

Having navigated the main corridors, and after a brief detour to the restroom, they were soon knocking on Mason's office door.

"Come," Mason said, the bass of his voice carrying through the heavy English oak.

Raven opened the door and motioned Jessica in ahead of him. He followed her inside, where she stood frozen near the doorway, closed the door behind him, and with a hand on the small of her back maneuvered them both until they were standing in front of Mason's desk. For some reason she seemed shy and unsure of herself, a total contrast to the confident woman who had led him out of his own office.

Mason sat behind his roll top desk, seemingly oblivious to their presence, but he was like that. Raven knew he'd acknowledge them when he was ready, but he was anxious to get this interview started. He really wanted to hear her tell them what he already suspected. That she could see the future. And that the reason he was unable to erase her memory of their first encounter was because it wasn't *her* first encounter with *him*. She had many years' worth of that memory, which he would never be able to touch.

When Mason finally looked up at them, his dark eyes gleaming in the lamplight, Jessica gasped and dropped her eyes to her feet. Raven was more than a little pleased when she inched closer to him as if for protection, placing her hand over the pulse point at her throat.

Chapter Twenty-Eight

"Miss Sweet," Mason rose to greet them. "My name is Mason. Thank you for agreeing to see us." Like I'd had a choice in the matter? This Mason guy was incredible, though. Looking at him was like gazing into a solar eclipse—stunning and brilliant and hazardous to hold your eyes on for even a second or two. His dark hair was relatively short and slicked back, not a lock out of place, and his eyes were like black pools. I was sure if I looked directly into them, I'd be lost and no one would be able to find me again. And I didn't think that was necessarily a good thing.

He emerged from behind the desk area, his smile warm and relaxed, his hand extended for me to shake. I hesitated, afraid if I touched him I'd be hit with the nastiest vision I'd ever seen. Despite his easy manner, this was a man who exuded power.

Deciding it would be rude to ignore his greeting, though, I took his hand, bracing for the worst, and was relieved when nothing happened. However, he was studying me like I was a ninth grade science project, and that made me a little uneasy.

I bravely tried to hold his gaze, but when this became impossible, I angled my eyes downward on the pretense of sizing him up. He was tall—nearly as tall as Raven, and he was wearing tan slacks and a white, loose fitting shirt with the top two buttons undone, a sexy little tuft of hair peeking out from the V. (Romance novel sexy—not porn star sexy). His whole look was casual, but elegant. After what seemed an uncomfortably long time, Mason released my hand and bowed me toward a comfy looking sofa at the far side of the room. I snuck a peek at Raven, who nodded slightly, and then aimed myself for the couch, hoping I wouldn't be obliviously waking up on it anytime in the near future.

Mason's office was what I'd call country eclectic, with an old roll top desk propped against the wall, more modern looking work tables to either side, creating a den for the man to hibernate in while doing whatever work it was he did there. I loved roll top desks and admired this one as being quite old. The finish on it was worn and scratched, though, and I fought the urge to offer to spruce it up for him. Now might not be the best time to try and drum up business. But I'd keep it in mind.

The walls were done in a pale cream color, and paintings were elegantly spaced around the room. By the looks of the man I would have expected Degas or Monet, but these paintings belonged to the room. David Moss and Terry Redlin covered the walls with a variety of hunting scenes. Ducks, pheasants and quail were the center point of most of the works, with retrieving dogs coming in a close second. What was it with these men and dogs?

A small desk lamp sat to the left of the desk, and as in Raven's office, the paperwork was stacked in tidy piles. I noticed a leather in-box sat nearly empty, and couldn't help but wonder what was on this man's desk pad.

Then I noticed something on the corner of the far worktable that didn't seem to fit in with the southern décor—a flash of black silk. It was my handbag, completely forgotten in all that had happened. I must have left it in the Hummer in my eagerness to escape. And inside it was my cell phone, which reminded me that I really did need to call Piper and Alex. They would be so worried if they were unable to contact me.

I wondered, not for the first time, exactly how long I'd been there, and it occurred to me why I felt suspended in time. There were no windows in this place. There had been none in Raven's office, none in the halls, and there were none here.

My latest vision flashed in my mind, Raven standing strong and fierce, fangs extended, and the walls of the windowless room pressed in on me. My suspicions were humming now, all but confirmed in my mind.

I knew I should be scared. Knew enough of vampire lore to understand that these guys were probably not quite the *good guys* Raven was trying to convince me of earlier. I mean, if the sunlight thing is true, then they probably drink blood, too, and God only knew what else.

But my vision had been clear. I was safe with Raven, my very own knight in shining armor. No matter what, he was going to protect me. He had told me as much, but it was nice to have my own talent supporting his words. And I trusted my talent. That being the case, though, meant I was also going to get hurt before he could rescue me. Badly hurt, and I wasn't looking forward to that. But first things first.

I sat down on the sofa, crossing my bare feet at the ankles (I'd opted not to don the bloody heels again. Ick!), and Raven sat to my right. Mason chose the wingback chair to my left, leaving me feeling a little surrounded, with a rugged hard rock maple coffee table blocking my only path of escape.

After several moments of silence I couldn't stand it anymore, so I said, "Mr. Mason, I really appreciate all you're doing for me here. I mean, what with the white haired dudes trying to kill me and everything..."

"It's just Mason," he said, his smile seeming genuine, his voice smooth as silk.

"I'm sorry—Mason—but as I was saying, my friends are going to be looking for me. I left them rather abruptly last night, and if they've been by my house at all to check on me, I'm sure they'll be worried. Those things left quite a mess on my front lawn, and with the same thing happening on the Stuckey's property, chances are the police will be involved. I don't want to cause any trouble for you or for anyone, so I'd really like it if we could get this little interview over with so Raven can just...drive me home?"

Mason's eyes flicked to Raven the minute I said his name, leaving me wondering if that had been the wrong thing to say. For Raven's part, he just lifted his hands palms up and shrugged, a curious grin playing at the corners of that gorgeous mouth.

"You're property has been taken care of. There will be no evidence of what transpired last night." He was still looking at Raven, who was trying unsuccessfully to look innocent.

"Oh," I said, a little deflated, and wondering vaguely how they had managed to save my grass. So much for my exit plan. Well, if they weren't going to take me home, then it was time they started talking. I took a big breath and opened my mouth to demand some answers, but Mason beat me to the punch.

"Tell me, Jessica, how did you learn Raven's true name?"

I stopped, my mouth hanging open stupidly. I had been planning to ask the big question, not answer it. These people were strange enough, I was sure telling them my little secret wouldn't phase them in the slightest. Yet I hesitated. The image I'd seen of Raven protecting me notwithstanding, I knew I was still in a precarious situation. Not to mention the fact that I'd seen him kill with impunity. Sure, it was to save our lives, but the fact that the death didn't bother him, well it tells a girl something about a person. These were dangerous people, and though they seemed to be on my side at the moment, I really didn't want to tell them anything that was going to change that. My little talent could put me over the edge in either direction.

Finally, I figured I was already in this up to my armpits, a little further wasn't going to kill me. And if it did, no biggie. I was probably already dead anyway.

Taking a steadying breath, I looked first at Raven and finally at Mason. "I have visions," I said, a little defensively. Raven nodded, as if I were confirming something he already knew. Mason simply waited for me to continue.

"I've had them ever since I can remember. Sometimes they come as dreams and sometimes just out of the blue, like when I touch a person or just look into their eyes. It's never been something I can control—it just happens when it wants to. But no matter what, the visions always come true."

I had their attention now, so there was nothing left but to plough through. "One of the earliest dreams I can remember was of me as an adult finding a naked, bleeding man on my porch. When I was little, I didn't understand. The house was not familiar to me at the time, and the fact that the man was naked eventually just embarrassed me.

"Imagine my surprise when I woke up early Thursday morning to find my vision playing out live in Technicolor. I knew Raven instantly as the man in my dreams, recognized him as a person I'd known my whole life, even though we'd never met. But the vision never went beyond a certain point. I would reach for the man—Raven—and then I would wake up. I started to think it was just a recurring dream, especially when I grew up and started looking as I did in the vision. I hoped it was, because the man I kept seeing was so badly injured, I didn't think I'd ever be able to save him.

"Seeing him lying there like that scared the crap out of me, but I admit I was excited to finally know what happened next. I tried to figure out what I was supposed to do, how I was supposed to help him. But just like my vision, I reached for him and woke up. I tried to convince myself it was just the dream again—that it hadn't really happened, but too many things were out of sorts."

I was on a roll now, the words tumbling out of my mouth like they'd been rehearsed. It felt good to finally be able to talk this through with someone, and I seemed to have a captive audience.

"First, there was my toe." Raven and Mason both looked down, so I held my foot up for their inspection, my little toe still black and blue from the beating it had taken. "I stubbed it when I went to investigate the noise on the porch. Then when I woke up thinking it was just a dream, I bumped my toe again, reminding me quite painfully that this had happened before. There were no signs of Raven on the porch, though. Everything was as it should be.

"But then I went into town and Mr. Stuckey from across the road was saying how something had frightened his animals and that there was blood in his driveway. It seemed like too much of a coincidence, but still, I couldn't remember.

"Finally, when Raven came waltzing into the Mayor's ballroom looking very much alive, perfect in fact," I said, clearing my throat and trying to hide a blush, "well, I knew it had been real. We were trying to sort it all out on the way home, but nothing was making sense, to either one of us I suspect." Raven nodded agreement, still looking amused. "Then we were attacked and Raven brought me here," I concluded.

"And his name?" Mason repeated. "I'm assuming this was another vision?"

"Yes," I said. "Just a little while ago."

"So, what? A vision just came to you and said 'His name is Raven?'" Mason asked, not disbelieving, really. More like he was trying to understand.

"Umm...yeah, something like that. It's a little more complicated, a lot of symbolism, you know? But that's basically how it works." I didn't really want to go into the whole thing just yet. Especially the part about feeling safe with them, or at least with Raven. I needed to keep as much of an edge as I could. I had yet to determine if I was going to be friend or food for these guys.

Mason seemed to be deep in thought, considering what I'd said. I still had so many questions, but again before I was brave enough to ask one, he said, "Why do you think you don't remember anything after reaching for Raven?"

I thought about this for a second, then resignedly I said, "Mason, I know you and Raven are, well, different. Raven mentioned 'his people,' and I don't think he was talking about Europeans. I could feel him messing around in my head, so I'm guessing Raven did something to me to make me forget." I looked at Raven for confirmation, and he nodded once, his eyes soft with what looked like—guilt?

Mason studied me for a long moment before saying, "I realize you have become an unwilling participant in what for us will inevitably be a war. Whether by fate or by circumstance I do not know, but you are here now and without knowing who we are and what you now face, your life would be forfeit." More with the drama. I tried to swallow, my throat dry as the Sahara.

Mason seemed to be collecting his thoughts before continuing. "We are an ancient race, thousands of years old, immortal to a point and separate from homo sapiens. We were wild in the time of our creation, animals living by instinct for survival, much like early humans, yet with major differences as the sparrow differs from the hawk.

"The advancement of man has forced us to become more—civilized. For centuries we were perfectly happy to exist in the shadows, hiding from humanity and taking what was necessary for our survival, with little thought of how it might affect mankind. Unfortunately, this became increasingly difficult, forcing us to...evolve. A sagacious group of males assembled in Romania, where the basis of our—government, if you will—was created. The Legion, as it exists today, is in place to ensure that our people live in a sort of secret harmony with man, taking only what is needed to sustain our existence. Because of our laws, humans remain blissfully unaware of our presence, and in turn we are not persecuted because of our—differences, as you say."

Blah, blah, blah. With the vision I had of Raven earlier today, the windowless building he'd brought me to, and the gruesome but necessary murders of two non-human beings the night before, I was fairly certain I knew where Mason's guarded oration was going, which would be to confirm what I had reluctantly admitted to myself already. I really wished he'd just come out and say it. A few days ago I wouldn't have believed him, would have laughed in his face. But now I just needed him to verbalize it in plain English, without the bullshit and dribble history lesson.

"It's a lovely story, Mason, but if a war is coming, as you say, then I think we need the condensed version," I said, leaning back on the sofa and trying to look relaxed. I did my best to hold his gaze, hoping to mask my anxiety with a confidence I didn't really feel. Raven was watching me, his expression unreadable. Folding my hands in my lap and putting on my best all-business face I said, "So, are you Vampires are what?"

Chapter Twenty-Nine

Raven's eyes widened and he couldn't help himself—he laughed. This girl had skills. Not only had she learned his name from her vision, but apparently his race as well! Mason wasn't one to show emotion, but the expression on his face was priceless. His eyes were as wide as Raven's, though Raven was sure his leader was finally realizing the implications of what Jessica's gift could afford them. Or cost them.

For Jessica's part, she just sat there, patiently waiting for one of them to respond. When Mason hesitated, Raven controlled his laughter and reached a hand to Jessica, touching her shoulder to bring her focus on him.

"Yes," he said, his eyes still dancing with humor. "We are Vampire." He reached for her mind, and was surprised to find her less afraid than he would have suspected. Her pulse was thrumming in her neck, but it was more excitement than fear. She glared at him, obviously aware of what he was doing, and chagrinned, he dropped the connection.

Her eyes softened and she said, "Tell me, Raven. Please tell me what happened the night I found you. I really need to know." She was pleading with him now, and he wanted so badly to tell her everything. But not with Mason here. He wanted to tell her in private. With what he'd learned of her so far, the fact that he had fed from her was likely not going to go over well, and he'd rather not have an audience when that conversation went down. Besides, it was...personal.

Instead he said, "I will, Jessica, but first we have some more pressing things to discuss with you. Namely, the mess I inadvertently pulled you into."

"Oh, you mean the albino dudes?" she asked seriously.

"Yes," Mason chimed in. "As I mentioned before, we are on the brink of war with a race of Sorcerers, though at this time we are still unclear as to why this has come to be. Until recently we were only vaguely aware that they existed.

"The Sorcerers captured and tortured Raven several weeks prior to him appearing on your property, but for no discernable reason. His escape, and the aid you have already imparted, inadvertent as it was, have helped us to be aware of the threat. From what we can detect, these creatures are planning some sort of takeover. The Mayor of Fallen Cross has been compromised, which puts the entire town at risk. Whatever the Sorcerers are doing, this is probably just the beginning. We're doing all we can to stop this before it goes too far. But now I need to know. Jessica Sweet, are you willing to help us further?"

Chapter Thirty

I reached for Raven's hand to steady myself, and relaxed a little when his fingers wrapped around mine. If what Mason just said was true, then everything and everyone I loved was in jeopardy from these Sorcerer guys. Of course I would do anything I could to protect my friends, but I really didn't see how I could be of any help, and I said as much to Mason.

"You have a talent, Jessica, which could be very useful in helping us to determine what our next move should be."

"Yeah," I said, "but it almost never comes to me on command. It just happens when it happens. I've never been able to really control it. So how does this help you?"

"You seem to be connected to Raven. Tell me, since your first encounter, how many of your visions have involved him?"

My face turned seven shades of red as I recalled my vision the night of the fundraiser—was that really just last night? Mason had said so, but time seemed so relative just now.

"I've only had two," I confessed, "But yes, they were both about him." I felt Raven's fingers tighten reassuringly in mine.

"If I am correct," Mason replied, his gaze resting on our joined hands, "there will be more. Any information you could supply would be information we probably would not have otherwise. Your gift told you what we are and even provided you with Raven's true name. It seems you are given the information you need, when you need it. A protective measure, I'm sure."

"Does that mean I have to be in danger to get these messages? If that's the case, I don't know if I want to face one of those Sorcerer thingies again. Honestly, I got lucky the first time. A repeat of last night might not work out so well." I was getting a little panicky. My eagerness to know what was going on around me, to know who and what I was dealing with, suddenly seemed like a really bad idea.

Mason took my question as rhetorical, and I looked down at my free hand, as if I could find the answers etched in my palm. If my friends were in danger, and there was something I could do to protect them...They were all I had left. Frightened as I was, I knew there was nothing I wouldn't do to ensure the safety of my home and the people I loved.

I swallowed again, trying hard to be brave, and I raised my head to meet the cool darkness of Mason's eyes. "I'll do what I can," was all I could say, and he smiled at me.

"You are very brave," he said, as if reading my mind. "The Legion will do all we can to protect you from harm, but know that what you have agreed to today could mean the difference between success and complete annihilation. Not just ours, but humans' as well."

My head was still spinning when Mason stood up, signaling the end of our meeting. Raven helped me to my feet, keeping my hand in his as Mason led us to the door, confirming our dismissal. However, with all the thoughts swimming around in my brain, the obvious finally banged into the front, making me drop Raven's hand and stop in my tracks.

"Umm, Mason?" He stopped, turning curious eyes to me. "What happens to me now?"

"Happens?" He replied.

"Can I, umm, go home now?" I knew the answer before I even asked the question, but I had to know exactly where I stood. If I was a prisoner being held here to perform parlor tricks for their cause, they would find me less than cooperative.

"I'm afraid that won't be possible, but it's for your own safety." Figures. "Raven will escort you to your quarters, where you should be more than comfortable. Once we've established the threat level, then we can reevaluate the situation. Until then, we would rather have you here, where we can keep an eye on you."

Okay, it didn't sound like I was a prisoner *exactly*, but it still sounded like I wouldn't be sleeping in my own bed for a while. I started for the door again, and again I stopped. "Any chance I could get my purse back?" I asked, hoping my smile didn't look too scowly.

Mason walked to his desk, picked up my bag and returned it to me. "You'll find everything intact," he said, releasing the purse to my custody. "I understand your need to contact your friends, but I have to stress the importance of confidentiality where we are concerned. Bringing your friends in at this point would only make them targets." He would have continued, but I held up my free hand in the universal stop symbol, which seemed to take him back a bit.

"I get it. Tell them I'm okay, but keep them in the dark." He nodded once, then turned his back on Raven and me, returning to his desk and what must have been important Vampire business. I looked at Raven and he motioned me toward the door.

Chapter Thirty-One

We walked down the corridor, mostly in silence. Every so often Raven would tell me to turn left, or guide me to turn right. At one point we got on an elevator and he pushed the "up" button. The only other choice was down. Guess that explained why there were no windows. We'd been underground. So much for my brilliant deduction about Vampires and sunlight. It's like adding two plus two and getting five, but five still being the answer I was searching for. You know, common core math.

I still had so many questions, but when I tried to ask, Raven suggested I wait until we reached my quarters, then all would be answered. My quarters. Sounded way more permanent than I wanted to contemplate. I just hoped that this whole Sorcerer thing would work itself out quickly, and before anyone was seriously hurt.

The elevator doors opened into a hallway that was bright and cheerful, full of color, with decorations that leaned more toward residential than the stark halls of the floor below, but still no windows. Raven led me across the hall into another elevator, which had buttons for several floors. He pushed the three button, remaining silent as we arrived at our floor.

Upon exiting the elevator, Raven led me to the right where we walked to the end of the hall, turning right once more into a hall dotted with several doors on either side. We stopped at the third door on the left, where Raven let us in to a beautiful sitting room furnished entirely in Louis XV. The sofa was carved with flowers and scrolls, a simple cream fabric covering stiff looking cushions I hoped I wouldn't be waking up on any time soon. (I really needed to do something about this couch phobia I'd developed.) Two spindly legged arm chairs sat across from the sofa in a matching simple fabric, a delicate walnut coffee table occupying the space between. An enormous fireplace with a marble mantle and hearth took up one whole wall, a giant ornate mirror hanging above it. Various other period pieces were scattered throughout the room.

I noted with relief that tall windows spanned the far wall. However, they were heavily draped, not letting in a single ray of sunshine, meaning it was either still dark outside, or those suckers were completely lightproof. I wandered over to the nearest curtain, lifting the edge ever so slightly, and was relieved to see a bit of light shine through.

All in all it was beautiful, but not in any way a place I would choose to live. If I were a bazillionaire and lived in a mansion, this would be the room I just showed to people on the way to the areas where they were allowed to hang out.

Something of my thoughts must have been showing on my face because Raven, who had followed me to the window, said, "You don't like it." Not a question, and he didn't sound offended. Just a statement of fact. "I'm sorry, Jessica. For everything. I only chose these quarters because they were across from mine. I thought that perhaps knowing I was near..." He began to cough, like he was choking or something, and I caught a hint of pink in his cheeks as he turned away from me.

True, I wasn't happy to be here under the circumstances, but I really couldn't take this out on Raven. He had been more than accommodating, and was trying very hard to make me feel safe in a who-knows-what-kind of place this was, full of who-knows-how-many would-be monsters. I reached out and touched his shoulder, intending to apologize, but he flinched at my touch.

I left my hand where it was and said, "It's okay, Raven. Really. I'm just not used to all of this opulence. I'm assuming you've been in my house, so you know the kind of stuff I'm used to—or were you not able to come in without being invited?"

His shoulders started to shake, and concerned I'd said something wrong, I edged around him to try to see his face. The bastard was laughing at me. I slapped his arm—hard—and stalked to the other side of the room nearer the fireplace, anxiously aware that I'd just slapped a Vampire. Even if it was just in fun, and even if he did deserve it, it might not have been the smartest move I'd made lately. But on a long list of stupid moves, it was hard to say where this one ranked.

Fortunately, he'd taken it in the humor it was intended, but it rankled me that he only laughed harder. "It's not funny," I fumed. "You try being in a house full of people you know nothing about, except what other people have made up, and see if you don't say something stupid now and then." And he laughed harder yet as my scowl deepened.

His laughter became contagious, though, and before long I was smiling reluctantly. Finally he collapsed on the delicate sofa, the mass of him making me flinch, sure the whole thing would splinter under his weight.

"Sit, Jessica," he chuckled, patting the seat beside him. "I won't bite," he grinned when I hesitated, his teeth perfect and white. No sign of fang.

"I'm not worried about your bite," I retorted, not really sure if that were true. "But I am worried I'm going to say or do something that's going to be unforgivable and I'm going to end up as somebody's dinner, with or without your protection."

This had him chuckling again, but when I glared at him he did try to stop. "My sweet Jessica, I haven't laughed like that in decades! I've forgotten how misguided humans can be." Before I could get my ire up again he held up his hands defensively and said, "But you're right. There is much you need to know before I introduce you to the other residents."

"How many of you are there? Here, I mean."

"In the main house, there are six of us in residence. All officers. Mason is our Warlord, as you know, and I am his Second. Merlin is in charge of security, surveillance, and a variety of other computer geek stuff. Harrier is a pilot and a Warrior, though I'd stay away from him if I were you. He's got a bit of a temper, and he and I aren't exactly...friendly. I don't think he'd hurt you, since you're here as Mason's guest, but I wouldn't put it past him to try and scare you just to get under my skin."

"Good to know," I said, nodding, trying to take it all in.

"Tas is a good guy, though. He's in charge of the troops—the Soldiers who live in barracks elsewhere on the grounds. They patrol the neighboring towns and cities every night, keeping an eye out for signs of vamps living outside of Legion law, mostly just young ones trying to buck the system, but you run across a feral now and again, and they can make things dicey as far as keeping our race undetected goes."

"What's a feral?" I asked.

"Just what you would think—like a cat who's supposed to be domesticated, but decides it would rather be wild. Same thing."

I just nodded again, trying to understand. I knew some humans like that.

"And Viper is our munitions guy—he keeps us armed and dangerous," he concluded, with another flash of his teeth. These were Vampires. What on earth was this Viper guy supplying them with that made them more dangerous than nature had? The thought sent a shiver down my spine.

"Okay," I said. "Well I think the next thing we need to do is get the stupid questions out of the way, and I swear if you laugh at me again, I'm opening all the curtains!"

"Now that I would appreciate you *not* doing," he said, more seriously. "That's one they got right."

"So if you are exposed to sunlight, you go poof?" I asked.

"Well, not so much 'poof.' More like ashes to ashes. It takes a while, and by awhile I mean hours, not days, but yeah, eventually the UV rays will get us."

"How long can you be exposed and still survive?"

"It depends. The more pureblooded the vamp, the less exposure they can stand."

"So where does that put you on the spectrum?"

Raven glanced at the curtained windows. "I can survive about an hour of indirect sunlight, though I'd be in pretty bad shape. Direct sunlight, not so much."

"So you're pretty pure, then." It was more of a statement than a question, and I was curious to see him grimace.

"My blood is pure," he finally replied, his tone making it clear that subject was closed.

"I think I'm confused," I said, still curious about the general topic. "You mentioned young ones before, and I thought you meant the recently turned. Are you saying that Vampires are born and not made?"

"Vampires can be created in two different ways. True, a human male can be turned—Tas is an example of this—but most of us have been born, the pure among us having both Vampire mother and Vampire father. The blood lines thin when a female Vampire mates with a human male."

"What about the other way around," I asked. "A human female with a Vampire male."

"Fortunately, or unfortunately, depending on your viewpoint, a female human can neither be turned, nor can she conceive a Vampire's child. The genetic makeup of the human female is just not compatible with Vampire, giving her immunity all the way around."

"Immunity? Like, from diseases too?"

Raven smiled. "We don't get sick."

"Good to know," I smiled back. Well, that was one thing I wouldn't have to worry about. The turning thing, I mean. "So, you're immortal?"

"Not exactly," Raven said, shifting a little. "True, we live a very long time, but we do wear out eventually. And of course, we can be killed. It isn't easy, but it can be done."

"Hmm," I said, processing.

"What else would you like to know?" Raven asked, leaning back into the corner of the sofa and folding a leg underneath him, his arm stretched across the back.

"Well, obviously the invitation thing is bogus." I glared at him before the smile that played on his lips could turn into an all-out laugh. He schooled his face, but I could see he was struggling. "So let's go with the obvious. Crosses?" I felt my neck for the gold cross I'd donned what seemed like years ago."

"Nope."

"Holy water?"

"Uh-uh."

"Garlic?"

"Good in pasta sauce."

"You eat? Real food?"

"Yes."

"Okay. So the blood thing. That's crap too?" I said, hopefully. But he hesitated, sitting up straight again and dragging his fingers through his hair. He was stalling.

"Raven?" I asked softly, not sure I really wanted him to answer this one.

"Yeah. Look, Jessica, this one is true."

Chapter Thirty-Two

"Bummer," Jessica muttered, then seeming to sense his discomfort said, "Hey, it's a part of who you are. But I'm guessing the Legion has rules about this. That's what Mason was saying about 'living in harmony with humans' and 'only taking what we need,' all that?"

Raven got up and started pacing. He knew he was going to have to tell her all that had happened in their first encounter, and he hoped she maintained the open mind she was now displaying once she found out that she had already been "dinner," as she had put it earlier.

Jessica stayed where she was, her eyes following his every move, waiting for him to say more.

"Jessica, I need you to understand something about the blood thing," he began. "There is a particular magic, for lack of a better word, to the Vampire race. It is what makes us more than human. We have certain attributes common to our race, living extremely long lives and healing very quickly, among them. The blood that we drink, is the substance that helps us maintain this magic. We eat food to maintain our bodies, we drink human blood to maintain our magic. Without the blood, our powers would diminish, and we would become mortal, dying at an exponential rate, even more quickly than humans do."

She was still watching him, but to her credit, she didn't look too horrified.

"How often do you have to drink it—the blood, I mean?"

"Every couple of weeks...unless we are injured." The statement hung between them for a moment before Jessica's eyes widened, and she looked at him as though understanding something for the first time. Raven braced himself.

"Raven," she began cautiously, "the night I found you—when I reached for you and you did whatever you do to make me sleep. Did you...feed...from me?"

He turned away, unable to look into her eyes. Unwilling to see the horror that was inevitably going to be there, replacing the shock he had already seen. All he could do was nod. Christ, he was a coward. Who knew?

"Wow," she said, her voice unreadable. Was that a good wow or a bad wow? Preoccupied, he didn't hear her approach, but she was behind him in an instant, her hand on his arm. Her honeysuckle scent was playing with his senses, and that mixed with the memory of having his fangs in her wrist, her blood in his throat, was making it hard for him to breathe.

"It's okay," she said, turning him to face her. "I know I should be really ticked right now. Actually, that was my first instinct. But you saved my life last night, which I guess makes us even?" She was giving him more credit than she had before. Probably more than he deserved. "Besides," she sighed, "I'm just too tired and my brain is too frazzled to make a big deal out of this now when there is so much else to consider. What's a little blood theft among friends, right?"

He couldn't look at her, though. She was being cavalier about it, but he couldn't help feeling ashamed. He'd fed from humans for hundreds of years, and although his first hundred and twenty-five years had been beast-driven, he now believed in the laws the Legion had set forth, following them to the letter. Technically, he had done nothing wrong in taking Jessica's blood, although he had not counted on her remembering him afterward. Still, it seemed like an invasion with her. Like he had taken something that now he wished she had given freely, and it was unsettling for him to think that she would likely never do so.

"Raven, please look at me," she pleaded, and he raised his eyes to meet hers. He expected to see disappointment, however she simply seemed resigned. Tired, as she had said. "Seriously, it's okay," she repeated. "I don't remember it, and I'm still alive." She was absently rubbing the wrist where he'd fed, though he hadn't mentioned it specifically. "I know now why my visions always ended when they did. Your Vampire magic must work in visions too." She was smiling at him as she spoke, teasing, but seeing he wasn't convinced, she went on more seriously.

"Do I like the idea that you ate at my house without being invited? No. It's pretty rude, if you ask me." Her words were reproachful, but she still managed a hint of a smile, and her tone was matter of fact, giving him hope. "Of course my first reaction was 'Ooh! Ick!'" He flinched, but she pretended not to notice. "It's not every day a guy tells you he's had you for dinner, literally, but Jesus, Raven, you were dying, right?"

"Yes," he whispered.

"And drinking my blood kept you alive?"

"Yes."

"If I had known the situation, I probably would have offered anyway, so no harm, no foul, okay?" She patted him on the arm and returned to her seat on the sofa. "Now, come back here, sit down, and tell me the rest of your adventures in Jessie-ville, starting with what happened over at the Stuckey's. Really, it's okay. I won't bite," she grinned.

Raven walked back to the sofa, not sure how to continue. He had expected fear, revulsion, even anger, but not kindness. Certainly not forgiveness. For centuries he had dedicated himself to the Legion, working his way up through the ranks, trying to make amends to himself and his race for the evil he had spread in his youth. Out of necessity, he had denied himself any type of relationship with a female. His reputation kept anyone worthwhile at bay, and fighting the beast for a quick fuck that usually left him frustrated or worse—so not worth it.

Yet now he found himself not only fascinated by this woman, but drawn to her. He was a loner who'd spent his entire life avoiding closeness, pushing people away, but as he talked to Jessica, all he wanted to do was hold her close. What was he thinking? He could barely handle the few friendships he had, and he certainly wasn't interested in Linking with a woman, especially not a human woman. And yet...

Jessica listened intently as he filled her in on all that had happened. He reassured her that the blood at the Stuckey's was not his, but rather the remains of the two Sorcs he'd offed. And she seemed truly relieved that he had made it to her in time, though she did cringe again when he explained how he had fed from her wrist. She laughed when he said he'd spent the day in her cellar, horrified by the creepy crawlies she was sure he'd encountered. And she laughed even harder when he confessed to borrowing clothes from the cedar robe in her bedroom. The sound was exhilarating.

He didn't mention how he'd reacted to her scent, nor did he tell her how her blood had intoxicated him, giving him more energy than a normal feeding ever had, burning through him like a meteor in the midnight sky. And when she asked about her knees having healed from the night before, he confessed he had tended to them, but neglected to go into detail of exactly what that "tending" had entailed.

For the first time in his long memory he found himself wanting to be accepted by someone, and this put him off balance. He knew how to lead and he knew how to fight. He knew how to kill, and in spite of centuries of keeping the beast at bay, he knew he would still enjoy it, if he allowed himself. What he didn't know was how to love, and the idea that he was even thinking of going there was terrifying.

Chapter Thirty-Three

A knock at the door had Raven on his feet in an instant. He opened the door just a crack, whispered something to someone on the other side, and then closed it back again.

"I'm afraid I need to leave you alone for a moment. Will you be okay on your own?" He had come back to where I was still sitting on the sofa, and I stood up to get my purse.

"Sure—I need to call Piper anyway. Will...will you be back?" The thought of him leaving my side was overwhelming. I knew I was being a wimp, but I couldn't help it. It had been a really long day. Night. Whatever.

"Of course," he smiled. "I'll see that food and some clean clothes are sent up. I shouldn't be too long. Lock the door behind me."

I did as he asked, retrieving my purse from the table by the door where I'd dropped it when we'd come in. I fished out my phone and pushed the button on the top to get the time. It was almost noon—on Sunday—and I was starving.

First things first, though. I needed to call Piper. I figured she would be easier to fool with a "passions overcame them" scenario than Alex would, and since I couldn't think of a less scandalous cover story for me spending the night with Raven, that was going to have to do. I'd pay for it later, but I kept reminding myself that it was for their own good. God, I was starting to sound like the Vampires.

Piper picked up on the fourth ring, her voice rough with sleep.

"'Lo," she mumbled.

"Piper, it's me, Jess. You okay?" I asked.

I could hear Piper bouncing up in her bed, "Ohmigod—Jessica! Where are you? Alex tried to call you last night, but you must have been in bed already. You missed a great party, I mean the part that you missed. I swear, I haven't drunk that much champagne in forever! I had to have Daddy send a car for us, we were so toasted! Alex was really pissed you left with that guy, but I hope you didn't screw it up! Did you? Screw it up?" I swear sometimes the girl didn't breathe.

"Umm...I haven't yet," I said. "Actually..."

"Great, 'cause he was super-hot and I really think we need to get together, all of us, have a few drinks and get to know him better. I mean, you can't go on looks alone. And Alex needs to be softened up a bit. He really had a hard on for that guy. Too much testosterone. So, did he take you straight home? What did you do? Did you break your losing streak? Spill girl!"

"Piper—I, uh. Yeah, it was great," I muttered, hating that I was lying, especially about something I found myself wishing were the truth. "I just wanted to let you know, I'm not at home and probably won't be for a few days. Ra—Ramon and I are going to hang out at his place for a while and just see what clicks." God, that was terrible!

"Ooooh," Piper crooned. "You go girl! Keep me posted, and don't worry. I'll tell Alex you're fine so he doesn't have a canary. Okay, well, if you need anything, just let me know! Tell *Ramon* I said 'hey'!"

"Will do. Bye Piper." I hung up on her, knowing what I said would have never played with Alex. I checked my messages and sure enough, he'd left four, none of which sounded like he was very happy with me. I tapped the phone off, hoping Piper would be good at her word and let Alex know I was okay before he blew a gasket.

I looked down at myself, and then up in the mirror over the fireplace. I was still in my once pretty dress, my hair limp and tangled, though I'd removed all the bobby pins from my fancy up do during my earlier potty break. My hands were still sore and my head was starting to throb a little. I needed a shower. Bad.

I passed through the bedroom, barely noticing the ginormous bed, and entered a bathroom that must have been designed either for or by the gods. There was an enormous whirlpool tub that was more like a small swimming pool, and a walk in shower with dual shower heads (was that for sharing?). Everything was white and gold, and the place glowed like sunshine on a warm spring day.

I decided I was too tired for a shower, and turned the water in the bathtub on hot, adding a few bubbles from the bottle on the side of the tub. Stripping out of my ruined dress, I wrapped myself in a thick terry robe I found hanging near the shower, and sat down on the edge of the tub, waiting for it to fill. When the bubbles were near to overflowing, I dropped the robe, leaving it on the floor where it landed and stepped into several feet of bathing bliss. I located a knob on the side of the tub that turned on the jets, and I knew I'd died and gone to heaven.

I thought about all that Raven had told me, and I surprised myself by how easily I accepted all he revealed. What was it about me that made me capable of embracing all this strangeness without a second thought? True, I had my own strangeness to sort of prepare me for even more, but seriously—was I nuts? As far as I knew, I was the only human in a mansion full of blood sucking Vampires, and here I was, luxuriating in a pool-sized hot tub, fool enough to think I was safe.

Chapter Thirty-Four

Raven was gone for almost an hour. Mason wanted to know how Jessica was settling in, and if Raven thought she was going to be a problem. He explained that she seemed to be accepting the circumstances for what they were and that she was still eager to help.

Then Mason wanted to know Raven's take on the progress being made in the Sorcerer search. He knew it was his job, and that his input was important, and normally he would be all over that, but his mind kept drifting back to the sassy brunette he'd just left. Finally, Mason dismissed him, and Raven hurried back to the residential level.

First he stopped in the kitchen. He could have had a servant take care of this, but found he wanted to be the one to tend to her. Not knowing what she would like, he picked up a variety of foods: fruit, sandwich fixings, a bottle of water and a can of Pepsi. He hoped she drank leaded, because no one in the house went for diet anything. He placed everything on a tray and carried it out.

Next he stopped in his quarters across the hall from Jessica's. She had been rather amused when he'd told her about the clothes he'd borrowed from her home. He'd stashed them in his room, secretly wanting to keep a reminder of her, but under the circumstances he felt she might need them more than he did. Plus, the irony of her wearing them now wouldn't be lost on her.

Chuckling to himself, he walked across the hall, his offerings in tow, and knocked on the door. When she didn't answer, he let himself in. She might be in the shower and not be able to hear him.

The thought of Jessica standing buck naked, hot water sluicing her body, had his nerves, among other things, standing at attention, and he chided himself for it.

He dropped the tray on the coffee table, and headed into the bedroom, intending to leave the clothes on her bed, and then return to the other room to wait for her. However, the sounds of splashing caught his ear, and his curiosity got the better of him.

Jessica had left the bathroom door ajar, and a gentle nudge was all it took to afford him a view via the mirror that left him breathless. She was lounging in the bathtub, the jets running full on, thick, foamy bubbles dancing merrily across the water.

With a sigh, she slipped under the water, and when she emerged it was with a lazy stretch, bubbles clinging to her firm breasts giving the allusion of lacy lingerie, and sending his heart into overdrive. She reached for the shampoo, and soon had her hair in a thick lather. The bubbles on her breasts were melting, sliding seductively along her skin to return to their brethren in the pool of water at her waist.

Closing his eyes, Raven tuned his senses to her heartbeat, the strong, steady pulse reminding him of the first time he heard it—the night she unwittingly saved his life. He inhaled deeply, the scent of shampoo and bubble bath mingling with the sweet honeysuckle that was her unique scent. This was as close to paradise as he'd ever been.

Raven sighed quietly. He knew he should walk away, leave her to her bath, but the sound of her heart kept him riveted to the spot. Beat. Beat. Beat. So strong. So—enticing. He found his own heart adjusting to match her pulse. Slow—steady—but...

Raven opened his eyes, seeking her reflection, but she was gone. No, not gone, he could still feel her heart, but it was different—faster. She had slipped under the water, presumably to rinse her hair.

He watched the tub reflected in the mirror, waiting for her to emerge. How long had she been under? He listened to her pulse growing faster with each beat, and he waited, but the bubbles on the surface remained undisturbed.

Surely she was fine, but her heart—it was pounding in her chest—begging her to breathe. How long could a human hold their breath? Raven had no idea. He reached out to her mentally, but found her mind a blank. Was she having another vision that prevented her from knowing the situation she was in?

Her heart rate continued to increase, and yet she remained beneath the water. What the hell was she playing at?

Finally, Raven could stand it no longer. Blinded with irrational panic, he burst into the room, dropped her clothes to the floor, and was tub side in two strides. He thrust his arms through the warm, sudsy water and searched frantically. When his hands clasped around her shoulders, he pulled her up and out of the water. She fought him, though, scratching and kicking, drenching the rest of him with soapy water. His own heart was racing now, with what he realized was relief. She was fine, and even more, she was protecting herself.

He relaxed his hold on her only to receive a right hook on his jaw. Christ, she was a strong little thing! Raven tightened his hold on her again, wrapping his arms around her and pulling her to him as he sunk to the cool tiled floor.

He held her in his lap, probably squeezing too tightly, but he was struggling not only to calm her, but to calm himself of a combination of emotions that had him reeling. Relief, embarrassment—hell, the fact that he had cared at all was freaking him out. He realized he was shaking as much as Jessica as they sat on the floor, water and bubbles pooling on the tile around them.

She was screaming at him now, her words finally breaking through the confusion clouding his mind.

"What the hell do you think you're doing?" she shrieked. "Jesus, Raven, if I hadn't realized it was you—I nearly clawed your eyes out!"

He didn't care. He just needed to feel her close, to know she was still there. He couldn't speak, couldn't move, and most puzzling, couldn't understand his own reaction. He just held her to him, needing time to regain control of his emotions. This was so not cool. She was still trying to slap at him, to get him to let her go, but that wasn't going to happen. He needed her close—needed to understand.

Finally, she stopped moving, stopped fighting, and she relaxed against him, her firm body going soft in his arms, and he laid his cheek against her wet hair.

"Raven," she whispered in his ear. "Please, let me go. I can't breathe." He loosened his grip on her a little, but not enough for her to escape his arms.

"You were under so long," he said, struggling for a voice.

"I just wanted to see how long I could hold my breath," she said. "You could do laps in that thing."

"I just..."

"I know, I get it," she replied. "You just scared the shit out of me, that's all."

"Yeah," he whispered, pulling back so he could see her eyes. "Jessica?"

"Yeah?" she looked back at him, wet hair clinging to her face, her icy eyes still showing irritation.

"Don't ever do that again," he sighed, his mouth claiming hers in a kiss that he hoped would last well into the next millennium. She stiffened in his arms, then relaxed again, first accepting then seeking to control their embrace. She wrapped her arms around his neck, pulling him closer as she pressed her bare skin against him. She ran her tongue against his teeth and he felt his fangs throb. She had no idea what she was doing to him, but he didn't want her to stop. Instead, he deepened the kiss, tightening his hold on her, his canines not the only thing throbbing.

Her hands were in his hair now, pulling, stroking, and he thought he could die from these unfamiliar emotions. Reluctantly, he pulled his mouth from hers. He needed to see her. When she turned her eyes to him, they were smoldering, full of passion, and wordlessly he asked what he needed to know, asked what he'd never *asked* before. She nodded, licking her lips seductively, and he had them in the bedroom before she could consider changing her mind.

Chapter Thirty-Five

Before I could blink we were across the threshold and into the next room, where I was dropped unceremoniously onto the luxurious bed. Both of us were soaked from the bathtub fiasco, but neither of us seemed to care. I was already naked, and found it completely unfair that he was still clothed. So as he pulled off his black t-shirt, I tugged at the button on his trousers, wanting him so badly I couldn't see straight.

After what seemed like hours, we finally freed him of his clothing and he was on me before I got a chance to appreciate the sight of him. The last time I saw him naked he was covered with blood, and I remember being ashamed of myself for being turned on in spite of it. Oh, well.

He kissed me gently at first, my eyes, my cheeks, then finally our mouths were fused, tongues searching, probing. I ran my tongue over his teeth again—I couldn't help it. I was fascinated with his teeth.

"Jessica," he moaned, "Please, don't." But I couldn't stop. I wasn't surprised to find his canines sharpening around my tongue. Cripes! It was a hell of a turn on. I gasped against his mouth, my hands busy exploring the rest of him, especially that fine rear I'd admired inappropriately as he'd lay dying on my porch.

Raven's hands were equally busy, finding places on me I'd forgotten existed, setting my nerve endings on edge and sending me over more than once. I wanted him inside me fiercely, but when I reached for him, he grasped my fingers and pulled my hand above my head, his mouth now exploring my breasts, my stomach, and lower until—oh, shit!

"Raven," I cried. "Oh, my God!" but I don't think he was paying attention. I screamed when the mother of all orgasms rocked me, grabbing his shoulders and pulling him back up my body so I could claim his mouth again.

Instead, he kissed my neck, his tongue and teeth playing over my pounding pulse, and I absently wondered what it would feel like were he to sink his teeth in that tender flesh. The mere thought of it sent me over again, and I wrapped my legs around him as I shook with ecstasy.

"Raven, please!" I begged. "I want you in me, now." I ran my fingers through his hair, grabbing a handful of the inky silk and pulled his head back to show him I was serious. He raised his head, and when he looked at me his eyes were shining like amethyst, bright and alien, his teeth—no, his fangs—fully extended, smooth, white and lethal.

I gasped at the sight of him, not afraid, really, just shocked by the unexpectedness of it. He was so beautiful, otherworldly, and all I could do was gape, eyes wide. But before I could say a word, he was gone.

Chapter Thirty-Six

Dammit! He'd gone too far. Raven fled her rooms and found his way across the hall to his own, banging his head against the door he'd closed behind him.

He was an idiot to think she had needed his help—and as much as he admonished himself for that, his stupidity went even further. What the hell was going on?

The need to protect her was intense, but then seeing her like that, all naked and wet, struggling in his arms, had awakened the animal inside him. And when they'd kissed, that need was replaced by the need to possess her. To claim her as his own.

What was he thinking? That's just it—he *wasn't* thinking. He knew that by getting close to her like this he would be exposing her to a side of him no one had seen in centuries. But with her scent wrapped around him, and her sweet voice begging him, all he could think about was burying himself in her, fangs and cock, both to the hilt. He'd let himself forget what he was, forget that they were different, forget how dangerous he was to himself as well as her, and by doing so he'd frightened her—showed her the monster he was capable of being.

This feeling, caring what a woman felt about him, was going to drive him insane.

In his earlier years he was wild and out of control, and for a Vampire that was saying something. The thought of what he had done, what he knew he was capable of doing, was repugnant to him now.

A strange course of events had brought him to the Legion, desperate and searching for a new purpose. The Legion was created by the Primeval, a group of the oldest, disputably the first of the Vampire, when it became clear things were getting out of hand. They had been struggling for more than two centuries, trying to gain control over a race that had run amok.

While vamps in the Primevals' home areas were unwilling to challenge their strength, and chose to fly under the radar, those outside the Primeval realms ran wild, killing humans for the sheer pleasure and power of it, and coming dangerously close to exposing the entire race.

Raven was one of these feral vamps, the kind that other ferals tended to steer clear of. His reputation for the savage rape and mutilation of his victims was a source of nightmare to the more civilized vamps, a thing of legend to other ferals. At the time, it was a status he was quite proud of.

This reputation was also something that Mason and the Legion felt would be useful in their attempt to gain ground in controlling the ferals outside the Realms. Tame the Rapist, and the others would fall in line.

Of course, by the time they'd found him, Raven had been altered, no longer emotionally, or even physically, capable of the brutal murders he was once famous for. A bizarre encounter with a beautiful mark for hire had left him nearly mad, incapable of violence of any kind for a very long time. He had fled Europe and come to America, hoping to either regain some control over himself or die, and that's where Mason had found him, convincing him he could use his talents for the good of the race.

It had been a long road, but with Mason's help and a tremendous amount of training, Raven was eventually able to balance his animal urges instead of suppressing them. He was able to feed without killing, fuck without raping, and eventually kill again, so long as the pleasure was repressed. In fact, any attempt to find pleasure in an act of violence was a guaranteed trip to hell. The strong desire to control and possess another being, to be a god, had not left him with the passing of the mysterious white haired woman—the last person he'd killed for pleasure—but any attempt to enjoy the execution of his violent urges left him incapacitated for hours.

And Jessica had awakened something of that beast in him. For the first time in centuries the need to control another being—to possess, to own—was nearly too strong to suppress. It was different than before—not necessarily violent, but definitely testing the control he'd worked so hard to establish, and it stroked the beast lying within him, opening the creature's eyes and making him want to come out and play.

Not only was he having "beast issues," but Raven also felt a powerful need to feed from her, and only her. It was as though only she could sustain him, keep him alive, though unlike with other humans' blood, which could sustain a vamp for sometimes weeks, hers seemed to intoxicate him and then burn away exponentially, filling him with immense energy, but leaving him starving much more quickly, more intensely.

He could still feel the echoes of her blood running through him from the first time he'd taken her vein, let alone the little snack he'd treated himself to the previous night. Christ! The thought of that little indiscretion made him furious with himself, even more so when he realized the strength of his need.

Raven stalked into his bedroom, the sight of his bed pulling unwanted memories of Jessica lying magnificently naked across the hall, fear etched in those beautiful eyes. Fear of him.

He hadn't taken the time to dress before his escape, but he had gathered his clothes, which he threw at the headboard of his king sized bed, his boots making a satisfying *thunk* when they hit. He stormed into the bathroom, and straight for the shower, turning the jets on full blast and ice cold.

Leaning his head against the cool glass blocks of the shower wall, he closed his eyes, hoping the frigid water would wash away some of his shame.

Mason would kill him if he'd frightened the girl so badly that she refused to help them with the Sorcerer situation. But that wasn't what bothered him the most.

What if he'd frightened her so badly that she could never look at him again?

Chapter Thirty-Seven

Okay, what just happened here? I was still laying on that monster bed, propped up on my elbows, staring at the door where Raven had just disappeared, the sheets damp around me. I was still panting for chrissakes, and more than a little afraid that I'd screwed up. Again. I could hear Piper now. *Way to go, Jessica. I hold out hope that someday you'll meet a man you can't scare off, but you even managed to scare away a Vampire! Jeeze Louise, you're incredible!*

No, Raven was incredible. I sighed, dropping my head back on the pillow and wondering how I was going to fix this. Maybe—maybe I shouldn't even try. I'd obviously done something wrong, and let's face it. I was going to keep screwing up. It was in my nature. Pulling a pillow over my head, I let go with a silent scream, kicking my heels against the mattress in sheer frustration.

This was getting me nowhere. I really wished there was someone else in this blasted house I could talk to, but Mason and Raven were the only one's I'd met so far. Raven was out of the question, and Mason just didn't strike me as the kind of guy you could pop in on for tea and advice. Besides, it was kind of personal. Weren't there any women around here?

Shaking my head, I decided lying there feeling sorry for myself wasn't accomplishing anything. So I got up and headed to the bathroom to finish what I had started—bathing, that is. On the way to the tub I stepped over some clothing that I didn't remember seeing before. Raven must have been bringing me something to wear. I reached for them, hoping they weren't too soaked, and was relieved to see that they were mostly dry. Then I started to laugh. These were my dad's sweats. The ones Raven had borrowed last week. When I turned the t-shirt over and saw the "I Fly" logo on the front, I lost it. I was laughing so hard I ended up on the floor again, hugging the soft cotton to my chest.

At some point the laughter turned to racking sobs, and I don't know how long I sat on the floor, rocking myself with my Daddy's clothes in my arms, the events of the past few days finally catching up and overwhelming me. Life sucks for everybody in a million different ways, but right now, mine was the worst.

I just wanted to go home.

Chapter Thirty-Eight

Raven punched the large bag in front of him with such ferocity, he felt the bolts suspending it from the ceiling above give a bit. He knew they were secured with a Vampire's formidable strength in mind, but right now, he felt he could pull the thing down with his teeth. Several more punches were followed by a sequence of kicks—front, side, roundhouse—and then more punching. He didn't know who or what he was fighting at the moment. He only knew he had to win at all costs.

The cold shower had helped relieve his sexual tension, but Raven was still struggling with the uncontrollable urge to hurt something. It had been a very long time since he'd had to fight this hard to maintain control, and it unnerved him to realize the beast was so close to the surface. He had decided that maybe a little time with the heavy bag was in order, toweled off quickly, and dressed in his regular work out attire: a pair of black sweats and an old t-shirt with the sleeves and neck cut out for maximum mobility. After lacing up his high tops, he was ready to rock.

The Soldiers referred to this room as the Club, mainly because you had to be pretty high up the ranks to be able to use it, but really it was just a glorified gym. The Soldiers' facilities were elsewhere on the grounds, and admittedly, not as nice.

Free weight benches lined one entire wall, one hundred pound plates filling a rack nearby. They didn't bother with the traditional spa fare of strength or training machines. The most advanced weight training equipment was only a warm up for them, even on the highest setting.

Along another wall, treadmills, ellipticals, stationary bikes and stair climbers provided them with a variety of cardio choices, and a fighting ring took center stage in the room. The heavy bags were hung on one side, and mirrors lined the walls from floor to ceiling.

Raven's current workout was intense bordering over the top, but it did help him gain some focus. Right now, all he could think about was killing this fucking bag. Violence against inanimate objects never seemed to bother him, so he at least found pleasure in destroying something.

The mirrors behind the bag reflected his image back to him. His eyes were still glowing, his fangs still extended, the tendons in his neck standing out in stiff cords as he continued the unrestrained assault. He looked like a fucking animal, which only fueled his rage.

"Yo! Rave!" a voice, heavy on the Aussie, called from just inside the doors. "You pull down another bag and Mason's gonna go postal on your ass." Tas sauntered in, a picture of serenity in a pair of powder blue sweats and a white tank top, his blond waves pulled back in a hasty tail. Many opponents underestimated Tas because he was so pretty, but it was something they only did once. He was small for a Vampire, probably because he hadn't been a very large human, but he was lethal now, make no mistake.

Raven didn't care who it was, though. Right now all he heard was a challenge, and pulling his last punch, he spun to confront the male, eyes blazing, fangs bared.

Tas threw his hands up defensively and laughed, "I'm just saying, dude, you seriously need to calm down. You look completely rabid!" Tas had an easy way that radiated out to everyone around him. He was different from most males Raven knew, and not just because he'd been turned Vampire rather than being born. His nature was calming to those near him, which came in handy with a house full of egomaniacal Vampire males. True, it was a talent Tas could call upon in grave situations, but really, it was just his nature. When he was around, you just wanted to sit back and ride the waves. Probably another reason people underestimated him.

At the moment, however, Raven didn't give a shit about how the male's talent worked. He just knew that within moments his fangs had retracted and he could feel his heart returning to a non-lethal rate.

Raven walked across the room to the nearest bench, picking up a dumbbell on the way, and sat. As he extended the weight to begin a set of bicep curls, he glanced up at Tas, who had begun a complicated *kata*. The man moved like water, his motions smooth, his focus unwavering.

"Thanks," Raven whispered, and Tas was good enough to pretend like he didn't hear.

Chapter Thirty-Nine

I don't know how long I sat on the wet floor, bawling my eyes out, but eventually the tears dried and I pulled myself up off the floor. The water in the tub was cold by now, so I pulled the drain plug and headed to the shower. I didn't waste time thinking, just steamed and soaped myself up, rinsed, and then dried as quickly as I could.

I put on my dad's old sweats, savoring the scent that reminded me of him, and a hint of something different, something musky, that I recognized as Raven. After giving the floor a quick once over with my towel, I headed back to the sitting room, where I was surprised to find a tray of food. It looked like it had been there awhile, and it occurred to me that Raven must have brought it with the clothes. Hmm...Raven. Nope. Not gonna go there.

Instead, I picked up an apple and absently rubbed it against my shirt. I thought about the orchard on my property that my father had loved so much. It was small—just a dozen or so fruit trees. Mostly apple, but there were also two cherry trees, and once upon a time a tiny pear tree Dad could never get to bear fruit. Though he pampered the poor thing almost to the exclusion of all else, it had eventually died, and Dad was forced to refocus his efforts on the other trees. Not that he minded. He was pretty easy going about stuff like that.

In the summertime he had a vegetable stand set up in the barnyard where he sold the tomatoes and other vegetables he'd grown from seeds. People came from two counties over just to buy his produce. But in the fall, it was all about the apples. Red

Delicious and Golden Delicious, sold in half bushels or by the stem. He'd laugh with his customers and they would share local gossip, then they would be on their way. When he died, Dad left quite a void in the community. People still shake their heads with shame that I never learned his secrets to keeping the garden. The truth was, he just had a way with plants that made them want to grow for him. I think they knew they were loved and they returned the affection with their fruit.

I glanced down at the apple I was still holding, and raised it to my lips for a bite. The flesh was crisp and sweet, the juice spraying out from my mouth and then trickling down my chin. I wiped it away with the back of my hand and chewed thoughtfully, enjoying the flavors and the memories they invoked.

I walked over to the fireplace and smoothed my empty hand along the marble mantle. Glancing up in the mirror above the massive stone piece, I couldn't help but wonder again how the heck I'd gotten here. I leaned my cheek against the protruding shelf, soothed by the coolness it shared with me.

Taking another bite of the shiny red apple, I headed back to the bedroom. I was exhausted, and a nap was sounding pretty good to me, but as I crossed into the room I hesitated. It may be the most comfortable place in my suite, but I just couldn't bring myself to lay down on that bed.

Grabbing a pillow and blanket, I retreated back to the sitting room. I eyed the spindly sofa warily, then decided on a corner of creamy carpet near the window. I fluffed the pillow up, wrapped the blanket around me and lay down on the floor, hoping to find a few minutes of peace.

As my eyes drifted shut, I was relieved to find the darkness so peaceful, so complete. I was out—floating in that dream place between sleep and awareness—that place where, for whatever reason, fate chose to grace me with her secrets. I hovered there for a minute or hours—time really was relative.

Then I sat bolt upright, my heart thundering in my chest, my breath coming in shallow gasps. I was hyperventilating, I was going to pass out, and I buried my face in the blanket. Finally, I was able to drag a long breath of air deep into my lungs...and I screamed.

# Chapter Forty

Piper parked her BMW in Jessica's driveway, looking around at the property that was her dearest friend's home. On the outside, the barn she'd parked in front of looked like it would fall down in a slight breeze, but Jessie's father had shored up the structure from the inside, making it a safe workplace for them, while maintaining the old building's rustic appeal. He'd done that with all the out buildings here, telling her and Jessica it was a piece of history. He'd even restored the old outhouse, which of all the buildings was probably in the best shape. The walls were sturdy, and there was even a little moon carved in the door. Mr. Sweet had painted the whole thing white, to match the house. Piper had only ever been inside once, and in spite of Mr. Sweet's attentions, it still smelled like, well, an outhouse. Ick.

As the sun set over the orchard, Piper wondered at how quiet everything was. Usually Jessica had music blaring, either some rock opera from the Seventies or some other crazy band her parents had listened to. Piper actually liked Big Pig—go figure.

Apparently, Jessica was still with *Ramon*! Piper couldn't help but sing his name, even in her mind, and she smiled at the thought of her BFF taking a walk on the wild side for a change. This guy was absolutely gorgeous, so continental—and in her always humble opinion, he was perfect for Jessica, even if it was just for a few nights (and days!) of fun in the sack.

Piper had told Alex about Jessica's astonishing hook up with the mystery man from the party, and predictably he was frantic. She had always thought that Jessie and Alex should get together, but Jessie just couldn't wrap her mind around that one. Alex, on the other hand, was completely smitten, and had been for years. Piper had tried often to explain this to Jessica, but Jessie always poo-pooed her and made her drop the subject. Well, Jessie couldn't say she wasn't warned. Alex's behavior at the party was so obvious, even Ramon picked up on it.

Piper got out of her car and headed toward the house, passing by Jessica's old Honda on her way through the barnyard. Two giant maple trees framed the small yard near the road, their towering boughs joining high overhead, creating a natural arbor over the tiny patch of grass that Jessica insisted on maintaining. Piper would have just graveled the whole thing, but it was where Mr. Sweet had sold his apples and veggies, and though Jessica had been unable to keep up the garden and the orchard, she still kept this area immaculate as a sort of tribute to her dad.

Piper had gone back and forth with Alex, who kept coming up with excuses to go to Jessica's house and check up on her. It was obvious he was hoping Jessica would be home by now, even though Piper had repeated their conversation to him several times. Jessica said she wouldn't be home for a few days, and that was that.

Then Alex insisted that the cats needed taken care of. She knew this was just another excuse, but he did have a point about the critters. So to keep him out of Jessie's hair, Piper promised to drive over this afternoon. She had to do something to keep Alex from going all mother hen over the poor girl. That would come soon enough, and Jessica deserved a few days to languish in a sexual stupor before having to explain herself to their overprotective friend.

Piper strolled along the old black sidewalk, wondering not for the first time what they had used way back then to make this thing. She remembered as children seeing Jessie's father out there with an oil can, fighting back the ant hills that gathered in the cracks. She'd asked him once why he just didn't get a new sidewalk put in, but like the barn, he insisted on keeping things "authentic."

The porch door was unlocked, as usual, and Piper knew from years of experience where the cat food was kept. King Kat was sitting on his wicker throne, and gave an exasperated yowl when the spring loaded door slammed shut behind her.

"Sorry boy," she mewled back at him. "Are you hungry? Huh? Want some food?" She reached for the metal trash can that held the tons of kitty grub Jessica always kept on hand, and opened it, jumping and shrieking when a mouse leaped out at her.

"Jeeze Louise!" she exclaimed, her hand on her heart as she watched the little rodent disappear behind a flower pot. "Jessica really needs to get an exterminator out here. Or maybe she just needs a good mouser," she said, giving King Kat a meaningful look. The threat apparently failed to move him, as he was meeting her glare with one of his own.

After kicking the can a couple of times to make sure there were no more surprises, Piper peered over the side from a safe distance, just to be sure, then filled up the old coffee can with kibble. Turning on the spigot for the hose, Piper exited the side door carrying her can of cat food to the patio where Jessica kept several bowls for the feline buffet.

"Heeeeeere kitty, kitty, kitty," Piper called, and in seconds she was surrounded by meowing, purring BFFs. "Yeah, I know. Mommy's away, so the cats can play. Don't worry though. Auntie Piper's got your back," she crooned as she poured the cat food into several bowls, then retrieved the hose and filled the water bowls on the other side of the patio.

King Kat had followed her out, but was still watching her from a perch on a nearby picnic table.

"Hey boy, aren't you hungry?" She asked. He answered by raising a hind leg and ceremoniously cleaning his nether regions. "That's just gross," she scolded. King Kat ignored her and continued with his ablutions. That cat was strange, but Jessie just loved him to pieces. Frankly, he gave Piper the heebie-jeebies.

Walking back through the side door onto the porch, she leaned down and turned off the water. Before she could straighten up completely, a hard hand was over her mouth, and an arm was stretched around her throat, a low voice muttering in her ear.

She lost consciousness before her scream was barely a thought.

Chapter Forty-One

What the *fuck*?

Raven had finished his workout and returned to his quarters for some much deserved rest. It was still a few hours before sunset and he finally felt calm enough that he might be able to sleep. It was hard to say if Tas's presence in the Club had been coincidence or not. Mason had a way of looking out for his officers, but either way it didn't matter. Raven was just glad to be in control again.

He stripped off his clothes, stretched out on his giant bed, and closed his eyes. His breathing went deep and even almost instantly, and the last thought that drifted through his mind was of her.

Now, he found himself sat bolt upright in the bed, his fists grasping handfuls of black satin. His breathing was labored and his heart felt like it would leap from his chest with the next pounding beat. His blood was absolutely burning within his veins, burning with panic and despair.

He scanned the room, certain he was not alone, that danger was imminent, but there was nothing there. That's when he heard the first screams coming from across the hall.

By the time he'd pulled on his jeans, there was a pounding at the door, sounding desperate and frantic.

"Raven!" It was Jessica. Christ, what the hell had happened? "Raven, please let me in!" He opened the door and she nearly fell into his arms. Her hands grasped his bare forearms, the unexpected weight of her putting him off balance. Her face was drenched with tears and her eyes were filled with the panic that still rippled through his blood. He regained his balance and tried to lead her into his suite, but she pulled at him, crying, begging unintelligibly.

Finally, unable to interpret her ranting, Raven grabbed her face in both of his large hands, forcing her eyes to meet his. "Jessica, please. You have to calm down. What the hell is going on?"

"It's Piper!" she cried. "Oh, my God, Raven, they've got Piper!"

Chapter Forty-Two

I was hysterical, and I knew I wasn't making any sense. Raven was the last person I wanted to see, but the first person I ran to. Thank God he was in his room across the hall. What would I have done if he'd been elsewhere in the Compound? I was completely lost in this place and had no idea how to contact anyone. I had a fleeting thought about the vulnerability of my situation, but right now that wasn't important.

The Sorcerers had Piper, and God only knew what they were doing to her. Why, though? Why would they take Piper? My vision had been typical, clear and vague at the same time. I saw Piper in a dark room, bound hand to foot, and struggling to see, to hear. I saw her try to scream, and she was puzzled by the lack of sound. Then the Sorcerer had come in and...oh, God! The terror on her face was the last thing I saw.

Oh, Piper! Why did they take you? *How* did they take you? It just made no sense!

Raven was saying something to me, but I couldn't focus. I needed him to help me. I needed him to *do* something! I was starting to hyperventilate again, and then his hands were on my face and he was forcing me to look into his eyes. I swear, if he knocked me out again, I was going to stake him! I wasn't sure if that was a real life way to kill a Vampire—we hadn't gotten that far in my lessons—but I was pretty sure it would hurt.

After a few seconds of eye contact, I found myself relaxing, my breathing coming easier, the panic subsiding somewhat. But the tears wouldn't stop. I just fell into Raven's arms, sobbing. He sort of put his arms around me and gave me a vague pat. I'm sure he was trying to comfort me, but I think I was scaring him again, his discomfort quite apparent.

Finally, I hiccupped, and with a shuttering breath I said into his shoulder, "Raven, what are we going to do?"

He pulled away from me and looked into my tear ravaged face again. "We'll find her," he stated calmly. "But first, we need to go to Mason with this new information. He'll want to know you had another vision about the Sorcerers."

"Can he help?" I asked, doubt in my voice. "*Will* he help?"

"We have to stop these things, Jessica. It's not just about your friend—it's about our race, the humans, and races you have only imagined."

Most of that little speech went right over my head, and it wasn't until I thought about it much later that I realized what he had said. My only thought was of my friend in the hands of those monsters. If talking to Mason would find her sooner, then we needed to go right now.

Raven pulled on a shirt and some shoes, and we were on our way through the labyrinth of halls. We rode the main elevator to the ground floor and then climbed into the subterranean elevator, or Sub-T as they called it, where Raven pushed the down button. "Is there a way you can check—make sure she's been taken?" he finally said, breaking the tense silence that had settled upon us.

I was incredulous! "I know she's been taken—dammit, Raven, I *saw* it!"

"What I mean is, maybe it hasn't happened yet. Is that possible? If so, then perhaps we can prevent them from taking her."

Oh. Well, that made sense. "I could try her cell, and Alex's. What time is it?"

"It's about 10:30."

"At night?" I asked. My clock was totally off.

"Yes."

"Okay. Crap! I didn't bring my cell!"

"We'll set you up in the war room. There's a phone there you can use—untraceable." Of course it was.

I didn't think we'd ever get there, but eventually we were in a large conference room with a big oak table and lots of high-back executive swivel-tilt chairs. The walls were bare, except for a smart board at the head of the table, an old-school retractable projection screen secured above it.

Raven set me up with a sleek, black multi-lined office phone, telling me what I needed to dial to get an outside line, and then promising to return with reinforcements soon.

The door snicked closed behind his retreating back, and I reached for the phone, my fingers hovering over the handset for a moment. Please, please, please let her be okay! I picked up the receiver and dialed Piper's cell. She never left home without it, and I knew she would answer if she were able. Not even sleep could stand in the way of Piper and potential gossip.

The phone rang three times—four times—and I was greeted with Piper's voice—or should I say voice*mail*. Crap! The next logical step was to check with Alex and see if he knew anything. Maybe if we were lucky, they were together, at a movie or something.

"Alex here. Talk to me."

"Alex, it's me. Jess."

"Christ on a cracker, Jessica—where the hell have you been?" Wow. That was nice.

"Alex, I..."

"You know I've been worried sick about you! First you have a vision that puts you on your ass, and then you disappear with Mr. I'm All That? He could be a serial killer or anything, and you just go off all high and mighty and climb into a Hummer with a complete stranger!"

"Alex, please, I...you saw the Hummer?" Serial killer—hah! He had no idea.

"Are you home? I should come over there and give you a wakeup call you won't forget. I've got web sites with pictures of girls who went off with strangers and ended up dead or worse! I swear, if that guy has hurt you in any..."

"ALEX! SHUT UP AND LISTEN!" I shouted into the mouthpiece. Jiminy Cricket. At least it seemed I had his attention...finally. "Alex, is Piper with you?"

"What? No. What's Piper got to do with anything? This is about you and your complete disregard for..."

"Alex, FOCUS!" I snapped. "Have you seen Piper at all today? Please—this is very important. I promise, you can yell at me all you want later, but we need to find Piper *right now!*"

I think the hysteria was returning, and something of it must have been apparent in my voice, because finally Alex was paying attention. "Jess—what's wrong?"

"Piper—where is she?"

"She—I don't know!" He sounded confused now, and I think my panic was contagious. "I, um, talked to her earlier. After she talked to you? I admit, I was upset about your decision to, uh, hang out with that guy. I told Piper I was going to go to your house and wait there for you to get home so I could, well, you know?" I'll give him credit. At least he had the good graces to sound contrite.

"Anyway, she talked me out of it by promising to go and check on your house and feed the cats. She said she didn't think you would be there, but that the cats shouldn't be left without food and water."

"Christ, Alex, they're *feral* cats! They would be okay for a day or two." Now I was off topic. "What time was that? When was she going to my house?"

"Hell, it was probably around 7:00—why? Jessica, what's this all about? Is Piper in some kind of trouble?"

"Oh, Alex," I groaned. "This is all my fault! I had another vision, and I'm afraid that Piper has been kidnapped. Rav—Ramon has some friends who he thinks will be able to help us find her, but I'm scared, Alex. What if something happens to her?" The thread of control I'd gained from Raven was gone and I was crying again, long wet tracks etching my cheeks, little puddles of tears forming on the burnished wood of the conference table. But Alex was a lifeline, and though he was overprotective, he was still my family, and the sound of his voice on the other end of the phone helped to ground me a little.

"It's okay, Jess. We'll find her. I'll make some calls, check around town and see if anyone's seen her. And I'll drive out to your place and see..."

"NO!" I cried. The last thing we needed was for him to get caught up in this too. "Stay away from my house. I'm sorry Alex, but for now, it's just not safe."

"Seriously, Jessica, this is beginning to piss me off. What the hell have you gotten yourself into? Does it have something to do with this Ramon guy?"

I drummed my fingers on the table, thinking of how I was going to get around this. Alex wasn't stupid, so I needed to come up with something plausible. I decided to stick with as much of the truth as I could, without betraying Raven.

"Alex, promise me that what I'm about to tell you will be just between us. You can't say anything to *anyone*, okay?"

"You know you can trust me, Jessica," Alex huffed.

"Do you remember the vision I told you and Piper about? The one I've had since I was little, with the naked guy on my porch?"

"Yeah," Alex said thoughtfully, "the one where he's all bloody and you wake up before you find out who he is or anything?"

"Uh-huh, that one," I said, hoping he'd cotton on and I wouldn't have to go into great detail.

After a few beats he said, "*Ramon?*" as if the thought of it was ludicrous. Guess I hadn't been as forthcoming as I'd thought with the naked guy details.

"Yeah, it happened early Thursday morning. I didn't tell you guys," I rushed on before he could accuse me of withholding information, "because at the time, I wasn't really sure it *had* happened." Oops—that was getting dangerously close to too much information, so I redirected. "What I mean is, even after it happened, it still felt like it could have been a dream or a vision, so I figured I'd just sit on it for a while and see if anything came of it." Alex was still listening quietly, but his breathing was getting harder and I could tell he was biting his tongue.

"And nothing did, Alex, until Saturday night at the Mayor's house, when much to my surprise the Naked Man walked into the ball, all dressed up and alive! It really happened, Alex, and I left with him because I needed to know exactly *what* happened."

"And?" he was still biting his tongue, and the word came out a little garbled.

"And nothing. He said that there had been some bad guys after him, but he was okay, and then, um, one thing led to another, and I decided to stay with him for a while, to see if I could figure anything out about the vision."

"Piper said you were..."

"I know what Piper said," I snapped. " Exactly what I told her. Alex, she'd be so disappointed if she thought this was something other than sex. You know how badly she thinks I need to get laid." I was starting to think she was right, but I kept that to myself.

Alex muttered something that sounded like, *mind her own damn business*, and then said, "So you think these bad guys Ramon dragged into your life took Piper?"

"I don't know," I whined. "Alex, I just don't know. All I know is that I'm scared. If we lose Piper—I just don't know how much more I can take. And Alex, remember you promised. Not a word about Ramon to *anyone*."

Alex's silence was not reassuring.

Chapter Forty-Three

When Piper regained consciousness, she was stiff and disoriented. She tried to look around, but when she opened her eyes she was in complete darkness. Her hands were tied behind her back, her ankles also bound and connected to her wrists. Great—she was hog tied.

Usually, Piper was able to reason through most situations and come up with a solution to any problem. This wasn't a talent she broadcast—sometimes playing the dumb debutante was really useful, and she tried hard not to ruin the reputation she worked so hard to maintain. She also wasn't one given to panicking, her father having taught her that the best way to solve a problem was to look at it objectively. Since she didn't appear to be in immediate peril, other than severe cramping and discomfort, she decided to take her daddy's advice to heart and see what she could come up with.

She had just fed the cats and come back onto the porch to turn off the water, when someone snuck up on her. Her first thought was that Alex had somehow caught her off guard, trying to scare her into not scolding him for driving out there to check up on Jessica when he had promised to stay away. But that was obviously not the case.

The ground where she lay was cool and hard. She rubbed her cheek against it to see what it was made of, and was pretty sure it felt like wood. Not fancy hardwood like her parents had just had installed in the dining room—no this felt like something you would find in a cabin or something. But cabins had windows, and this place smelled musty, as though it hadn't been aired out in a while. Given the complete darkness she was submerged in, there were either no windows or else this place was sealed up for secrecy, and probably intimidation. Or, it could just be an old shed.

She tried to listen, to see what she could hear from outside her prison, but there was complete silence. No traffic, no birds, no people. Nothing. This place was definitely chosen with great care, confirming Piper's suspicions that this was a kidnapping for ransom. It had to be, right? What other reason would anyone have for taking her?

Only, if that were the case, then how did they know where she would be? Alex was the only person who knew she'd be at Jessica's, and he certainly wouldn't admit to anyone that he was so crazy about Jessie being with another guy that he had to have Piper go and check up on the place. So how did they know? She supposed they could have followed her, but surely she would have noticed. Wouldn't she have?

Piper tried struggling, but it only made her bindings tighter. Her mouth was dry and her joints were aching from the awkward position she'd been lying in for God knew how long. She tried to scream, but found she had no voice. That was odd. She tried again, and again—no sound.

Without warning, a door flew open and the room was flooded with bright light, blinding her even more than the darkness had just seconds before. Unable to cover her eyes, she squeezed them shut as tightly as she could, hoping this was a rescue and not the alternative.

If her eyes had been open, Piper would have seen that there was no sound when the door slammed into the wall, and just when she was beginning to think she'd gone deaf, her hearing returned. What she heard, though, was enough to completely shake loose the calm she'd just willed herself into.

What she heard was a blood curdling scream, human, assuming a human could make a horrible sound like that. It left her skin prickling and her hair standing up on her neck. She peeked through her lashes, trying to get a look at who or what had come through the door, and then wished she hadn't.

Lying on the floor in front of her was a child, screeching at the top of her lungs. She had been beaten to the point that her features were indiscernible, her hair pasted to her skull with blood from her numerous wounds.

Standing above her was a tall man who looked vaguely familiar. He had long, pure white hair that floated around his head like a swimsuit model with a fan blowing in her face. He was dressed in white robes, the light beaming in from the door creating an unholy glow around him. Except for the blood covering his hands and spattering his sleeves, he looked completely harmless, like somebody's grandpa. Well, except for the eyes. Even if she squinted, Piper couldn't convince herself that it was the light making his eyes glow red like that.

The man walked toward Piper, kicking the child as he passed, intensifying her screams. The red glow of his eyes began to pulse, and for the first time since she realized she'd been kidnapped, Piper was terrified.

Chapter Forty-Four

When Raven returned to the war room, Jessica was just ending her call.

"I know, Alex. I will, don't worry. I love you, too." She sobbed the last as she replaced the receiver, and Raven's heart clinched. Alex was the guy who had stood up to him at the Mayor's party. The one who acted as though he had claims on Jessica. The one Raven didn't like. At all. He stifled a growl, and continued on into the room, Mason and Merlin close on his heels.

Raven sat beside Jessica, laying a hand possessively over the one she still had resting on the telephone. In the middle of beating the crap out of the heavy bag he had decided to let her be, forget about her, but now the old green eyed monster reared its ugly head, and he was right back where he'd started. Obsessed.

Once Merlin and Mason were seated and the necessary introductions had been made, all eyes turned to their leader, whose gaze was fixed on Jessica. He blinked several times before speaking.

"Raven tells us you've had a vision, of the Sorcerers this time." Jessica nodded, her face etched with pain. "Tell us about it." Jessica did as she was told, explaining to them again that the visions weren't always clear. She didn't know where they were holding Piper, only that it was dark and secluded. She was fairly confident the Sorcerer she saw was *not* Helmut Fuhrmann. She was also convinced that Piper had been hurt. Or was going to be hurt. Time was a fluid thing in her visions, something very hard to discern, as Raven had reminded her. The things she saw could have already happened or be about to happen, or maybe not happen for twenty years or more. (The last she said with a meaningful glance at Raven.) But with what Alex had told her, she was convinced this was a current event. One that left them very little time if they were going to save her friend.

"Merlin, how's the recon going?"

"It's hard to say, since we've been limited to what we can see from the air, but with the intel we've gathered so far, it looks like the area north of the gravel pit is definitely host to something that's killing off anything alive within a mile radius. The trees are browner than they should be this time of year, and the air has a sickly feel to it. It's like the area has a pulse, completely unnatural."

"Have you heard from the Weres?"

"Yeah. They were already aware of something off in their forest, same location. Plus, last full moon, several wolves went missing from the reserve. Young ones. The adult who was with them was found dead, mid-change. Cause of death undeterminable. They were running separate from the main pack—apparently that's what they do with their young—and no one has seen or heard from the little ones since. They were too young to be able to control their shift. Chances are they were taken as they changed. They would be most vulnerable at that point, especially if their guardian was killed first—no one to protect them. No clue what the Sorcerers are doing with them, though."

"Have there been any reports of missing vamps in the area?" Raven had been deep in thought, but this comment pulled him back to the present.

"No," Merlin replied. "So far as we know, Raven's the only one who's been taken. However, it seems like things are heating up in the Mayor's office. Supposedly, they're trying to pass some kind of law making it legal to hunt "wild dogs" in and around Fallen Cross. Apparently, there have been some complaints of livestock going missing, or being mutilated, and they're blaming it on packs of wild dogs. That little incident with you and the Sorcs at that farm?" Merlin focused on Raven.

"You're kidding," Raven shook his head.

"Nope, not kidding. They're blaming that on the "dogs." Seems to me, this could be Fuhrmann trying to pin stuff on the Weres, manipulating the Mayor into doing some dirty work for him."

Mason drummed his fingers on the table. "Merlin, didn't you say that the Weres were responsible for the repression of the Sorcerers in the early 1800's?"

"Yes, sir."

"Then it would appear we've been operating under false assumptions. In spite of the fact that one of ours was taken, this was not meant to be our war. It seems the Weres were the targets all along. I don't know where Raven falls into this, but his abduction gives us a reason to lend our support to the Weres. If they can take him down, they could take down any one of us, and that sort of threat cannot be ignored."

Jessica looked up, seeming to just be catching up to the conversation. Her eyes were wide with a sudden realization and she seemed to be having trouble forming the words. Finally she said, "Wait a minute—are you talking about *Werewolves*?"

Chapter Forty-Five

My mind had been wandering, the Vampires' talk of intel and recon going right over my head, when all I was really interested in was the part where they would say, "This is where Piper is," and "This is how we're going to rescue her." Certain words began to register, though. The things they were saying started to sink in and I couldn't believe what I was hearing, although I don't know why I was surprised.

Werewolves? You've got to be kidding me! But when I voiced my question aloud, all eyes turned to me, making me feel small and intimidated. Mason's black eyes bored into me, as though my question were ridiculous and this new guy, Merlin, barely looked up, his focus still on the laptop in front of him. He seemed like a nice enough guy, as far as Vampires went. He was good looking, which I was beginning to think was a prerequisite, though where Raven and Mason were more European this guy was definitely from the Asian contingent. He had long, straight black hair that he kept tucking behind his ears, dark almond shaped eyes, and flawlessly smooth skin. Dressed in black trousers and a white cotton V-neck shirt, he was smaller than the other two, probably not even six feet. In spite of his nerdiness, you could tell he was still put together. I wouldn't want to run into him in a dark alley, that's for sure. Then again, with Vampires, I'm sure alleys were something you'd want to avoid, altogether.

Raven was kind enough to answer my question, the other males in the room barely tolerating the interruption.

"Yes, Jessica, we're talking about Werewolves, or Weres. There's a pack in the woods we were discussing as a potential gathering place for the Sorcerers. North of the gravel pit. They are pretty common, actually, as far as supers go, and they do tend to blend in pretty well with humans. I wouldn't be surprised if you knew a few of them, though it would probably surprise you to know who they were."

"Well, tell me then. Who are they?" If they told me Mable at the Diner was a Werewolf, I wouldn't be too surprised.

"It's not really our place to out the Weres," Mason interrupted. "If they wanted you to know, they'd have told you themselves. Now, if you would like us to get your friend back, I'd suggest you let us continue."

Yes sir! I thought, though I kept that bit of sarcasm to myself. It just seemed like every time I turned a corner, something newer and stranger was getting thrown at me, and as open minded as I liked to think I was, it was getting harder and harder to believe this was all real. Except, if it were a dream, I know for sure Raven and I would have...

"So, if I've got this right, the Weres are missing some Werekids? Do they think the Sorcerers have taken them?" I asked, trying to refocus.

"They do now. They knew something was lurking in their forest, but the Sorcs must have some kind of glamour up around their area. The kind that keeps them invisible and undetectable, from the ground anyway." Merlin said. "However, I don't know how they expected to keep their magical activities hidden. Any creature with an ounce of magic in them, Were, vamp, whatever, would feel the reverb in the area. I think even a human might feel something off there. It's disturbing."

"So we have the area narrowed down. How do we get in?" Mason asked Merlin.

"Viper and Tas are on that now. They've taken a Squad of Soldiers out to the woods, presumably for survival training. Tas got clearance from the Weres, so there shouldn't be any problem from them. The Soldiers they've taken are a special unit, trained in magical defense and detection. They went out at sunset. We should be hearing from them soon.

"Also, Viper's developed a new weapon, something that can disrupt the Sorcerers' magic, sort of like an EMP disrupts electricity. It's been hard to test without having the exact magic available, so they're hoping to get a chance to try it out tonight. If it works, it will be a definite advantage."

"Very good," Mason said. "So now, we wait."

"Wait?" I cried. "What do you mean, wait? My friend is out there and she's in trouble. How can you just sit here and *wait*?" I was on my feet now, positive I didn't just hear the man say he was going to hang out in the comfort of his little fortress while my best friend, my family, was being tortured or worse by those evil Vegas act wannabes!

"Calm down," Raven said, a strong hand resting on my shoulder. "Mason's right. There's nothing more we can do. Once we've pinpointed the exact location of the Sorcerer's we'll be able to go in and take them out, but until then, our hands are tied."

"Has anyone been to my house? To see if they left any clues?" I asked, desperate for something constructive to do, rather than just wait.

"Yes, Harrier went out just after dark. He said there were a few pots knocked over on the porch, but otherwise, all was quiet," Merlin answered, barely glancing up from his computer.

"Well, there has to be *something* we can do," I cried. "I can't just sit here and do nothing. I'll go crazy!" I turned to Raven, hoping for some kind of support, but he was making a determined effort to look anywhere but at me. Coward.

When he did look at me, something in his eyes gave me hope. "Jessica," he hesitated. "You've got a cat..."

"I've got about a dozen cats," I deflated. "You'll have to be more specific."

"This one's big—all black—acts like he owns the place."

I couldn't help my smile. "That's King Kat. And I'm pretty sure he *does* own the place. Why do you ask about him?"

Raven hesitated again. It seemed like there was something he wanted to tell me, but didn't know how. Seriously, if telling me he was a Vampire didn't scare me off, nothing he said could. I waited though, giving him time to gather his thoughts, though that tiny bit of patience nearly killed me.

"I want to try something. Mason, any objections to a quick trip to Jessica's?"

"I'm coming with you I said," jumping up and heading for the door before Mason had a chance to nix the idea. I didn't know what Raven had in mind—didn't really care—but I wasn't about to miss a chance to pick up some real clothes and some freakin' shoes.

Mason didn't say no. Instead he said, "You need backup?"

"No," Raven smiled. "I think I'm in pretty good hands."

I heard Merlin chuckling as we headed out the door.

Chapter Forty-Six

Piper's fear intensified as the tall man approached her, his features blank, his movements determined. She struggled and screamed when he got near, grateful to hear her own voice again, but the man just reached down and slapped her—hard—reducing her screams to silent sobs.

He reached down and detached her legs from her hands, her muscles crying at the release. Then he picked her up underneath one arm and carried her toward the door, going out of his way to kick the little girl again on his way out. As he closed the door behind them, the girl's cries became muffled, and Piper wondered vaguely if the child would be okay.

The man had taken her into another room—it was, indeed, a cabin—with a fire dancing merrily in the fireplace, and the smell of food permeating the air. Piper's stomach grumbled, and she was ashamed to admit she was hungry, as frightened as she was. She could seriously use a margarita, too, but she didn't see that happening any time soon.

The man dragged her into the center of the room, where she was unceremoniously dropped into a chair, her arms still tied behind her, now draped over the chair's back. Like an interrogation scene from an old war movie, a bare light bulb hung over her, extending from a long cord that stretched up to and along the ceiling, then down the wall to a socket located near the door. Piper was certain she heard the rumbling of a generator outside, which meant this place was off the grid. She must be pretty far from civilization.

Without warning, the door to the outside swung open, and in walked a man she definitely recognized. The same man she had mistaken the surly guy behind her for earlier. It was Helmut Fuhrmann, the Mayor's new assistant! What the heck was this all about? Now she was sure there had been a mistake. The Mayor would never stand for this.

Piper opened her mouth to say as much, but Fuhrmann cut her off. "Silence." he said, and something in his voice made it impossible to disobey. "You will speak only when commanded, and you will answer all questions truthfully. Do you understand?"

"I...yes," Piper squeaked. Why hadn't she noticed this guy being so scary at the party? He was dressed much the same as he had been the night before, though his suit was less tuxedo, it was still very Armani, and unlike grumpy guy, his hair was pulled back in a slick pony tail, with hair bands strategically placed along the length of the tail in a totally Eighties do. Based on the other guy's floating locks, Piper figured this was to keep Fuhrmann's hair under control. These guys had serious static issues.

"Are you Jessica Sweet?" Fuhrmann asked her. Piper shook her head, confused.

"No, of course not. My name..."

"Do not lie to me!" His voice boomed throughout the room, like it was coming from everywhere at once, and his eyes were red now, like the henchman who still hovered behind her.

"I am NOT lying to you," Piper insisted, adamantly shaking a red curl out of her eyes, forgetting for a second to be terrified. "As I was saying, my name is Piper Penelope Pendleton, thank you very much, and if the Mayor knew you had me, you'd be in some big trouble, mister!" Piper didn't like to be yelled at.

"The Mayor is insignificant," he said, his voice normal again, but his words disconcerting now. "If you are not Jessica Sweet, why were you at her home?"

"I just went to feed the cats," Piper said, feeling a little put out. "Hey, is Jessica in some kind of trouble?"

"She has been seen in the company of my enemy, and they must be destroyed."

"Who, Jessica or the enemy?" Piper needed to get this right, but Fuhrmann just gave her an incredulous look.

"You will lead us to her." Fuhrmann commanded, but Piper just shook her head.

"No, I don't think so. I don't even know where she is." Thank God Jessie hadn't told her where Ramon lived, but if he was the reason they were all in trouble, Piper was going to have to reconsider her previous endorsement of him.

"She will come to you. You will call her." This Fuhrmann guy was really getting on her last nerve, his thick German accent giving her the willies. She felt like she was in *Raiders of the Lost Ark* or something.

"I won't do it!" Piper insisted, and then she screamed in agony. She was being lifted by her wrists from behind the chair, her shoulders screaming with the pain of nearly being dislocated. Grumpy was standing too far away to be the one implementing this punishment, and Fuhrmann was still in front of her. Was there someone else in the room?

The light bulb over her head flickered as Piper screamed, still shaking her head, the tears flowing freely now. "I can't!" she cried, and then out of nowhere something connected with her cheek, and she was blinded by the stars created from the blow, the chair rocking back on two legs.

The more she refused, the harder they struck, drawing blood on more than one occasion, until finally, thankfully, she lost consciousness. Her last thought before the darkness took her was that with all the blows she had received, she had never seen who or what was striking her.

Chapter Forty-Seven

Fuhrmann was livid. The stupid little human was refusing to cooperate, and his brand of magic was not changing her mind. The Sorcerers were able to do many things, but for whatever reason the Gods had chosen to give unrestricted compulsion to the Vampires. Memories he could tamper with, and he could make suggestions, but they only worked if they wouldn't cause the person to cross a moral line or do anything they would find offensive. He couldn't affect free will. This rankled Fuhrmann to no end, especially when he needed an unwilling party to do his bidding.

Humans were usually simple enough. Pull the right strings, or limbs as the case may be, and they were willing to do or say just about anything. This one, however, was protecting the Sweet girl as she would herself. That sort of self-sacrificing attitude was beyond Fuhrmann's comprehension. There had only been one person he would have died for, and she was taken from him. Everyone else was insignificant.

Not that he minded this kind of work. He had enough anger in him to continue beating the girl until she was nothing but a bloody pulp, but circumstances being what they were, he knew that would not be possible. He could take his rage out on the pup in the other room later.

Or not. Damn, if she hadn't already had her beating for the day. Unfortunately, her pack mates had been made of lesser stuff, having succumbed to the rigors of their daily "training" several days ago.

Fuhrmann had adopted a training method for the young Weres that he learned about in the underground dog fighting rings. The animals were kept hungry and frightened and ready to bite anything that came near them. The strongest survived the training to fight. Amazingly, the small female had been the strongest.

As his magical blows landed again and again on the red-headed human in front of him, he allowed his thoughts to continue wondering.

The little blonde female was truly ferocious! She'd been kept in a cage for hours each day, where Fuhrmann and his men could poke sticks at her as they went by, and she would snarl and yell at them, in spite of her precarious situation. Sure, she cried when they beat her, but her anger was near to the boiling point, just where he wanted it. Fuhrmann had no doubt she would attack the first living thing she encountered the moment she changed, and he couldn't wait!

Bringing his focus back to the present, he realized the human had lost consciousness. With a final blow, just because he felt like it, he left the cabin.

Chapter Forty-Eight

Raven was silent as he navigated his Corvette through the back roads that led from the Legion's Compound to Jessica's house. After much argument, it was finally agreed that they wouldn't put Jessica into trance again, but only if she agreed to be blindfolded until they were far enough away from the Compound that she wouldn't be able to find her way back.

After about fifteen minutes, he reached over and pulled the cloth hood from Jessica's head, the static in her hair reminding him of the Sorcerer's who'd held him captive.

"So where are we?" she asked. Raven just smiled. Like he was going to tell her. Eventually she'd get her bearings, but he had driven around randomly for about ten minutes just to confuse her. Mason had insisted on this.

"What's the deal with my cat, anyway? Don't get me wrong—he's great—but I just don't understand what King Kat has to do with anything."

"It's hard to explain. I told you about my own gift, the mind touch?" When she nodded, he continued. "Well it doesn't just work with humans—I can use it with animals as well. It's not like I can hear words—it's more like intentions, feelings. I can tell if they are upset, happy, hungry, frightened. And I can convey my own intentions to them."

"Okay, but how can that help us find the Sorcerers?"

"Your King Kat seems to be different from other animals. When I was here before, I could swear he was asking *me* questions." Raven glanced sideways at Jessica and wasn't surprised to see the disbelief on her face. "I know it sounds unlikely, but I think there is more to King Kat than meets the eye. I figured it wouldn't hurt to investigate further, assuming he'll cooperate. He seems to have an attitude."

Jessica just shook her head. Vampires, Sorcerers, Werewolves? Why not a cat who can communicate with a Vampire. "So what do you think he can tell you? I mean, we already know what the Sorcerers look like, and surely King won't know where to find them."

"No, but he may be able to tell us if Piper was taken from here, and maybe even when."

Chapter Forty-Nine

Fifteen minutes later we were pulling into my driveway. My heart fell when I saw Piper's BMW sitting next to my little Honda. This was definitely not a good sign. Raven made me wait in the car while he searched the property for intruders. After a couple of minutes he came back for me, opening the door and helping me up from the low riding vehicle.

My spine tingled as we neared the places where the Sorcerers had been dispatched. I was pleased to see that Mason was true to his word. You really couldn't tell that a non-human had disintegrated there, not even in the yard. They must have some heavy duty goo remover back at the Legion.

King Kat was in his chair when I stepped onto the porch, and he greeted me with his normal disdainful meow, as if to say, "Where you been, lady?"

I reached down to scratch his ears, and he rubbed his inky cheek all over my hand. When Raven entered, the rubbing stopped and King Kat sat straight up, his focus now on the Vampire. "So that's how it's gonna be," I scolded the cat. He bumped my hand and then jumped to the picnic table to get closer to Raven. Whatever.

I left them on the porch to bond, anxious to be inside my home again. The microwave clock read 12:49 am, and my stomach rumbled, reminding me that all I'd had to eat since the party last night was an apple. I opened the fridge and pulled out a bag of deli ham and one of Colby cheese. Pulling out a slice of each, I rolled them together and ate them like that.

I walked around the kitchen, touching my things. It had only been a day, but it seemed like a lifetime since I'd been home. Remembering that I wouldn't be here for long brought a lump to my throat.

I walked back to the door and peeked out at Raven and King. Raven had sat down on the swing and King was on his lap, his front paws planted firmly on Raven's chest putting them at eye level with each other. Piper always said King Kat creeped her out, but I just thought he was peculiar. He showed up on my porch the day after my mother died, and unlike the rest of my strays, he had been friendly and approachable. He made me feel like I wasn't alone in the house, like I had a friend who would always be there, one I could tell anything and he would never judge me. Watching these two together had me wondering where he'd come from.

The lump in my throat was swelling at an alarming rate, and I was afraid the tears were going to start soon, so I turned away from the happy reunion and headed upstairs to pack up some clothes. Raven was unable to say how long I'd be gone, so I decided on a week's worth. I could always do laundry.

I nearly had my clothes together when I heard the door open downstairs. "I'm up here," I called to Raven. When I turned toward the door less than a second later, he was standing there watching me, which naturally made me jump.

"What the hell, Raven?" I cried. "You scared the crap out of me. Again!"

"Sorry," he said, but the smirk on his face told me he wasn't really. "So this is your room?"

"Like you don't already know that." He shrugged and I continued, dropping the sarcasm. "When my dad died, Mom couldn't bring herself to sleep in here. She and Dad were inseparable, and the thought of being in here without him was more than she could take. She moved to the room on the other side of the house, and told me I should move my things in here." I folded up the last of my clothes and put them in the suitcase I had sitting out on the bed, the memories of my mother's pain palpable in this room.

"I argued with her, tried to tell her that maybe she'd feel closer to Dad if she stayed in here, but she just couldn't do it. Turns out, she couldn't do much of anything. She lasted about a year without him, but in the end she just couldn't be in a world where he didn't exist. She died a couple of months ago." I looked up to see Raven watching me, a strange look in his eye.

"If someone tells you it's not possible to die of a broken heart, don't believe it," I choked. "I've seen it first hand, and Raven, it's the saddest thing you could ever imagine."

"Are you in love, Jessica?" His question caught me off guard, and I hesitated. I knew I was feeling something for him, but it seemed a little soon to be asking for a true love vow.

Before I could answer he said, "You hesitate. The man from last night—Alex? It is true then. He is your...mate?" He looked so sincere, and if I wasn't mistaken there was a tinge of anger in the way he'd said "mate."

I blinked once. Then I blinked again. Then I laughed my ass off! I fell on the bed next to the rollaway I'd just zipped closed, and I just couldn't help myself. *Alex?*

"I heard you tell him you loved him," Raven said defensively, but I still couldn't stop laughing. How this man could make me laugh when so much was wrong in my world, I didn't know, but he kept doing it. Finally, I wiped my eyes and sat up, only to find him glaring at me from where he stood leaning against my closet door.

"Sorry," I said. "It's just that Alex is my friend." Raven started to say something but I interrupted him. "No, you definitely heard me say I loved him, and I do—with all my heart. But not *that* way! Alex and Piper are the only family I have left now, and I love them as I would a brother and a sister. I would do anything in the world for them, and they for me. But Alex and I never have been and never will be—what did you call it? Mates? Uh-uh. Not gonna happen." I was still smiling, though trying to be a little more delicate. Who knew Vampires were so sensitive? He did seem to believe me though, his demeanor more relaxed than it had been moments ago.

I picked myself up off the bed and reached for the suitcase, thinking I needed to get downstairs and pack my sundries. Raven was there before I could blink and to my credit, I didn't jump this time. I just looked up at him and shook my head.

He didn't say anything—just kept staring at me, and I was beginning to get a little uncomfortable under his intense glare. I moved to go around him, but he moved with me, blocking my path. I moved back the other way, and, sure enough, he was there again.

I decided maybe conversation would help, so I said, "Did you and King Kat get everything straightened out?" He just kept staring at me, and then I saw something that took my breath away. His eyes—those beautiful sapphire irises—were ringed with tiny purple sparks. The other times I'd seen his eyes go all purple it had happened in a flash, instantaneously, or else I'd happened upon it after the fact. This was different—the outer ring was a multitude of tiny starbursts of purple light surrounding the natural blue of his iris. I was spellbound, fascinated by the intricacy of it.

Then somewhere in the back of my mind I remembered that with Raven, purple meant passion and power. He was either going to kill something, trance me out, or else I was going to get another chance to see him naked sans blood. The mere thought of it made me tingle in naughty places. My mouth went dry, which I found amazing since I was fighting to keep from drooling.

My hand reached up to his face, seemingly of its own will, and my fingers traced invisible lines from his eye to his jaw, feather light against his olive skin. "Raven," I breathed, captivated still. "Your eyes."

Without warning he pulled away from me, grabbed my suitcase and headed down the stairs, leaving me trembling in the middle of my bedroom, gasping for air.

Chapter Fifty

Helmut Fuhrmann paced the length of the cabin, fury burning through him. The entire situation was turning into a giant cluster fuck. The idiots had captured the wrong girl! Not only was she the *wrong* girl, she was a *connected* girl. He'd thought, *no problem*. He could use her to contact the Vampire's concubine, but this one was being quite uncooperative. And if her parents were friends of the Mayor, then she would surely be missed, so he couldn't even kill her to ease some of his frustration. The ramifications of her disappearance would be catastrophic, a distraction to the Mayor that Fuhrmann couldn't risk. They were at a critical juncture in their plan, and the Mayor's involvement and complete attention were imperative.

The door opened and two lower Clansmen were escorted into the room. These were the two responsible for this ungodly screw up. Fuhrmann turned to face them, his control wavering as they closed the door behind them. They were typical of his race, tall and reedy with the weightless hair that was a side effect of their use of magic.

Pointing at the slumped form of the red-headed girl, now lying curled on the floor, he said, "Who is this that you have brought to me."

The two men exchanged a glance, each hoping the other would speak first. Finally, the taller of the two opened his mouth and said, "Sire, it is the girl you asked for. The Sweet girl."

"And what makes you so sure that she is who you say?" The one who had spoken kicked the other, who yelped. Fuhrmann rolled his eyes, swallowing his fury.

"She was at the house you sent us to. The one where our brothers were murdered. She was feeding the cats—seemed very much at home. It had to be her!" The smaller man was sweating now, realization dawning on him quickly. "Are you saying this is the wrong girl?"

"Ah, welcome to reality my friend." Fuhrmann smiled at the pair, an evil, pointy toothed smile that did nothing to calm their nerves. His voice was calm, barely audible, when he said, "This one is useless to me. Bring me the Sweet girl. You may go."

The pair breathed a hesitant sigh of relief as they strode quickly to the door, but as they reached the center of the clearing outside, their master's voice stopped them in midstride.

"I've changed my mind," was all they heard before exploding into a million bits. Fuhrmann glanced around the clearing, wiping a bit of subordinate goo from beneath his eye.

Turning back to the interior of the cabin, he pointed to Piper's surly guard and said, "You—clean that up."

Chapter Fifty-One

Raven didn't speak to me again until we were well on the road. I wasn't sure what I'd done wrong, but apparently there had been something, and I was feeling a little sulky because of it. My best friend was missing, and here I was having relationship problems with a Vampire I'd just met. Just ducky.

I was still pouting, my arms crossed over my chest and my head turned toward the window, when something landed in my lap. I screamed, flapping my arms in front of me to fend off my attacker, my seatbelt being the only thing that kept me from jumping completely out of the car. A sound registered through my terror that I eventually interpreted as swearing—it sounded something like *sonofabitch*. At about the same time, something soft began rubbing against my face. I stopped flapping long enough to open my eyes. King Kat? What the hell?

"Why didn't you tell me King Kat was coming with us? Is he safe? I mean, you're not going to eat him or anything are you?" Raven glared at me, but I didn't care. I was still a little miffed from the silent treatment I'd been receiving, plus I knew I was just moments away from donning the hood of ignorance, and my mood wasn't getting any better. Finally, Raven spoke.

"Look, Jessica. I'm sorry about earlier. I just needed a moment to...clear my head. As far as Malcolm goes, I didn't realize he was coming myself until he made his presence known to me about five minutes ago." Raven didn't seem pleased with our stowaway.

"He told you?" I said skeptically. "Wait a minute. Who's Malcolm?"

"The cat. He prefers Malcolm. He said King Kat was fine, and it did do wonders for his ego—not that he needed it—but he's been Malcolm for too many years to change now."

"So you guys are on a first name basis then?" Could my life get any stranger?

"You could say that."

"Do I even want to know what you two 'talked' about?" I said, making bunny ear air quotes with both hands.

Raven hesitated before saying, "I'm sorry to say that he did see the Sorcerers take your friend. He said to tell you he's sorry. He knows what the girl means to you and if there were anything he could have done to help, he would have."

I decided just to roll with it and said, "Does he know what time she was taken, or is time a relative thing to him, like summertime or dinnertime?"

Raven glanced at me, giving me a look that said I should be ashamed of myself and to show a little respect. The cat in my lap stopped rubbing long enough to give me kind of the same look. "It was around 7:15 in the evening. She had just fed the rest of the cats when she was abducted by two Sorcerers who put a sensory spell on her and dragged her away."

"Did he see which way they went?" Not that it made much difference. We were so far out in the country, they could have gone anywhere from here.

"Unfortunately, no. He said he'd considered tagging along with them, but decided against it, hoping I would return with you so he could tell someone. He witnessed our little scuffle the other night and knew that I had...um...taken you with me." King Kat—I mean, Malcolm—had stopped rubbing his face with mine, and was glaring at Raven as he said this. Raven cleared his throat, seeming embarrassed.

"Am I missing something here?" In answer, Raven reached for my hand looking apologetic, but Malcolm hissed at him, causing a hasty retreat. I rubbed Malcolm's ears making kissy noises at him, and he reached up his cute little feline nose and pressed it against my puckered lips. Raven growled, and Malcolm started to purr. These two were going to drive me crazy.

With a jerk of the wheel, Raven pulled over into the entry path of a corn field, tires screeching. I was afraid there was about to be a throw down between my cat and the Vampire, and I held Malcolm tightly, turning him as far away from Raven as I could get.

But Raven just handed me the hood. Guess it was time to get blindfolded again. I'd be so glad when this was all over. "What about Malcolm?" I asked, only half serious.

Raven reached across and had Malcolm away from me in the blink of an eye. Before I could protest he had pressed a button on his key fob and was out the door. Malcolm's yowling became muffled with the slamming of the trunk. Nice. Real nice.

Raven returned to the driver's seat and looked at me as if to say, "What?" I just pulled my little hood over my head and showed him what the silent treatment felt like.

Chapter Fifty-Two

Piper woke up with something cold and wet pressing against her face. Her entire body was one big giant ache. It hurt to even open her eyes, but the sliminess was really starting to irritate her. She moved her head and for some reason was surprised when she was able to lift her arm to bat away at whatever was nudging her. Her hand connected with fur, and her eyes flew open.

Now she wished she was unconscious again. Staring her right in the eye was the biggest, scariest dog she had ever seen! Its coat was shaggy and black with silver streaks through it. It had teeth the size of her little finger, and its eyes looked like demon eyes, gold and shining and aware.

She tried to scramble away, startled to find she was in the woods, leaves crumbling under her hands and feet, briars sticking to her hair and her sweater. How did she get out here? The last thing she remembered was being at Jessica's and feeding the cats, but she felt as though she had been beaten with a club from head to toe. She backed into the base of a tree and leaned there, gasping with fear and confusion.

"Stand down, Butch." The voice came from behind the animal, and she jumped at the unexpected noise. The dog sat down, tongue lolling out of a huge canine grin.

"Are you okay?" the voice asked. She couldn't see who was talking and was still so disoriented. She looked around wildly, her hands clutching fistfuls of leaves and weeds.

"I'm right here," she looked up and saw the man as he kneeled down beside her. The dog backed off some, and now she could see the man clearly. He looked like a hunter, although she didn't know what he could be hunting this time of year. He was tall and lean, with light brown hair and an easy smile. He was dressed in jeans and a red flannel shirt that would have been hot during the day, but was probably fine at night.

That's when it occurred to her that it was dark out. The moon was shining brightly—a day or two away from being full—but that was the only light she could see. And even that was being sifted through the trees making the forest seem eerie and alive, the shadows of the trees dancing in the filtered light.

The man was still looking at her, waiting for an answer she supposed.

"Where am I?" she asked, hoping she didn't sound too silly. "How did I get here?"

"Well, little lady, I was going to ask you the same question. As to where you are, you're in the woods."

This answer irked her a little—she could see she was in the woods—but since he had just saved her from being eaten by a huge, vicious dog, she supposed she could give him a little latitude. She glanced over at the offending animal to see him rolling on the ground, apparently enjoying the feel of the dead leaves scratching his back.

The man saw her looking and said, "That's Butch. He didn't mean to frighten you. He was just standing guard until I could get here. Do you remember anything about what happened to you, how you might of ended up in our forest?"

"No," Piper said. "I was at my friend's house out on Reserve Road, feeding her cats, and then I woke up here. Am I...am I going crazy?" She was starting to get hysterical, and the man seemed aware that she was on the verge of a panic attack. He reached out to help her up, but she flinched away from his touch.

"I'm not going to hurt you, Piper. I'm just going to get you home."

"How...how do you know my name?" Piper rubbed her eyes and looked down at herself. Her clothes were filthy, and her sweater had a rip up one side. And was that blood? It was hard to tell in the shadows of the moonlight, but by the pain throbbing through her entire body, she wouldn't be surprised if there had been some bleeding involved.

The man laughed, rubbing his chin. "Everybody knows you, Piper. Your granddaddy owns the Sand and Gravel just south of here. Half my family works for him. My name is Patrick Dane. Let me see about getting you home. Can you walk?"

"I don't know," Piper said, struggling to stand. The man reached for her hand again, and this time she took it, appreciating the leverage. With his help, she managed to get to her feet, and when she looked into his eyes, she knew she could trust him. "How far are we from a phone?" Piper asked.

"Not far," Patrick said. "I have a place just around the bend there. We'll have you home in time for breakfast. You coming, Butch?" Piper looked at the dog in time to see him shake his head as if in answer, and then run off in the opposite direction.

Chapter Fifty-Three

Raven felt like a complete idiot. First there was the unexpected realization that King Kat was *way* more than he'd appeared, and Raven was annoyed with himself for not recognizing the creature for what he was on their first encounter. Even more peeved that the bastard had managed to stow away in his car without Raven's knowing.

He thought they had come to an agreement—Raven would look out for Jessica, and Malcolm would watch the house. But Malcolm reneged. Evidently, Malcolm's word was crap. Jessica would never have forgiven him if he'd put the cat out by the road, so Raven had taken not a little satisfaction in throwing the son of a bitch in the trunk.

Though Raven didn't want to admit it, the real issue here was that Malcolm had seen what he'd done to Jessica in the Hummer, and the cat was more than a little miffed at him. As Raven was still kicking himself over that little incident, he didn't need a fucking pussy cat to remind him.

Then, there was the situation with Jessica, which had almost gotten out of hand again. If she hadn't spoken...If she hadn't mentioned his eyes, he would have...

Damn! He snuck a glance at her hooded form in the seat next to him. Even with her head covered, he could tell she was upset with him. Her arms were folded defensively across her chest and she had turned to face the window, even though she couldn't see out.

He'd tried talking to her, but she was having none of that. He thought about telling her the everything. Telling her about the animal he had been and was still too capable of being now. Telling her that she could be his undoing, the one thing that could cause him to regress to his old ways, and if he hurt her he would never forgive himself. He thought about telling her all this, but when it came down to it, he was afraid. He'd been a lot of things in his excruciatingly long life, but he'd only been truly afraid twice.

The road flew beneath the tires of his Corvette, an inky black ribbon in the darkness of the countryside, and he couldn't help but remember how his journey had begun.

His first taste of fear had been when his parents died, or rather had been killed. Some villagers had decided that his family was evil, though he was sure there had never been proof. They were very careful, but such were the times, and things like that happened. Someone said you were bad, rumors spread like crazy, and you were pretty much toast. Raven had been out playing in the woods and returned to find the slaughtered bodies of his mother and father lying twisted in the ground level of their home.

Raven was alone and small, only ten years old, and though he knew there were others of his kind, he had no idea how to find them, nor how to survive on his own. His parents had loved the serenity of the forest they called home, and though they promised to take him to Court at some point when he was older, for the time being they were content.

An older Vampire found him weeks later, running panicked and starving in the woods, and took him in, showing him the ways of the race. He was from a Primeval realm and knew how to survive without human detection, and he taught Raven much.

But Raven's anger with the humans was palpable. He hated them for what they had done to his family, and he privately vowed that when he was older he would take his vengeance out on them. Until then, he bided his time, learning the mind tricks his race excelled at, and discovering a few that were personal only to him.

When he reached the age of twenty, he was nearly his full height, and his strength was incredible, even for Vampire. He took his leave of the old vamp who had raised him, and despite the male's objections, set off to mete out the justice he felt his family deserved.

He returned to his old home, finding the meager structure barely standing, an elm tree growing where the fireplace had been.

Aliya DalRae

The memory of his parents' broken bodies lying across the floor, now littered with the detritus of the forest, infuriated Raven. After several long moments, he walked away, and never looked back. Never returned.

The first house he came to was that of an old spinster woman. Looking back she hadn't been that old, maybe thirty, and for a human, she still looked completely doable. He knew she lived alone, and since he didn't care who he hurt first, she would do just fine. And hurt her, he had. He had used her fear as an aphrodisiac, raped her and beaten her, then drank her blood to quench his hunger. Not for energy. No, this was a hunger for something more. This was a hunger for vengeance, and he sought to sate that hunger with his first victim.

What happened to him that night surprised even him. He became intoxicated with the power of dominating this woman. Her fear elevating him to a confidence level he never imagined. He held this human's life in his hands, and in that moment, he knew he was special. Before he tore out her throat, he gazed into her eyes, her blood smeared across his rage and ecstasy contorted face, drops of the red liquid dripping from his fangs onto her ashen skin, and he asked the woman, "Am I a god?" Her only response was a blood curdling scream, which he silenced with the removal of her larynx.

He was flying now, convinced this was how he was meant to live. By the end of the night, not one villager remained alive, all of them slaughtered by his hands and fangs, their mangled and abused bodies strewn across the countryside. That night, the Rapist was born.

Chapter Fifty-Four

I could feel the car slowing down and knew we must be nearly there. I heard some clicking, like Raven was pushing some buttons or something, and then we picked up speed again as the car angled into a steep descent.

After a minute or so, Raven said, "You can take the hood off if you want." I ignored him. God forbid I should see a tree I might recognize later. Screw that. They wanted me in the dark, then by golly, I'd stay in the dark.

Yeah, I was still pretty miffed. The thing that happened in my bedroom just had me confused. I was getting used to that. But when Raven threw my cat in the trunk without so much as a 'by your leave"—who does that? It was rude and cruel, and I wasn't speaking to him again until he apologized. Or unless he had information about Piper. Or if he was going to explain what the heck was going on with us. Otherwise, my lips were sealed.

"Jessica, please. Take the hood off so I can see your face." I ignored him. I could tell by the change in sound that we were inside a garage now, and Raven was parking the Corvette. He cut the engine and I could feel him turn toward me. I gave him more of my back, as I turned my entire body toward the window.

I flinched when I felt his hand brush my shoulder, but then the hood was lifted from my head. I lost a few hairs in the process, making me yelp and slap at his hand. I really needed to reevaluate this slapping-the-Vampire habit I'd developed.

"Jessica, I'm sorry." It was a start. I glanced over my shoulder at him, my look suggesting he go on. "I'm sorry for wigging out on you at your house, and I'm sorry I put your cat in the trunk." I turned to face him, leaning my back against the door. Still I was silent.

"The secrecy of the Legion's location must be upheld, and since I wasn't prepared with a kitty blindfold, I did the only thing I could think of. I put him in the trunk."

"But who's he going to tell?" I finally broke my silence. "He's a freakin' cat for chrissakes!"

Raven sighed. I could tell I was testing his patience, but I didn't care. "Please understand," he said. "Malcolm is not your typical cat. He's something...more. I can't tell you what—he made me promise, and unlike him, I keep my promises." I raised an eyebrow in question. "Just suffice it to say that there are others he can communicate with, and it was the only option. I'm sure he's fine, but we can't let him run free around the Compound. He'll have to be confined to your quarters."

A muffled yowl erupted from the area of the trunk, and Raven and I both looked between the seats in the direction of the sound. Raven said loudly, "You know I'm right, Malcolm. If you don't like it I can either leave you in the trunk or take you back to Jessica's. Your choice." We heard Malcolm spit and I rolled my eyes.

"Well, let's get him out of there, then. I'm assuming you can conjure up a litter box and food and water bowls? Some kitty chow?"

"He doesn't like that crap you've been feeding him," Raven said distractedly as he exited the car, leaving me nonplussed. "I'm sure I can find something for him in the kitchen."

So we retrieved my cat and my suitcase from the trunk of the car and headed back to my quarters, where Malcolm explored every inch of space, crawling over the furniture, and under the bed. Finally, he climbed up on one of the spindly chairs and curled into a ball, rumbling with contentment. I still didn't know what was going on between Raven and Malcolm, but decided to let it rest for now. We needed to get back on point with finding Piper. These other little mysteries were going to have to wait.

Raven carried my suitcase into the bedroom and laid it on the bed. I followed him in, intending to put my meager things in the closet and dresser, but the sight of him near the bed where we'd almost—you know—well, it was a little disconcerting. Instead I stood in the doorway and said, "Just leave that there—I'll get to it later," and I retreated to the sitting room.

Raven followed me out, but headed for the door. "I need to tell Mason what we learned. If you need anything, I programmed my number into your cell phone. Just call and I'll return immediately." Malcolm sneezed and I nodded. Raven took a second to glare at the cat, and then he was gone.

Chapter Fifty-Five

Fuhrmann was furious. Eliminating the idiots responsible for the kidnapping snafu had been therapeutic, but it did nothing in the way of repairing the damage that could result from their incompetence.

Pacing the length of the spacious cabin, he went over again the plan that was now set into motion. A quick memory erasing spell and a dump in the forest would have to do. Compulsion would have been cleaner, but there was that moral issue he couldn't get around, and the girl was one hundred percent selfless when it came to her friend. Turning on the Sweet girl was something this one could never do. He probably shouldn't have beaten her as he had—but he'd been frustrated and he found violence to be amazingly, well, therapeutic in such circumstances. He called in his personal healer to do what could be done to mend the cuts, but quite a few bruises remained. The girl would no doubt try to remember what had happened to her, and trying to explain her injuries could tug at the memory spell, but that couldn't be helped.

It took some creative wording, but Fuhrmann was eventually able to fashion a loophole in the compulsion problem, which made him smile. After laying a suggestion on the girl that she seemed to accept without question, he'd had Pallman take her to the center of the Werewolves territory. She would either be found and returned home, where she would complete the task he'd given her, or with any luck one of the bloodthirsty animals would have her for a midnight snack. The compulsion spell would be wasted, and her death would do nothing to bring that butcher to him, but it would be optimal for the greater plan, providing more proof to the Mayor of the existence of the "wild dogs" that needed to be eradicated from the area.

He nearly had the Mayor convinced of this problem, having regaled him with stories of the lunar creatures from his own country, warning him that they had been spotted in this area and that something needed to be done to exterminate the beasts before they started killing the neighbors.

Mayor Diggs wasn't a complete idiot, though, and while Fuhrmann had him wondering, he still wasn't entirely won over. Even if the girl was found mangled by animals, the stubborn man would still need the upcoming demonstration. Full moon was in two nights, and the little creature caged in the holding room would be the perfect example.

He smiled as the memory of her "training" played in his mind. The Werewolves had been responsible for the near extinction of his race many years ago, and retribution was long overdue.

The plan was intricate, and this was merely a trial run, to see how easily the humans could be turned against the wolves. Humans were simple, and if you could get the right ones to believe, they would lead the rest, thanks to their very human "mob mentality." The wolves would become extinct, and the Sorcerers could rise again to their full power.

If this worked, if he could manage to incite a panic in these small-town humans to the point of eradicating the wolves here, then he could tell his master that the plan was a go, Sects would be mobilized across the globe and the wolves would be annihilated. Revenge for the years lost in an exile his race had been forced to endure.

Finding the Rapist in this Podunk town had been a bonus. His capture had been serendipitous, and Fuhrmann had enjoyed torturing the Vampire, only regretting that those imbeciles had let him escape. He had had big plans. The torture was to have gone on indefinitely, until the Vampire was begging to be put to death. Entertainment for Fuhrmann after a long, frustrating day of dealing with humans, and a small price to pay for the torture the Vampire had inflicted upon Fuhrmann's own wife.

It had been centuries ago, but he would never forget the sight of her ravaged body. She hadn't been dead long when they found her, and her hair still moved from the magic that had yet to burn out of her. Her face had looked amazingly peaceful, considering all she had endured at the hands of the Vampire race's most savage spawn.

Fuhrmann had been devastated by the loss, and spent many decades searching for the animal who had destroyed all the beauty in his world. However, the Rapist had disappeared. The telltale killings that he carelessly left as a trail for so many years, daring others to follow, stopped inexplicably. He had neither been seen nor heard from in Europe for centuries.

Finally, Fuhrmann returned to his people, determined to help them rebuild the race, his revenge reluctantly put on hold, but not forgotten. Never forgotten.

Now, he knew the Vampire was near, had held him in his grip, and he was determined to retrieve him again. To finish the punishment that he had only just begun to mete out.

Seeing the Rapist waltz into the Mayor's fundraiser, healthy and whole, infuriated Fuhrmann. It had taken all his will not to fly at the monster and tear him apart right there with the entire town looking on. It would have been fitting, but his master would not be pleased if Fuhrmann were to ruin the experiment for his own personal piece of revenge. When he saw the animal dancing with a human girl, he made some inquiries as to her identity. The fact that she lived so close to where the Rapist had escaped was not lost on Fuhrmann, and playing a hunch, he sent two of his best men to her home to lie in wait. If she were alone, they were to take her, bait to lure the murderer to him. If the Vampire was with her, they were to subdue him and kill her while he watched.

Unfortunately, things hadn't worked out as he'd planned, and he'd lost two good men because of it. He had no idea how the pair had escaped and it infuriated him to no end.

He still planned to take the girl—an eye for an eye as the human's Bible said. But with her friend's abduction, she would probably be well guarded, so acquiring her might prove difficult. Unless the Piper girl survived her night in the Were's forest. If that should happen, then he merely had to wait. The full moon was in two nights. And he would have his vengeance.

Chapter Fifty-Six

Raven nearly ran through the hall leading to Jessica's quarters. Mason had received word from the Werewolves that Piper had been found and was currently resting at the home of their Area Alpha. He could have called, but he inexplicably wanted to see Jessica's face when she learned her friend was okay.

He burst into her room without knocking, causing her to jump to her feet in alarm and Malcolm to jump in front of her, hissing and spitting. The cat needed to get a life.

"She's okay!" he blurted before she had a chance to recover. "We just got word! Your friend is safe!"

She walked toward him, disbelief painted on her face. "Really? Raven, you're not just saying that?"

"Of course not! The Weres have her!" The smile that had started to form on those beautiful lips changed back to a grimace, her eyes etched with worry. "It's okay," he said. "She's safe with Patrick—he's their Alpha. Apparently, one of his pack was out wondering the woods, getting a head start on the full moon, when he ran across the girl passed out in a clearing. He called for Patrick, who went and collected her. They were cleaning her up and promised to have her home before breakfast."

Jessica still looked worried, and Raven's heart fell a little. He thought she would be ecstatic to know that her friend was safe. Instead, she just looked more concerned. Slowly, she turned away from him and sat back down on the sofa, pulling her knees up to her chest, her face buried in her folded arms.

She had changed into some of her own clothes—a comfortable looking pair of jeans and an old college sweatshirt—and she looked incredibly small all curled up like that. Raven moved to join her on the sofa, but Malcolm jumped in his path.

"Don't make me kick you," he whispered to the cat, who glared at him for a moment before jumping on the sofa and laying as close to Jessica as he could get. Raven sat down next to Jessica, ignoring the cat between them, and reached a hand to her. He breathed a sigh of relief when she untangled one of her arms and extended her hand to join with his.

When she looked up, her face was wet with tears. "Are you *sure* she's safe with them? I mean, I don't know them. I don't really know your people very well, and while I'd trust her with you, I just...are you sure she's safe?"

With his free hand, Raven extracted the cat from between them and closed the space before Malcolm could regroup. Then he reached up and wiped a stray tear from the corner of her eye. "I promise you, she is safe. We know this pack, and though I wouldn't call us friendly, we do what we can to maintain a peace between our species. They were alerted when we discovered she was taken, and knew exactly what to do. Her family has been contacted and..."

"What did you mean, they got her cleaned up?" Her voice was calm but there was a hint of panic in her eyes.

"She, uh, had some bruises, and apparently couldn't remember a thing about who had abducted her or how she had been hurt."

"But...she's okay?"

"Yes, *amante*, she's okay."

Jessica broke then, throwing herself at Raven, crawling into his lap and wrapping her long arms around his neck. Malcolm yowled at them, but Raven told him mentally to buzz off, which he did, his tail standing straight up and flicking in the air as he made his retreat.

Raven folded his arms around Jessica, her relief so intense it melted into him with her body. She was sobbing now, and he stroked her hair, crooning soothing words in her ears. Just when he was convinced he could stay like that forever, she pulled away from him, just enough to look into his eyes. Hers were red and swollen, but she was smiling and the room was brighter for it.

Raven wasn't sure how long they stayed like that, eyes locked and searching, but at some point hers changed from shiny to smoky, and the tension between them thickened, a fog that enveloped them, secluding them from the rest of the world. Her hands were on his shoulders, her thumbs absently rubbing circles on the pulse points on his neck.

And then her lips were on his, soft and delicious, her tongue probing the depths of his mouth. He repositioned them on the sofa, sitting up in order to meet her mouth straight on, and then she was straddling him, her knees pressed against his hips, her breasts crushed against his chest. Her tongue was insistent, toying with his elongating fangs again, making him swear, praying for restraint.

Just when he thought he could take no more she tested him, her hand between his legs, massaging him to an erection that was already out of control. If she kept this up...shit! He growled as he stood, her arms and legs still clutching him, their mouths fused in explorative passion. He couldn't get her to the bedroom fast enough.

Soft music sounded somewhere in the back of Raven's mind, and he thought that it was—right. That she made his whole world sing. But in that instant she released him and was running toward the door.

Chapter Fifty-Seven

"Hello? Piper?" I nearly screamed into the phone I'd retrieved from the table by the door. If this wasn't Piper, I was going to kill someone!

My body was still humming from once-again-interrupted passion, and I glanced at Raven, who was now pacing by the fireplace. I tried to get his attention, to tell him I was sorry, and I truly was, but he wasn't looking at me. At least he hadn't run out again.

And then I heard it. The most beautiful sound in the whole wide world. Her voice was shaky and she seemed tired, but it was my Piper and I'd never been so relieved in my life.

"Jessie?" She sounded so small when she said my name, her usually strong and bubbly voice reduced to a shaky whisper.

"I'm here, sweetie, I'm here!" I cried. Fresh tears were streaking down my cheeks like a dam had broken behind my eyes, but I didn't care! "Are you okay? Please, please tell me you're okay!"

"I'm...I'm fine," she said, but she seemed confused.

"Are you home? Have you talked to Alex?" I'd spoken with him earlier, but that was before Raven had told me she'd been found. Alex hadn't slept all night, having been either on the phone or out physically looking for her. He'd been frantic with worry, as was I, and I hoped that she had called him first, seeing how I seemed to have the inside track on all things Sorcerer related.

"Yeah, I talked to him a couple minutes ago and he's on his way over. I just got home. Mom and Daddy were frantic, and they're still talking with the police, but Jessie?" she was hesitant, her voice so soft I had to strain to hear. "I don't know what happened! I was at your house and then woke up in the woods, and oh! Jessie—it hurts so bad!" She was crying again, and I wasn't there to hug her, to tell her it would be okay. That's what we did for each other. She was battered and scared, having no idea what had happened to her, and here I was, safe and sound, a horde of Vampires to protect me, and, oh yeah! I nearly had one of them in bed! I sunk down on the floor, my back sliding along the wall, feeling like just about the worst friend ever. I was hesitant to ask but I had to know.

"Piper, what hurts, honey?"

She didn't hesitate before crying, "Everything! Mr. Dane had a doctor come and look at me, and there are some bruises, and my clothes are covered with blood—Jessica, my pink Gucci is *ruined*!" That was so typically Piper, I could have shouted with joy.

"But Jessie—I don't know where the blood *came* from!" She was whispering again, and she sounded so frightened. "They couldn't find any cuts—just the bruises and the blood. The police took my clothes and they are testing them for DNA. Jessie—could I have hurt someone?"

I couldn't believe what I was hearing. "Absolutely not! Piper—you don't have a cruel bone in your body—there's no way you could have hurt someone like that. No way." I was emphatic, and I hoped she would believe me. I don't know what the Sorcerers did to her, or even worse—made her do—but they definitely screwed with her memories, and I was furious.

"Piper," I said, "It's going to be okay. I'll be there as soon as I can. I promise."

"Are you still with Ramon?" she asked, and I could almost hear a smile in her voice.

"Yeah. Look, Piper, I'm so sorry this happened to you. It's all my fault! If I hadn't run off with the hot guy at the party, you would never have been at my house and this never would have happened!"

"Jessica," she scolded, almost sounding herself again, "I don't even know what happened, so you certainly can't be blaming yourself for it. Being at your house was just the last thing I remember. Obviously, it wasn't the last thing I did."

She was being practical again, a side of her she kept well hidden from the public at large, but that she hadn't been able to hide from Alex and me. You'd think she would be the hysterical one, but here I was blubbering like an idiot. Of course she had no idea just how much my fault this was, and the guilt was tearing me apart. I'd never be able to make this up to her. Heck, I'd probably never be able to tell her just how much I'd screwed up.

We hung up with me promising again to come as soon as I could, but now I was in a state of complete self-loathing, and I just sat on the floor where I'd landed and cried. I wanted to be with my friend, but I knew if I said anything to Raven, he'd just tell me how it wasn't safe and that I should just stay put.

I slammed the back of my head against the wall in frustration, and when I opened my eyes, Raven was finally looking at me, his expression unreadable. I stood up and ran both hands through my hair, preparing myself for the next conversation. I'd just thrown ice water on a hot, passionate fire, and he couldn't be too happy with me right now. I knew he probably understood—it was Piper, after all—but that's still got to dampen the old ego.

I started to apologize again, but he was already at the door. Uh-uh. Not again.

"Stop!" I pretty much screamed at him. And for a wonder—he did. "You're not running out on me again!"

He turned to face me, and waited silently as I dragged myself to my feet.

"Come back in here, sit down on that god-awful sofa, and talk to me," I demanded, pointing firmly at the offensive piece of furniture, and again he did as he was told. If he kept this up, I was going to think I had a pet Vampire. Nice upgrade from a cat.

He sat back on the sofa, draping his arm casually across the back, and looked at me, still saying nothing, his lips pressed together in a thin line. His eyes remained blue—apparently I hadn't pissed him off yet—so I sat beside him and held his gaze for a moment.

"Look," I began haltingly, not really sure what I wanted to say. "First of all, I'm sorry about a little bit ago. It's just, it was Piper, and I so needed to talk to her!" He nodded, his face placid, his demeanor calm.

When he didn't say anything, I continued, "I know things keep happening, and we keep getting interrupted, or—whatever—but I just need you to know that when I said yes, I meant yes. I'm not a tease—I wouldn't do that to a regular guy, and I certainly wouldn't lead on a guy who I know firsthand could snap my neck without even blinking." He blinked at that.

I prattled on for another few minutes, pretty much just saying the same thing over and over, but when he did nothing more than nod at me, I lost it.

"Dammit, Raven, why won't you talk to me?" I was livid, but when he looked at me, he seemed embarrassed. He lifted his lips in what I'm sure was supposed to be a smile, but with big ol' fangs like that, it looked a little more sinister.

A small "Oh," was all I could muster.

Chapter Fifty-Eight

Raven had struggled the entire time Jessica was talking to her friend, trying to get himself back in control, but his damn fangs were having none of it. He'd felt his eyes return to normal as the passion eased, but for whatever reason, he couldn't get the fangs to retract. He'd just fed from her four days ago, but it felt like it had been weeks. The way her blood had energized him initially, he thought he would be set for a while. True, he'd expended a lot of that energy in healing, but it shouldn't be this way. He was starving for her, and it was becoming impossible to suppress his instincts.

He didn't want to leave her, not when she was finding out what happened to her friend. Who knew how upset she would be, and for reasons he still couldn't comprehend, he wanted to be there for her. God, he was losing it. Her pulse was pounding, her whole body a steady vibration, thunder to his sensitive ears, and that was making things worse, his fangs an aching throb he was barely able to conceal.

She was starting to get grumpy, though, so he had no choice but to show her why he'd remained silent. He was determined not to frighten her again, but she was being very insistent. He knew he probably looked like a snarling monster, and relief flooded him when she didn't run screaming from the room.

"Um, is that from before?" she asked innocently, rolling her eyes to examine the ceiling.

"Yeah, sorta," he muttered, his speech somewhat altered by the bulk of his extended canines. "Look, Jessica," he said, turning his head so she wouldn't have to see him this way. "If you're okay, I should go until I get this under control."

"Do you need to—um—feed?" She asked timidly. "I mean, have you fed since the other night when you...when we...on my porch?" she finally concluded.

"No, I haven't fed since then, but I shouldn't have to. It's just that you have an effect on me. One that makes me crave you, crave your blood, as though yours is the only blood that can keep me alive. Jessica," he rushed on when her eyes grew wide. "I don't mean to frighten you, and I will never feed from you without your permission. Never again, I mean." Her heart picked up pace, which did nothing to diminish his need.

He watched her eyes, searching for something of what she was thinking, and was shocked when she pushed up the sleeve of her scarlet and grey fleece, and extended her bare wrist to him.

"Christ, Jessica. You're killing me."

"On the contrary, Raven. I want to keep you alive," she stated calmly, moving closer to him on the couch, her arm still stretched in front of her. "If you recall, I had a vision. And I need you to be there. To keep *me* alive."

Raven could see the pulse point jumping in her wrist, calling to him with its steady rhythmic beat. He reached out, wrapping her wrist in strong fingers. His need was extreme, her willingness exhausting the last of his resolve.

"I'm so sorry, Jessica. But if I start, I don't think I'll be able to stop should you change your mind."

"I don't want you to stop," she whispered. She was practically panting now, but her eyes were sharp with awareness. "And stop apologizing for who you are."

"What if I go too far?" Raven whispered, alarmed by the strength of his need and the memory of his past.

"You didn't before, and you were dying and didn't even know me. Do it, Raven. Take my blood." Raven lowered his mouth to her wrist, his fangs brushing her delicate skin, and he hesitated.

"I swear to God, Raven, do this!" She was breathless now, pressing her wrist to his mouth enticingly. "I need you inside me, and since it doesn't look like we'll ever get to make love, I'll settle for this. Please, let me help you!"

At these words he withdrew his lips from her wrist, and raised his eyes back to hers, an impossible idea taking form. Maybe he could make this better for her. Give her everything she wanted, and take what he needed at the same time. He hadn't mixed feeding and sex since, well, since the last time his beast had been in control. When the strange woman had cursed him with her dying words. Even the possibility of doing this again was an incredible turn on, and his animal side was nearly vibrating with anticipation. The question was, could he do this without hurting her? Without hurting himself, and frightening her even more? He never combined his passions now—hadn't since he was cursed. Or perhaps it was more accurate to say, he was unable to.

The first time he tried after the incident with the woman, the fantasies of the kill, which had been half the fun before, were replaced by the image of her serene face, dying at his hand. He tried to erase her from his memory, but the harder he tried, the longer the image remained.

By the time he'd hooked up with Mason, he had been practically starving, not knowing how to feed without killing. Feed without brutal sex. The physical pain triggered by the attempt was so severe it left him writhing, as though his entire body were on fire. And the recovery time for each attempt increased exponentially.

He'd done the only thing he could, which was to abstain from everything, and the process had nearly destroyed him. Once he had begun his training with Mason, though, he had discovered how to perform each act separately, dispassionately, allowing him to feed to stay alive and to even kill when necessary. Balancing the beast with the need was difficult, but Mason had worked with him personally, devising a system, a meditation of sorts, that focused the beast on the desire at hand, allowing Raven to do whatever was necessary without too much problem, so long as he found no joy in it. However, if he tried to combine the acts of passion, as he referred to them now, if the beast managed for even a second to push him over the edge with his violent desire, the visions of the woman would enter his mind, and the excruciating pain returned in spades.

But now he had a chance. He had a woman who was offering herself to him, body and blood, and he knew, at least in theory, that this could be enjoyable for her. For both of them. In theory. He'd never combined the two for anyone's pleasure but his own, perverted as it had been, and let's face it—his "partner" never lived to know the difference. The thought of giving pleasure had never occurred to him.

Could he do this for Jessica? Or would the attempt result in him convulsing on the floor, as it had so many times in the past. There was no way he could make love to her—feed from her—without enjoying it. His cravings for her were insane, and the beast within him had raised its head, sniffing at the opportunity, the combination of which was quite disconcerting.

Jessica was staring at him questioningly, silently begging him to do *something*. He still held her wrist in his hand, and holding her gaze, he wrapped her fingers with his own, his mind made up, though he was trembling with the uncertainty of the outcome.

His decision, however was moot. As he moved to stand, Malcolm jumped between them, and before Raven could throw the bastard into the nearest wall the cat placed his front paws on Raven's chest, sending two words that echoed in his mind.

"They're coming."

Chapter Fifty-Nine

I was waiting for him to say something. To *do* something, my heart nearly beating out of my chest in anticipation, when all of a sudden, Malcolm was between us. I nearly swatted him myself, and the look on Raven's face told me he had something more permanent in mind. However, his anger instantly turned to focus, and after a moment I knew why.

It sounded like an entire army was marching down the hall toward my suite. I looked at Raven, terrified. They'd never come up here in a group before, and it sounded like the whole household was waiting outside my door. (Funny how quickly you start to think of a place as *yours*.)

Raven jumped up and was at the door in a flash, Malcolm fast on his heels. I got there in time to foil Malcolm's escape, scooping him up before the door opened and depositing him in the bedroom, firmly closing the door behind me.

When I turned around, the room I'd thought of as cavernous moments before now seemed claustrophobic. Raven was standing by the door, talking to Mason and Merlin, the only other people I recognized. Among the others crowded around was a tall, sinewy guy with a shaved head, emerald green eyes and tattoos covering most of his exposed body. He moved very smoothly, putting me in mind of a cobra or a python or something.

The snake man was talking to a big—and I mean *huge*—guy with red-brown hair and a sinister demeanor, and a smaller man who was absolutely breathtaking. He had the most beautiful golden blond hair I'd ever seen on a man, his eyes the blue green of the ocean, and at least twice as deep.

Mingling around were about a half dozen more guys, all in black uniforms, black boots, their bodies in various levels of disrepair. One guy was heading toward the sofa with blood running down his arm and I squealed before I could stop myself. Bad move. Where there had been chaos a moment before, now there was silence, and all eyes were on me.

"I-I'm sorry." I said to the room in general, but looking at the guy who was about to ruin my sofa. "Let me help you." I ran to his side and redirected him toward the bathroom, where the blood wouldn't do as much damage. The poor guy looked bewildered as I led him away from the group, and when someone growled behind us, his head whipped around and I swear he went from pale to gray.

"How badly are you hurt," I asked, directing him to sit on the side of the tub while I took my towel from the hook I'd hung it on earlier. It was still damp, but I ran it under warm water anyway, ordering the guy to remove his shirt.

He didn't reply, and when I turned toward him, ready to administer aid, he just stared at me.

"I can't help you if you don't show me where you're hurt," I demanded. He blinked at me, looked behind me, swallowed hard and then looked back at me. I felt the hair on the back of my neck prickle and it hit me.

I reached for the Soldier's shirt and began pulling on it. Then without turning I said, "Raven, he was about to bleed all over that fancy sofa out there. I realize he's probably one of you and this is probably not necessary, but if I'm going to be staying here, I'd like to make myself useful. If you want to stand there, fine. But stop glaring at the poor guy. In fact," I whipped around and reached for the bathroom door. "Maybe it would be better if you didn't watch!" And I slammed the door in his face.

I turned back around to see the Soldier's face had gone from gray to deathly white, a stark contrast to his dark brown hair, panic etched in his cocoa colored eyes.

"If you're going to die on me, I'd appreciate fair warning. If it's *him* you're afraid of, don't worry about it. I'll take care of it."

Finally, he spoke.

"Do you have any idea who that is?" he whispered, his voice so quiet I could barely hear him.

"I know who he is. What I don't know is who you are. What's your name, Soldier?" I was getting into this whole military medic thing. I think I was pretty good at it.

"I'm...I'm Peregrine, but he...he..."

"He'll be fine," I assured him as I peeled his shirt off the rest of the way, revealing an ugly gash across the upper segment of his left arm. It was about six or seven inches long, fairly deep and still bleeding, and I wondered if Vampires ever got stitches. "What happened to you guys?" I asked him as I pondered my next medical move.

He leaned toward me and inhaled deeply. "You...you're human?"

"Peregrine, in a minute or so I'm going to ask a question I'll really need an answer to. Any chance you'll ever respond?" I smiled at him in what I hoped was a reassuring manner and was rewarded with a shy grin. That was better.

"Perry," he said.

"I'm sorry?"

"Call me Perry. Everyone does."

"Okay. Perry. I'm Jessica, by the way. And in answer to your question, yes, I'm human. Now, quid pro quo. What happened to you guys out there?"

"I'm not sure I can discuss that with you." I was mopping up the blood from his arm and he hissed when I pressed a little too hard on the wound itself.

"Sorry," I muttered, but I didn't ease up. "Listen, Perry. My friend was out there. She's okay now, home and I hope safe. But those Sorcerers had her and they need to be stopped. Please tell me you stopped them."

Perry was looking at me like I'd just grown horns. "You're *that* human?"

I blushed, realizing that rumors of my escapades with Raven must have reached the lower ranks, and I nodded. Perry straightened his shoulders, his eyes reflecting a respect that hadn't been there a moment before. "I'm honored," he said and bowed his head to me.

"Why?" I asked, continuing my ministrations. "Don't tell anyone, but I got lucky. Those floaty-haired bastards are scary vicious, and if Piper hadn't made me buy those freakin' spike heels, we wouldn't be having this conversation.

"I'm honored," he said, "because I've fought them. I know what they can do, and I've been trained to confront magic. You are human, and yet you managed a kill and an assist. That's more than impressive."

I looked up from my work to see him smiling at me. I smiled back humbly, and eager to be on to another subject said, "Please don't laugh, but you're only the second injured Vampire I've ever encountered, and I didn't do much for the first one, so if you don't mind...what do I do now?" I had cleaned the area around the wound, but didn't know if I should go with the alcohol or hydrogen peroxide for the main attraction, both of which I'd found in the medicine cabinet. I held both bottles up to demonstrate my dilemma, and Perry pointed to the alcohol.

"It hurts more, but it's a stronger disinfectant. Not that we worry much about infection, but it never hurts to clean it out," he shrugged. I opened the clear plastic bottle and, holding the now bloody towel under his arm, I splashed about half the contents into his gaping wound. He jerked away from me, roaring in pain, and I backed off immediately when his brown eyes flashed amber.

"Sorry," he panted after a moment, his eyes melting back to chocolate as the pain ebbed.

I looked at him warily from across the room, and when he nodded that he was back in control I said, "Okay, now what? Do you need stitches or should I just tape the wound closed? I'm assuming you'll heal quickly?"

"Yes," he said, "we do heal quickly." He examined the gash which, if I wasn't mistaken, was already looking better. "I think if you just tape it together, then wrap a bandage around it, it will be fine. And keep the blood off your furniture," he added sheepishly.

"Sorry about that," I said, pulling lengths of Steri-Strip from the package I'd found with the other first aid supplies. This medicine cabinet was disturbingly well stocked. "I was just a little overwhelmed when the Vampire contingent swooped in and took over the one place I was feeling safe. When I saw the blood, I just freaked out. I don't even like that couch," I finished weakly.

Perry chuckled as I applied the tape to the gash and then wrapped a boatload of gauze around his upper arm. It was probably overkill, but he looked at it approvingly, flexing his arm to test the bandage.

"Thank you," he said, bowing his head to me again. He picked up his torn shirt, and stood to return to the living room and the rest of the crew, but then he stopped and turned back to face me.

"I like you, Jessica. I see many humans in my patrols, but few possess the kindness that you have shown. You seem not to fear us, and that is refreshing. Because of this, I feel," he lowered his voice to that barely whisper again and continued, "I feel you should be warned. I don't know what you know about Raven, but he's dangerous."

I just looked at him and whispered, "Duh—Vampire!" but he shook his head.

"No, Jessica, please hear me. Raven is the Vampire that other Vampires fear. He seems protective of you, and that's to your advantage, but the things he is capable of, the things he has done...You're a sweet girl, Jessica. Please. Take care of yourself."

And with that he was gone. My heart was pounding so hard I could hear it echoing throughout the room. I turned toward the bathtub, where the echo was the strongest and realized it wasn't my heart I as hearing. Malcolm had been there the whole time, and was now beating his tail against the porcelain bottom of the bathtub.

I reached down to rub his head, thankful for a friendly face, Perry's parting words reverberating alarmingly in my mind.

Chapter Sixty

Raven was furious! She had no right to go slamming doors in his face, let alone secluding herself in a closed room with an injured Vampire. Was she *nuts*?

Mason had all but dragged him from outside the closed door, and when that Soldier's roar had disrupted the meeting taking place in Jessica's living room, Viper and Tas had physically restrained him, the lack of her blood scent the only thing that really kept him from tearing down the flimsy barrier and ripping that fucking Soldier into a million pieces.

The band of Soldiers Tas and Harrier had taken into the forest in search of the Sorcerers' lair had come across several perimeter guards, and a skirmish had ensued. The Sorcerers had eventually been taken out, but Tas's men had taken a hit, four dead and three times that seriously injured. The fucker in the bathroom with Jessica may have survived the battle with the Sorcerers, but he was dangerously close to joining his fallen comrades.

Raven was pacing, wearing a path in the plush carpet, trying to ignore the drops of blood that led into Jessica's private bath.

"Raven, do we need to restrain you in your quarters?"

Raven looked up to see Mason staring at him, his face stony, his body tense. A glance around the room confirmed every eye on him, every Vampire ready to pounce. Hell, the Soldiers were practically cringing! Raven peered up into the mirror over the mantel and understood their tension. His eyes were sparking purple, his face contorted in rage. It wasn't pretty.

"Fuck it," he said, and stormed out of the room, crossing the hall to hole up in his own digs, where he continued his pacing.

When a knock sounded on his door, he knew who was there. Mason needed him to be in control, and he was anything but. Tas was the only one Mason would trust to reel him back in, so Raven wasn't surprised to see the blond vamp standing on his threshold. He opened the door wider, and walked back into his living room.

The layout of his quarters was a mirror to Jessica's rooms across the hall, but the décor was substantially different. Where her suite was antique Louis XV, his was sleek and modern, the furniture sporting black lacquer and leather, the lines sleek and smooth. Gold framed mirrored sconces dotted the walls, the candles springing to life at a thought.

Tas followed him inside, closing the door behind him. He was unusually silent, and Raven knew the male was having trouble deciding how to proceed. Hell, he didn't know, himself.

He had obviously just made a complete fool out of himself in front of not only the Team, but a group of Soldiers as well, and over a female. A *human* female. Had he kept his cool, they would have just assumed she was a snack, or a toy he'd brought home to play with for a while before erasing her memory and sending her on her way.

But no, he had to act the jealous fool. He fell into his favorite leather chair, propped his feet up on the glass table in front of him and crossed his arms over his eyes. He heard Tas settle onto the sofa nearby and they both remained silent for nearly half an hour.

Finally, he couldn't stand the quiet any more. Puffing out a breath of air, Raven peeked through his arms at Tas, expecting for the male to be studying him like a bug. Instead, Tas was stretched out on the couch, one arm curled behind his head, his eyes closed as though he were asleep.

Raven just shook his head. He'd been up against the Sorcerers—he knew what it demanded of a Warrior. His people had taken a beating, and here was Raven, pouting over a girl.

Tas was his best friend, and Raven knew he would have come even if Mason had not ordered him to. He thought the only reason they were able to be friends was because Tas hadn't been around when Raven was—how he was before. Every Vampire Raven encountered treated him with either awe, contempt, or fear. They all knew the stories, the legends, the horror of who he had been, and few had been able to overcome them. No one believed he had changed. But then, no one knew what had happened.

The Primeval had come to him, seeking his unique brand of violence to take care of a little problem they had in the form of a woman. They never said what the problem was, but Raven didn't care. He'd been killing for pleasure for decades now. The fact that there was a paycheck involved, that was just icing on the cake.

The woman had been beautiful, everything he could ever ask for when it came to his type of fun. He looked forward to the fear in her eyes, the panic and the pain. His fangs had dripped with saliva as he stalked her, imagining how she would taste, her blood on his tongue mingling with the sex he would enjoy. And yes, he would enjoy her. He imagined every thrust, every withdrawal, every humiliation, and his inevitable release as he drilled her to insanity, drained her of her life's force and then ripped her throat to shreds. Imagining himself picking bits of her from his teeth as he rested afterward, he was nearly giddy with excitement.

Once he had her, he discovered she was even more beautiful up close, her hair so pale it was nearly white, so silky it seemed to float around her, creating a coronal effect encircling her perfect, pale face. She was tall but fragile, with delicate cheekbones, and full luscious lips. Her beauty and scent drove the beast within him into an animalistic rage that filled him with the closest thing to happiness he'd ever known.

Eager to begin, he dragged her deep into the woods. She struggled at first, but after a while she had hung limp in his arms, no longer fighting the inevitable. This had amused him, as he carried her to the area of woods he had chosen for this particular kill. He knew he would have her screaming soon. Begging for mercy, which he conveniently was lacking.

When they reached their destination, Raven threw her to the ground, shredding her dress from neck to hem, his claws leaving deep gashes the length of her body. He was ready for her screams, his body hard and anxious for the sexual stimulant her fear would provide him. But she remained silent.

Infuriated, he tortured her, beating, clawing, raping and debasing her in a wild frenzy, and still she remained silent. Finally, he knew he could do no more without killing her. He was completely frustrated. No one—man, woman or child—had ever been able to remain silent through his violent attentions, and he felt death was too good for this one. He needed her to bow to him. To acknowledge him for the god he was.

Out of frustration, he grabbed two fistfuls of her hair and raised her head, forcing her to look him in the eye. She didn't flinch, and her stare never wavered. Raven growled his demand, "Acknowledge me. I am a god!"

A single tear slid down her cheek, the first she'd shed in all the hours he'd been destroying her body. Raven reached out with the mind touch, knowing that finally he would get at least a bit of the reaction he craved. The reaction he deserved. But he was shocked to discover that her tear was not for herself. It was for Raven. In pity for Raven.

He lowered her head slowly back to the ground, and stared at this bizarre woman. In that moment of stillness he hesitated for the first time he could remember, and she lifted a hand to his face. He trembled at her touch, fear enveloping him for only the second time in his life, and she whispered to him, soft words, words of sadness and words of hope. Words that left him feeling something he'd never felt before. Remorse.

Chapter Sixty-One

I knew I could only hide out so long in the bathroom without having the Soldier, Perry's, injury as an excuse, but I couldn't bring myself to face Raven just then. Perry had been so sincere, and he seemed so young. What could he possibly know about Raven's history?

Unless, of course, that history was so horrible that every Vampire in the world knew it.

Crap!

Malcolm was winding his way through my ankles as they dangled off the edge of the tub, where I'd sat to contemplate my next move. I reached down and picked him up, rubbing my cheeks in his soft fur.

"What am I going to do?" I asked the cat, really hoping I'd get an answer. He talked to Raven, dammit. Why couldn't he talk to me?

Instead he just rubbed me back, his soft cheek soaking up tears that I couldn't stop from falling.

I pulled the cat away from me, and looked him in the eye.

"I know you understand me. I heard Raven talking to you and he was using plain English. Please, nod if you can understand me." I knew I was seriously losing it, but Malcolm was the closest thing I had to an ally here, and I desperately needed an ally.

Malcolm just stared at me, though, and I huffed out a sigh, knowing I was being stupid. Raven obviously had special abilities with animals, but regardless of his insistence otherwise, in the end, Malcolm was just a cat.

I got up and washed my hands, removing the remainder of Perry's blood, then dried them on the last clean hand towel that was hanging on a rack above the commode.

Finally, bracing myself, I returned to the living room, carefully locking Malcolm in the bathroom with an apology and a promise to get him home soon.

I was ready to be accosted and berated by an overprotective Raven, but instead I was met with the kind of silence that only occurs when you inadvertently walk in on a conversation where you are the main topic.

I looked around and found the room nearly empty. The Soldiers, including Perry, had vacated the premises, and there were two men noticeably absent from the room: Raven, and the hot California stud muffin.

Mason approached me, always the aristocrat, and said, "Miss Sweet, I do apologize for moving in on you the way we have. We had intended to meet in Raven's quarters, but when we found he was here, well, our news couldn't wait.

"What news?" I asked, fearing the worst.

"The good news is, we've located the Sorcerers. Viper's weapon was successful in disrupting the magic that was protecting their encampment, and our team was able to recon the area, although at a great cost."

"Cost?" I said, sinking into one of the uncomfortable spindly chairs. I didn't think I wanted to know what cost.

"Yes," Mason replied. We've lost four Soldiers, and have twelve in the infirmary. The men you saw here escaped with minor injuries that will heal with alacrity. Peregrine's was probably the most severe, however he had been unwilling to join the others for medical treatment. He is...friendly...with the Werewolves and is desperate to help them retrieve their young."

"Where is he now?" I asked. "Did he go to the infirmary for better treatment? I'm sorry," I apologized to the Warlord. "I just needed something to do."

"Actually," a voice sounded from the corner near the fireplace, "we sent him to the barracks to clean himself up. Your scent was all over him, and the last thing we needed was for Raven to catch a whiff of that. It was so fuckin' strong, we'll have to keep them separated for a week! What the hell were you thinking, female?"

This was coming from the russet-haired giant I'd noticed earlier. He was dressed in black leather from head to toe, and I swear he made the Hell's Angels look like pussy cats. Leave it to me to piss off the biggest guy in the room.

"Harrier, back off!" The tattooed man said this, actually placing a restraining hand on the giant's arm. Merlin was still on the sofa tapping away at his computer, completely oblivious to the trouble brewing around him.

"Fuck you, Viper," the big man said, throwing off the male's hand and taking two menacing steps toward me. "It's obvious you weren't thinking at all! You waltz in here like you own the place, ordering our males around like servants? Who the hell do you think you are?"

"I'm s-sorry," I squeaked, scampering up from the chair and putting it between us. "I didn't ask for this!" By now, Mason had put himself between me and the giant—Harrier—and Viper was at the big man's side, struggling to hold him back. I took a quick moment to register that the guy who looked like a snake was named Viper. I knew I was nearing hysteria when I had to fight the urge to giggle.

"Back off, Harrier," Mason said calmly, his hand on the other male's chest. "There are things at work here you know nothing about, and it would behoove you to treat the lady with respect, as she is here as *my* guest. If you can't manage that, then I suggest you excuse yourself. We're meeting in the war room in an hour. Take the time to compose yourself."

With that and a muttered "Fuck you all," the Harrier dude stalked out, slamming the door behind him and leaving me to crawl around and sink back into the chair I'd been hiding behind, my legs unable to hold me up any longer.

Merlin looked up at the sound of the slamming door, glancing from me to Mason, to Viper, and then with a shrug, he returned his attention to the computer on the table in front of him.

Chapter Sixty-Two

Raven woke with a start, surprised to find he'd been asleep in his chair. Rubbing his eyes, he glanced over at the sofa to find Tas still there, snoring quietly. It had been a tense night for the team in the field, and Tas tended to internalize the emotions of those around him. He'd lost men, and that was never easy for anyone, but for Tas it was especially difficult. Add Raven's meltdown on top of that, and the guy had to be exhausted.

Raven rose from the chair, stretched, and headed to the shower. A glance at the clock told him it was nearly noon. Looks like they missed the meeting. No big. If Mason had needed them there, he would have sent someone. More likely he thought it better they weren't present. At least Raven, anyway.

Christ, he was a mess!

Jessica was right across the hall, the thought of which made him wince. He'd nearly fed from her earlier. Nearly exposed himself, his weakness, in an attempt to please her, knowing that the chances were very real that by trying to mix passions he would end up in pain so excruciating he wouldn't even be able to tell her what was wrong. But he'd wanted so much to do that for her. For both of them, if he were being honest.

How do you go from being a male with no sense of value for human life to one who would die to please a woman? Die to protect her.

Shaking his head, Raven stripped and turned the shower on full jets, waiting until pillows of steam surrounded him like a puffy cloud before plunging his head into the scorching stream. As his hair plastered around his face, he thought of Jessica as he'd seen her last, just a few hours ago. She had been angry with him, and probably rightly so, but the sight of her tending to another male had been maddening. The utter fear on the Soldier's face had been the only thing keeping Raven from obliterating him right there in front of the girl. It was obvious the male knew who he was and what he was capable of. Raven knew the young Soldier wouldn't dare harm her, and even if he'd considered anything more asinine going in, by the time Jessica had slammed the door, the male knew if he touched her he was a dead man. Raven had made that clear. His mind touch didn't work with people of his own species, but that wouldn't have even been necessary. Raven had been pure fury, and any Vampire worth his fangs would have sensed that immediately.

Once Raven was thoroughly scalded, he soaped up and rinsed quickly, thinking a few more hours of sleep were in order. He knew plans were underway regarding the attack on the Sorcerers, but it likely wouldn't be tonight. Full moon was tomorrow night, and the more they learned, the more likely it was that the enemy's target was not the Vampires, but the Weres. Logically, if something big were to happen, it would be during full moon.

Of course, that didn't explain why they had taken Raven, probably something he would never know. Maybe they were just bored that night. Wrong place, wrong time.

He grabbed the bath sheet hanging behind the door and roughly toweled off, still curious as to why he had been a target. He thought of Jessica and what he'd nearly done with her. To her. Which made him think of the woman so long ago, her white-blonde hair floating around her head as he'd ravaged her. Her pale, slender features, and how she'd touched his face. The electricity he'd felt in the touch, and then the emotion, as though he'd been cursed. As though he'd been touched by...fuck!

Raven staggered at the memory, falling to his knees as he realized what he'd done. That was no ordinary woman he had killed all those years ago. The Primeval who hired him had known what she was, and Raven had been too buried in violence to understand. To even care.

He had been set up.

Raven absently ran his fingers through his wet hair, trying to focus.

The Sorcerers would have had no way of knowing it had been a murder for hire. Raven's reputation was for killing randomly and at will, not as an assassin. They would have no reason to attack the race as a whole, but every reason to hunt down Raven and to kill him in retaliation. He had been such a liability to his own race that they had set him up in hopes that he would be eliminated, and they wouldn't have to deal with him anymore. Wouldn't have to risk one of their own. It was a brilliant plan, except it understandably had never occurred to the Primeval that the Rapist would stop killing. That he would go underground, become untraceable, and that their plan would fail because of it.

As the reality sank in, Raven started to tremble. The woman he murdered, his last act of selfish violence, had saved his life with her curse. He'd always known this to some level, known that his life was better without the indiscriminate misery he had dealt to others and embraced as his birthright. He was stronger for the control, and though the evil still lived within him, he knew that the curse would never let him be as he had been.

The Primeval would have assumed their plan a success when the killing stopped. Assumed that the Sorcerers had destroyed the Rapist, and washed their hands of him completely. How they must have congratulated themselves for their cleverness.

The idea that he had been so disposable—the thought made Raven furious! With the Primeval, yes, but more so with himself. He had placed himself in that position, had chosen his path of destruction, and yet, they had no right!

They must have been livid when they discovered he was still alive. The Primeval had their hands in all things V, and the Legion was one of their favorite ventures, so there was no way Raven could hold his current position without their knowledge. And approval.

Mason had found Raven, nearly mad from starvation, and had literally handed him his life again. Raven saw him as his savior in a sense, and always as his friend. He was here, alive, because of Mason.

But Mason would have had to report to the Primeval. It would have been their call to either eliminate the Rapist, which would have been easy given his condition, or to use him to frighten the feral vamps into submission. The Rapist was still a legend, after all.

The big question though, was how much did Mason know? Was he aware that the Primeval had tried to eliminate Raven? Mason had fought for him, had to have convinced the Oldest to spare Raven's life. Under the new laws, Raven would be considered an outlaw.

But the question remained—did Mason pull Raven out of the gutter because he believed in him—or was he just following orders?

Raven was still kneeling on the bathroom tile when Tas knocked on the door. He looked toward the sound, and realized that he'd shredded his towel into stringy bits, and they were laying scattered all around him.

How could they have done this to him? They were predators, too. Surely he wasn't so much worse than the rest, especially hundreds of years ago when the race was young and wild, that they felt the need to eliminate him in such an underhanded way. Was he so disposable they felt they couldn't dirty their own hands with his death, or were they just cowards, afraid of the fallout should their attempts fail? Even as the whys swept through his mind, he knew the reality. He had simply been too dangerous.

The knock sounded again, more urgently this time, and Raven could sense Tas's anxiety. But he couldn't respond.

In order to eliminate the Rapist, they had hired him to kill. To kill an innocent woman. Someone's mother, perhaps, or sister. Or wife. And he had agreed to do so with great pleasure. Just another human, as far as he knew. Nothing personal. Just business.

But to someone, her murder had been very personal, and that someone was here, now, in Fallen Cross. Raven's capture and torture *had* been personal. It was about revenge, and the pisser of it was, Raven was quite certain he deserved it.

Chapter Sixty-Three

Mason and Viper were very kind, apologizing all over themselves for Harrier's outburst. They didn't offer any explanations, though, which made me wonder what had happened between Raven and Harrier to make the latter hate me without even knowing me.

I mean seriously, did I ask to come here? Did I ask to be brought into the middle of a Vampire/Werewolf/Sorcerer war? No—fate tangled me up in this with my stupid visions and I was just about as pissed off about the whole thing as anyone could be.

Raven had been right, though. Harrier was pretty scary, and I definitely didn't like the idea that I was on his shit list. I kept these thoughts to myself, though, and was happy to see the backs of my visitors as the last three showed themselves out of my suite.

After a little while, there was a timid knock on the door. Unsure of who or what I would find on the other side, I went with the traditional, "Who's there?"

A small, female voice replied that she was there on the Warlord's orders, with food and fresh linens. They had maid service? It occurred to me then that the tray from the day before had been removed and my bed had been made. I didn't know if the sheets had been changed, since I had yet to sleep in the darn bed, but something told me that when I finally collapsed I'd find that they were fresh.

I opened the door a crack to find a small framed girl with long blonde hair tied back in a sleek ponytail. She had a cart with her, stacked high on one end with towels and sheets, the other end laden with a tray of the most delicious food I'd ever smelled.

The girl smiled at me, and I opened the door to allow her access. With a shy curtsey, she headed in with her cart in tow.

"Where would you like the tray?" she asked meekly, and when I indicated the coffee table she was quick to place it there. I removed several covers to find eggs, bacon, toast, bagels, croissants, and fruit. A final cover revealed two bowls—one with tuna, the other plain water, presumably for Malcolm. It was nice of Mason to remember his guest had a guest. Two pitchers balanced out the tray, one with juice, the other milk, and I didn't hesitate to tuck in.

The girl disappeared into the bathroom while I chowed down, and I was glad for it as I couldn't help being rude. My stomach rumbled even as I ate, and the thought of having to make polite conversation when all I wanted to do was cram fistfuls of food into my pie hole made me want to growl like Raven did sometimes.

By the time the girl returned to the sitting room, I'd slowed down to the point that I was merely shoveling, and I felt I could take a moment to at least be courteous.

"Wow," I said as she went about her chores, dusting and whatnot. "I was starving, and this food is delicious!" She merely nodded at me and continued around the room.

"What's your name?" I tried again.

"Tabatha," she replied quietly, lifting a lamp from a table near the heavily draped window and running a dusting cloth beneath it.

"I guess I'm just surprised to see another woman here," I said, nibbling on a croissant, considering how to ask what I really wanted to know. When she didn't respond I dove in. "Can I ask you a personal question?" She stopped what she was doing to consider me for a moment. When she nodded, I took a deep breath.

"Are you...human?"

Tabatha tilted her head at a curious angle. "I am Vampire, of course," she finally replied. "My family has served Warlord Mason and the Legion since the Legion was formed in...many years ago," she corrected. "We are honored to serve, and if there is anything we can do to make your stay here more comfortable, please let us know. The phone by the bed has Service on speed dial. Have you finished with your meal?"

I nodded, moving Malcolm's bowls to the floor and reaching for a final gulp of OJ before she whipped the tray efficiently from the table and placed it back on the cart. She gave another short curtsey, and was out the door.

I leaned back on the hard sofa, patting my finally full tummy and wondering about the Vampire family that was apparently living in servitude to the Legion. Or maybe, they got a paycheck each week. I wondered if they lived here, or if they had homes away from the Compound, or maybe just elsewhere on the property. I found myself wishing Tabatha had stuck around for some conversation.

My eyes began to droop, though, and the thought of sleeping on this uncomfortable excuse for a sofa was less than appealing. I dragged myself up and after a quick visit to the bathroom to deposit Malcolm's breakfast, I found myself staring at the huge bed that loomed in the center of my sleeping quarters. I could still see Raven lying there, naked and wet and beautiful, the purple light in his eyes shining with passion. I could feel his fangs as I stroked them with my tongue, could feel his heart beating in rhythm with mine.

And it made me want to cry. He'd run out of here without a word. True, I probably shouldn't have slammed the door in his face, and if what Harrier had said were true, all I'd really succeeded in doing was endangering the life of another male. I hoped Perry would be okay, and not just with his shoulder. But I worried more about Raven.

Had it really been just four days since he'd shown up on my property? There was still so much I didn't know, and so many opportunities for me to screw up. I'd just met the guy, but I felt like I knew him. Probably because I'd been dreaming about him since I was a little girl.

But it was more than that. I was drawn to him like moth to flame. I wanted him, not just in my bed, but in my life. Christ—I'd offered him my *blood* today! The frightening thing was, I think I wanted it more than he did. Don't get me wrong—his desire was pretty strong, those enormous fangs making that clear. But I was desperate to feel his teeth sink into my wrist, eager for it, frantic with desire of my own. I think I wanted it even more than I wanted to make love to him, if you could imagine that.

This line of thinking was making me more exhausted, so I fought back the memories and, after pulling off my shoes and jeans, I crawled under the heavy quilt. I was right. The sheets where crisp and cool and perfect. I closed my eyes, but when I did, all I could see was Raven's face as I slammed the door on it. He'd been furious, which at the time I'd found ridiculous, though I think I had a better understanding of it now. What bothered me, though, was just before the door obscured his face from view, I could have sworn he looked...hurt.

Chapter Sixty-Four

Piper lay on her bed, curled into a little ball. It was nearly 3:00 PM, and she knew she should get up, but her mind was playing catch up. She had slept some, a fitful sleep full of strange dreams of bloody children and surly white haired men. She dreamed of forests and cabins and of bare light bulbs hanging over her head. She dreamed of children screaming, then of her own screams, and she had awakened racked with spasms, her body aching, tears streaming onto her pillow.

She sat up and looked around her room. It was pink and frilly, and so typically her, but it didn't seem like home anymore. She was frightened, and she knew she had reason to be, yet she couldn't remember why.

Alex had come to see her before she'd come up to bed. He had been frantic for her safety, and she was moved by the tears of relief he'd shed when she walked into his arms for the best hug she'd had all day. He really was a good man. A wonderful friend, and for a minute, Piper could see what Jessica meant about him being good boyfriend material. For a minute.

She was surprised that Jessica hadn't shown up yet, though. Piper knew that her parents would have let her come up, whether Piper was sleeping or not, and the fact that she wasn't here made Piper anxious.

Alex had been closed mouthed on the subject, and when Piper had brought up Ramon, he'd become frigid. Surely Jessica wasn't dumping them for some guy she'd just met? She wouldn't do that!

But then, why wasn't she here?

Piper swung her feet over the edge of the bed and fished around for her slippers. The pink bunnies were pushed too far underneath her bed and she ended up having to get up to get them. Slipping the fluffy footwear on her feet, she dragged a frilly robe around her shoulders, and headed toward the stairs.

She hoped her parents had gone into the office—surely her dad had patients to see, and her mother often worked the office for him, just for fun, she said—but it wasn't a surprise to see them both sitting at the dining room table, drinking their favorite coffee blend.

She was surprised, however, to see Alex asleep on the sofa, a throw pillow under his head and a pink afghan her grandmother had crocheted tucked up underneath his chin. Piper swallowed a huge lump and rubbed at her eyes to stop the tears that were threatening to fall.

"Sweetheart! You're up!" Piper's mother, Amber Pendleton, leapt from her chair and rushed to her daughter's side, pulling her into a frantic hug.

"I'm okay, Mom, really," Piper whispered into her mother's ear, but she clung to her nonetheless.

Finally, after what seemed like hours, Piper asked, "Has Jessica called?" Her mother's face was hard to read as she considered her daughter.

"I'm sorry, honey. We haven't been able to reach her since you talked to her this morning. I know you'd like to see her, and I'm sure she'll be here as soon as she can..."

"We can't find her," Alex's voice was rough from sleep, but his anxiety was still apparent.

"Alex!" Amber exclaimed, making "don't upset my daughter" motions behind Piper's back.

"It's okay, Mom. I know where she is. Sort of. I'm just surprised she hasn't come by yet, that's all. I'm sure she'll come when she can."

Piper stumbled into the kitchen and retrieved a mug from the tall cabinet left of the sink. The coffee smelled delicious and she couldn't wait to get some of that caffeine pumping through her veins.

After adding tons of milk and sugar substitute, Piper lifted the steaming mug to her lips and took a long, searing sip.

Alex had joined the elder Pendleton's at the dining room table, and they all jumped at the sound of a ceramic mug crashing onto the stone tiles. They leapt up in unison, rushing into the kitchen to find Piper standing trembling in the center of the room, staring at the pool of milky liquid now staining her fluffy pink bunny slippers.

Chapter Sixty-Five

I woke with a jerk, my heart hammering in my chest. Malcolm was lying on my stomach, alert almost the moment I was. I lifted him up with one hand, pushing myself to a sitting position with the other, then sat him back on my lap, stroking him absently, his lithe little body arching with every stroke.

What had startled me awake? I don't think I had a vision—I usually remembered them—but something was off, and then it hit me. I'd been dreaming of Piper. She was frightened and alone in the woods surrounded by Werewolves. Snarling, drooling, megawolves with red eyes and razor sharp teeth. It *was* just a dream, thank God, and not a vision, but it was scary nonetheless.

I desperately needed to talk to my friend.

I got up, ignoring Malcolm's protesting yowl, and retrieved my phone from the other room, returning quickly before somebody came barging in and saw me in my underwear.

I pulled the covers back over my lap, Malcolm reclaiming his spot, and hit one on speed dial. It was just after 3:00 pm and I hoped that Piper was up and around. I was sure she had slept most of the day after all she'd been through, and so wasn't feeling too guilty about not being there with her, but now I felt that she needed me, and the guilt was creeping back.

"Hello!" Piper sounded frantic, and I was immediately on guard.

"Piper—are you okay?"

"Ohmigod, Jessica! I'm SO glad you finally called! When I talked to you earlier this morning I was a mess, I was confused and

I just didn't remember. I would have told you then, but I was so freaked out over waking up in the woods with that dog, and it must have slipped my mind, but then there were the dreams, and the babies were crying, and then I was drinking coffee and I remembered and I'm so sorry—I think I ruined the slippers you got me for my birthday. But Jessica—"

"Piper! Slow down—you're losing me, girl!" She sounded like Piper on crack, and Piper doesn't do crack. I had a feeling the Sorcerer's had done something to her and I was about to find out what it was. Piper giggled and shushed someone in the background. It sounded like Alex.

"Sorry, Jessie. It's just, they told me they couldn't get hold of you and when I realized I had something very important to tell you, I panicked, and I spilled my coffee all over my bunny slippers, but then the phone rang and it was you—"

"Piper, please," I begged. Piper was a chatterbox, but she was nearly hysterical, her voice higher than normal, and her prattle more nonsense than I was used to. She was scaring me.

"It's okay, Jessie," she said, reassuring me. "I'm okay. It's just I had to tell you. You have to go to the Sand and Gravel. Tomorrow night. At nightfall. It's really important, 'kay? Will you go?"

That wasn't exactly what I expected, but okay.

"Piper, why do I need to go the Sand and Gravel? Who told you to tell me that?"

Piper hesitated, seeming confused where she had been so confident a moment before. "I don't know," she finally said, "but I know it's important. Life and death important? The babies need you!"

"It's okay," I told her. She was starting to get upset and I didn't want her worrying. "I'll be there. You just take care of yourself, okay? Promise?"

"Of course," she said, coming back to herself. "Hey, Alex wants to talk to you. Want me to tell him to bug off?"

"No, Piper, I need to talk to him. Thanks." Didn't really *want* to talk to him, but—

"Jessica—where the hell are you," Alex was whisper-yelling at me, and that's never good. "Piper's been asking for you, and I couldn't tell her anything. Now she's giving you instructions to save some babies at the gravel pit, and it sounded like you said you were going? Please, Jessica. Call the police. Let them handle this." He sounded even more hysterical than Piper had.

"Alex, please don't worry. Ramon and his friends have this under control. I promise you, I won't let anything happen, but if we involve the police, more people are going to be hurt. I can't come now, and *no*, it's not because I'm having sex! These men, Alex," I huffed out a breath and took in another to try and steady my voice. "Just promise me you'll keep Piper away from the gravel pit. Promise me you won't let anything happen to the two of you."

"I promise, Jessica," Alex said, the grief in his voice obvious.

"And Alex, I may need your help tomorrow. Keep your cell phone close, okay?"

"I will," he promised, hesitantly. "Just remember, it goes both ways. We need you, too," he said, and hung up.

Crap! Now what was I going to do. If I tell Raven, he's just going to want to go in my place. It was obvious the Sorcerers had some sort of beef with him, and I absolutely would *not* let him do that. But then again, what could they possibly want with me? Whatever it was, it didn't matter. I was confident I knew who the babies were, and if my going would keep the people I loved safe, then I was going. I'd killed one of them before. Who knew? Maybe my luck would hold.

Chapter Sixty-Six

I peeked out into the hall and was pleased to see Tabatha pushing her cart out of Raven's rooms.

"Hey, Tabatha," I whispered. I didn't think I was ready to see Raven yet. When she looked up I said, "Can you tell me if there is a gym in this mausoleum? Someplace a girl can work up a sweat?"

"Of course," she replied, glancing over her shoulder into Raven's living room. Great, *everybody* knew. But then she proceeded to give me detailed directions to a place called "The Club".

Having showered and changed into sweats and a cutoff tee, I secured Malcolm in the bedroom and headed out the door. Raven hadn't given me a key, so I was careful not to lock the doors, hopeful that security was as good inside this place as it was outside.

After wondering around for about fifteen minutes, I accidently found what I was looking for. It was on the Sub-T level, but away from all the offices, which I was thankful for, seeing how I wasn't really interested in running into Harrier again. Or Raven, for that matter. The idea crossed my mind that either one could be in the gym, but I figured I could peek in first and if there was anyone else there, I'd just skedaddle.

So that's what I did—I opened the door, which had a hand painted sign hanging over it reading "The Club," reminding me of the sign my mom had painted for the shop, and I peeked in. The room was *huge*, but then again I wasn't surprised. Huge was the order of the day in this place.

I called out a tentative *hello*, and when no one answered, I headed for the treadmill. I hadn't worked out in what seemed like years, and I was eager to work off some of the tension that had been building inside me. I had an idea what I was going to do about getting to the gravel pit the following night, but I had to get through this night first.

And damn Raven for screwing up my days and nights. I should be winding down about now, not winding up!

I climbed on the treadmill, which was, of course, top of the line. After programming a relatively difficult run, I pressed start and moved my feet with the belt beneath them. There was a brief warm up, followed by a gradual increase in angle and speed. After ten minutes I was well into my groove and feeling great.

Sweat was pouring from my brow, and I wiped it with a yellow towel I'd brought from my bathroom. Tabatha had taken away all the bloody towels and left me a nice pile of fluffy clean ones.

My breathing was even, my pace steady, and the endorphins were starting to kick in. Life was good and nothing mattered. Not Raven. Not Piper. Not the Were babies. And not those damned Sorcerers. All that mattered was I was alive and running. My muscles were loose, my mind was clearing. I was in heaven. When I finished my run, I promised myself a round or two with the kicking bags I'd seen hanging in front of a mirrored wall, and I couldn't wait to whack something.

That's when the air in the room stirred, and I felt the hair on the back of my neck prickle. My first thought was that Raven had found me and come to apologize, and I did all I could not to turn around. I closed my eyes and concentrated on my pace, one foot in front of the other, breathe in through the nose, out through the mouth.

When I opened my eyes, I nearly tumbled off the treadmill. Harrier was standing in front of me, his hands braced on the treadmill hand bars, his face livid. Without a word he reached over and hit the emergency stop button. The belt beneath my feet slowed, and I knew I was in some deep doo-doo.

Chapter Sixty-Seven

Raven and Tas were just leaving Mason's office when they heard the screams.

He had been feeling pretty good, that euphoric exhausted feeling he usually got from a good workout. The sleep and shower had helped, and it never hurt having Tas around. Mason had filled them in on the plans for the following night, and though the two had a few suggestions, the plan was pretty solid. It had been difficult not confronting Mason with his recent realization, but there would be time for that after the Sorcerers were dealt with.

Mason had told them to take the night off, get some rest and be ready to rock tomorrow night. Raven planned to round up Jessica, lock them up in his bedroom (away from Malcolm) and not come out until she either hated him or loved him. Either way, she needed to know the truth. Somewhere between realizing his race had betrayed him and facing Mason for the first time since that realization, he'd come to another conclusion.

He was in love with Jessica. It was ridiculous—she was human for chrissakes! But it was there, and the last thing he wanted to do was fight it.

Raven also realized that in just over twenty-four hours he would be squaring off against the race of the woman who had cursed him. Someone among them knew what Raven had done, and they would be gunning for him personally. It was difficult to know how to face such a foe. Righteous anger was a hard thing to battle, especially when you knew you were in the wrong.

He had to tell Jessica how he felt before the raid, just in case. If he didn't come back, she had to at least know what she meant to him.

And then she screamed. The euphoria he'd been feeling instantly changed to terror. Raven and Tas exchanged a quick glance, and then both were off and running at top speed. The screams were coming from the Club—what was she doing in the Club?—and they were there before the next scream sounded.

They burst into the gym to find Jessica on the mats, Harrier straddling her, her hands pinned above her head with his left hand, his right moving familiarly along her throat. His fangs were bared, his eyes blazing like molten lava.

"Raven," the giant male drawled. "Glad you could stop by. I was just about to find out how *sweet* this tasty twit of yours really is." Jessica struggled beneath him, but that was only enticing him. As if to prove a point, Harrier lowered his mouth to her neck, his eyes locked with Raven's, and slowly licked her pulse points. He raised his head again, daring Raven to move, the saliva dripping from his fangs blending with the tears on Jessica's face.

Jessica was kicking and bucking, trying to rid herself of the weight that had settled on her, but she was wasting her time.

"Jessica, stop moving," Raven ordered, and was relieved when she did as he said. Tas was doing his thing, trying to ease Harrier down, but his thing took time—time Jessica might not have if she kept encouraging Harrier like that. Hell, all that struggling was turning *Raven* on, much as he hated himself for it, and his senses told him even Tas wasn't entirely unaffected. It was a Vampire thing.

Tas was talking to Harrier now, but Raven kept his eyes on Jessica. He'd kill the bastard if he had to, but he knew Mason would be pretty pissed if he did. Then again, Mason had been part of the great betrayal. He'd do what he had to in order to keep her safe.

"Hey dude," Tas was saying. "What's going on?"

"Fuck off, Tas—I know what you're trying to do!" Harrier spat, his one hand tightening on Jessica's wrists, his other moving lower toward her breasts. Raven growled, but Tas put a hand on his arm to steady him. One wrong move, and Jessica was done for.

"No big to me, man. I just don't understand why you're all over this chick. She do something to you?"

"I said fuck *off!*" Harrier was hissing now, his hand changing directions again, now going for her throat. Never a good thing, Harrier hissing. Raven looked to Tas for a sign, anything that would tell him Tas was in control, but he got nothing. Tas was totally focused on Harrier, and Raven knew to leave him to it.

They stood like that for five long minutes, Raven and Tas watching—ready to intervene. Jessica lying as still as she could, and Harrier taunting them all with his touching and his threats.

"She's a fucking *human*," Harrier sneered, his voice tight with anger. "She's dinner, Raven, you're favorite kind. How is it she's still alive? I know you like to play with your food, but your reputation isn't for dragging it out. Not this long, anyway. She should be dead, and you should be staked. You shouldn't even be here," he spat.

Raven was practically vibrating with fury, Jessica's safety the only thing keeping him from leaping on the bastard. He reached out with his mind, to try and reassure her, but was disappointed to find her mind completely closed to him. Her eyes were squeezed shut, and he wished he could say something. To let her know that Harrier was screwing with her...with all of them. But he didn't dare. And what if he was wrong?

"Why *are* you still alive?" Harrier bantered, and Raven knew he was talking to him. "Rumor is you were to be eliminated centuries ago. You were to be put down like the rabid feral you are. How did you escape the punishment for your crimes? How is it you are here, living high in the Legion, and taking humans for pets?" Raven saw Jessica flinch at these words. He hoped he'd have a chance to explain.

After another five minutes, Harrier's hands started to relax. The roving hand became still, and the fire in his eyes faded. Finally, he leaned down again and licked the side of Jessica's face before planting his palms roughly on her shoulders and pushing himself up.

"Fuck you both, and your human pet too," he spat as he shouldered between the two males and out of the gym, the doors banging loudly in his wake.

Jessica was still lying on the mat, her eyes closed tight, her arms still above her head, just as she'd been held. Raven looked at Tas, who was already heading for the door. "I'll get him settled," he promised, and Raven was finally free to go to her.

Raven knelt beside her and touched her face, his thumb wiping the dampness from beneath her eye, the other male's saliva from her cheek. She cringed first, then before he knew what was happening, her fist was planted squarely in his jaw, and he was seeing stars. What he didn't see was the second punch, nor the third, nor all the ones that followed. She was beating the shit out of him, and all he could do was laugh.

Chapter Sixty-Eight

I whacked that bastard as hard as I could with a right, and then followed it with a quick left. It was hard to get leverage from down on the floor where I was, but if he was stupid enough to give me my hands, he was going to pay.

Actually, I was probably the one who would pay in the end, but I was a fighter, and I wasn't going to make it easy on him.

I thought I'd heard Raven telling me not to move, and I'd stayed still for a very long time. But then he didn't say anything else. No *it's going to be okay, Jessica,* or *hang tight Jessica,* and he did absolutely nothing to stop my attacker. Maybe I'd imagined hearing his voice. Maybe I just wanted him to come to my rescue so badly that I'd made it up in my head. Or maybe, after hearing what Harrier said about Raven, my heart was pounding so loudly in my ears, I couldn't hear anything else.

None of that mattered. Right now, this fucker was going to pay. My hands were still free and I was striking him for all I was worth. He was no longer sitting on me, so I struggled to my feet, staying low so I could continue to pummel him. I was blind with fear and anger and I couldn't really see what I was hitting, but I could *feel* it. And it felt good.

I knew my mind was playing tricks on me, because I could swear I heard him laughing, which was impossible because I'd struck him in the face so many times he should be anything but amused. I found my balance and did what came naturally. A swift roundhouse to the mother fucker's jaw should put a damper on his humor. My foot landed with a satisfying thud, and I saw his head snap, saliva flying as he landed Rocky-style on the mats.

I stood at the ready, prepared for his recovery. He was a Vampire, so I was sure my time was coming, but I still had more in me. More anger and more humiliation, and I would take every ounce of it out on him before he got the chance to kill me.

When he didn't move, I thought I'd gotten lucky again. I was going to have my feet registered as a deadly weapon. But then he stirred, and by then the fear was abating, my eyes beginning to focus on my opponent.

Who wasn't Harrier.

Fuck!

Raven was lying on the mat, bleeding and laughing silently. At least I hoped he was laughing, because I'd feel *really* bad if I'd made my Vampire cry!

"Uh...oops?" Was all I could come up with, and he started to laugh for real.

"Is it safe to come out now?" Raven chuckled, rising to his elbow and patting his lip with the back of his hand.

"I, oh Raven, I'm so sorry!" I cried. Literally cried. The tears were flowing freely again, this time out of guilt and embarrassment, and relief that I wasn't going to be killed, right now anyway. At least I didn't think he was going to kill me.

"Jessica, I've been blinded by rage before. I know what it looks like from both sides now, and let me tell you, it's not pretty. If I were human, I'd be dead. Of course, if I had decided to protect myself, you would be." He had stopped laughing and was looking at me like my mother used to when she'd caught me doing something dangerous or foolish. I started to say something, I didn't know what, but Raven continued.

"If I had been Harrier, or any Vampire, for that matter, you would have been dead after the first strike. More likely, before. Promise me, Jessica, you won't try to fight one of us. You're good, for a human. Beyond good, but I'm probably the only Vampire who will ever let you get away with that. And even I would prefer if you'd pull your punches next time. This fucking *hurts*!" he said as he leapt nimbly to his feet, thumbing blood from beneath his nose.

He held his non-bloodied hand out to me, and I hesitated. I was still a little freaked out from the encounter with Harrier. That was one scary Vampire. And Perry's warning was still clanging in the back of my mind, only he had warned me about Raven, not Harrier. He'd said that *Raven* was the one other Vampires feared, but other than his willingness to kill Sorcerers, I hadn't seen anything to verify Perry's story. Well...except for how Raven reacted to Perry.

When I didn't take his hand, Raven walked past me to the treadmills and picked up the towel I'd been using. He wiped the blood from his hand, and then from his face, and I was relieved to see the cuts on his face and lips already healing. Obviously, I hadn't done as much damage as I'd tried to. My own knuckles would be aching for days.

Raven watched me, seemed to be struggling for something to say. The adrenaline that had been pumping through me as I pummeled him was waning, and all of a sudden my legs didn't want to keep me standing. I didn't want to show weakness—not to one of *them*—so I managed to find my way to a weight bench as far away from the treadmills as I could get, and I half sat, half collapsed onto it.

"You know I won't hurt you, Jessica." Raven said this from across the room. He'd remained by the treadmill, giving me my space.

"Yeah," I said, "See Raven, I *don't* know that. I *think* I know, but I don't really, do I? You're like him," I said, nodding at the doors where Harrier had disappeared. "You're one of them, and I'm just a girl." I wasn't angry, and most of the bravado had drained out of me by now. But the look on Raven's face said my words had struck more deeply than my physical blows ever could. I didn't care, though. At this point, I needed some clarity.

"But your vision—" he began, and I cut him off.

"Yeah, I know what the vision showed me, and I trust my visions. I do. But that *Vampire*, he didn't care who I was or what I could do. He's not even afraid of Mason, who told him mere hours ago to leave me alone. I'm not safe here, Raven. I know you think you can protect me, but you can't be there twenty-four/seven."

"Go back," Raven interrupted me. "What do you mean, Mason told Harrier to leave you alone? Why would he have to do that?"

"You *weren't there*," I stressed, bolstering my point. "After I kicked you out of the bathroom, you disappeared. Then when I came out, Harrier jumped all over me, saying I acted like I was superior or something."

"You are a little pushy..."

"Raven, please! I can't stay here anymore. You just made it clear to me that I can't protect myself against one of you. I killed a Sorcerer and...and got an assist on another one," I said, using Perry's phrasing from earlier. "Seems to me my chances would be better at home."

"Mason won't let you leave."

"Why are they afraid of you?" I parried. Mason thought I was an asset, even though I hadn't really done anything to demonstrate that presumption, so Raven was probably right. Or maybe he thought I was a threat. Either way, I didn't want to argue that point just now. I planned to be out of here by tomorrow night and I needed some questions answered.

"Who is afraid of me?" Raven asked, his face turning to stone.

"Perry. The Soldiers. Why, Raven?"

"What did that Soldier tell you?" He was sounding more sinister now, edging toward me, and I almost regretted mentioning Perry's name.

"He told me they are afraid of you and that I should be careful. Why, Raven? Why are *you* the one that Vampires fear? Harrier, I could understand, but why you?"

"That's what he said?"

"Yes. That's what he said. And Raven, if you harm one hair on his head because of this, I swear I'll...I'll never speak to you again." Lame, I know, but it was the strongest threat I could come up with on short notice.

Raven was getting closer and I edged back on the weight bench. I didn't like the way he was looking at me. I'd touched a nerve, but I couldn't seem to shut up.

"And what did Harrier mean about human pets, and killing, and playing with your *food*, and having you put down?"

Raven was at the end of the bench now, his glare still hard as rock, but he didn't touch me. And then just like that, his face softened, and his shoulders sagged a bit, and he knelt where he stood, his hands clinging to the end of the bench as if for balance.

"I'll tell you, Jessica, everything you need to know." I raised my eyebrow and he said, "Everything you *want* to know, but not here. Come with me to my rooms and I will explain."

Chapter Sixty-Nine

She still seemed frightened and on edge, but when Raven rose and extended his hand to help her up, she took it readily in her own, swinging her long legs over the bench and standing shakily beside him.

"I want to trust you," she whispered, almost too low for even him to hear.

Raven clasped her hand in his, and they walked in silence back to his quarters. He opened the door and stood aside for her to enter first. She glanced across the hall at her own door, before finally crossing the threshold.

"Nice couch," she muttered, and claimed a corner of it for her own. Raven sat beside her, but not too closely. He didn't want her to feel cornered, and with what he was about to tell her, he wanted her to know that she was free to leave whenever she chose. Leave his rooms, anyway.

"So, you want me to ask a question, or are you just going to spill?"

Raven hesitated. He'd been planning this most of the day, but now that they were here, he had no idea how to begin. Finally, he decided to start at the beginning.

"When I was very young, my parents were murdered...No," he said when her eyes softened toward him. Don't be sympathetic yet. Please wait until I've finished, then draw your own conclusions. And know, I will understand if you then find my presence distasteful. You are free to return to your rooms at any time." She nodded, and he swallowed, wishing he didn't have to continue.

But he did, and though the compassion she had first displayed soon turned to revulsion, she never made a move to leave. He left nothing out, painting a picture for her of the vicious creature he had been, describing his acts of rape and murder in detail. He told her of his first kill, the one that had released the beast inside him, convincing him he was a god, and he explained to her how during this time he was happiest when he was committing violence upon humans. He had no desire to stop, ever. It defined him as a powerful Vampire, a god above humans. Above all Vampires. He would have been content to live his entire life in this manner, and never regret a single moment.

"But you did stop," she said, more a statement than a question. He nodded and she asked, "Why?"

"Why did I stop?"

"Yes, why did you stop? You were happy, or whatever, just doing what Vampires do. Why would you ever stop?"

"Jessica, I don't think you understand. I wasn't doing what most Vampires do, not even then. We are more civilized than Hollywood makes us out to be, as a race, at least. But like humans, there are those of us who," he shrugged, "go bad, I guess."

"But you all drink blood, right?" She had tucked herself into the corner of the couch, as far away from Raven as she could get, her knees pulled tightly to her chest. But she was still listening, asking questions, and a flicker of hope sparked in Raven's heart.

"Yes, we all drink blood, but we're not all murderers. We're not all monsters. We've always leaned more toward predator, but the Primeval, the oldest among us, learned early that if we destroyed the humans, we destroyed our primary food source. It was better to live in secrecy, keep our existence hidden from humans."

"But then, how do you feed? I'm assuming that little trance thingy works to make the humans forget they've been, you know, the main course."

"Exactly, and with the use of the mind manipulation we were able to exist side by side with man. To thrive, even. But there were always those who fought the new ways. They enjoyed the violence and the power. They are the main reason the Legion exists, to keep the ferals in check." He watched her intently, needing to see her eyes as he said the next. "Think of the worst you've ever imagined a Vampire could be, multiply that by a hundred, and you would have me."

She studied his face, and he wondered what she was looking for. What she saw. "So, you were like the Charles Manson of the Vampire race," she finally said, and he knew she understood.

"Yes," he stated simply, "With a little Ted Bundy, Jack the Ripper and Hannibal Lector thrown in."

"You still haven't answered my question, though." He raised an inquisitive brow and she said, "Why did you stop?"

Raven rose from the sofa and began pacing around the room. She watched his every move, waiting silently. He didn't know how much he should tell her. How much he wanted to speak aloud. Harrier had all but confirmed his suspicions. The race had wanted him gone, but how much should he share with a human, even if she was his human.

He stopped pacing and leaned against the wall opposite the fireplace. He'd promised her full disclosure, and he wouldn't break his word.

"I had become a liability. The Primeval couldn't control me, no one could. The Legion was still fairly young and had their hands full. There was a large number of ferals back then, and they tend to move around, making them hard to manage. I, on the other hand, made no effort to hide. You only had to follow the trail of bodies, and you could be guaranteed to run into me sooner or later. Unfortunately, I was fairly indiscriminate in who I killed. I'd kill a Vampire just as soon as a human. It wasn't as much fun, and usually only out of self-preservation, but it made no difference to me. I was a god. I was all powerful, and no one could stop me, not even my own kind.

"Near the end, they tracked me down with an offer. I was told that they, the Primeval, needed a woman killed, and they wanted their hands to remain clean. I was more than happy to be their weapon, and they paid me well.

"What I didn't realize was that they were setting me up. I've only just begun to put the pieces together, but Harrier basically confirmed it down in the Club. They set me up to be murdered by another race. A strong and ancient race. I still don't know who the woman was, but I've figured out *what* she was."

"Let me guess—tall and thin with white floaty hair?" Jessica asked.

"Right in one."

"Oh, Raven."

"So, I guess that explains why I was in the Sorcerer's sights. One of them is pretty pissed at me, with good reason. If I'd known, I don't know. Maybe I'd have just let him kill me and be done with it."

"What?" Jessica cried, incredulous. "It's obvious I don't know as much about you as I thought, but I never took you for a quitter!"

"It's not quitting, Jessica. Death would be a fair punishment for what I have done. But I haven't answered your question yet. You asked why I stopped killing. She was why. The whole time I...tortured her...she never cried out. She was calm and stoic, and I was furious with her. I was ready to rip her apart out of sheer frustration, but then she touched me and spoke to me, and it was like being touched with electricity.

"And then, Jessica, it was as if I were seeing her for the first time. The blood and the damage, her body broken in my hands, by these hands," he said, offering his palms to her.

He shook his head, and lowered his hands, raising his eyes to meet hers. "And I was...sorry," he whispered, lowering his gaze.

"What did she say?" It was a whisper, one Raven nearly missed, drowning in his own misery, his own memory. He stole a glance in Jessica's direction and was surprised to see her eyes shining with tears.

What did she say? Raven closed his eyes, those words imprinted in his mind, etched there along with the woman's ravaged face. And when he glanced back at Jessica, her beautiful face shiny with tears shed for him...*for him*...he realized that the woman, the Sorceress, wasn't cursing him. She was blessing him. And she made him wait over four hundred years to understand.

"Raven, what did she say?"

Raven shook his head, dragging a hand through his ruffled hair, and when he looked up, a single red tear traced a path down his cheek.

"She said, 'No more. Find love.'"

Chapter Seventy

I was standing in front of him before I was aware I had moved. He was rigid and unbending, his arms at his sides, and it broke my heart. The man had just bared his soul to me, told me things that probably should have had me running screaming for the door, but there was one problem.

No matter what he'd done, it was in his past. I knew there was more to be told, and I had a million questions to ask, but the bottom line was, I was already in love with him. I can't think of much worse he could have confessed, but if he had come up with something, it wouldn't have changed that fact one bit.

I loved him.

Raven's wall was still up, and I couldn't blame him, but I had one more question to ask before I made a complete fool out of myself.

"Raven?" When he lifted his eyes to mine, they were pink with Vampire tears. "When?" He just looked at me, puzzled. "How long ago did this all take place?"

"Four hundred and ten years ago. Next May."

"But who's counting, right?" I smiled for the first time in what seemed a year, and his face softened. A little. He spoke of this as though it happened last week, but it was *four hundred years ago*! He'd been trying to make up for his horrible past for four hundred years.

I lifted a hand to brush away his tears, much as he'd done for me in the Club, just before I went all Bruce Lee on his ass, and his hand closed over mine.

"How old *are* you?" I whispered, unable to keep the fascination from my voice.

"Five hundred and seventy-two. Next month." He smiled, and my heart did a back flip.

"Hope you don't mind a little age difference," I grinned, stretching to my full height and then some so I could claim those beautiful lips with my own.

Well, I tried. He was really tall, and I stood like that for an embarrassing lifetime before he finally leaned down to me and pressed his lips to mine. It felt like Christmas and the Fourth of July, all wrapped into one. I wrapped my arms around his neck to ensure he couldn't pull away and I kissed him thoroughly, hoping to convey all my feelings in this one embrace. Within moments we were both gasping for air.

"Raven," I panted. "Is there any chance you'll be running out of here in the next few minutes?"

"Got the night off," he gasped, his mouth busily exploring my neck, my hands tangled in his inky hair.

"Are you expecting visitors?" I moaned when he hit a particularly sensitive spot behind my ear.

"None," he whispered. "Where's your cell phone?"

"Don't know—don't care," I couldn't get close enough to him, barely resisting the urge to throw my legs around him. "That door lead where I think it does?" I gestured vaguely to the closed door behind him, reluctant to lose physical contact with him on any level.

In answer, he picked me up, planted his lips firmly on mine and, after a brief struggle opening the door, he carried me into what I would soon refer to as *heaven*.

Chapter Seventy-One

Raven couldn't believe this was happening. He'd just told the woman he loved that he was a monster, and *this* was her response? Maybe she'd misunderstood...No...she couldn't have—he was very clear. His mind was reeling, her acceptance far beyond anything he could have imagined, could have hoped for. Hell he had just been hoping she didn't run screaming from the room. But *this*? Only in his wildest dreams!

He carried her to his king size bed, laying her gently on the satin comforter, where he could do no more than stare at her. She was still in her sweats and a t-shirt that was all too similar to what he worked out in, her chestnut hair lying in tangled curls around her angelic face—and it was the most erotic thing he'd ever seen.

He moved to her, but she said, "No," her palm planted firmly on his chest, and his smile faltered.

"I want to see you," she whispered. "All of you."

"Yes, you are most definitely pushy," Raven grinned, but he stood back to do her bidding. Jessica didn't seem to hear him, her teeth biting seductively into her lower lip as Raven pulled the black cotton tee over his head, shaking his hair out of his eyes so as not to lose sight of her.

He kicked off his boots, and when he reached down to unfasten his trousers, she was there, her hands holding his in place. "Let me," she said, and he did what he imagined any gentlemen would do. He let her.

Jessica's hands were warm and her tongue was soft, tracing circles around his nipples as she toyed with the button. She was deliberately and painfully slow in the process, and Raven was gasping for breath by the time she finally released him from the confines of his pants.

Her eyes were soft and smoky as they scanned every inch of him. She ran her hands across his broad shoulders and down his chest, thumbing his nipples in passing. Her exploration continued down his sides and around to his smooth back, sliding down until her hands were cupping his muscular rear. He shuddered when she knelt in front of him, her soft cheek nuzzling the curls at the base of his arousal.

When she took him into her sweet mouth, he nearly collapsed, fisting his fingers in her hair and struggling to remain standing. Raven's mind was in overdrive, crazed with a sensation he'd never experienced. Sex for Raven had never been like this. First it had only been about taking, the woman merely an object for him to abuse for his own pleasure.

After he'd learned to control the beast, to separate his passions, sex was simply a release, and one that was difficult to come by. With a reputation like his, it was all but impossible to find a Vampire female willing to submit to him, let alone pleasure him. Even the prostitutes refused him service, not eager to chance a union with the beast.

Human women had proven to be less than satisfying, as well. They were certainly eager—charming a human had never been a problem for him, proven by his tremendous success as the Rapist. But the act was empty, the beast never satisfied, being denied the final, rapturous release of the human's death.

In the end, he had simply given up on sex altogether. Which was why the attraction he felt toward Jessica had come as such a surprise, and this...*this*...was...

Her tongue was dancing patterns along his thick shaft, her teeth gently scraping his throbbing head. If she kept this up...Raven's fingers were still tangled in her hair, and gently he pulled her away from him and drew her to her feet.

"One of us has entirely too many clothes on," he whispered, claiming her lips in a fiery kiss before pulling the flimsy cotton over her head in a quick, fluid motion. She was impatient and the rest of her clothes were in a pile at their feet so fast, Raven could have teased her about having Vampire-like speed. Could have, but there were more pressing matters at hand.

She was so beautiful, her hair tousled, her lips swollen with passion. Her breasts were perfect mounds, generous and heaving as she struggled to catch her breath. Her hips gentle curves flowing into long, athletic legs.

Raven reached out to her, and she closed her eyes, her head falling back as she arched her body toward his. He took a moment to cup a breast in his palm, her nipples hard and taunting, then lifted her to the bed, where he joined her, his body pressing the length of hers as he lay beside her, his shaft pulsing against her smooth hip.

Raven needed to touch her, to feel her, and he began at her face, tracing the lines of her cheeks, her nose, her jaw. When he reached her lips, she opened them invitingly and drew his finger into her mouth, sucking and pulling, making his cock leap in anticipation.

He moved to her throat, laying thumb and forefinger along the pulsing lines of her arteries, his fangs extending, biting into his lower lip as her blood called to him.

He realized he could do this all night—explore her, watch her, discover every hidden pleasure point she possessed, and that would be fine with him. But when he reached her core she was slick and burning. Raven slid an experimental finger into the wetness, cupping his palm against her mound and she exploded in ecstasy, calling his name and crying out with pleasure.

Her hands were everywhere, pulling him to her, and he had no choice but to follow. He hovered over her, supported on his elbows, and was truly frightened now for the fourth time in his existence. But she gave him little chance for thought. She held him firmly in hand and arched her hips to meet him, to pull him inside her as though she starved for him. Raven closed his eyes, unprepared for the electricity that was coursing through him at the mere touch of their sex. When he opened his eyes again she was looking at him, her icy blue eyes soft and pleading, and he could not deny her.

He entered her, slowly and as gently as he could, and when he was completely sheathed, she pulled him down to her and held him closely, her body convulsing in erotic tremors. With each pull and thrust, she cried out with pleasure, her fingernails raking his back, her body arching to meet each thrust with one of her own, until their bodies exploded in mutual climax, leaving them breathless, sweaty and clinging to one another.

When his mind cleared somewhat, he found that his fangs were pressed against Jessica's throat, her pulse beating against his tongue where he'd been kissing her, loving her. And the beast was there, eager and longing.

This was what he had wanted earlier. To be able to make love to her and feed from her, giving them both the kind of pleasure he'd only read about. But now he wasn't so sure.

Jessica's hands were everywhere, touching him, petting him, and the beast was practically purring with anticipation, ready for its own murderous release. Raven prepared himself for the Sorcerer woman's face to appear, hoping for the failsafe to enter his mind and push the beast back. To stop him from taking the next glorious step in reclaiming his past. To stop him from hurting this woman who had become so precious to him.

Jessica pressed her throat to his mouth, taking him by surprise, and one razor sharp fang accidently broke her skin. A tiny drop of blood, honeysuckle and sweet, fell on his tongue, and he prayed to the gods for the trigger to stop him. He prayed for the pain that would prevent him from hurting her. He was enjoying this, and if he fed with the passion, the pleasure he knew lay just beneath the surface, it was just a tiny step more to letting the beast free. Frantically, he searched his mind for the woman's face.

And for the first time in four hundred and ten years, she wasn't there.

Chapter Seventy-Two

Oh. My. God. I've heard of having mind blowing sex, but can honestly say I'd never had it before just now. Raven was an animal, all right, but by recent experience, not the evil one he described to me. Whatever that woman did to him, I truly wished I could thank her. He was sweet and loving and tender and with him still inside me, his teeth grazing my neck, I could almost orgasm again.

I lifted my neck to greet his lips, my hand on the back of his head, holding him there, loving the feel of him there, and I felt a pinprick, but thought nothing of it until Raven went utterly still. "It's okay," I said, stroking his hair. I lifted my hips toward him and could feel him growing again inside me. Vampire sex was *amazing*!

Raven made a guttural sound, low in his throat, and I matched him with one of my own, the pleasure of him on me, in me, nearly more than I could bear. When I opened my eyes, though, the room was bathed in violet, pulsing light, and my heart rate actually increased, which I didn't think was possible.

Raven was peering down at me, his eyes illuminating the entire room with their strobing, amethyst glow, his lips curled in a feral snarl, revealing fangs that could have belonged to a saber toothed tiger. At least they looked that big to me, up close like that. I'd seen him vamped out before, but this was different. This was the face of a monster.

I told myself not to be afraid—that it was still my Raven—but it wasn't until that moment, looking into those cold, hungry eyes, that I realized the impact of the stories he shared with me mere moments ago. He wasn't talking about a stranger, and he wasn't talking about a past version of himself. He was telling me, warning me, that he still fought with this side of himself every day. And right now I was seeing what his victims had seen, and it wasn't sweet and it wasn't tender. It was downright frightening. And I was a naïve idiot.

But there was a failsafe, he'd said so. The lady wouldn't let him hurt anyone anymore. He was just waiting for that to kick in, I was sure. I closed my eyes and lay as still as I could, but when his hips started moving again, I was lost. He felt so good and my heart was having trouble catching up with my mind, never mind my libido, and I was still unable to separate the incredible sex with the man I'd fallen for, from the starving animal salivating over me like I was a dessert bar at the all-you-can-eat buffet.

I tried to think what Raven would tell me to do, to keep from encouraging his beast, as he'd helped me with Harrier, but my hips had a will of their own—Cripes, he felt good!—Or maybe he was in my head again, controlling me—I didn't know. But before I knew it I was clinging to him again, screaming through another mind-blowing orgasm, sweat dripping between my breasts, and my throat aching for...oh, God. For him to bite me!

Raven stilled inside me again, his body rigid, his muscles roped beneath my hands where I clutched him, my nails biting into his skin. I opened my eyes and he was staring at me, that amethyst light a beating pulsar, but behind the light, behind the feverish desire was something more. Something behind the hunger. Raven was panicking, and that was not a good sign. I was beginning to think the lady wasn't going to show tonight, and apparently so was he. He was well and truly afraid, and that did nothing for my confidence.

I watched saliva run down one ginormous fang and fall menacingly toward me as his lip curled in a fierce snarl, and then the look of panic was gone. Crap! I forced myself to hold his stare, hoping that what I had seen was not an illusion, that he really was fighting the urge to beast out on me, and praying to every god I could think of for some help.

Raven lowered his face to my neck, breaking our gaze and I squeezed my eyes shut as he inhaled deeply, the velvet softness of his tongue licking the frantic pulse in my neck making me shudder. He tensed, forcing himself away from that tempting spot, and when he opened his eyes again there was a bit of, well, humanity for lack of a better word, lurking in there.

A tear leaked out the corner of my eye and I thought, *help us, please!* Raven's arms flexed around me.

"Jessica," he whispered through clenched teeth. "I'm sorry..." and as the small bit of humanity faded from his eyes, I felt myself fading as well, fading into that place I alone knew. I blinked and evil Raven was replaced with the Raven from my vision, the one I had at the Mayor's gala. His face was buried in my throat, and we were making love like nobody's business. The first time this vision came to me, I thought we were just sexing it up like crazy, and that in itself had put me on the floor. But I didn't understand then. I didn't realize the significance. It wasn't just about us being together—it was so much more than that. It was showing me Raven loving me and feeding from me at the same time. It was showing me how tonight was supposed to go. How it would go. As I watched Vision-Raven feed from me in my mind, Real-Life-Jessica relaxed. I knew now what had to be done. The only problem would be convincing Raven.

As my eyes regained focus, it was like I'd never left. Raven was still holding me, staring at me, but he was fighting again, fighting himself, his past. Panic was not just a shadow—now it blazed in his eyes as he fought to keep his beast at bay, but when his lips curled in another snarl, I saw blood on one of his fangs. Was it mine or his? If it was mine—no wonder he was freaking out. I had to make him hear me. Make him understand.

"Raven," I whispered, and he growled in response. "Raven, listen to me." His head shook slightly, his eyes narrowed, but his body was still a vibrating ball of tension.

"Raven, you have to feed."

His hands dug into my shoulders and he shook his head and growled again. "No!" it was low and guttural and my heart clenched.

I wrapped my arms and legs around him to keep him from running, and whispered, "Raven, you don't understand. I saw it. You *have* to feed from me, now. I promise, it will be okay. You won't hurt me, I swear on my life."

"She's...not...coming," he snarled through clenched teeth. "I can't stop it. If I lose control..." His voice was strangled and tormented, and my heart ached for him.

"I know, Raven, I know. She's not coming, and that's okay. She's not supposed to. This is what she was telling you. Her words that cursed you—this is what she meant. *Find love*, Raven. And I'm right here."

He hesitated only a brief moment, then he rose over me, his face contorted in agony, his fangs flashing in the pulsing light of his eyes, and he lunged at my neck with a ferocious, tortured growl. It took every ounce of control I possessed not to scream with terror.

I don't think I was really prepared for how it would feel, his enormous fangs sinking into that tender skin at my throat. It hurt, yes, but only for a moment, and then *holy shit*! It was the most amazing pain/pleasure feeling I ever experienced, and I couldn't possibly begin to explain it. I exploded immediately, my core clutching at the male still sheathed inside me, and I'm pretty sure he came with me, based on the fact that he released my neck and roared like a crazed lion.

But then his fangs were back inside me, and the suckling sent multitudes of baby orgasms screaming through my body. My every nerve was on fire, and I trembled and writhed beneath him, hoping he would never stop.

Sometime between almost forever and not nearly long enough, Raven slowed, pulling his fangs from my neck and dragging his tongue along the punctures there, and I nearly cried at the loss. He then collapsed panting on top of me, my blood dripping from his lips and fangs, forming tiny pools on my chest. I reached up to stroke his hair, furtively feeling my neck en route, and was surprised to find my skin unmarked.

After a few moments of catching our breath, Raven rose above me again, and I saw that his eyes were fading, more sapphire than amethyst now, and I realized that the blood on my chest may not have been mine. Raven's bloody tears were stinging my skin, tiny pinpricks of fire that frightened and exhilarated me.

"Hey," I whispered as he rolled from on top of me and curled against my side. I shifted to face him, gently fisting my hand in his hair, but he refused look at me. I shuffled around until my face was close to his, and I pressed my lips to first one eye, and then the other, his tears salty and metallic as I kissed them away.

Raven shivered at my touch, and when he finally opened his eyes I said the first thing that came to mind.

"I love you, Raven."

And his tears began in earnest.

Chapter Seventy-Three

Raven woke with a start, his arms and legs wrapped around something unfamiliar. Something soft and warm, his head resting on two perfect pale pillows. Breathing deeply, his senses were besieged by the sweet scent of honeysuckle, and the past few hours came rushing back to him.

Jessica.

Slowly, careful not to disturb her, he rose up on one elbow and watched her as she slept. Her lashes lay in long, dark fans on her cheeks, her full, gorgeous lips curved in a half smile as she dreamed a secret dream.

His gaze drifted down, and Raven was embarrassed to realize her chest was stained pink from her blood and his tears. He swallowed hard as he remembered the emotion that had wracked him, wrapping him like a gift and exploding through his soul like a roman candle. Never had he felt such happiness. Such release. Big bad Vampire—yeah, right.

During his feral days, his actions had provided him with what he thought was ecstasy, bliss personified. He had felt strong and powerful, and his body had surged with the rapture of his newfound supremacy. He had felt nothing after his parents' death until he had taken that first life. *That* had made him feel something for the first time in years, and he equated that feeling with happiness. Satisfaction, at the very least.

After the experience with the witch, he had put away thoughts of happiness. He was content just to be alive, and if he could do that without being an animal, then that was a bonus.

But tonight, he learned what true happiness was.

Jessica said she loved him, and for the first time in centuries, he felt whole. The emotions that enveloped him surged through every fiber of his being, and they could not be contained, escaping in the form of tears.

Before Jessica, he'd never shed a tear. Not when he found his parents, not when he was a lost child in a hostile world. Not even for the witch whose curse had turned into this incredible gift. But tonight, it was as if a dam were bursting, freeing nearly six hundred years' worth of unshed tears. First he cried from fear of losing her. But when Jessica said she loved him, he couldn't breathe, couldn't speak. He could only weep like a fucking baby, and the memory of it had his eyes welling again.

Raven studied the bloody patterns on Jessica's skin, absently licking his thumb and swirling the moisture through a crimson streak on Jessica's breast, creating a creamy path through the scarlet stain.

Jessica moaned and shifted her body provocatively, her lips opening in a soft O, making Raven wonder what she was dreaming. He hated poking around in her mind. For one reason, he considered it an invasion of her privacy. More importantly, though—and he hated to admit this—it was because she could tell when he was doing it. It didn't make him less curious, though, and with her sleeping so sweetly, he convinced himself a peek into her dreams wouldn't be *that* much of an intrusion.

Closing his eyes, he reached out to her with the fingers of thought he used for his mind touch, and when their consciousness connected he nearly gasped at the image he received.

She dreamed of him, and what he saw was as hot as his own real memories of their recent lovemaking.

In her mind, he saw himself naked, lying across her lithe body, his lips suckling gently at her breasts, first one, then the other, her body writhing in pleasure.

Outside the dream, his hand still lay on her breast, and he pinched her nipple absently as he watched them in her mind.

She dreamed of him.

"You're in my head," a sleepy voice broke into his reverie, and he jumped from guilt, hastily retracting his hand from her breast, ashamed of himself for intruding.

Somehow, she caught his hand before he could remove it completely, and she pulled it back toward her, placing it firmly back on her breast, keeping it in place with her own. And she was smiling.

Not knowing quite how to apologize, Raven leaned in and kissed her gently and fully on the mouth. "I love you, Jessica," he whispered against her lips.

"I love you, too," she smiled and pressed her lips more firmly against his.

After a moment he drew away from her and cupped her face in his hand. She was still smiling. At him. "What time is it?" she asked. He leaned over her to retrieve his watch from the nightstand, laying on her heavily and laughing when she feigned suffocation.

"6:00 AM. Why, you got some place to be?" he teased.

She sighed and looked at him, apprehensively.

"Raven, I need to talk to you about something." After all they'd discussed regarding his past, the seriousness of her tone made him uneasy. He rolled off of her and sat up, setting his back against the headboard, and putting some space between them, trying not to panic.

Jessica hesitated, and Raven knew he wasn't going to like what she had to say.

"It's nothing *bad*," she insisted, sitting up and crawling next to him. She lifted his arm and snuggled herself beneath it, letting his hand rest once again on her breast. She reached down with her right hand and stroked his bare thigh, the fingers of her other hand wrapped gently around the arm draping her.

"It's just, I really need to see Piper."

"That's not possible," Raven responded instantly. His arm tightened around her, pinning her to his side. It wasn't safe, and there was no way he was letting her out of here until it was. For chrissakes—he just found her. He couldn't—wouldn't—let her do anything that could take her away from him.

"Raven, please," she begged. "You don't understand! She's my family, and I should have been there for her yesterday when she got home. But I wasn't. I've been sitting in this fancy mausoleum for more than two days, and I've been neglecting my life. I have work that needs done, and people who worry about me."

Raven said nothing. Could think of nothing to say.

"Don't get me wrong," she purred, "I'd love nothing more than to stay here in bed with you for the next week or six, but the fact is, you're going to be going out tonight, for sure, to face the Sorcerers, and your job requires who knows what other kind of military responsibility. I'm sure you don't just work when you feel like it." Raven remained tense and silent.

"And what if something happens to you? What if I'm stuck here and you don't come back to me?"

"Mason would see that you were protected," Raven insisted. "He would see you home safely." He tightened his hold on her, but Jessica wriggled away from him and turned, sitting on her knees to face him, her luscious hair falling in tangles around her face, her chest still stained with their mingled blood.

"Maybe," she said, drawing his eyes back to that beautiful mouth, "but what if *he* doesn't come back, and I'm left to fend off that Harrier maniac by myself. You know I'd never survive him."

Raven sighed and reached for her, but she stubbornly avoided his touch, and his heart clenched. "I know you don't believe it, Jessica, but I don't think Harrier would harm you. I think he was messing with me down there, and you were just a means to an end. If I were out of the picture, he wouldn't give you a second thought."

"Raven, even if that were the case—and I have serious doubts—you still know that I'm right." Jessica held her hands out palms up and shrugged her shoulders. "Even if that were true, the Sorcerers are still going to be taken care of tonight, after which, things will go back to normal, right? I still have a life, friends, my job and I need to get back to them, sooner rather than later."

Raven stiffened. Normal. She wanted her life back. Her life the way it was before he showed up and turned everything upside down. But he wasn't going to let her go that easily. He would lock her in his office again, if he had to. There was no way he could let her just walk out of his life. Still, her words stung. The euphoria he felt just moments before faded in a cloud of rejection.

"You said you loved me," he whispered accusingly, not looking at her, hating how weak he sounded.

"I do love you, Raven, but that doesn't change the fact that I have things to do, and that there are other people out there who care about me."

"So you would just leave—go back to your life. To 'normal'?"

"I don't know what you want me to say, Raven." She was getting frustrated, he could tell. "You just want me to forget everything that came before you? Forget the rest of the world exists, just so you don't have to worry about me?"

"Yes," he leaned toward her menacingly, hissing through his fangs. Her eyes widened, then narrowed, but she did not retreat from his threatening approach.

"I'm sorry," she said, anger leaching into her tone, "But I won't do that—not for you. Not for anyone. No matter how much I love you, I won't stop being who I am."

This was too much. Raven didn't do emotions. He was a murderer first, and Warrior second—he had absolutely no frame of reference when it came to impossible women. He couldn't kill her, Christ that would be anti-productive, so Warrior mode it is. Raven jumped from the bed, reached for his clothes and said, "Jessica, I know this is hard on you, but as you say, this will be taken care of tonight. Once the Sorcerers are gone, I'm sure Mason will release you to do as you please. To go back to your life as it was, before," he waved his hand vaguely at the bed, "any of this," and though he tried to make his voice hard, authoritative, he couldn't keep the hurt from leaching through.

Jessica sat up, realization hitting her. "Raven, I didn't mean…it's just that I need to see Piper. Please, try to understand!"

"Tomorrow," was all he could manage as he headed toward the bathroom. He was shaking, furious, and knew he needed to calm down before talking to her. Before trying to make her understand how much he needed her to be here. Needed her to be safe. Hell, even calm he wasn't sure he would be able to explain, and though it killed him to walk away from her, it was all he could manage right now.

He tried hard not to notice the hurt and confusion in her eyes as he walked by, but the tear tracing down her cheek was impossible to miss.

Chapter Seventy-Four

Raven was in the bathroom for a really long time, and it became obvious he didn't plan to finish our conversation. When I heard the shower start, I reluctantly got dressed and headed back across the hall.

I walked into my own bathroom, and Malcolm followed me in, rubbing against my legs and nearly tripping me in the process. I sat down on the tub and patted my lap in invitation, which Malcolm instantly took me up on, jumping on my legs and digging his claws in just a little too hard to have been just for balance.

He looked up into my face, his sweet little whiskers twitching at me, his eyes all too knowing. I don't know why I was feeling like I'd betrayed the cat by sleeping with Raven, but the look on his face seemed to merit guilt.

I plugged up the giant tub and turned the water on full blast and super-hot. A nice long soak was in order, my body aching from the night's activities. It was still an hour or so before sunrise, so I figured I might as well relax. A plan was forming in my mind, and common sense said I would be better served implementing it during daylight hours. I was going to see Piper and I was going to the gravel pit, Raven be damned. I was crazy about the jerk, but all this "it's for your own good" and "you're safer here" crap was really getting on my last nerve. Walking away from me like he did, well that just pissed me off.

I would have liked a chance to explain myself further to Raven. I think he thought I meant I didn't want to be involved in his world anymore, but nothing could be further from the truth. I just need it to be balanced. I'll never be a Vampire, Raven made that perfectly clear. It would be metabolically impossible, even if I *wanted* to change my whole life.

Honestly, I had absolutely no idea how this was going to work. My heart ached with only a hallway separating us. How could I bear having a whole world between us? I didn't know what to do, but I was determined to at least try. If Raven could be flexible, that is.

But none of that mattered right now. Piper said that I had to be at the gravel pit tonight at sundown. That it was a matter of life and death. She may have had her memory altered, but the dreams she mentioned about screaming children were enough information for me to put together whose life was at stake. It was the Were children. The Sorcerers were using them to lure me to the gravel pit. And the only purpose I could serve would be to bring Raven along for help. To lead him into their trap. Once I saw Piper I'd hopefully have a better idea what I was dealing with. But one thing was certain. If the Sorcerers wanted Raven, they'd have to find another way, because there was no way I would knowingly betray him like that, even if he was being an ass. I'd do what I had to do to save the Were kids and protect my own. They knew who Piper was—that she was special to me, so if I didn't do as they said, my friend would never be safe. And the best way to keep Raven safe was to keep him in the dark.

A noise in the living room had me out of the tub and drying off at record speed. I threw on my jeans and a fresh shirt, and ran out to see who had come in, hoping for once that it was *not* Raven. Malcolm was fast on my heels.

My luck was running. Tabatha was in the living room, her little cart parked just inside the door stacked high with fluffy, fresh towels.

"Good morning!" I called to her, and she jumped. "Oh—sorry!" I smiled and she smiled back as Malcolm transferred his attentions to her.

"Good morning, Miss Sweet," she half bowed, her blonde ponytail swinging with the movement. "I'm sorry to disturb you. I was told to make sure your stay here was comfortable, but I wasn't sure what hours you keep. Are you rising or retiring?"

"To be honest, I'm not really sure," I sighed. "My days and nights are so confused," and I laughed as I plopped down on the fancy sofa. "So do you and your family live here?" I asked absently as I reached for the tray Tabatha had set on the coffee table. There was coffee this time, and it was calling to me, plus it gave me something to do with my hands.

"Oh, no. We have a home...elsewhere. However, we are always available for the Legion. There is someone on staff twenty-four hours a day, to cook or clean or whatever the Warlord and his Team requires. The Soldiers take care of their own quarters and meals. We have no responsibilities there."

More information than I was digging for, but helpful nonetheless. I sat back with my steaming coffee mug, blowing across the top before taking a tentative sip. It was strong and flavorful, just the way I liked it.

I watched the young vamp go about her duties and decided to jump in. I had to trust someone, and Tabatha was pretty much my only hope.

"Tabatha, I need your help," I said finally. The cloth she was using to dust the armoire halted in mid swipe.

"Anything you need, miss," she said hesitantly.

Setting the coffee back on the tray, I walked over to her. "I need a car," I said quickly, "and a vague idea of where I am. I promise, I won't tell anyone about this place. I have no desire to put you or your people or the Legion in any danger. I have great respect for all of you, but I really need to get home. I have things I need to do, and it's imperative I do them today."

Tabatha remained still and I held my breath, hoping she was considering helping me, and not ratting me out to Raven or Mason. Finally she said, "I can't let you leave here on your own." My heart dropped and I started to beg, plead, whatever I had to do, but Tabatha held her hand up and I waited.

"As I say, I can't let you leave on your own. It would be more than my life's worth to expose the Legion in that way. But once you are settled, I'm done for the night, and will be leaving here shortly. I can take you with me, drop you off at your home. If we are discovered, I'll still be in trouble, but you seem—kind. I want to help."

"Wait a minute," I said, pulling my cell phone out of my pocket and checking the time. "The sun's up—I thought you were, you know?"

Tabatha giggled. "I am not pure blood, not even close. I can spend several hours in the sun before its effects take a toll on me. At least in the mornings or evenings. We'll have plenty of time to get you where you need to be and me home and safe in the dark." Her laughter was like chimes in a gentle breeze, and in that instant I trusted her completely.

"When can we leave?" I asked, anxious to get going before Raven showed up again.

"Depends," she replied. "Are your quarters to your liking?"

"Absolutely," I nodded. "Let's roll."

Chapter Seventy-Five

I waved to Tabatha as she drove off, feeling oddly out of sorts on my own property. Malcolm was running around sniffing everything, reclaiming his territory, I supposed. The maple trees were swaying gently in the soft breeze and the early morning sun shone brightly through their leaves.

I stood outside the porch, staring at my home. Here I was, gazing at what had been my life for nineteen years, and in this moment it all seemed strange to me. Like going back to your elementary school after you'd graduated from high school. Everything seemed so small and insignificant, like you just didn't fit anymore.

Getting here hadn't been easy—the blasted Legion had cameras everywhere, and Tabatha had to do some fancy camouflage on me, the largest part of which was an old maid's uniform we hoped would pass for current, just to get me to the car. Once there, I slipped onto the floor of the backseat with Malcolm, who was being extremely cooperative for a cat, and Tabatha covered us with an old blanket, which I had carried Malcolm out in, pretending I was helping her carry things to her car for dry cleaning.

No one stopped us, and no one asked any questions. Fortunately, I didn't see any of the Team members, only a few servants and a Soldier or two. But as Tabatha reminded me, until we were well off the property, until we were well away from the Compound, we wouldn't know if we'd been seen. Even then, it was probably more a matter of when, not if.

I shuddered at the thought of what Raven would do when he discovered I was missing. He was going to be pissed, but it was his own fault. He walked out on an important conversation, and the more I thought about it, the madder I got. My back was up now, and since anger is usually a good motivator for me, it was just what I needed to get my butt moving.

Taking a deep breath, I unlocked the front door and entered my home, seeing it as though it were through someone else's eyes. I shook my head to clear out the cobwebs and made a mental checklist. First on the agenda—see what kind of damage was on my answering machine.

About a million calls from Alex, covering his bases in trying to find me, two telemarketers, and one call from Mr. Peterman, wondering when I'd be done with his chair. Sorry Mr. Peterman. You're going to have to take a back seat for now. I got bigger fish to fry.

First I called Alex and asked him to meet me at Piper's around 2:00. As it turned out, he was already there. Apparently, after her abduction, Alex had taken several days off work and was sleeping on the Pendleton's sofa to be close to her. Weird.

Once that was all set up, I went upstairs to change clothes. I found an older pair of jeans and a T-shirt that wasn't too shabby to wear out, but also wasn't one of my favorites. I didn't know what I would be getting into tonight, and I didn't plan on coming back here before heading out to the gravel pit, just in case Raven sent a day crew looking for me.

I went back downstairs and did a couple loads of laundry, checked my mail and e-mail, and cleaned out my refrigerator. My phone rang a couple (hundred) times, but the number was blocked so, assuming it was Raven, I ignored it.

I tied up the garbage bag with all the fridge castoffs, set it on the porch to take out to the trashcans by the barn when I left, and glanced at the clock. It was time to go.

I grabbed my everyday purse from the washstand by the front door and replaced the items from the fancy bag I'd been carrying since Saturday, back where they belonged. I locked up behind me, fed and watered my kitties, grabbed the bag of garbage and headed for my beloved Honda.

Malcolm was sitting on the hood of the car when I got there, and I waved a hand to shoo him away, but he just looked at me.

"You can't come, Malcolm, I'm sorry." More cat staring. "I swear, I'm just going to Piper's, if that's okay with you." He cocked his head, as if considering the veracity of my statement, then walked to the edge of the car hood in my direction. I held my hand out to him, and he rubbed it lovingly.

"I don't know how I'd get through this without you, Malcolm. Promise me you'll never run away?" Malcolm began to purr as he continued rubbing, and I bent my nose to his for an Eskimo kiss. He looked at me for a moment after that, then leapt off the car and headed toward the orchard to reclaim the rest of his realm.

I climbed in the car and headed off to Piper's, Andrew Lloyd Weber's *Aspects of Love* blaring from the tape deck of my ancient ride.

~~~~~~~~~

Malcolm sat in the shadows of the brooder house, watching intently as the silver Honda drove away. He had been sent here as eyes and ears, to watch the girl and make sure she fared well. His Overlord had recommended him for the job, and he was glad to have it.

Since his wife's death, he had no desire to walk in human form. He felt closer to her like this, as a feline. They had run and hunted together, and it was this form he wanted to remain in for eternity. Nearly two years had passed since Anna died in childbirth. Two years he mourned for her and their stillborn child, denying his humanity.

His Clowder had tried to bring him back, forcing him to change several times—which was painful as hell! But when they realized it did no good—he just changed back as soon as he was alone—they finally gave over. Two months ago, the Overlord offered him this position, which suited him perfectly. He didn't know who wanted this girl watched or why, and truly when he accepted the job, he didn't care. It was an opportunity for him to stay as he desired without having the whole group begging him to come home. He had hoped this assignment would last forever, but now he wasn't so sure.

As the old Honda passed out of his sight he sneezed in frustration, rubbing a massive paw along his nose and whiskers, trying to get the scent of her out of his head. When she rubbed noses with him like that, it could be overwhelming. Besides, she still reeked of the bloodsucker.

He stretched out in the shade, crossing his long forepaws in front of him, his head held regally, his eyes nearly closed. And he thought of her. He liked when she talked to him, and she did so often, telling him about her day, her thoughts, her fears. Often she spoke of her parents, both of whom had died. He understood her mourning and gave her what comfort he could. Of course, if she knew he wasn't *just* a cat, she might not have been so open with him, but he chose not to think of that.

And she was a cuddler, this one, which he had to admit he didn't mind at all, especially when she rubbed him and nuzzled him. Didn't mind? That was probably an understatement. She, of course, had no idea that by rubbing his whiskers against her he was marking her as his. Then again, if she did know, what would she care? He was just a cat, right?

When the Vampire showed up on her porch, Malcolm was curious, mostly just hoping the male would wipe her memories and disappear with no one the wiser, so long as she remained uninjured. He tried to ask him what was going on before the vamp left the next night, but he was apparently too startled, or too dense, to reply. (Probably the latter.) Then he'd shown up with Jessica after the fancy dress party, only to be attacked by the Sorcerers.

Malcolm was very proud of how Jessica had protected herself, and he begrudgingly confessed, if only to himself, that the bloodsucker had fought well, too. He had been willing to give the male some leeway, until he'd pulled that stunt in the Hummer. A low rumble started at the back of Malcolm's throat as he remembered. Fucking Vampires.

Even so, he had to concede that she had been safer in the Vampires' lair, in spite of the obvious sparks that flew whenever she was in the same room with the one called Raven. It was bad enough to know she was hot for a bloodsucker, but when the injured Soldier had exposed who Raven was? The thought of her in the hands of the Rapist almost had Malcolm shifting on the spot! The Rapist was legendary, even among Malcolm's people.

His assignment was to watch and report, and he'd been happy with the simplicity of the job. But things were changing, and now she was showing a sudden penchant for danger. Escaping the Vampires as she had was gutsy on one hand, suicidal on the other. Sure, part of him was thrilled to have them both on their own turf (he considered this property as much his now as hers), but he knew her leaving without the Vampires' consent would have consequences. Potentially, dire consequences. She had left in haste, and though he was sure she was anxious to see the Piper woman, he was just as sure that there was more to it than that.

Whatever Jessica was up to, one thing was certain. Malcolm would be of no use to her like this. Blinking at his furry legs stretched out before him, he flexed his razor sharp claws.

And for the first time in two years, found himself longing for his human form.

Chapter Seventy-Six

When Raven finally returned to his bedroom, it was only to find Jessica gone. He assumed she'd returned to her quarters, and it was probably just as well. He still didn't know how to take what she'd said about things returning to normal, and still didn't trust himself to ask. The thought of her going back to her old life, Sorcerers or no Sorcerers, scared the crap out of him.

But Raven wasn't a complete idiot. He knew that there was no way to protect her from everything, and there was no way she'd let him keep her caged up. Her independence was part of what made her so attractive to him.

He lay down on his bed, her scent surrounding him, and began to meditate. Once he was calm—completely calm—and had perhaps rationalized his way out of losing her, he would go to her and explain himself. They would figure out how things would be between them, and they would find a way to make them work. They had to. He simply couldn't live without her.

Raven's breathing was deep and slow, the meditation doing wonders to clear his head. A sound from the other room registered somewhere toward the outskirts of his mind. He ignored it.

It sounded again, and again he ignored it, though what it was, was beginning to register more clearly.

The third time he realized that the sound was that of insistent pounding on his door and all he could think was, *Jessica*. He ran to the door in nothing but his sweat pants, and swung it open, expecting to see her there. However, the face that greeted him was not only not Jessica—it wasn't even friendly.

Harrier stood there, his lips arched in a disgusted snarl, his russet hair falling into his eyes. At the sight of Raven, he just shook his head and said, "War Room. Now," and turned to walk away.

"Harrier, what's up?" Raven called, but the male kept walking.

When Raven arrived in the War Room, everyone was there. He'd taken time to change into work clothes, black fatigues and combat boots, and so wasn't surprised to see Harrier there before him, sneering in the corner. Merlin was at his usual spot with his nose in his computer; Tas, Viper and Mason spread in chairs around the table.

It was barely mid-day, so Raven had no clue why they were all awake, let alone assembled here. Nor did he understand the looks he was getting from the others. Not hate, really, more disdain, as though he were a friend who'd become an utter disappointment. As though he'd betrayed them in some way.

The tension in the room was thick, and Raven stopped just inside the door. The atmosphere was definitely not welcoming, and he was hesitant to cut off his only escape.

Mason motioned toward an empty chair, though, and Raven had no alternative but to take it, reluctantly closing the door behind him.

No one said anything. No greetings, no banter. The only noise in the room was Merlin's keyboard clicking away. After what seemed hours, Merlin said, "I've got her." And a fist clamped tightly around Raven's heart.

"Got who?" he barely whispered.

"Your pet has escaped," Harrier scoffed, and Mason glared at him across the room.

Certain he hadn't heard correctly, Raven looked to Mason for an explanation. When Mason remained silent Raven said, "What do you mean, escaped? She was never our prisoner! And she was in her quarters. Have you searched everywhere? She couldn't possibly have left the grounds, Mason, she doesn't even know where she is, let alone have transportation to get her away from here."

Mason, sensing the panic that was rising in Raven, held up a hand for silence and Raven reluctantly obeyed. He needed to be out there, looking for her. She had to be on the grounds somewhere. They were just overlooking her. She could be outside. She could be in danger!

They had a few day walkers among the Soldiers and staff. Why weren't they looking for her? Raven made to stand, but a look from Mason kept him in his seat. Merlin was talking again, but Raven's head was spinning and he had to concentrate to keep up.

"Early this morning the young maid, Tabatha, left with another servant. Both were carrying large piles of blankets and things. The second could easily have been Jessica. Tabatha's car was not in a direct line of sight of our cameras, but the second servant must have left with her. We see her entering the garage with Tabatha from the lifts, but she doesn't reappear anywhere afterward. She doesn't return to the Compound."

"This is ridiculous!" Raven shouted, slamming his palm on the table in frustration. "She wouldn't do this, Mason."

"So she said nothing to you about wanting to leave?" Mason asked calmly. The others were still avoiding his eyes, except for Harrier, who seemed to be enjoying this.

"No!" Raven said hastily, but then, "Well, not like that, anyway. She said she wanted to visit her friend, but when I told her it wasn't possible, that it wasn't safe, she accepted that. She wouldn't do this to me, Mason!"

All eyes were now on him, and he realized that his meditation had been wasted. He was shouting again, and he could feel the anger burning through him. Realizing he was on his feet, he slowly lowered himself back into his chair, raking a hand through his hair.

How could she betray him this way? How could she tell him she loved him, and then run away?

But then, wasn't that exactly what he had done to her when she mentioned wanting to leave? He ran from her to avoid the conversation. Still, this was different. After last night—everything was different.

"There's nothing to be done until dark," Mason was saying, "so we might was well calm down and try to figure out where she is heading. Raven, you said she wanted to visit her friend. Could it be that simple?"

Raven thought for a moment, struggling to regain his composure. "Yes, it could definitely be that simple." He really hoped it were that simple. "She was upset with me when I said it wouldn't be possible, and Jessica is strong willed. I wouldn't put it past her to do this with her only motive being to see her friend. She won't betray us, Mason."

"We'll find her tonight, then. And Raven, I hope you're right. I don't have to remind you of our conversation concerning the liability she causes."

"Of course not, Warlord," Raven growled through clenched teeth, Mason's threat to Jessica clear, and unwelcome.

The Team arose and shuffled toward the door, Harrier's pleasure over Jessica's fate leaving a nauseating stench in the air.

"Tough luck, Raven," Tas whispered as he followed the others out. "I really liked her." The finality in his voice was ominous.

Chapter Seventy-Seven

Sitting in the Good Times Bar and Grill with my two best friends in the world, working our way through an order of Good Times' famous beer batter fish and chips, some chicken wings and a bucket o' beer, it was easy to pretend like the last week or so hadn't happened.

I had arrived at Piper's right on time, and it hadn't taken much to convince the two to join me for an early dinner—or late lunch. Whatever. Recent events had us all pretty shaken, even though they knew very little of what was actually going on, and we agreed that we need some "us" time.

I envied them their ignorance—wished like hell I would be going home after dinner and curling up on the couch with my favorite cat and a good book. But wishing was useless, so for an hour or two, I was going to hang with my friends and pretend like my world hadn't been turned on its ear.

The pub was small, but it was a popular watering hole for the Fallen Cross locals. The bar was mahogany with an old fashioned mirror hanging behind it that put you in mind of an Old Western Saloon. Roughhewn beams were spaced along the ceiling, alternating with the hanging fans that turned the stale air. The barstools and chairs were upholstered in dark red Naugahyde, the tables left bare and sporting the carved initials from decades of patrons' covert shenanigans. After a while it had become something of a badge of honor to have been able to carve your initials into a Good Times' table, and the owners, having been unsuccessful in quashing the activity, finally threw in the towel.

That's when they hired me to come in every couple of months to throw another coat of polyurethane on the most recent works of art.

My initials were on the table in the corner farthest from the bar, along with Alex's and Piper's. I had been paranoid about getting caught, but my partners in crime had been relentless and apparently I was not good at standing up to peer pressure. I was so relieved when we weren't discovered, yet I couldn't help a tinge of pride when I came in the following month to seal my work for posterity.

I tuned back into the conversation going on around me, and Alex was talking about work.

"...Mrs. Perkins' palsy was making her false teeth clack together, and apparently she could only hear it in the car! Harry told her to get some denture adhesive, and if that didn't work to call her dentist!" Alex slapped a palm on the table, laughing so hard tears were forming at the corners of his eyes, and Piper was laughing right along with him, one hand on his arm, the other holding her stomach.

I just smiled along with them, happy to be here, not really caring what we talked about. It was all so normal, I didn't want it to end.

Piper looked at me and her eyes softened a little before going devilish. "You're thinking about your *man*, aren't you?" she teased.

I just smiled and raised my eyebrows a couple of times, egging her on.

"So are you going to spill, or what? Is he gorgeous all over? Is he amazing in bed? Did you use a condom?"

I just continued to smile, which made Piper relentless.

"I'll bet he's hung like a mule," Piper said offhandedly, which had me slapping at her and Alex looking like he was going to hurl.

We laughed and carried on like this for a while longer, but it was getting late and I knew my reprieve was about to end. I had to get down to the gravel pit before sundown if I was going to avoid being stopped by Raven. Because there was no doubt he would be looking for me as soon as he could.

When Alex left the table to visit the little boy's room, I leaned closer to Piper and said, "Piper, I hate to bring this up, but I need to ask you about what you told me the other day."

Piper just looked at me with a big question mark on her forehead, so I went on. "You know, about the dreams you've been having and how I need to go to the gravel pit?"

"Oh, yeah!" she said cheerfully, as though the whole concept of screaming children and night time visits to a giant hole in the ground were a day at the park. "What do you need to know?"

"Piper, you're *sure* I'm supposed to go tonight? At sundown?"

"Yep!" she replied, though as I watched her it seemed she was no longer herself.

"Do you know *why* I'm supposed to go?" I asked.

"Life and death," she responded matter-of-factly, reaching for another wing.

"*Whose* life and death, Piper? Please think." Her perky little nose wrinkled up a bit, and panic was building behind her eyes. "It's okay," I said, reassuring her, and the panic subsided a little.

"Jessie, you just have to go, okay? The babies need you," she added in a whisper as Alex sauntered up and put his hands on Piper's shoulders, giving her a little massage before retaking his seat.

"My turn!" Piper chimed as Alex sat beside her, and she was up and gone in a flash. Alex was watching me.

"So are you going?" his face was somber, almost sad.

"Yeah, I have to, I think," I said. "Did she say anything else to you? Give you any idea what's going on?"

"No, she doesn't remember anything. The DNA tests came back, and the blood on her clothes was definitely hers, but there wasn't an open wound on her. And the only thing she will say is that you have to go to the gravel pit. She doesn't know who wants you to go there, who had her, nothing. And she wouldn't say anything to her parents or let me tell the police. All she will tell me is that you have to go save the babies, whatever the hell that means. Jessie – you can't do this."

"Alex, I have to! If I don't, they could come after Piper again, or you, and I can't lose anyone else."

"What about us, though?" he was getting angry now, his glare boring holes in me. "Do you think it would be all sunshine and puppies for us if you got yourself killed? You don't know what you're facing out there. It could be a murderer or a rapist—anything!"

I grimaced at his words, thinking *No, I made love with* that *guy earlier. These ones are much worse.* I knew exactly what they were—and pretty much what they wanted from me. I hoped beyond hope that they would be disappointed when I showed up without Raven, and that somehow I'd be able to rescue the babies Piper kept dreaming of.

The more I thought about it, the more hopeless it all seemed. If Raven were with me, then maybe I would have a chance of helping the kids, but that would just be leading him into their trap, and I couldn't very well do that, could I?

I let out a breath I hadn't known I'd been holding and realized that Alex was watching me, waiting for some kind of response. "This is Ramon's fault, isn't it?" he asked me quietly, and I flinched.

"Alex, it's just not that simple. Yeah, his people are involved, but you know it's not his fault. This was all going to happen, no matter what. You know about my," I whispered, making a gesture to indicate the vision, "and you know they always come true. There was just no getting around it. He's in my life now, and I'm good with that. This other stuff—well, all I can do is try to protect you guys. If that means I go to the pit, then I go to the pit."

"And if you don't come back? What then?" The sorrow in his eyes was heartbreaking.

"I'll come back," I promised him, but I wasn't really convincing.

"At least let me come with you."

I looked at Alex for a long moment, and then shook my head. "You have to take care of Piper. She needs you, you know." He glanced over my shoulder, nodding in that direction to indicate she was coming. "Promise, me, Alex." I whispered in a rush. "Promise me you'll stay with her until this is over."

"How will I know?" he asked. "That it's over."

"You'll know," I promised. "You'll know."

Piper sat down then, patting me on the head before plopping into her seat. She was bubbly and excited, and Alex and I tried to shake off the seriousness of our conversation to keep her from suspecting.

My stomach was starting to churn as I considered what I was about to do. I kept telling myself this was the only way, and that I wasn't really as stupid as it seemed I was, but I had to protect my friends. If I didn't do this, the bad guys could easily hurt someone I loved, and I would never forgive myself. I just hoped that Alex would keep his promise to stay with Piper.

On top of everything else, I had a real bad feeling about Raven's reaction to my disappearance. Not only was he going to be furious with me, but Mason and the others would be none too happy either. I wouldn't be surprised if they were already planning my assassination. Well, probably not Raven, but the others certainly were. Hopefully, Tabatha wouldn't be in too much trouble. It was sweet of her to help me, but she really did put herself out on a limb.

I wasn't helpless, though, and I wasn't afraid of them. Well, maybe a little afraid, but these were *children*. Were children, yeah, but they were probably scared to death. Whatever the Sorcerers had done or were planning to do with them was surely vile and evil, and I couldn't just stand by and let it happen. Especially when I had a personal invitation.

Chapter Seventy-Eight

Raven was pacing a path in the carpet outside the Sub-T elevator doors. He was dressed for battle, his clothing black from head to foot. Under his oversized leather duster he wore a weapons harness packed with ammunition, hand grenades, his favorite silver blades, and his Glock. Viper had even given him a couple of his magic EMPs, M-bombs he was calling them now, so Raven was feeling locked and loaded, and looking absolutely lethal. Now if the sun would just freakin' go down!

Mason had sent a daywalker to Jessica's home, but naturally, she was nowhere to be found. Hell, the cat was even missing. Malcolm had probably gone back to his own people by now, leaving Jessica to fend for herself. If Raven ever got his hands on the bloody furball, he'd rip his fucking legs off.

Finally, the sun slipped below the horizon, and Raven was up the elevator and out the door running. He would have preferred the speed of his Corvette, but he'd learned many years ago that battle gear and bucket seats did not go well together, so instead he jumped in the Hummer, ramming it in reverse.

The tires screeched as he slammed on the brakes to avoid running over the Vampire standing behind him, hands plastered against the rear window. Raven growled as Harrier stalked to the passenger door and jerked it open.

"You're not going out there alone," he snarled, and Raven flashed his fangs.

"Stop me, asshole," he hissed, but Harrier was already in the Hummer. "What the fuck are you doing?" Raven shouted at him.

"You don't give a *fuck* about me and you certainly don't give a *fuck* about Jessica!"

"I have my reasons," Harrier said quietly. Strapping on his seatbelt, he said, "Buckle up, Rapist."

"Fuck you, Flyboy."

Raven didn't have time for this shit. If he wanted to come, fine, but the bastard better not get in his way. It occurred to him that Harrier's lack of feeling for Jessica could very well be why he was sent—to eliminate her if it were necessary—but Raven couldn't think about that now. If it came down to it, he'd slaughter the male without a second thought.

Jessica was all that mattered, and he had but one guess as to where she might be. Piper Pendleton wouldn't be hard to find.

Chapter Seventy-Nine

Helmut Fuhrmann stood stoically at a window just inside the small office space located near the entrance to Anderson Sand and Gravel, his eyes closed but all other senses alert. He had six men with him tonight, which one would hope to be plenty enough to capture one human. The rest of his Clan was on standby nearby.

The Were child was in a gravel pile not far from the entrance, buried up to her shoulders and unable to move. A spell ensured she would not be crushed by the weight of the pebbles, nor would she be able to dig her way out. Her presence was necessary for the night's festivities, and Fuhrmann couldn't afford to lose his last example before the meeting with Mayor Diggs. She was awake though, and screaming relentlessly, which was giving Fuhrmann an incredible headache. He clenched his teeth and tolerated the screams, though, as they would be beneficial in ensuring that the Sweet woman not be deterred. He would take no chances that she might change her mind. If she heard the screams, she would come. Humans were interesting that way.

The sun was just inching below the horizon, and Fuhrmann was getting what a human might call antsy. He lamented not having had time to produce more of the tranq potion—things would have been so much easier with it. But nonetheless, he would soon have his bait, his trap would be set, and his beloved's murderer would be at his mercy. And this time he would not escape.

It wasn't long before he felt a stir in the alarm spell he'd cast around the property. Someone was breaking his perimeter, and he didn't need to guess who. It seemed the girl was either incredibly brave or incredibly stupid. Either way it was a shame she would be terminated. She also happened to be incredibly beautiful, but who really had a need for that?

As the alarm spell tickled at the base of his neck, he opened his eyes, not surprised to see the girl squeezing through a gap in the chain link gates. Fuhrmann had arranged that they be open just enough for her to squeeze through. He didn't want it to be *too* easy for her.

He laughed to himself at her gullibility. The fact that she would come, knowing as she must that it was a trap? How incredibly *human* of her. What surprised him, though, was that she came alone. Fuhrmann stifled his disappointment at the lack of Vampire presence, but it would just make baiting the trap all the more fun.

She would be well bloodied by the time he finished with her, her blood scent would carry for miles, and the murdering Rapist would come.

Chapter Eighty

This was probably the dumbest thing I'd ever done in my entire life! I'd parked my car about a mile down the road, in a neighborhood with lots of houses and lots of lights. I figured it would be safer there than on the side of the busy state route where the gravel pit was located, or worse yet, anywhere near the Sorcerers.

Raven would be looking for me, and my car parked mere feet from where I stood would be like a freakin' neon sign. No, this way he'd be going door to door, scaring the neighborhood, but at least not in any danger himself.

I'd come to some realizations as I'd made my plan. I was in love with a Vampire, and we all know how that's going to work out. Even if he *did* decide to give up killing and running around sucking other humans' blood and stuff, he was still going to live for another bazillion years, and stay hot the whole time. Me, I was going be old in less than twenty years, my hair going grey and my face going all wrinkly. I knew, with my pride, I wouldn't be able to stand that kind of humiliation, not even for twenty years of awesome Vampire sex with the most amazing man I have ever met.

It wasn't fair, but those were the facts.

On the other hand, I was quite certain I couldn't live without him. Okay, I *could*, but I absolutely didn't want to. I'd be 'til the day I died wondering what if? What if I'd taken a chance? What if I'd stayed with him? What if the Vampire Chemists come up with a way to alter human female DNA to the point where we could someday make the change—where I could become a Vampire and we could have babies and live happily ever after?

Right—and in a minute I'd start spewing fairy dust out of my ass.

With those my only options, I'd done what I knew was right. I left Raven—he'd be fine without me; I said good-bye to my family, though they didn't know it. And now I was off to save the Were kids, protecting Piper and Alex in the process. Exactly *how*? No idea. But I thought if I could at least get the kids free, then it would be okay if the Sorcerers killed me. I wouldn't have to face a life of lies and secrets and disappointment. I'd die a hero, and I'd see my parents again on the other side. It all sounded pretty good to me at the time.

The walk had taken longer than I'd planned, and the sun was just touching the horizon when I neared the edge of the gravel pit property. A deep ditch angled down from the road, and then back up to the chain link fence that surrounded the property, concertina wire edging the top of the fence, making climbing out of the question. It seemed like overkill to me, but the Anderson's had gotten tired of kids climbing the fence and skinny dipping in the near bottomless lake they dug the gravel from. I suppose some sharp razor wire next to your bare ass and bits as you tried to escape getting caught *would* be a deterrent.

I inched along the ditch near the base of the fence, hidden from the road traffic by shadow and depth, and came upon the entrance. Two huge chain link gates were connected by a giant chain and padlock. The chain was too long, leaving an uncharacteristically inviting gap between the gates, but then, I knew they wouldn't leave me to my own devices. What kind of set up would it be if I couldn't get in?

I squeezed through the gates, regretting that last piece of fish I'd practically inhaled, and once through I crouched to the ground, trying to get my bearings in the growing darkness. I knew the place was surrounded by motion lights, but either I hadn't triggered them or they'd been disabled. Either way, it was getting darker by the minute, and I was starting to wonder about my whole self-sacrificing plan.

As I crouched on the ground, mulling over the sanity of being on private property where I was fairly confident I was going to be murdered, I heard the screams. Terrifying, terror filled, bone chilling, childlike screams coming from a dark mound of what I assumed was gravel just a few yards from where I knelt.

So there was nothing to it. I had to go on.

I tried to stay in the shadows, crouching low, making myself small. It was probably a waste of time—if I were a Sorcerer who was trying to capture someone, I would probably know the moment they stepped onto the premises.

The screaming continued, and my blood was curdling in my veins. After what seemed like hours, I was close enough to make out the source of the screams. A tiny head seemingly placed at random on the side of the mound of gravel. I could only assume that the body that went with the head was *underneath* the gravel, and the thought terrified me.

I forgot about my made for TV crouching and ran to the child's aid.

"Shhh," I said, trying to calm her, for it was a little girl's face staring up at me, once-blonde hair now the color of filth and blood was plastered to her pale, heart-shaped face. Her eyes were wide with terror, tears streaking the grime that covered her cheeks. When I spoke she hesitated, gasping for breath, and then she let out another ear piercing scream.

I bent to her and started digging, whispering reassurances, trying to quiet her screams, to let her know I was going to help her, but this kid was too far gone. The Sorcerers had had her for weeks, and apparently had wasted no time in teaching her to fear. I wanted to kill the bastards!

She must have finally realized I was trying to help, because the screaming stopped, although her sobs were persistent. My hands were aching already, my nails torn and bloody, and I didn't seem to be making any progress. Trying to distract us both I asked, "What's your name?"

"Allie," she sobbed.

"How old are you, Allie?"

"Six."

"Allie, do you know where the others are? The others like you?"

She choked on a sob and I was sorry I'd asked. "You're by yourself now?" I asked, as gently as I could.

When she nodded, I said, "Well, Allie, my name is Jessica, and I'm going to get you out of here."

"You can't," she whispered.

"Of course, I can," I insisted, digging harder, putting my forearms and shoulders into it.

"You can't," she whispered again. "You should run away fast," she added, and her voice was eerie, unnatural. I froze, struggling to see her face. The moon was rising behind us, and I was well aware what that was going to do to her. I had hoped to get her away before the moon rose completely, but apparently that wasn't going to happen.

As things went from bad to worse, the hair stood up on the back of my neck, and I sensed we were not alone. My heart fell to my stomach when I heard a sinister voice behind me, accented heavily with German.

"Welcome, Miss Sweet. So nice of you to join us."

Chapter Eighty-One

Raven maneuvered the Hummer through the residential neighborhood, fighting the urge to break every traffic law in the process. The Pendleton girl had been less than cooperative, especially with the man, Alex, running interference. They had just returned, having parted ways with Jessica at a bar downtown, and were quite reluctant to share any information about Jessica with him.

Of course, the appearance of Raven and Harrier probably didn't instill the humans with too much confidence, two huge strangers, dressed for battle, popping up on your doorstep and demanding information on your best friend. Yeah, Raven would have cooperated about as well as they had.

Piper had hidden behind Alex, suddenly not so eager for her friend to be connected with *Ramon*. And Alex hadn't liked him from the beginning. Of course, he was jealous, his feelings for Jessica making him rank with the emotion.

But fortunately, Raven had other ways. Alex's mind was crowded with thoughts of what he'd do to Raven if anything happened to Jessica. Useless. But from Piper's mind he learned where Jessica had gone.

Dammit! He slammed his palms on the steering wheel as an SUV crossed his path, causing him to slam on the brakes at the stop sign he'd intended to run. Why would she do this? Why would she meet the Sorcerers on her own? She had to know it was a trap—had to know that they were using her to get to him. Why would she put herself in that kind of danger? To save the Werekids? She didn't even *know* the Weres.

And now the Legion thought she was a traitor.

Raven accelerated quickly as soon as the intersection was clear, and headed east through town, contemplating his companion.

Harrier had been silent through most of the search. They had gone to Jessica's first to find Piper's address—the fucking cat was still missing—and Harrier hadn't said a word. Then he'd joined Raven in the interview with Jessica's friends, and though he lent an intimidation factor, he had again remained quiet. True, he wasn't much of a talker, but his silence didn't bode well for Jessica. At the least, he should be taunting Raven in some way. He never missed an opportunity to make his disdain for Raven's past known. But tonight, he was quiet.

Raven couldn't stand it any longer. "Talk," he said, veering left onto Main Street. Harrier turned his golden eyes from the road and focused them on Raven.

"What do you want to know, Rapist?"

"Why do you hate her?" Raven struggled to keep the emotion from his voice.

"I don't hate her," Harrier stated blandly, returning his eyes to the front. "I hate you."

"So, what, you aren't allowed to kill me, so you would hurt her to get at me?" Raven was incredulous. He knew that Harrier had no love for him, but what he had done to Jessica was unforgivable.

"I don't want to hurt her, you idiot. I'm trying to protect her."

"You're not making any sense, flyboy. Protect her from what? From the Sorcerers?"

"No, from you, asshat. And from herself."

"And you do this by attacking her in the Club? By frightening her?"

"Yes, by showing her what she has to look forward to in any kind of relationship with you. It's only a matter of time before your old ways resurface and she becomes yet another human casualty in the Rapist's war against mankind. Everyone knows it." Harrier's voice rose with passion as he continued, though his eyes remained straight ahead.

"The Legion thinks they've tamed you. They think that they have the Rapist on a leash, but they're naïve. A leopard doesn't change his spots, and a feral doesn't change his ways. Sure, you pretend to be in control, but I've seen the way you look at the girl. The hunger in your eyes is more than just, 'Hey, I need a snack.'

"Your feral beast is waiting just below the surface, and your ability to abstain from your favorite pastimes is being strained. She will push your buttons, *my friend*, and you will kill her. You will rape her and mutilate her, and yeah, you might even feel bad about it later, but it *will* happen, and I don't want to be around to witness the whole thing.

"And I certainly don't want to have to clean up your mess, so yes—I'm protecting her. Her, the Legion, the fucking world! You should have been put down years ago, and if the Primeval hadn't fucked it up, you would have been.

"But here you are, acting all noble, trying to save the girl and get the bad guy, when we all know that you're just a ticking time bomb, waiting to go off."

Raven wasn't surprised by Harrier's revelations, but was a little stunned that he had the guts to admit it all out loud. He'd known the male hated him, but until now he hadn't realized how deeply that hatred was seated. And Harrier knew about the plot to have Raven eliminated—he had intimated as much in the Club. But, did everyone know? Was he the only one to just be figuring this out?

"Did Mason send you tonight, or did you come on your own?"

"Your actions have been erratic since meeting the human. Mason is concerned, as are the rest of the Team, that her presence could push you over the edge of control. Let's face it. Without Tas, you wouldn't have made it this far."

"You don't know," Raven whispered, whipping the vehicle east on the State Road. No one, outside of Mason, knew about the curse. Mason had sworn an oath, and in spite of all Raven had learned recently, he was sure his Warlord would not break his word.

But now, it would seem the curse had been lifted. He'd mixed passions with Jessica, had fed from her, made love to her—enjoyed it!—and no one had died. He had controlled the beast without the failsafe. What if Harrier was right? What if it was up to Raven to control the beast from now on—and what if he failed?

"I know that she will be your undoing," Harrier said, more controlled. "And if we can't trust you to have our backs, you're useless to the Team. Not that I've ever trusted you, but for whatever reason, the others have. Now trusting you is a risk, one we can't afford to take."

Raven inhaled deeply. "Have you ever been in love?" he asked, bringing Harrier's attention around with alacrity.

"What does that have to do with anything?" Harrier asked, suspicion coloring the question.

"Everything. Nothing. Never mind," Raven replied, shaking his head as he willed a red light back to green and sped through the cleared intersection.

"No, wait," Harrier turned to face Raven completely. This turn in the conversation was the last thing he expected. "Are you saying you are *in love* with this human? That Raven the Rapist is what? Cured by the love of a good woman?" His words dripped with sarcasm, and he laughed when Raven didn't respond.

"Tell me," Harrier continued. "Is this why you are so eager to run to the girl's rescue, knowing it's a trap?"

Raven remained silent.

"No," Harrier said, shaking his head. "This is just a show you're putting on for the Legion, to convince them of your integrity. You just march into a situation where you know you're a target, take out the bad guys, and oh, save the girl while you're at it, proving your worth and how truly you've changed? We had a plan, Raven, and a good one too. Now the whole thing has had to be scrapped because of your entanglements, our Soldiers standing by awaiting new orders because your pet chose today to escape and throw herself in the middle of something that is none of her concern. Not that I blame her for running from you. Probably the smartest thing she could have done."

Raven glared at him, and Harrier returned the stare, evaluating the other male's reaction. When Raven returned his attention to the road without a word, Harrier watched him for a moment longer, then pointed to the left.

"Look. There's the gravel pit, and it certainly looks like it's the place to be tonight."

He was right. Though the security lights were unlit, their enhanced vision allowed them to see that there was more than a little activity in the place. Traffic was approaching from behind, so they drove on slowly enough to see the two dark vehicles enter through the gates they had just passed.

At the next chance they turned around for another pass, and Raven took the opportunity to feel the area for consciousness. There were seven Sorcerers, five humans, one Were, and Jessica. And she was terrified.

Chapter Eighty-Two

Helmut Fuhrmann smiled at me, his white, pointy teeth making it look more like a snarl. "The rest of our party will be along shortly. And you may as well cease with the digging. The young Were is held in my snare, and only I can release her. Ah, it seems our guests of honor have arrived.

I glanced over my shoulder and saw two pair of headlights pulling in through the gates. I couldn't see who had unchained them, but that was just as well. The lights were extinguished, and two dark sedans materialized from the shadows. The moon was rising behind the massive pile of pebbles, the light now illuminating the top of the hill, bathing the scene in a warm glow. It was only a matter of time before the direct moonlight touched Allie, and then all hell would break loose.

I started digging again, knowing it was a waste of time, but I was desperate. Voices murmured behind me, too low for me to hear, and I knew what they were here for. Fuhrmann was going to use Allie as an example, to turn the humans against the Weres. Mason had mentioned something about the Weres and the Sorcerers having it out years ago, so this finally made sense. I was positive that one of the people behind me was Mayor Diggs, and as the voices drew near, I wasn't disappointed.

"Jessica Sweet?" Mayor Diggs asked, his voice shaking with disbelief having realized I was there.

I stopped digging, stood in front of Allie to block her from their view, and gave the Mayor a friendly little wave and a smile. I'd met him many times through Piper's family, so I wasn't surprised he recognized me.

"I don't understand," Diggs was saying to Fuhrmann now. "I've known Jessica for most of her life—there's no way she can be what you're claiming!" Diggs was puffed up with self-importance, his extensive forehead sweating in the stifling heat of the night. Still, I was touched that he would try to protect me like that.

"Ah...you misunderstand, Mayor. Miss Sweet is merely here as, shall we say, a distraction. Once the animal turns, she will hunt, and it would be best to have her prey close at hand, her attention away from us. We wouldn't want any accidents."

Diggs was really flustered now, his thick eyebrows narrowed into a V, his mouth working silently, like he couldn't figure out what to say. "But, she has nothing to do with this!" he finally blurted out. If the light was better, I'd swear he was beet red.

"She has, more than you know *Mr. Mayor*, and you will accept what I tell you as fact. This woman has been consorting with monsters—it is only fitting that she sacrifice herself as payment for this betrayal to her race. Besides, you said she has no family to speak of, that she wouldn't be missed. That makes her perfect for our little experiment."

I wasn't sure I heard that right, but it sounded like the Mayor was telling people I was *disposable*? Wow. That sucked. Just when I thought we were going to be friends.

A noise behind me had me turning back to Allie. Her eyes were amber now, and the moonlight was mere inches from touching her sweet little head. She looked at me, knowing what was going to happen, and she was absolutely petrified.

I leaned down to her as the Mayor and Fuhrmann continued to bicker about my disposability factor, and I stroked her matted hair. "It's okay, Allie. It's going to be okay.

"How?" she asked in a tiny voice, way too small for the power that was emanating from her. Her face had taken on a more adult appearance, and I could feel the gravel that was holding her tremble with the energy her little body was emitting.

She looked up into my eyes, the amber of hers taking on an unearthly glow, and she said, "Let me smell you." I just looked at her until she said, "Please, give me your hand." I reached toward her, allowing her to sniff my fingers, and she closed her eyes as if trying to memorize my scent. "You smell like flowers," she said, "like my mom." Her unexpected smile was so radiant it took my breath away.

"Stand back, now," she whispered, closing her eyes. "It will happen soon. And Jessica? Just make sure I can smell you, okay?"

I nodded, marveling at how grown up she seemed, then backed away just as Fuhrmann and the Mayor and his other cronies gathered around to see the show. When I looked back at Allie, the stones that had been holding her prisoner had fallen away, her tiny body filthy and battered, lying atop it now. Her skin was twitching as though something was trying to get out, and I suppose that was just the case. Her face was tortured, the pain evident, and more than I could bear to watch.

I averted my eyes, but the sound was still horrible. It was like her bones were crunching and grinding, her skin ripping and tearing, and in my imagination that was happening. I heard someone in the Mayor's party gasp—someone else screamed. I stole a glance at the Mayor, but he was just standing there, enraptured by the process of this beautiful little girl being transformed into a snarling beast.

I heard Allie panting and peeked back in her direction. Where the child had been, now stood a beautiful wolf. She was snow white, though her coat was dingy and matted, her amber eyes glowing in the moonlight, and she was larger than I had anticipated, given the size of the child. She stood and sniffed the air, rounded on the small group standing just a few feet away and without hesitation, she lunged at them, full of snarling, monstrous rage—

Only to be stopped by an invisible wall, a sickening thud echoing through the area as she bounded off the wall, falling and landing on her side. I gasped and started to run to her, but thought better of it. She was probably pretty tough in this form, and I was still waiting for her to realize I was there and to decide to have me for dinner.

I knew nothing of what the Weres took with them when they changed—how much of their human side they remembered—and why would I? I wasn't real confident a single sniff test was going to be enough to keep me off the menu.

Allie picked herself up and threw herself at the barricade again and again, and the Mayor seemed almost as impressed with the wall as he was with the wolf girl. The woman who had screamed was now laughing and clapping her hands in delight, finding Allie's attempts at escape entertaining. I didn't recognize her, but if she held an elected position, she was definitely not getting my vote!

I backed away a little more, giving Allie room to do what she needed to do, get her aggressions out, exhaust herself, pass out—whatever—and I ran into another of those invisible force fields. Great. I was in an invisible box with an angry Werewolf, who, if like most baby animals when they were frightened or hurt, would probably lash out at whatever it found.

I sunk to my knees and closed my eyes. I half hoped Raven would show up and save my stupid ass, but the other half of me still wanted him to stay away. Seriously, why did I care about the Werewolves anyway? I had nothing to do with them, right? But I reminded myself that I was also trying to keep Piper safe, and if I hadn't come, then she would have been in danger again, and I couldn't live with that.

Plus, Allie was just so *innocent*. I reevaluated that thought as the sounds of snarling, snapping teeth and heavy breathing ceased being far away.

With my eyes tightly closed, I waited for Allie to snap. I wanted to speak to her, but that could be the wrong thing to do. The only thing I could think of was to be submissive, let her know I wasn't a threat. That's what they do on the Nature Channel.

So I lay down on the ground and curled into the fetal position. The creepy woman with the Mayor said, "Aww," and I nearly growled at her myself.

A puff of air blew at my face, and I realized that Allie was right there. She wasn't snarling anymore, but she was still breathing heavily. I opened my eyes a crack to see what she was doing, but she was just sniffing me. Her nose was cold and damp when it touched my cheek, and when I jumped, she bounced back, her forelegs and chin nearly flat to the ground, her tail end in the air, and her tongue was hanging out.

She approached me again, touching my face with her nose, and then jumping back into the same playful position. Ohmigod! She remembered me! Well, that was a relief. I sat up slowly, still not wanting to startle her, and I held out my hand. She approached slowly, sniffing my hand, and then lay her furry cheek in my palm. Her coat was magnificent. I didn't think white wolves were common, but she was extraordinary. As I scratched at her ears with my free hand, I wondered how big she'd be when she grew up.

I was so fascinated with what was happening right in front of me, so focused I nearly missed it when the voices behind me turned on Fuhrmann.

"I thought you said they were ferocious?" I heard the Mayor ask accusingly. "You had me all paranoid about these "dangerous" animals running among my constituency, and *this* is what we're supposed to be afraid of? Thank you, Mr. Fuhrmann. Thank you very much for wasting my time. Now at least I know who's paranoid." And on and on it went.

Fuhrmann looked absolutely livid and started shouting at Allie. Something shocked me—shocked us both I think, because Allie jumped as much as I did—and Fuhrmann screamed at her to get on with it. He taunted her, but the barrier that had been intended as a death chamber for me turned into a sanctuary for both of us. We just ignored him as best we could, although Allie did throw a snarl or two his way.

"We'll see how dismissive you are with the barrier removed," Fuhrmann shouted, and the air crackled and sparked in a large circle around Allie and me.

I caught Allie's eyes and hoped she would understand when I whispered, "Run home, Allie! *Run home!*" Her eyes were deep and soulful, and she whined at me, looking over my shoulder and then back at me. Apparently, the Mayor and his cronies didn't realize the barrier had been removed, because they were still yelling at Fuhrmann, and distracting him, I hoped.

I fought back tears and said, "Go now, Allie, I'll be okay. You get home, NOW!" and I waved my arms at her, hoping the Sorcerers weren't paying attention, and that she would have a chance to get away. The moment she bolted I jumped up and ran the opposite direction, screaming and waving my arms, trying to draw all eyes to me.

It worked. The voices that had been arguing heatedly went deathly silent, and then someone shouted something like, "Where's the wolf?" and the lady was screaming again, and the Mayor was flapping his hands like a chicken, his minions bustling around him, trying to shoo him back to the safety of the cars.

Fuhrmann, however, only had eyes for me. Aren't I the lucky one?

I tried to run behind the big pile of gravel where Allie had been buried just moments ago, but before I got very far, I felt my legs fly out from under me and I landed flat on my face. Or rather my boobs. My breath was knocked out of me, and I was vaguely thankful I'd never considered implants, even though I think one of the girls popped anyway. Is it physically possible to break a boob?

I struggled to my feet and started to run again, only to run right into another one of those freaking force fields. I changed directions and tried again, but the barrier was everywhere, and I was truly stuck. I beat my fists against the invisible wall, sending sparks flying with the contact, and screamed at the top of my lungs.

And that's when things got crazy.

Chapter Eighty-Three

Harrier had called in the location of the Sorcerers to the Legion, and Mason was quick to dispatch a Squad of Soldiers, as well as their Special Forces, aka the Team. Viper, Tas and Mason joined Raven and Harrier in a field east of the gravel pit, where they were updated on the situation. Merlin had remained at the Compound, taking the position of command central, as usual.

A Were child was being held with Jessica in the center of a group of buildings and the gravel dunes, with one Sorcerer and five humans in close proximity. Six Sorcerers were spread around the pit, hidden discretely from the humans. Their positions were easily determined, and the Soldiers were dispatched to each location, standing ready, waiting for the signal.

As they approached the perimeter, Raven felt his skin crawl. A magical barrier was in place, most certainly there to warn the Sorcerers of potential intruders. He sent mental messages to the team, and they all halted, awaiting further instruction. Time for Viper's little invention to come into play.

When he looked again, Raven could see Jessica, beating her hands against the air, her anger overpowering her panic, but she was okay. The humans had scattered, now diving for their cars, and the Were was gone, or at least beyond Raven's range. Moments later the vehicles tore out of the gates, gravel spraying behind their tires. Soldiers would be dispatched to take care of the memory alterations. But for now, at least the danger of human casualties was eliminated. Almost.

Mason gave a signal, and Viper detonated the M-bomb. The atmosphere went completely electric, sparks and bolts of lightning piercing the air as all magic in the area was nullified. The barrier holding Jessica back dissipated, and she fell forward with the momentum she had created pounding on the invisible wall. As she landed on all fours, Raven felt her surprise at her sudden freedom, but he and the rest of the team were already in motion. The Soldiers were attacking the Sorcerer sentries, and the Team was headed for Fuhrmann. Unfortunately, Fuhrmann was headed for Jessica.

All around them chaos reigned, Soldiers fighting Sorcerers whose magic was impotent from the M-bomb, screaming their battle cries, celebrating as each Sorcerer was exterminated. Out of the surrounding woods, wolves teemed, joining the Soldiers in their attack on the sentries. Raven, however, was focused solely on Jessica, every step a mile long and an hour slow. He dodged a wolf aiming for something behind him, and leapt over a Soldier who lay injured on the ground. As he grew closer Jessica looked up, her eyes locking with his. Panic mixed with relief washed over her face, the same emotions kicking through Raven's soul. But before Raven could reach her, Jessica was pulled into Fuhrmann's grasp, and they disappeared right before his eyes.

Chapter Eighty-Four

Allie ran as fast as her young wolf legs would carry her. She ran for the forest, for the safety of the trees, as far away from the monsters as she could get. That's what the *human who smells like mother* had told her to do, and her wolf agreed, so she ran, even though she didn't know exactly where she was—she'd never been this far away from home without adult supervision, regardless of form.

After what seemed like hours, her lungs burning and her tongue lolling in fatigue, Allie collapsed behind a boulder. With space and time between her and the monsters, she was able to let her wolf get her bearings, her nose in the air, scenting the wind.

The monsters were nowhere near, apparently they had not followed her, and the fragrance that filled her senses was sweet and clean. The smell of earth and trees, of a rabbit that had stopped, frozen under a bush, the musk of a deer whose antlers had scraped the bark of a nearby tree trunk. And the scent of pack.

These woods belonged to Allie's pack, and it was full moon, so they would all be out running, hunting. All she had to do was let wolf take her where she needed to go. To find her family.

Allie took off running, her nose guiding her to where the pack scent grew stronger, a crooked wolf grin decorating her face. In spite of the filth, her white fur was luminescent in the pale glow of the full moon, and as she ran she felt freer than she had ever been. The pains of her capture were healing quickly now that she was wolf, and *human who smells like mother* had given her this freedom.

With wolf in control she could only be happy, content to enjoy this moment of independence, and eager to scout her way home. But later, when her small human form returned, she would mourn not knowing how her savior had fared.

Chapter Eighty-Five

When the barrier disappeared I nearly fell on my face again, but fortunately just landed on my hands and knees. The air around me was going nuclear, like Fuhrmann was shorting out and all his magic was exploding around him. He was absolutely furious—his face contorted in a gruesome mask of anger.

The Mayor and his cronies had lit out like their asses were on fire, leaving me to fend for myself (guess who else isn't getting my vote this year?) and I hadn't heard any yelping, so I truly hoped Allie had gotten away before the fireworks started.

I looked up, trying to catch my breath and figure out which way to run, and my eyes met Raven's as he desperately fought to reach my side. But he was too far away, barely a shadow, and then Fuhrmann was there. He grabbed my arm, pulling me to my feet, and before I could blink, the world was fading around me. The last thing I saw before all went black was a group of men and wolves coming out of the shadows, Raven leading the way.

When things refocused again, I was in a moonlit clearing that seemed all too familiar. The surrounding trees were humongous, but they were dying, diseased, their dead leaves scattered on the ground and blowing around us in an unnatural wind.

Fuhrmann threw me unceremoniously to the ground and kicked me in the stomach as he walked by. He was muttering to himself, what could have been crazy-man talk, but more than likely was some magical mumbo jumbo. I had my answer soon enough.

Without preamble I was jerked in the air by unseen hands, my arms stretched above me as though tied to a post, my toes barely scraping the ground. This wasn't good.

Fuhrmann approached me, still mumbling, still glaring at me, and I couldn't help myself. I had to ask, "Why are you doing this? I didn't do anything to you!"

"You stupid bitch," he spat at me, literally spraying my face he was so close to me. "It's not about *you*! It was *never* about you! You're just bait. Your lover will come for you and then he will be mine. He'll pay for what he's done, starting with you.

That sounded ominous.

"But he's not even here!" I argued. "You left just as he showed up! That doesn't sound like you're too anxious to face him. And you should be afraid. If you damage one hair on my head, Raven will—" but I didn't get to finish spewing. An invisible gag filled my throat, and I was silenced. That was a handy trick.

"Oh, he'll come, human. The best way to lure a Vampire is to give him the scent of blood. Want a specific bloodsucker? Use specific blood. Yours will do nicely." With that, he tore my clothes from my body, taking care to rake my skin with vicious claws I hadn't noticed before, causing bloody streaks to form down my torso. I couldn't speak—couldn't scream, though I tried. Tears sprang to my eyes, and I realized too late that I didn't want to die.

I was crazy to think that sacrificing myself for my friends, my town, for Raven, was a good idea. I was a fucking moron! I was no hero—I was just a girl. Already, this hurt like nothing I'd ever experienced, and I could tell by the mad gleam in Fuhrmann's eye that he was just getting warmed up. I had no idea how far he'd brought us, or how, but it was obviously a brand of magic not covered by Viper's M-bombs. And it was far enough away that the magical interruption the Legion had caused was not affecting things here.

My arms jerked higher above my head, leaving my feet to dangle in the air, and Fuhrmann disappeared briefly, only to return with something that made my blood curdle. A cat-o'-nine tails? You've *got* to be kidding me! The Sorcerer had changed from his civilized suit to the white robes from my vision, and he was grinning maniacally at the fear now contorting my face. He held the whip in one hand, and a redwood staff in the other. When he leaned the staff against a nearby tree and stroked the barbed straps of the cat-o'-nine-tails, I could tell he was eager to begin putting the scent out for Raven to follow.

"It's time, human," he sneered at me as he walked circles around my dangling form. I tried to struggle, to kick out at him, but I was frozen in space. As quickly as it had appeared, I felt the gag dissolve from my mouth, and my arms and legs swung out, leaving me hanging spread eagle in the air, my bare skin pebbling in the magical wind. Fuhrmann's robes were floating around him like Moses in *The Ten Commandments*.

"May I watch?" A soft voice sounded from somewhere behind Fuhrmann, and my jaw dropped when Tabatha, the Legion maid, strolled into view, a white silk gown floating around her ankles. I don't think anything could have surprised me more. I had trusted this girl—she had *helped* me! What in the world was a Vampire doing in league with the Sorcerers? When I asked as much, she laughed her soft, tinkling laugh before speaking in a hardened voice.

"My family has been in service to the Legion for centuries. We may as well be slaves, for all those animals care. I met Helmut in town and he knew my true nature. Accepted it. And offered me an opportunity to escape. My future and the future of my children will not be to play servant to the Legion. We will be our own people, live our own lives, and I have Helmut to thank for this."

Tabatha walked to Fuhrmann's side, the innocence and shyness of the girl who had aided my escape absent in the young woman standing before me. This woman was confident and...bitter.

"When our work here is done, Helmut will take me with him to start our new life together. He has offered me the world and all I had to do was make sure you were able to make this...appointment." She giggled again, eyeing me up and down as I hung crucified in midair.

"I trusted you!" I spat, and she laughed harder.

"Well, I suppose that was your mistake. One of many, I might add. What in the *world* were you thinking, getting involved with the Rapist of all creatures? Really, I knew humans were stupid, but that is just silly!"

"And you think you're better?" I cried. "This person who you say is *saving* you? He's a murderer, just the same as Raven was, only that was Raven's past, and this asshole is still a murderer. He killed *children* for chrissakes!"

"Yes, but they were just *Were* children, really no more than animals. And now he's going to kill you. And I get to watch—and maybe even taste!" Tabatha clapped her hands and licked her lips, obviously thrilled with the prospect of seeing me bloodied.

Fuhrmann was still stroking his whip when he yelled for us to shut up.

"Sorry, baby," Tabatha crooned, but when she reached out to stroke Fuhrmann's arm he dodged her touch. I didn't think he could look any more disgusted than he did when looking at me, but I was wrong. His eyes were absolutely pulsating now, and his teeth looked like needles in his mouth.

Tabatha hesitated, confusion distorting her pretty face.

"You've served your purpose, you bloodsucking whore!"

And with that he flicked his fingers at her and she erupted into blue-green flames. Her screams echoed throughout the clearing, and I was certain that the horror and pain on her face were only partly due to the way her flesh was crisping in the magical fire.

Unable to look away, I closed my eyes tightly, but the smell was unavoidable. Poor Tabatha. At least this explains why she wasn't in my vision.

"My apologies for the interruption," Fuhrmann sneered when the screaming stopped, "but your respite is over."

I squeezed my eyes tighter, waiting for the first strike, and to my surprise it landed across my breasts instead of my back. The fucker wasn't even going to torture me nicely! I heard a blood curdling scream, and as another strike from the leather whip sliced through the tender skin on my stomach, I realized that the screeching voice now echoing through the decaying trees was my own.

As I let loose another shriek, that wicked voice said, "Yes, scream, my dear." He was circling me like a vulture. "It will add to the blood scent, pulling him to us. You will draw him to me like a human magnet, and then he will watch you die." Another strike, this time across my hips. I couldn't help it. I screamed again.

He continued to circle me, striking at will, my body becoming a latticework of bloody welts and flayed flesh. Before I lost consciousness, I thought decidedly that I could have gone my whole life without first-hand knowledge of the cat-o'-nine-tails.

Chapter Eighty-Six

They just *disappeared*! Raven stood in the parking lot of the gravel pit, staring at the spot where Fuhrmann had dematerialized with Jessica. It should have been impossible, the magic had been nullified. Where could they have gone? *How* did they go?

The fighting continued around him. The Sorcerers had called in reinforcements, and though the six they had detected initially were most certainly dead, these new ones were putting up a fight. The M-bomb had done its job, giving the Soldiers and wolves enough time to engage the enemy in the old fashioned way, without the threat of magical retaliation, but its effects lasted only a short time.

When the newbies arrived, Viper set off another M-bomb, so even the new Sorcerers were deprived of that unfair advantage, at least for a time. But where the Legion had begun with superior numbers, that was no longer the case.

Raven searched the grounds—they couldn't have gone far! A Sorcerer jumped him from behind, and he barely hesitated to throw the bastard from his back, twisting the sinewy neck with a deathly snap that registered no more than the disintegration process that began almost instantly. His duster, including many of his weapons, had been ripped from his back along with the Sorcerer, and when another enemy tore at his shirt, Raven disposed of him as well.

There were so many piles of rock and gravel, Fuhrmann could be hiding Jessica behind any of them, but Raven would be able to sense her if she were near. He would sense her emotions, feel her fear—he didn't know how, simply knew that it was true. It was impossible, but she was nowhere near. In a flash, the Sorcerer had taken her beyond his reach, beyond his touch. They could be anywhere!

Raven began to run wildly. He would run until he found her. He had no idea how Fuhrmann had done this—why hadn't the M-bomb prevented this?—but the fact remained, they were gone. He ran through the trees, as fast as his vampiric powers would carry him.

A piercing in his heart brought him to a halt. He was terrified, pain wracking his body until he was writhing on the ground, screams filling his head. Her screams. Her pain.

The fire in his body eased, and he lay on the ground gasping for air, tears streaming into his hair. The bastard was hurting her. He didn't know how he knew, but he knew it with a certainty. Just as he knew it was the scent of her blood floating to him on the breeze, filling him with fury.

Chapter Eighty-Seven

Helmut Fuhrmann was enjoying himself so much he nearly went too far. The girl was well and thoroughly bloodied, her scent undoubtedly wafting through the forest on the winds that he had wrought.

Each strike of the multi-strapped whip brought a sense of euphoria to him. Each mark on the human's body retribution for his mate. He was so focused on revenge that he was oblivious when the human lost consciousness, unaware that her life force was draining quickly, and he cursed himself for his carelessness. He needed her alive. He needed the Rapist to witness her death. If she died too quickly it would ruin everything.

Reluctantly and with great effort, he stilled his arm, the urge to continue the punishment difficult to contain. He realized his breath was coming in great heaves and he walked away from the suspended human form to regain some control, dropping the whip next to a decaying tree and retrieving his redwood staff. His hair had escaped from its binding and was floating around him like a mass of silver serpents, alive with his magic. He was alive. For the first time since Sylva's death, he felt truly alive!

Fuhrmann paced to keep himself occupied, kicking absently at the pile of smoldering ash that had once been a Vampire. How gullible females could be. But Tabatha had served her purpose, and as he toed the pile of her remains he had no misgivings. Means to an end was all, and certainly no great loss to this world.

He glanced back at the human still suspended in the clearing and admired his work from a distance. He knew if he examined her too closely he'd start beating her again, and that would be antiproductive. Blood was flowing freely from her body, forming crimson pools on the ground where her feet dangled. Her head was lying to one side, her hair falling over a face that he had intentionally disfigured.

Even if she lived, which she most certainly would not, she would never be the same. Her beauty had been erased, just as the Rapist had erased the loveliness of Fuhrmann's beautiful wife. He nearly giggled with the anticipation of seeing the bloodsucker's face as he gazed upon his lover, mutilated beyond recognition. And Helmut Fuhrmann was not one given to fits of giggling.

What was taking that monster so long? He was a Vampire, for chrissakes—he should have been here by now!

And just like that, the air around him sizzled, sparking with electricity. His hair, so alive a moment ago, fell limp around his shoulders as his magic dissipated. The suspended girl fell to the ground in a bloody pile across the clearing from Fuhrmann, and in the instant it took him to comprehend what was happening, the Rapist appeared between them, his fury and pain a good starting point to Fuhrmann's revenge.

Chapter Eighty-Eight

Raven was livid. Jessica was now lying in a pile at the edge of the clearing, her body bloody and broken, her heart barely beating. The M-bomb had released her from the grisly binding in which the Sorcerer had held her, but the sight of her spread naked to this bastard's eyes was nearly his undoing.

The man would die for this. Badly.

"Took you long enough," the Sorcerer taunted boldly.

Raven roared at him, his eyes flashing violet, his fangs stretched fully and gleaming in the moonlight. He started to lunge, but something held him back. For no reason he could comprehend, the woman's face appeared before him and a wave of agony swept through his body, the pain searing his very bones, and the shock of it more than the pain itself, gave him pause.

This should not be happening—the curse had been lifted! He had found love and combined passions with Jessica—all bets were off. And even if that weren't the case, the woman had never stopped him from killing in need before. He was defending the defenseless. His passions weren't confused or mixed—why was she here now? Was it because he faced a Sorcerer? Impossible. He'd killed Sorcerers before this one, several just tonight, and she hadn't stopped him then.

He struggled against the pain, each step toward Jessica's tormenter sheer agony. The man laughed a maniacal laugh and Raven roared again.

"What is it, Vampire? Are you a coward?" Raven struggled forward another step. "Does your fear make you incapable of defending this *woman*?"

Another step, another struggle, Raven's entire body shaking from the effort, the feelings of helplessness more excruciating than the pain.

"Why do you wait to attack? You didn't hesitate to kill my mate, you soulless bastard! Why do you hesitate to kill me?"

Raven stopped cold, the pain of a thousand invisible knives piercing his skin abruptly dulled with understanding.

"She was yours?" he asked, comprehension ceasing his struggle more than a curse ever could.

"Yes, she was mine!" Fuhrmann hissed, "And you destroyed her! My Sylva hurt no one. She was innocent and pure, and you took her for no other purpose than to sate your vicious needs."

"Her name was Sylva," Raven closed his eyes briefly, the woman's face floating behind his closed lids. Not as she had been near her death, but as she was in life. She was beautiful, with a smile that could still the earth, her eyes deep pools of love and acceptance. *This* was her mate? This man, this Sorcerer, who was so full of hate that he could murder children and torture women?

But then, that was exactly what Raven had done, wasn't it? No one had been safe from him.

Raven still stood between Fuhrmann and Jessica, shifting to maintain the separation each time the Sorcerer moved, but he made no further attempt to approach him, no further effort to attack.

How could he kill the man for doing no more than he wanted to do for Jessica? How? With pleasure! However, even if he could get beyond the twisted irony (and he could, have no doubt), Sylva would make Raven's revenge impossible. It seemed more than one curse was twisted on him that night.

He felt, however, that his enemy may not be working with all the facts. It probably would change nothing, but it was important to him that Fuhrmann know why his wife had died.

"Are you aware of the circumstances surrounding your wife's death?" he asked quietly, matching Fuhrmann's movements.

"I know that you killed her," hissed the Sorcerer, his eyes blood red and shining like stoplights.

"Do you know *why*, though?" his voice was still quiet, but Fuhrmann reacted as thought the question had been screamed. He swung to face Raven, his face contorted in a vicious scowl, his white robes billowing around him.

"There is no *why* with you, Rapist. It is what you do," he howled, pointing at Raven with the redwood staff.

"No, it is what I *did*." Raven's eyes and fangs remained sharp, but when he tried to approach the Sorcerer again, his body was wracked with another round of pain that nearly drove him to his knees.

The woman would never allow him to destroy her mate. There was definitely another curse at work here, or perhaps it was all part of the same. The first part had been to change Raven, to make him know what it meant to feel, to love. The second was to ensure her mate was able to take that away from him, the way he had taken her from Fuhrmann. What he had believed was an unselfish act had been anything but. She wanted her mate to avenge her, and her final act was to ensure Raven would not be able to fight back. So the Primeval's plan would finally be played out, unwittingly aided by their innocent victim.

"I was hired," Raven said, though his mind was still reeling with the realization of what had been done to him.

Fuhrmann had begun pacing again, and Raven paralleled his movements keeping himself between the Sorcerer and Jessica's still form. "Your wife was a target, and I was paid handsomely to eliminate her. Of course, at the time it meant nothing to me to take another life—I admit that freely. However, she was not of my choosing."

Fuhrmann raised his gaze from where he had been studying Jessica, lying helpless and exposed behind Raven. For a moment his fierceness shifted, but it returned in an instant.

Chapter Eighty-Nine

"Who?" Fuhrmann hissed through clenched teeth. "Who would want my Sylva dead?"

"It wasn't about her," Raven continued, his voice reflecting a calm he did not feel. "It was about me. I was to kill the woman, and in turn, she would be avenged by her family. By her race. By you, as it turns out. But the true target was always me. She was simply a means to an end."

"So what, this was another of your victims' families seeking retribution? Too cowardly to take you on themselves?"

Raven fought the urge to lower his eyes in shame. Instead he met Fuhrmann's gaze squarely, violet lights meeting the scarlet red of his enemy's, and he said, "No, it was my own race, seeking to destroy me. You were to be the hand that struck me down, but your wife had other plans. Do you know why you were unable to find me Fuhrmann?" Raven used his name, hoping to distract him. It didn't work.

"You disappeared. You became more skilled at covering your crimes, hiding the bodies. Many assumed you were dead. *I* assumed you were dead, until you were literally dropped at my feet."

Raven laughed cynically. "I was *never* concerned with hiding the bodies. I *wanted* them to be found. No, I disappeared because your wife willed it so. I took her life, but she took mine as well. The evil parts, anyway. You couldn't find me because she changed me with a curse. Recently, I thought she was doing me a favor, as well as any future victims I may have had," he added with an ironic smile. "But I think there was another reason. I think she wanted me to know what it was like to know love. And I think she was saving me for you."

Fuhrmann's smile grew slowly. From the grave, his wife was going to help him destroy her murderer. She had always been the clever one, the devious one, and he had admired this about her. Even in death, she was playing her wicked games, and had given him a gift as well. Vengeance was so sweet.

"So, kill me if you must," Raven continued, "but I fear your wife would be devastated to see what you have done to the innocents. She stopped me from creating more bodies, and yet you seem to have taken up where I left off." The Vampire was clueless—Sylva would be impressed with his efforts. It was difficult to keep the smile from his lips.

"Leave Jessica," Raven was saying, his voice shaking with his pathetic need to protect the human. "She's done no harm to you."

"She ruined my demonstration," Fuhrmann spat. "My Elders will be furious when they hear of my failure."

"She didn't ruin it. It was never meant to be," Raven said, his eyes focused on the Sorcerer's hair that was now lifting gently around his face. "My life would be forfeit without her, so to see her die would make me welcome death. Do you want me to die so willingly? Kill me alone, and I will go to my grave knowing what I will be leaving behind. Kill her first and I will gladly follow."

The Sorcerer considered this, taking a second to wonder if Sylva would approve. It took no time to conclude that she would, and he nodded at Raven. The girl would be dead soon anyway. And the Vampire wasn't the only one to realize that his magic was returning.

"Very well, bloodsucker. You shall have your death, and I shall have my revenge."

Fuhrmann raised his hands to his sides, the redwood staff glowing with power and magic. Whatever device was used to interrupt his magic had indeed worn off, and he reveled in the sensory pleasure that coursed through his veins with the power he called. Slowly, he approached the Vampire, savoring each step toward the end he'd been searching for. For his Sylva.

Chapter Ninety

Raven met the Sorcerer's bloody gaze, knowing that his time on this earth was nearing its end. He only hoped another Vampire would find Jessica in time to save her. He glanced over his shoulder at her crumpled body and wished with all he was that things could have been different. He wished he could have held her, kissed her one last time, and for the first time in his life—a life that had lasted entirely too long, yet had truly just begun—he knew he had a heart, because it was breaking for the loss of what could never be. Christ, would she ever forgive him?

Turning back to Fuhrmann, Raven squared his shoulders, his tattered shirt flapping in the unnatural wind Fuhrmann's magic had created. The Sorcerer was almost upon him—he seemed to be taking his sweet time about it, drawing out each step like the monster in a bad horror movie. Raven tried to step toward him, to meet his destiny step for step, but Sylva's last act of love for her husband held him in place. If he tried to take Jessica and run, Fuhrmann would strike her down faster than even Raven could move, and he could not let that happen.

So he stood his ground. After all the lives he had taken, the senseless acts of evil he had committed, it was ironic that he would die so easily for another. But Raven could imagine it no other way.

When Fuhrmann was less than five paces away, he lifted his redwood staff and lightning flew from its ends. His eyes blazed like bloody fire, and he laughed maniacally as he lowered the staff toward Raven, its lightning striking the surrounding trees sending black smoke rising into the night air.

Raven closed his eyes briefly, trying to imagine Jessica living a long and happy life, and the thought calmed him. But when he looked again, he was unable to comprehend the scene now in front of him. The smoke from the burning trees had taken shape into a form that now obscured his view of the Sorcerer. He was still trying to make sense of it when a voice sounded in his mind.

Get her out of here, Rapist—I've got this.

Raven hesitated no longer. He had Jessica in his arms and was racing through the trees in less than a second, leaving a large bird doing some serious claw and beak damage to Fuhrmann's face, and giving them their escape. He ran as he'd never run before, and within moments, the bird—a raven, ironically enough—was ahead of them, leading them to safety.

Chapter Ninety-One

I woke up on a bed of grass and leaves, my entire body on fire, my head perched on a leather pillow, and something warm and coppery trickling down my throat. Whatever it was, I wanted more, and I brought my hands to the source and held it firmly to my lips, sucking like it was an extra thick Polar King milk shake.

~~~~~~~~

The next time I woke up, there were voices. I was still on the ground, but my pillow had been taken away. I didn't hurt as much, but the voices were bothering me. They were whispering, but they might as well have been yelling for all the good it was doing. My head was pounding, and I just wanted them to shut up.

I opened my eyes, just a crack, to see three men standing in a semicircle not far from where I lay. One was clad in tattered leather—the other two were nude.

Cripes! If I kept waking up in the presence of naked men, I was going to get a reputation.

One of the naked men was Harrier, and I was aware enough to be ashamed that my first thought was of how awesome he looked in the buff. The male was a monster, but damn, he looked good!

The other man I'd never seen before. He wasn't a large man like the other two, and he appeared as a dark shadow in the midnight sky, but he was nothing short of beautiful. He had long dreadlocks, falling freely around his shoulders, and his eyes were an emerald green that went to glass when they caught the moonlight. I thought he seemed familiar, but I was certain I would not have forgotten a man like that, with or without clothes. He was especially impressive without.

I squeezed my eyes shut, trying to get these new images from my brain, and opened them again when I heard Raven's voice. Of course, he was the only one with clothes on, tattered as they were. No big. I'd already seen him naked.

"Now, you show up? Where were you when she needed you? Why didn't you stop her from this foolishness?" Raven was really mad, but my head was woozy, and I didn't know which man he was talking to.

"I had no idea what she was up to, and I did the best I could." The voice was deep and soothing, and I relaxed as he spoke. "When my Overlord informed me of the trouble in this area, I feared she might be involved, but forgive me. Getting here without a car took some doing, and it's been a while since I took this form."

For some reason the man sounded really sarcastic, but...wait...what form?

"Mason needs us," Harrier was saying as he pulled on a pair of leathers. Bummer.

Raven looked at the striking black man and said, "Stay with her, Shifter, but I'm warning you. You *will* respect her."

"I always have, bloodsucker. *I* always have."

And then it all went dark again.

Chapter Ninety-Two

Malcolm had shown up just as they reached the edge of the woods. The freaky little shifter had changed into human form the moment he saw them, choosing this moment to make himself useful, and Raven could have flattened him.

The little bastard had flaunted his closeness with Jessica, all that rubbing and sliding against her, sleeping with her when she had no idea what was in her bed. He couldn't tell her, of course. The unspoken rule among Supers was that you not out one another to the humans. Still, it would serve the bastard right if he *did* tell Jessica who was sharing her home. Knowing her, though, she'd welcome him with open arms, just as she had Raven. The girl was entirely too accepting of beings who were "other".

The slur about Raven not respecting Jessica had cut, though. *Come clean*, the fur ball had said as Raven left him to tend to Jessica. Christ.

Raven had confessed so much to Jessica in the short time he'd known her, he wasn't sure how much more the girl could take. Would this one thing Malcolm was so hung up on be the one that would make her crack? It was a small indiscretion, in the grand scheme of things, but it was so personal. There was no telling how she would react.

Of all the sins he had committed in his long life, taking advantage of Jessica for his own selfish pleasure was the one he was most ashamed of. Harder to confess even than feeding from her. She understood he had needed her blood to heal. And even with his past being what it was, she had never held it against him. The woman was baffling, amazingly so.

But this one thing he had done he would gladly forget. She would never have to know—no harm, no foul. But the furry little bastard knew, and if she ever discovered Malcolm's true form Raven was sure he wouldn't hesitate to rat him out. Bastard.

Raven hated leaving her in Malcolm's care, but there was Legion business to tend to, and Raven had disappeared on them once tonight. He was second in command, and he'd left his Soldiers to fight while he ran off to find Jessica. Plus, the bad guy got away, which didn't look good on a guy's resume.

So, for now he'd do his job, overseeing the clean-up of the battle grounds, staging the explanation for the damages and directing the debriefing of the Soldiers who had participated.

Though the Sorcerers were definitely on the losing side tonight, the Legion had taken their share of casualties. Some promising males had been lost, and even more were injured beyond what a little blood and rest could heal. Some things just didn't grow back.

Raven had done what he could for Jessica. Her injuries were extensive—Fuhrmann had been extremely thorough in extracting his revenge on Raven through her. He had beaten her until barely an inch of flesh was without damage. Her heart had been scarcely beating and she had nearly bled out.

Without Raven's blood she would have surely died.

Then again, if it hadn't been for Harrier's intervention, Raven and Jessica would both be dead.

Harrier had been ordered to keep an eye on Raven, and he took his orders seriously. He had followed Raven through the woods, remaining hidden when Raven entered the clearing to face his foe.

What baffled Raven was that Harrier had intervened at all. Here was his opportunity to send Raven to the hereafter, without ever lifting a finger. He had a front row seat to the assassination the Primeval had set in motion centuries ago. The assassination he had made clear should have been carried out by any means, rather than taming the beast and putting a military leash on it.

Yet, instead of pulling up a chair and a bag of popcorn, Harrier had helped him. Raven would never have been able to fight Fuhrmann. The woman's curse, Sylva's curse, would never allow it. She had been quite meticulous with the thing, protecting her family even as she died. So Harrier's intervention was the only thing that saved them.

He hadn't killed Fuhrmann, though. He did some damage, to be sure, but the Sorcerer had dematerialized before he could be mortally wounded.

That was another puzzle. If Harrier was going to jump in, why not do it with both fangs? Why the shift? Few knew of the Warrior's heritage, the shifter blood, but he had the element of surprise on his side—had he attacked at full Vampire strength he may have been able to kill the bastard. Why wouldn't he do that?

Of course, Raven had asked him this, but Harrier had given him the standard, "Fuck off," routine and walked away. With everything else they were dealing with, Raven had just dropped it.

The Soldier, Peregrine, had been employed to collect Jessica and Malcolm, who had reverted to his feline form, and take them back to her quarters at the Legion to heal. He was to stay with her, until she woke or he was relieved. Raven felt he owed the young male an opportunity to prove himself. He had been pretty hard on the guy when Jessica had asserted her will to help the Soldier—hell, Raven could have killed him!—and the things the male had told Jessica still rankled.

But he'd proven himself trustworthy with Jessica before—she would have told Raven had anything untoward happened in that bathroom. So now he was trusting Perry with the most precious thing in his world. Given Jessica's lack of attire, however, he still felt a stern warning about conduct was warranted, and so delivered.

Perry had swallowed a wave of fear, but in a moment his fear scent shifted to determination, and Raven clapped his shoulder to convey his confidence.

Harrier had returned to the Compound with Viper and Tas, leaving Raven to drive home alone with his thoughts. By the time he pulled into the underground garage, the sun was peeking over the horizon.

Raven was beat, but his only thoughts were of Jessica. Mason would want a report, but he would have to wait.

He entered Jessica's suite to find Perry standing guard at her open bedroom door. The male looked exhausted, blood caked on his forehead and in his closely cropped hair; but his eyes were alert. The tension left his stance as he acknowledged Raven's presence as friendly.

"Relax, Soldier," Raven walked toward him, hand extended in greeting. Perry looked at it for a moment before grasping it in his own. "How is she?"

"She's fine, sir. I mean, she's sleeping—has been the whole time."

"Good. That's good. Go home, Perry. Get some sleep. You look wasted."

Perry looked at Raven, meeting his eyes for the first time, and Raven was surprised with what he saw. He was used to being feared by his race, though after all these years he didn't understand why they couldn't just let it go. Very rarely, however, did they meet his eyes, and only a minor few did so with the respect he saw now. The Soldier bowed slightly to him before turning for the door.

"Perry," Raven waited for the male to turn. "Why do they fear me?"

"Sir?"

"The Soldiers—you—Jessica said...," Raven shook his head. "Why?" he asked. "Why still?"

Perry hesitated, not sure how to respond, then squared his shoulders and said, "They don't know you, sir. Only your reputation. Otherwise?" He shrugged, glancing at the still open doorway to Jessica's bedroom, and then back at Raven. Perry held Raven's gaze for a moment longer, then turned back toward the door. Raven watched him disappear into the hall, then turned back to the bedroom. To Jessica.

She was laying beneath the comforter, her bare skin covered properly, thanks to Perry. Malcolm was curled in a large black ball at her shoulder, his head laying possessively on her neck. Raven growled and Malcolm looked up at him, twitching his long, inky tail.

"Yeah, it's me, furball," Raven snarled at him. Malcolm just looked at him smugly and rubbed his cheek against Jessica's chin, drawing another growl from Raven.

Raven reached his mind to the cat and Malcolm bared his teeth with a hiss. *She's sleeping, bloodsucker. Leave her alone.*

You know I can't do that, Raven thought back to him.

The black cat tilted his head, studying him for a moment, then thought, *Yeah, I know*. And with that, Malcolm leapt off the bed and retreated to the living room, Raven closing the door quietly behind him.

Chapter Ninety-Three

More talking. I really wished people would pipe down so I could get some sleep. My head felt like a little man with a hammer was trying to whack his way out, and I ached all over. Even the tip of my nose hurt.

A cool breeze hit my neck, which had been toasty warm a moment before, and I rolled over and cracked my eyes open, looking for Malcolm. I don't know what I'd do without that cat. Always there when I needed him. Except now. Now, Malcolm was gone and Raven was standing over me in his place.

Raven was always there when I needed him, too. I was such a lucky girl. I reached my hand to him and beckoned for him to join me. When he moved toward the bed I croaked, "Too much leather," which made him smile.

After shucking his leather pants and a severely tattered t-shirt, Raven crawled under the covers with me and wrapped me in his massive arms. I snuggled my back against his chest, as close as I could get, and let him cradle me in a spoon.

"How're you feeling?" he whispered into my ear.

"Better now," I sighed. "Sore, but I'll live. Raven?"

"Mm-hmm?"

"What happened?" I turned in his arms to face him, needing to see his eyes. I remembered going to the gravel pit, but after that things went all fuzzy. I recalled bits and pieces—mostly hot, naked men, which I undoubtedly dreamed. I mean seriously—Harrier?—But as for what went on with Fuhrmann? Not a clue.

"Sleep now, *amante*. There is plenty of time for talk later."

"What about Piper and Alex?" I struggled to sit up. "Damn, I have to call..."

"I spoke with Alex on my way back to the Compound," Raven gently pushed me back against the pillows.

"What did you tell him?" I asked, my eyes narrowed. The thought of those two talking made me wary.

"The truth. That you are safe and well, and that you are resting in my home. He asked that you call when you arise, and I assured him you would. Good enough?"

"Good enough," I smiled, snuggling back into his warmth, his heart pulsing against my bare skin, and I was asleep in a heartbeat.

Epilogue

It felt strange to be home again. I was outside feeding the cats, enjoying a pleasant breeze that had blown in just as the sun dipped below the horizon. September had sauntered in on a cool front, which was a pleasant break from the sweltering heat of August in Ohio. Clouds were rolling in with the breeze, and I hoped we'd get some rain to perk up the grass, which had gone brown in the semi-drought.

I picked up the hose to fill the cats' water dishes and glanced up at my house. Everything was the same—same white siding, same Pella windows, same big ol' porch. A light was on in the kitchen, and the TV in the living room was on the Food Network. My normal house. My normal life. But it all seemed small and simple and empty compared to the Legion's Compound, and I missed having Raven right across the hall from me all the time. Not that he left me much time to miss him.

It was agreed that things had progressed rather quickly with us, and though I knew I loved him, and he absolutely loved me, I also knew I didn't want to screw this up. We still weren't sure how this would work, what with the whole Vampire/human thing, but we were determined to find a way.

We had regular date nights where Raven would take me out to a movie or dinner, or he would join Piper and Alex and me for drinks at Good Times. (We told my friends that "Ramon's" nickname was "Raven" because of his black hair, just to make things simpler.) And sometimes we'd just stay at my house, laughing and talking and learning all we could about each other, though he had a lot more experience and a lot more stories to share than I did.

And we had incredible, mind blowing sex. Just like a new couple was supposed to.

Alex was coming around regarding my new relationship. Raven could be extremely charming when he wasn't growling at people, and it turned out he and Alex had much in common when it came to literature. Who knew? I didn't even know Alex had a library card.

They still glared when one thought the other was mistreating me in some way, but they were always imagined slights, and a well-aimed glare from me was enough to set them straight.

Piper was recovered from her abduction, still thankfully oblivious to what she had endured. I didn't know for sure what the Sorcerers had done to her, but at least they left no obvious scars. She and Alex seemed to be closer than before, but when I asked, they both denied anything romantic going on between them. I hoped they were just sparing my feeling or whatever, and that they had finally hooked up, but they were keeping it to themselves if they did.

Apparently the Weres had fought bravely beside the Vampires, in spite of a certain lack of trust between the races. The enemy of my enemy and all that. Raven told me that Allie had made it back to her family, and that the Were pack was extremely grateful for what I and the Legion had done to rescue their little one from the Sorcerers.

I really wished I could see Allie again, just to make sure she was okay, but Mason seemed to think it better if I kept my distance. The Weres could be prickly about their identities, and it was bad enough I knew they existed. As it were, I could only identify Allie, and they wanted to keep it that way. Actually, they asked Mason to remedy that, too, but thankfully he'd declined.

I begged Mason to convince the Weres that I could be trusted. After all, the Legion was trusting me out in the world with their secret, and I hadn't told a soul. Not even my best friends. Oh, I talked to Malcolm about them all the time, but seriously. Who was he gonna tell?

Mason seemed to agree with the Weres, though, and felt that he was doing me a huge favor by not trying to erase my memories of her completely. However, I believe that he knew it might not take, so it was a feeble gift at that.

My memories of that night were coming back gradually, and Raven filled me in on the parts my memory still blocked out. He had followed my blood scent, just as Fuhrmann said he would, but he also had felt my pain. We weren't really sure why that was happening, but assumed it might have something to do with him taking my blood the night before. No other human's blood had caused such a connection, but we were grasping for answers that may never be found.

Raven told me that I had been injured badly, which I already knew from my vision, and he confessed to giving me his blood to save my life. I couldn't be mad about that, but I did find myself craving my steaks even rarer than I had before. One more thing Raven was hard pressed to explain. Other than my senses being maybe a little more acute, I had no serious side effects from this hematic elixir, besides being alive of course, and was left relatively unscarred. In the end, I just smiled and said, "Thank you."

Harrier's part in the whole thing remained a mystery. I truly thought he hated me, and Raven was certain Harrier hated him, but he saved us anyway. Maybe someday he'd explain it to us. Until then, I just smiled and said, "Thank you."

The Sorcerers had taken off for parts unknown. Raven seemed to think the Legion and Weres had destroyed a large number of the Clan that had been holing up in Fallen Cross, and what was left of them were nowhere to be found. Fuhrmann, unfortunately, had not been among the deceased. I hoped that he and the rest of them had gone away for good, but one thing I knew for certain was that it never paid to get too comfortable. The world's a crazy place, full of crazier things, and you never know what could drop out of the sky at you next. Or land on your porch. Just saying...

I finished up with the cats just as the last bit of sunlight slipped into the West. Raven had been in my cellar all day, sprucing it up for those times when an over-dayer was in order. I replaced all of my window sheers with heavy drapes, but he still ended up dodging Mr. Sunbeam. So after a day or two sleeping on the dirt floor in the cellar (I gave him blankets and a pillow, of course), he decided to make it into a real room. He said he felt like a Hollywood vampire sleeping down there with the spiders, and I offered to buy him a cape, or even a coffin, if he wanted. He was not amused.

With my critters fed and watered, I put up the hose and went to the porch to turn off the water, stretched as I straightened, then headed inside.

As I walked into the kitchen, I nearly ran into Raven, who was coming through the cellar door, muscles bulging beneath a black t-shirt with the sleeves and neck cut out, a smudge of dirt on his cheek marring his beauty only just.

"How's it going down there?" I asked, licking my thumb and rubbing at the smudge. He glowered at me but didn't pull away, and I laughed, throwing my arms around him and pressing my lips to his.

"Things are looking up," he rumbled when my lips moved down his neck. "Christ woman, you know what that does to me." He ran his hands down my back, settling them firmly on my rear.

"Yeah," I sighed into his throat. "I have an idea."

Raven gave a throaty growl as he picked me up and carried me into the living room, where the butter lady was whipping up a Butterfinger cake on TV. Raven hit the mute button before lowering me to the floor, grabbing a throw pillow from the couch and placing it gently under my head.

"So it's going to be that kind of night," I said as he slowly removed my white t-shirt and jeans, then stared at me as his own clothing fell to the floor at my feet. Sometimes we were all *Fast and Furious*, but it looked like this was going to be more of a *Slow Ride*. Yowza!

Raven joined me on the rug and put his fabulous lips to work, kissing, sucking, licking and I almost giggled with the memory of his latest confession. Apparently, the night after the Mayor's party, when we'd kicked the Sorcerers' butts together, he'd made a bit of a sexual faux pas regarding the manner in which he'd "tended to my wounds" while I was knocked out in the Hummer. I thought it was funny, and it certainly explained the hot dreams I'd been having prior to waking in Raven's office, but he was so mortified with what he'd done that I had to stifle my first reaction. I assured him that I was not upset, and for some reason that put him in even more of a mood, which he took out on Malcolm, glaring at him and mumbling something that sounded a lot like, "fucking furball."

I'll never understand what transpires between those two, and right now, I didn't really care. Raven's lips had reached a critical, central position, and things were about to go from *Slow Ride* to *Oh My God*!

I reached down and wove my fingers into his silky black hair, encouraging him to halt his explorations right where he was. In seconds he had me screaming with ecstasy, sending Malcolm racing from his favorite sleeping spot beneath the couch and up the stairs to his room. Malcolm was an indoor cat now.

As I tried to catch my breath, I wound my hands tighter in Raven's hair, pulling him up to share a passionate kiss.

"Raven," I gasped as his lips found my throat.

He made a noise that I took to be, *yes, my love*?

"You truly are a god."

Raven raised his head to look at me, his eyes spreading that radiant, amethyst light throughout the room, and then he roared as his fangs unsheathed. My legs opened to receive him, his mouth lowered to claim my throat, and I was in absolute heaven.

Vampire sex was a-*mazing*!

~~~~~~~~

Maggie watched the two from the study doorway, her mate and her young, as they cuddled in the leather chair behind his desk. The child's eyes were closed and she seemed fine—thank God for that—but Maggie couldn't stop the shudder that wracked her body at the thought of having nearly lost her little girl.

She'd given up everything once and it had nearly killed her. She was certain she couldn't bear to do it again.

Maggie and Patrick had been together since, well, forever. She couldn't remember not loving him. They had married young and though they struggled, they were in love and they knew that nothing would ever tear them apart.

When Patrick disappeared several years into their marriage she had been frantic. He wouldn't leave her without good reason, which meant he had to be in trouble or dead. She searched for him, to the exclusion of all else in her life, and even after the police had filed him away as a cold case, she continued to search. She had abandoned everything and everyone she loved trying to find him, her despair eventually dragging her into drugs and alcohol, a feeble attempt at dulling the ache in her heart that his absence had caused.

She had been on the verge of suicide when, as if in a dream, he returned to her. It was at night and she was stoned to a near catatonic state in an alley behind a bar she frequented, so she wasn't even positive he was real. But he had taken her away, and when she'd sobered up and realized it really was him, none of what he told her mattered. He was sorry to have left, although it had not been his choice, and he had prayed every day for a time when he would be strong enough to reclaim their love.

However, to do this, she had to be willing to sacrifice everything—to leave it all behind. *No big*, she'd thought at the time. Her mind still muddy from the drug use, she figured she had pretty much already done that. There was nothing in her life she wouldn't abandon if it meant they could be together again.

And that's precisely what she had done.

Eventually the drug haze wore off, and the realization of what she had abandoned hit her like a freight train, but by that time there was no going back. Patrick had been clear that a clean break was the only way, and she hadn't thought twice about it, not with him back in her arms. But eventually...yeah, she had regrets.

Now looking at Patrick, their daughter, Allie, on his lap, and realizing how close she had come to losing it all again, Maggie's heart clenched in her chest. Others had not been so lucky. Two children never came home, and poor Lucy had died trying to protect them.

"How is she," she whispered from the doorway.

Patrick looked up and gave her a weary smile. "I think she's okay. She's tough—more so than I could have ever hoped."

"She's very much her father's daughter," Maggie smiled, walking to their side and stroking the child's silky hair. She had been a mess when they found her. Her coat was matted and dull, and she was panting from fear and exhaustion. Butch had been the one to find her, and she had been so happy to see him, she had nipped at his flanks and his ears the whole way home, which, knowing Butch, would have been really irritating.

But word had spread through the forest that one of the lost had been found, and once the Sorcerers were under control, the wolves answered Butch's call, all eager to escort the youngling home. She had fallen into an exhausted sleep in front of the fireplace, her father's wolf wrapped protectively around her, and Maggie had watched them sleep, afraid to close her human eyes for fear they would disappear on her.

She watched until they shifted back to their human forms, and then had joined them on the rug, her arms wrapped around as much of them as she could gather to her.

"Have you talked to Butch and Marcela?"

Patrick shook his head. The oldest of the children who had been taken had belonged to them. Allie had sobbed uncontrollably when asked about her young pack mates. Butch and Marcela, and David and Sandra, the parents of the other young, had howled mournfully with the news. The others had been strong young males. Why Allie had survived when the boys couldn't, or didn't, they would never know. Maggie just hoped that the bastards who were responsible would be brought to justice. Many of them had died, but unfortunately not the right ones.

Patrick's chin was resting on Allie's head, and Maggie raised her spare hand to stroke him as well. He seemed well and truly spent, the stress and sadness of the past month having taken its toll. He stared at his desk, his dark eyes full of an intense, soul-deep sorrow. Maggie followed his gaze, and was not surprised to see the source of his pain.

A photograph lay on the desk, a little girl with chestnut curls and ice blue eyes, so much like Allie's, so much like Patrick's, smiling up at them. She was no more than six, Allie's age now, and walking proudly down the steps of the old county courthouse in Dayton, each of her hands clasped firmly in the palms of the older couple flanking her. The love in their eyes as they both stared down at the little girl still tore at Maggie's heart. Patrick's as well. It was so not fair.

But then, life wasn't always fair. They had done what they thought was best at the time. At least they didn't lose Allie, too. That would have been more than either of them could have survived.

The girl in the picture was a young woman now, and they owed her, big time. Allie could remember her scent, saying she smelled like Maggie, but she couldn't remember her name, and she had cried when she realized she had forgotten it in her panic to get away. Patrick and Maggie knew, though.

Fate was a fickle bitch.

about the author

Aliya DalRae is an avid reader whose love of books began practically at birth. As a young child she spent countless hours in the small town library, where the children's section consisted of three narrow shelves next to the check-out desk. Needless to say, it wasn't long before she was making up her own stories to keep her imagination engaged. Now living in the Midwest with her immortal beloved, Aliya spends every spare moment breathing life into her imaginary friends.

Visit Aliya at:

WWW.GOODREADS.COM
and
WWW.FACEBOOK.COM/ALIYADALRAE

Made in the USA
San Bernardino, CA
01 March 2016